MAGICIAN'S LAW

'Let me help you.' The voice was masculine, though soft and gentle, and came from almost directly before her. Something rubbed against the staff and it suddenly blazed with the cold blue fox-fire of the goddess. The congregation cried out, and one or two swords were raised to strike at the figure revealed in the eerie light.

'No,' the priestess gasped, raising her hand, pushing down the swords by her side. She looked over her shoulder at her congregation, using the opportunity to regain her composure. 'No, he must be one of us.'

She turned back and coolly appraised the stranger. It was a man, of that she was certain, although the long, black, hooded travelling cloak almost completely concealed his face and most of his body. He was tall, for he topped her by a head and she was standing on the altar steps, and though the wand blazed with stark light the stranger was still partially in shadow, almost as if he absorbed the luminescence. And she knew that it was he who had activated the wand. She looked down at the rod she still held in one hand and gasped: there wasn't another hand above hers on the length of wood, but rather a flat silver hook, intricate runes and delicate tracery winking in the pulsing light.

'Who are you?' she asked finally.

'I am Paedur, a bard,' the stranger replied softly.

Magician's Law

Tales of the Bard
Volume One

Michael Scott

SPHERE BOOKS LIMITED

Sphere Books Limited
27 Wrights Lane, London W8 5TZ

First published in Great Britain by Sphere Books Ltd 1987

TRADE
MARK

Set in Times Roman by The Word Factory Ltd., Rossendale

Printed and bound in Great Britain by
Collins, Glasgow

For
the Three that are One

List of the Gods

PANTHEON OF THE OLD FAITH

Lady Adur   Goddess of Nature; sister of Quilida
Alile   the Judge Impartial; Judger of Souls
Bainte   Winged messengers of Death, servants of Mannam
Baistigh   Lord of Thunder
Buiva   God of War and Warriors, the Warrior
Cam   God of Bridges
C'lte, Qua'lte and Sa'lte   The Triad of Life
Coulide Dream-Maker   God of Dreams
Lady Dannu   Prime female deity
Ectoraige   God of Learning and Knowledge
Faurm   Sea God; brother of Faurug
Faurug   The Nightwind
Feitigh   The Windlord, father of Faurm and Faurug
Fiarle   The Little God of Icy Spaces
Hanor and Hara   The first Great Gods
Huide   The Little God of Summer Rain
Luid   Fire Sprite
Lady Lussa   Goddess of the Moon
Maker and User   The Early Gods
Mannam of the Silent Wood   The Lord of the Dead
Maurug   The Destroyer
Nameless God   God of Madness and Delusion
Nusas   The Sun God
Ochrann   God of Medicine and Healing
Oigne and Uide   Gods of Cities
Quilida   Goddess of Growth
Shoan   The Smith
Sleed   The Maker of Mountains
Snaitle   The Cold God
The Stormlord   Unnamed God of Storms

Taisce   The Dewspreader
Tatocci   God of Fools
Uimfe   The Lord of Night
Visslea   The Spirit of the Mists

GODS OF THE NEW RELIGION

Aiaida   Lord of the Sea Wind
Hercosis   The Dreamlord; one of the twelve Trialdone
Hirwas   God of Far Seeing; one of the twelve Trialdone
Kloor   God of War
Libellius   God of Death
Quatatal   Bronze Sun God
Tixs   Bat God; a minor godling
Trialos   The New God

OTHER GODS

Aonteketi
   Six great birds that were once Gods of the Pantheon
   1 Scmall: The Spirit of the Clouds
   2 Kloca: Lord of Stone and Rock
   3 Aistigh: Lord of Subtle Harmonies; brother of Danta
   4 Danta: Lord of Verse
   5 Dore: Lord of Smiths (silver and goldsmiths)
   6 Fifhe: Lady of Beasts; daughter of Lady Adur
Bor   The Man God
Chriocht the Carpenter   Halfling carpenter of the Gods of the Pantheon; brother of Toriocht
Lutann   Demon God
Quisleedor   Life Child of Sleed, the Maker of Mountains (*see* Pantheon of the Old Faith)
Sinn   Mist Demon, Sun God
Toriocht the Smith   Halfling smith to the Gods of the Pantheon

PRIMAL SPIRITS

Chrystallis   The wind that blew through the soul of the One; the Soulwind

The One   The first being

The Three Cords   Disruption, Annihilation and Chaos

Duaite   Collective name for evil spirits; Duaiteoiri (singular)

Auithe   Collective name for good spirits; Auitheoiri (singular)

Magician's Law

Tales of the Bard

Prologue

I have collected many versions of the life of Paedur the Bard in my travels, and since it is a tale which, with the embroidery of time, loses nothing in the telling I have yet to hear two which match in every detail.

When I attempted to recreate the life and wanderings of the bard, I went back to the original sources, and talked to the few who remained alive who had actually met him, or read the accounts they had left behind. So, in many ways, this is really their account, their impressions of a remarkable man.

Some storytellers begin with his meeting with C'lte, the God of Life, while some others start with his encounter with Mannam, the Lord of Death. However, I have always thought that to understand the bard, and why he accepted Death's quest, one must begin earlier – much earlier – and so I always start with a quote from Lilis' account of the last of the Nine Great Battles of Antiquity.

> For a day and a night the great armies had fought and when the mists of morning had cleared, nothing moved, save the tattered pennants on broken spears that fluttered in the rank breeze. Ten thousand men had given their lives in the last great battle between the Light and the Dark – but to no avail, for the Balance remained.
>
> And the ravens and wolves gathered and fed.
>
> Now in the afternoon of the third day after the battle, Lugas the Bard rode through the Vale of Anfuile and out on to the Plain of Goride – but which was thereafter known as the Bloodplain – and the carnage, the reeking dead, the butchered lives, and the senseless waste sickened him.
>
> And as he rode away, he composed the Lay of Battle, and blessed it with the Old Magic, investing it with the power to quieten the most violent or maddened warriors.
>
> And later generations came to know it as the Lament of Lugas, or the Dove's Cry . . .

The bard wanted that magical lament. When he first took to the roads as a wandering bard, he used the opportunity to search through the libraries of the Tribes of the Seven Nations, the

1

archives of the monks and the Records of the Guild of Scribes –
but to no avail. When his fame became such that he was called to
the Imperial Court, many of his friends were surprised that he
accepted – but he only did so to gain access to the Emperor's huge
library. Again he was disappointed.

The years passed and he eventually despaired of ever finding it.
When the situation at court changed, and his position became
precarious, he retired to the solitude and silence of the forest and
he almost forgot about the Lament of Lugas . . .

Life of Paedur, the Bard

1   The Quest

Mannam is the God of the Dead, and his guise is that of a withered and blasted tree . . .

C'lte is the third part of the Triad of Life; he often affects the appearance of a brightly clad effete youth . . .

Pantheon of the Old Faith

The amber ball of the sun sank down behind the mountains in the west, briefly touching them with fire, while the forest that nestled beneath them slipped into shadow. There was a long moment of twilight silence as the forest composed itself for night and then the first rustlings began as the night creatures stirred from their burrows and nests.

Wood snapped, and silence fell again.

The tall shape of a man moved slowly through the trees, stooping now and again to pick up dead wood. His clothes had once been fine but were now patched and repaired, the ornate threadwork lost beneath a covering of filth and grime, and in the wan twilight only the bardic sigil high on his left shoulder took the light.

And it was difficult to recognise in the gaunt haggard face and sunken eyes Paedur the Bard, once Lore-Master to most of the kings of the Seven Nations.

A chill wind ruffled his long fine hair, and he turned his face into it; it was fresh with the tang of salt – a sign of rain. Paedur tossed his armful of rotten wood on to a rough oblong of cloth, stooped and gathered up the edges and then hoisted the bundle on to his back. He moved quickly through the thick undergrowth, leaves and dead branches crackling under his boots, heading back towards his shelter. Although it was only the afternoon of the year the weather had already turned unseasonal, changing towards the Cold Months, and there had been sleet and snow showers for the past few days.

The tall man came into the clearing just as the first heavy drops of rain pattered against the leaves. He swore briefly and made a dash for the almost invisible stone cell which nestled beneath a huge oak tucked in one corner of the clearing. He had his head ducked into the wind and had almost reached the shelter before he saw the figure standing in amongst the trees. Without breaking stride, Paedur dropped the bundle of wood and threw himself away to one side, crashing into the bushes. He rolled to his feet and his right hand found the long knife tucked into his boot. His left arm came up and the razor-edged and pointed hook that took the place of his left hand carefully parted the leaves as he peered out across the clearing.

The bard squinted towards the spot where he thought he had seen the shape; he wasn't sure, but he imagined the shadows were thicker there. He tilted his head to one side, listening, but the sound of the rain on the leaves and wet turf blotted out all other sounds.

The shadows suddenly moved. Paedur slowly backed out of the bushes and moved off to one side, his eyes never leaving the spot. If he could work his way around behind . . .

A figure stepped out from beneath the trees – and the bard stopped in his tracks. The shape was man-like, a head and more taller than Paedur, as thin as a sword – and completely enveloped from head to foot in a cloak of seared and withered leaves.

'Bard, come forth; face me.'

The voice was thin and high, a rasping whisper that set the bard's teeth on edge, and set the bats in the trees wheeling up into the darkening sky. The figure turned slowly and then a skeletal arm rose and pointed into the trees directly towards the crouching man. 'Come out bard, enough of these games.'

Paedur waited a moment, his hard dark eyes scanning the trees and bushes, alert for others, and only when he was finally satisfied that the stranger was alone did he step out into the clearing to face the sinister figure.

'Who are you?' he asked, keeping his trained voice low but projecting it across the clearing with as much authority as he could manage. He deftly reversed the long knife in his hand, holding it by the blade, gauging the distance across the clearing.

'I am Mannam,' the stranger whispered, his breathless voice whistling like the breeze through leafless trees.

'*Mannam*!' The bard felt his heart begin to pound, and he took a step backwards. Mannam, Lord of the Dead, Sovereign of the Silent Wood where the souls of the dead dwell until judged by Alile, the Judge Impartial. Mannam was Death.

The leaf-clad figure glided over the sodden ground until he stood before the bard. Paedur flipped the knife again and brought it up before the creature's face – if it had a face, for its head was mercifully shadowed beneath the cowl of its cloak.

'Put away your toy,' the creature whispered, 'it cannot harm me.'

The bard thought about the idea of threatening Death and then he smiled. 'Aye, perhaps not.' He wiped the thin blade against his woollen leggings and then slipped the knife back into his boot.

'We will talk,' Mannam whispered.

'What have I to talk to you about?' the bard asked. 'I will not bargain with Duaite,' he added quickly. He walked around the creature and strode over to his cell, calling back over his shoulder, 'But if you do wish to talk, then I insist that we do it in slightly drier surroundings – before I catch my death,' he grinned.

Lightning suddenly flashed across the heavy skies and it began to rain even harder. The bard ducked his head into the driving rain and ran for his cell. The Dark Lord turned, and followed him, his cloak rustling like aged branches rasping against stone.

The circular stone cell was small and stark; a pallet of straw lay to one side of the warped wooden door, a small writing board resting against a wall and a deep studded wooden chest comprised the furniture. Surrounding the writing board were scores of parchment scrolls, some loose but the rest neatly piled up in their wooden tubes.

Paedur crossed the earthen floor and settled by the glowing embers of the fire and then waited until Mannam had settled in a darkened corner, as far away from the small stone-enclosed grate as possible. The wind coming in through numerous cracks in the stonework moaned as if in pain, the sound curiously human.

The bard looked into the shadows. 'What is it you want?' he demanded, striking flint to stone, lighting a fire in the grate, for he knew the Duaite – the Dark Spirits – feared Luid, the Fire Sprite. He settled a bowl filled with a thick liquid on to the coals.

'I seek your aid,' Mannam whispered.

'My . . . what!'

'I seek your aid,' Mannam repeated softly, and then he added in the same sibilant whisper. 'I seek the Mandlethorn.'

'*The Bush of Life, the Thorn of Death*,' Paedur murmured. 'I have heard of it, of course, but I certainly do not have it.' In the shadows, his teeth flashed in a grin. 'Perhaps you should look somewhere else.'

The Duaiteoiri moved, his cloak rustling. 'Do not play with me, mortal – do not mock me. The Mandlethorn was stolen from me by C'lte the Undead. He burned the sacred bush which grew in the secret heart of the Silent Wood, but not before he had taken the twelve seeds from about the base of the bush. And beyond the Land of Mist, high in his kingdom, it flourishes – my Mandlethorn!' He gestured wildly, scattering leaves in all directions, some of them flaring and crisping in the small fire. His arm rose out of the shadows and he pointed at the bard. 'I want you to return the seeds to me.'

Paedur laughed; a rich melodious sound tinged with pity. 'Me? Now surely you mock me?' He leaned forward across the fire and squinted into the darkness that had gathered about the Lord of the Dead. 'Tell me,' he said quietly, 'are you Mannam, the Dark Lord?' He paused, and then added, 'Or are you perhaps the Nameless God of Madness and Delusion, or Tatocci, the God of Fools?'

There was a dull snapping sound, like a rotten branch breaking, and the myriad night sounds fled into silence. Mannam's voice, when he spoke, was barely above a whisper. 'You go too far, bard.'

In the long silence that followed, Paedur sat back against the chill stone wall of his cell and slowly stirred his supper of thin vegetable broth in a bowl of beaten silver. The wavering firelight painted his lean face in shades of crimson and bronze, flickered along the length of the silver hook set into the bone of his wrist and struck fire from the bardic sigil on his left shoulder.

'So . . .' the bard leaned forward, wrapped a thick cloth about the bowl and lifted it off the fire. He looked across at Mannam, his eyes points of amber light. 'Right then. You are . . . what you are. But why me?' he asked softly.

'You have been chosen,' the Dark Lord whispered stiffly.

'Chosen? By whom?'

'You have been chosen,' Mannam repeated.

Paedur brought the bowl to his lips, tilted his head back and drank deeply. A thin thread of liquid ran down his chin as he swallowed noisily. When he finished he wiped his chin and lips on his sleeve. He put the bowl down and looked into the darkened corner. 'I think we have nothing to say to each other. You are wasting my time – and I yours, I think.'

The Dark Lord shifted position, the brittle leaves of his cloak rustling sharply. 'You are a difficult man, Paedur,' he hissed.

'Tell me,' Paedur said suddenly, 'why do you have to deal with a mortal in the first place?' He leaned forward, shifting light dancing across his high cheekbones and forehead. 'Why do you not seek the Mandleseeds yourself? Surely you have the power?'

The shadows about the Duaite seemed to shift and stir. 'Your arrogance may be your blessing, but your stupidity will prove your undoing. C'lte is the Yellow God of Life, one of the Undead, the Undying. He is part of the Triad of Life, the least part of the three spirits created by Hanor and Hara. But on this plane, neither Sa'lte nor Qua'lte, his brothers, trouble themselves with the activities of mortals and only C'lte is concerned enough to watch over this world. He is my bane . . .' The whispering faded into the night and then the Lord of the Dead laughed with the sound of the wind soughing through rotting branches. 'And the only reason that I cannot recover the seeds myself is that he is Life and I am Death. The very essence of the Undying would utterly destroy me, aye, and the Yellow God also. And without life and death, what would be left?'

'Nothing,' the bard whispered, and he shivered in the chill of the night air, for Taisce the Dewspreader and Faurug the Nightwind were both abroad.

'Come mortal, your answer. Will you undertake to return the Mandleseeds to me or no? Your reward will be great,' the Duaiteoiri added persuasively.

Paedur placed a lump of turf to the fire and raked the embers with the point of his hook. 'You want me to make my way through the haunted Wastelands, climb the Broken Mountain, outwit the Yellow God, and find and return the seeds to you . . . is that all?' he asked sarcastically.

'That is all,' Mannam said quietly.

'But why me?' the bard persisted. 'And don't tell me again that I have been chosen.'

'Suffice it to say that you are a bard, familiar with the myths and legends of this plane, conversant with the mythos, the pantheons of the gods. Your knowledge of lore, your acceptance of the unacceptable will stand you in good stead.'

'If I refuse . . .?'

'Then there are others,' the Dark Lord murmured.

Paedur remained silent, although somewhere deep within himself he had already made his decision. He relished the very thought of the quest – it was the stuff of myth and legend, and the bard dealt in myths. Finally, he raised his head and scratched the stubble on his cheek with his silver hook, the sound rasping loud in the silence. 'And my reward?'

7

'I will give you the Lament of Lugas,' Mannam said softly.

Paedur felt the sudden pounding of his heart, the constriction in his chest. 'The Lay of Battle.' His voice sounded numb in his ears. He swallowed hard. 'You have it?'

The shadow in the corner rustled. 'I have it; Lugas and his companion Auigne the Harper passed into my kingdom – as do all men.'

The bard sat back, something approaching greed flickering in his dark eyes. 'You have the Harp of Auigne also?'

'I have.'

'I want it,' he snapped. He leaned forward again. 'Give me the Lament of Lugas and the Harp of Auigne and I will undertake to return the Mandleseeds to you.'

The Duaiteoiri straightened in a blur of rustling darkness. 'You are greedy, mortal, but you will have what you desire – if you bring me the twelve Mandleseeds.'

Paedur stood and looked down at the shadowed figure. 'And if I fail?' he wondered aloud.

'There is but one reward for failure,' the shadow whispered.

'That is?'

The Dark Lord remained silent.

'I will not fail,' Paedur murmured.

But Mannam, Lord of the Dead, was gone.

It was close to midday, and Nusas the Sun was high, blazing down upon the lonely figure of the man dwarfed by the huge bulk of the mountain which stretched upwards into the heavens. But at this height the sun did little to warm the man, it merely blinded him with raw, stone-reflected light. Icy fingers of wind plucked at his ragged clothing as he groped for a handhold on the slippery rock, threatening to tear him off. His silver hook – which he had worn for so long now that it was part of him – caught the light, splintering the pale sunbeams as he chipped rock and shale in an attempt to gain some purchase.

The bard slipped and his already lacerated palm was torn open again, streaks of blood staining the smooth stone. His scuffed and torn boots scrambled and found a toe-hold and he managed to snag his hook in a tiny crevice. His shoulder muscles cracked and threatened to tear with the strain. Summoning his last reserves of strength, he heaved himself upward, and his numb fingers brushed across a broad ledge. Paedur clung to the lip of the ledge, whilst his aching muscles bunched in a final effort to push himself up on to it. He prayed, warning Mannam that if he fell now he would never return the seeds, and then he pushed himself upwards. His hook screamed across the rock and then it caught, and then he was on to the ledge, feeling the stone smooth and cool beneath his forehead.

A month had passed since the visitation of Mannam. The bard had embarked on the quest immediately, setting out with a small bundle of provisions on his belt along the abandoned King Road that led to the Wastelands.

Once through the western fringes of Forest of Euarthe, the road had dwindled to a track, until it finally disappeared completely at the Bridge; a simple crude single-span bridge that crossed what was known throughout the Seven Nations simply as the Crevasse. This was an unfathomable gash that sliced through most of the western portions of the Nations from northern Thusal to southern Thusala without break. Beyond the Crevasse were the Wastelands, uncharted except in legends and myth, and uninhabited, except by the rumours that the gods of the Old Faith lived there.

Paedur had wandered through the Wastelands, using the myths as his guide; when he reached the fog-shrouded City of Souls, he knew he was on the right track. Although he avoided the city itself, his route led him along through the outskirts, and so he stopped his ears with beeswax against the beguiling cries and piteous wails that whispered and moaned through the tall hollow stones. The fog closed in then, and his only guide had been the warm fruit-scented breeze that blew through the ancient city from the Broken Mountain.

When he emerged from the mists several days later, he realised he had passed beyond the known world into the Shadowland which straddled the world of men and gods. Before him, the only feature in a flat sandy expanse stretching from horizon to horizon, was the Tulkaran Range, its once clean lines torn and shattered in the Demon Wars when the very planes of existence had heaved and bucked in turmoil. Towering over the dark mountain range he recognised the Broken Mountain, the legendary abode of C'lte, the Yellow God of Life, the Undead, the Undying.

It had taken the bard ten days to cross the desolate barren landscape between the fog wall and the mountains; ten days with little water and less food; ten days with almost no sleep.

The low rolling foothills of the Tulkaran Range quickly gave way to slopes of broken shale and scree, dangerous, treacherous ground where a foot or ankle could be easily trapped and broken in the crevices. It was slow, tiring work and he had been exhausted before he had even reached the first dark cliff faces of the Broken Mountain.

Paedur had rested there for two days, camping in a small cave by the side of a dried-up river bed at the foot of the first glass-like wall. The first night passed without incident, but his dreams had been troubled the second night. He had fallen into a light doze just as twilight was purpling the mountain above his head, softening its shadow on the plain that stretched out before him . . . and then the mountain's shadow had twisted and shifted. Suddenly creatures without shape, beyond dimension, had risen up from the rocky plain. He turned and ran but they pursued him with claws of sharpened thorns and he had fled down a twisting maze which was filled with the serpent-like hiss of dried leaves and the muted clacking of dead branches. They reached for him – he turned and awoke exhausted, trembling with fatigue and the pre-dawn chill, but, before the first rays of the pale sun had touched the mountains with bronze, the bard had begun his climb.

Time had little meaning on the mountain; he measured it by cliffs and slopes, boulders and ledges – each one a conquest, each one a mark of his progress. It had been relatively simple at first . . . but that had been a long time ago, and now his breath came in pained gasps and he was soaked in an icy sweat, his hair plastered to his head, fever burning in his eyes. The rock swam before him, and tiny crystals in the stone sparkled and blinded him like miniature suns. He cursed the day he had agreed to attempt to return the Mandleseeds to the Dark Lord – but greed had decided him; the same greed that would be the cause of his death.

He spent the night on the small outcropping of stone barely half a length across which projected out over the chasm. Faurug the Nightwind howled and plucked at his torn clothing with icy fingers and Fiarle, the Little God of Icy Spaces, caressed him with silken hands and razor talons.

And Paedur resigned himself for death.

It was in the darkest hour of night, that time when Uimfe, Lord of Night, hunted abroad, when the shade of Mannam came to the dying man. 'How fares the bard?' he asked, his voice faint, whispering.

Paedur pushed himself into a sitting position; he had lost all feeling in his feet and legs and his right hand was tingling painfully. Fever was burning in him – he knew it – and he accepted the Duaiteoiri's presence without question. 'You've t-t-tricked me,' he accused Mannam, his teeth chattering. 'I will die here.'

The shade drifted closer, floating half a span above the edge of the ledge, its leafy cloak blowing in some ethereal wind which did not touch the man. 'No,' Mannam whispered, 'no, you will not die here upon this rock; your death, when it comes, will be both wondrous and tragic. I have come to succour you.' The Dark Lord gestured with a hand that looked like twisted branches.

The outcropping was abruptly bathed in a coldly luminous fox-fire. Tendrils of blue fire snaked along the stones and gathered in the darkened corners, until the entire ledge pulsed with the witch-light. The bard felt the painful return of circulation to his legs, and the leaden exhaustion that had claimed him fell away, leaving him alert and refreshed. Mannam provided food also – although, having looked closely at it, Paedur decided not to question its origin – and the last thing he saw before drifting off into a deep and dreamless sleep was the image of Mannam, his garments flapping wildly in the ghost-wind, drifting out across the empty night sky into the darkness.

He awoke as the first light of dawn was sweeping in from the east in long streaks of light, fully assured that the visitation was only the product of a fevered dream. But he found that the ledge was blackened and the lichens and mosses were seared and crisped, and also that his alertness and renewed strength were anything but natural.

So he pressed on. The weather changed and Snaitle, the Cold God, sent ice and snow whirling through the upper reaches of the mountain and the temperature plummeted. The chill bit through the bard's thin, worn clothing and his every breath burned in his throat and lungs like liquid fire. But when the cold threatened to overwhelm him, he found a cloak hanging on a diseased and leprous bush which, he suddenly realised, was the only vegetation he had encountered since he had left the foothills. The cloak covered him from neck to heel; it had a high rounded collar and a deep cowl, and there was an ornate silver clasp in the form of a snake swallowing its own tail set into the stiff collar that would enable the cloak to be fastened across his throat. It was woven of a smooth silken fur that rippled and flowed with his touch, and the bard ran his fingers down its length trying to identify the material. It felt like human hair. He shuddered; he was not squeamish, but the very touch of it against his skin repelled him. He sorted through what his lore told him about the Silent Wood, Mannam's lair, and he thought he knew where the Dark Lord had obtained the hair to fashion the cloak. He suppressed the urge to fling it out over the abyss; he knew he needed its warmth if he were to survive. And so he wore it, and continued climbing.

Hanoresreth, the day set aside for the worship of the Pantheon, dawned bright and clear with Nusas shining from a sky of liquid azure and only a touch of the Cold God lingering in the air. Paedur stood on a broad shelf of rock he had found the night before and breathed deeply, savouring the sharp air. He ran his slim fingers through his fine black hair and tilted his face to the sky, feeling the warmth of the sun against his eyelids. And then he opened his eyes and looked down. Below him, the cliff fell away, sheer and seemingly unbroken, and he marvelled that he had even reached this far. On an impulse he knelt and prayed, something he had not done for many years, although he had always accepted the existence of the gods – the evidence of his bardic lore confirming that. The words and phrases came to him easily as he asked the Gods of the Pantheon to look down upon him and lend him their favour, and he prayed also that C'lte would at least understand his motives, and possibly even forgive what he was attempting to do . . .

C'lte, the Yellow God of Life, swore as the almost physical blow struck him. The saffron-coloured cloud he was riding fragmented and threatened to dissipate completely as his concentration lapsed. He threw up his mental shields and only allowed the merest whisper of the prayers and thoughts to trickle through to him – but the power and clarity were still tremendous.

The Undying urged his wind-born chariot lower, riding the winds and currents that lashed against the smooth basalt walls of his kingdom like waves against the cliffs of some sea-shore. The rise and fall of the prayers grew in intensity until the Yellow God was forced to blank them from his consciousness lest they shatter his mind, but he could still feel them battering against his shields like a hammer of metal. He pin-pointed the direction of the prayers and allowed his saffron cloud to be pulled apart by the wind and he dropped like a stone, his tight yellow leggings and short jacket of the same colour moulding themselves to his slight form. He saw the figure below him – a mortal by his size and arrogant stance – and then he re-formed the cloud just above the creature's head. C'lte dropped on to it like a stone into a pond. The cloud rippled and bucked before settling.

The bard looked up, startled; he stepped back until his shoulder blades touched the cold stone wall, and his knife slipped into his hand and his hook rose before his face.

The Yellow God surfaced from the depths of the cloud and smiled at the bard. 'You are a curious one,' he said in a high thin voice, like a boy's. 'You have neither the visage nor form of those emaciated holy cringers who climb upon my mountain and make my life a misery with their whining. But then,' he added, quietly noting the bard's strange cloak and sickle-like hook, 'no-one has ever reached this far before.'

'I am not a holy man,' Paedur said quietly, more startled and surprised than frightened by this foppish youthful-looking god.

'What are you then?'

'My name is Paedur, if it please my lord, and . . .'

'Your name is quite your own affair, and whether it pleases me or not matters very little.' The Undead shook his head slowly and sighed.

'I have come seeking your aid,' Paedur continued forcefully, suddenly annoyed at this effete creature whom men worshipped as a god. He rubbed the blade of the knife in his hand against the edge of his cloak and then returned it to his boot.

C'lte brushed back his corn-yellow hair with both hands. 'We gods really don't care to aid you mortals,' he said with a grin. 'Oh, certainly an awe-inspiring demonstration of power is called for every century or so just to keep you mortals in line, you understand, but we do have our own worlds to rule – and yours is but a minor plane of existence.'

The bard was nonplussed. He had expected many reactions from the god when he confronted him, surprise, anger, compassion, fear even – but certainly not indifference. 'But the gods need men,' he said almost absently.

And suddenly all the humour and boredom, the pretence, was gone from the Undying's lemon-yellow eyes. 'The gods and men are bound together, they need each other,' he snapped.

The bard smiled coldly, realising he had finally touched something in the creature. 'I have heard it said that when man loses faith in his gods then the gods die, for without faith the gods have no substance.'

13

The Yellow God stared at the man for what seemed like an eternity . . . and then he smiled. 'I like you, mortal. Here you are, obviously exhausted after your climb, and yet in your first encounter with one of the gods, you find time to argue.'

'I have not come this far to be put off.'

'What have you come for then? What brought you here?'

'I followed a dream,' Paedur said, dropping his voice almost to a whisper, looking away from the god.

The Yellow God nodded seriously. 'I have found that men often do; and yours led you here?'

Paedur launched into the speech he had prepared during his climb. 'I followed a dream planted in childhood, nurtured through youth until it finally grew and came to flower with my maturity. It is a dream which has brought me across the Bridge, through the blasted City of Souls, across the barren Wastelands, up past the Shaled Slopes, past the Shattered Stones and even beyond the Little Pinnacle. My dream has brought me here.'

'A pretty speech,' C'lte smiled. 'But now tell me why?'

'Because Lord C'lte, I am a bard – a poet also – and the tales and sagas I tell my listeners are full of the beauties of your domain, and I wish to fill my sight with images of life and beauty from your enchanted gardens . . . before I die.'

'A bard and a poet,' C'lte murmured, resting his pointed chin on his delicate long-fingered hands and leaning across the edge of the cloud. 'But why have you come to me now; you are a young man with many years of life before you. Surely there are many beauties on your own plane waiting to be savoured before risking all on this climb?'

Paedur looked at the god and then sighed, slowly shaking his head. 'Aaah, lord, I wish that were so.' He dropped his gaze, his eyes refusing to meet the god's hard stare. 'My lord, I have been informed that Mannam, Lord of the Dead, intends to call me from this world into the Silent Wood. I have a disease' – he rested his hook across his chest – 'and my physician tells me that there is no cure. I have not long left in this life . . .' his voice trailed off into a defeated whisper.

The Undying regarded Paedur steadily for the space of a score of heartbeats, and the bard shivered as those sharp yellow eyes bored into him. Surely the god would discover the deception? But then C'lte smiled bitterly. 'Ah yes, I know of the tiny life span of you Little Ones, and I have heard of disease, and, although it occurs in many of the prayers I hear, yet I fear there is little I can do about it since it is an absolute mystery to me.' The Yellow God of Life shook his head slowly. 'I cannot cure what I do not know.' He suddenly reached out his hand. 'Come then, come and I will guest you in my kingdom, and thus when you enter Mannam's dark lair, your memories will be of life and light.'

Paedur stepped forward to the edge of the outcropping and C'lte gripped his wrist and lifted him effortlessly across the divide that separated the ledge from the saffron cloud. The bard floundered as he sank into the billowing softness, but the god held him.

'Believe in it,' he said, 'have faith.' Then he added with a smile, 'Faith lends Substance.'

Paedur nodded dumbly, closed his eyes and imagined a sturdy fishing smack of heavy tar-daubed wood beneath his feet . . . and slowly the cloud took on the solidity and almost the shape of the vessel.

'You are a strange man, bard,' C'lte said quietly, observing the changes in the cloud. 'I did not think it was possible for a mortal to mould the *elementalis*.'

The bard grinned, feeling a tide of exhilaration surge through him. 'You forget my lord that I am a bard; if I cannot visualise strongly then my audience will find their tales and myths lacking and shallow.'

'Of course,' the Yellow God nodded, but his eyes remained hooded. 'Let us go then . . .'

They rose slowly until they were above the lower reaches of the mountain, and it was only then that the bard began to appreciate how vast it actually was. The endless wall drifted down before them, and when Paedur looked down he found that the base of the mountain was lost beneath a covering of cloud, while above them the pinnacle was still invisible in the dim and distant heavens. They passed huge gullies running in jagged rents across the slopes, ugly slashes and tears in the very fabric of the mountain opening out into giant craters and immense fields of shattered and broken rock.

C'lte nodded. 'That is why it's called the Broken Mountain.'

Paedur shaded his eyes, sure that he saw something moving in the blasted landscape. 'How did it happen?' he asked quietly.

The Yellow God shrugged. 'Oh, once long ago, in the war between the Usurpers and their allies the Demons against the Gods, the battle spilled over from Ab-Apsalom, the Battleground of the Gods, and its fury destroyed the lush green fields and wild forests that covered the slopes. And even now, many years after that battle, I will not touch it, for it is tainted and it taints all who come into contact with it.' The god laughed mirthlessly. 'Even if you had made it that far, you would not have come out of the Broken Fields a man.'

They rose further, the mountain flowing grey and monotonously before them, and then the bard suddenly took a shivering fit. Something cold slithered down his spine and nestled there. His vision blurred and he pressed the heel of his right hand into his eyes. He blinked, squeezing his eyes shut, and when he opened them again he found he could see – although his eyes still felt gritty and everything was blurred . . .

They rose past the Glass Cliffs, and the bard smiled ruefully when he saw them: he would never have been able to scale those glacial heights. As they slid past, he thought he could make out shapes – buildings, towers, walls – entombed within the crystal ice, but it was gone so fast he could not be sure. They rose past the huge circular nests of the Giant Eagles – empty now – cousins to the Roc and the Aontoketi, and as savage as the Gryphon . . . past the flimsy shelters of the Shepherds, who were once of the Culai, the First Race, demi-men, quasi-gods who ruled the world in the First Age . . . but those that now walked the heights were little more than brutes. But the gods used them in many ways, mainly to shepherd the thoughts and prayers of men – which by the time they had reached this far had assumed an almost identifiable form. The Shepherds gathered them together into neat bundles of desires . . . and then tossed them into the Gorge! Those garnished with the smoke of sacrifice and the blood of animals they put to one side and passed them on to the gods – if they remembered; but their memories are short.

And now the landscape changed, and the bard found it became even harder to distinguish between what he was actually seeing and what he thought he was seeing. His eyes were stinging again, and he found it easier to close them and listen to the Yellow God's voice as it rose and fell in a low drone as he listed the various sights. The bard found himself drifting into a light doze . . .

. . . They soared past the Eternal Fields where Youth and Childhood play hand in hand with Happiness and Joy, for there is no Sorrow in the Eternal Fields. They floated past the Gate of Years that leads to the Fields, and they rose over the Rainbow which hangs eternally over it, and the Road, of time-yellowed brick, which also leads to the Eternal Fields of Childhood . . .

Paedur struggled to free himself from the leaden exhaustion that now gripped him; his limbs trembled and ached and he could no longer feel his heartbeat or hear his breathing. And still they rose, and the Yellow God's voice continued remorselessly.

. . . They came to the Greater Pinnacle, where man's dreams gathered and howled defiance at a sneering Fate, and laugh and gibber through the small hours of the morning, for Coulide Dream-Maker stalks the minds of men then, weaving the Past with Present and Present with Future, granting desires a life and imbuing them with Joy or sometimes Terror, for his is a terrible power . . .

Paedur attempted to squeeze his eyes shut, but the images he saw and experienced lived within him, fired and fuelled by the Yellow God. The god's words, his descriptions of the Broken Mountain, were familiar, very familiar. The bard attempted to recognise the text the Undying was mouthing; he almost knew it; was it an ancient account of a man's journey to the heavens?

. . . They rose on the Silent Winds that sometimes blow through the soul with a soundless keening, and the saffron cloud tattered and frayed, but the Undying grasped the bard around the waist and, carrying him as if he weighed no more than a babe, soared above those mundane things which men hold important and which had gathered in ugly pools below the level of Dreams, while the cloud re-formed.

Up, ever upwards, past the Citadel of Man's Ambition which he builds in the Realm of Imagination; past the heights which he ever aspires to. A huge wall of roughly-hewn stones rushed past: the Wall of Ignorance which few men ever breach, but which must be surmounted if one wishes to attain life eternal . . .

'*Benedictus*!' Paedur suddenly shouted. '*The Vision of Saint Benedictus*.' And, as abruptly as it had started, the hazy visions and sights disappeared and revealed the barren slopes of the mountain beneath. He shook his head, attempting to clear the muzziness which still clouded his thinking. 'What did you do to me?' he demanded, raising his hook threateningly.

The Yellow God smiled and shrugged his slim shoulders. 'Well, it's such a boring journey up here, nothing to see but ugly grey rock and black stone, and I thought it might add a little . . . interest.' He bowed slightly. 'You are correct of course; in the main I took the "journey" from the *Vision of Saint Benedictus*.' He leaned forward and added confidently. 'A most arrogant man – a coward also – he spent nearly twenty days living just inside the fringes of the City of Souls, which were not nearly so bad then as they are now, before he returned and proclaimed to all who would listen that he had visited my kingdom.' The god shook his head, smiling coldly. 'I detest liars and fools – and he was both.'

'Had you anything to do with his curious death?' the bard asked, finding it difficult to remain angry for long with this boy-god.

'Who – me?' The god raised his hands in astonishment and then he grinned. 'Well, a little. He was very fond of his drink, you know?' He paused when the bard shook his head.

'I thought he detested alcohol.'

C'lte laughed. 'The only alcohol he detested were the drops he spilt on opening a bottle. However, to continue; it so happened that a tiny seed found its way into his cup. He swallowed it – and unfortunately it seems it took root in his stomach.' The god shrugged. 'A bush growing in his stomach; it was a miracle – and it gave him his greatest wish: it made him a martyr.'

Paedur smiled tightly, but inwardly he shuddered: C'lte was capable of exacting a terrible revenge on those who crossed him. And suddenly Mannam's words came back to him: *you will not die here upon this rock; your death, when it comes, will be both wondrous and tragic*. Benedictus' death had been both *wondrous and tragic* – a fully formed bush bursting out from his stomach – and the bard wondered if this was what Death had in mind.

They continued rising, and then they suddenly passed through a band of cloud, tinted billowing strands of differing colours which hid the cold, bare rock, cloaking it beneath a fiery mantle. The bard squinted into the shifting colours; he could see other multi-hued clouds nearby, and it looked as if all of them were joined by a thin silver thread.

Suddenly they were out of the coloured mist and C'lte's yellow cloud slowed and stopped. 'This way.' The god reached out his hand and took the bard's arm. He stepped over the edge of the fragmenting cloud – and on to a bridge; a bridge woven of gold and silver thread, rising and falling, joining the rainbow-hued clouds together. The Yellow God gestured with a translucent hand.

'The Bridge of Twilight,' he said simply, but Paedur detected a touch of pride in his voice. 'Here Dawn marches forth and Dusk stalks in silence. The bridge is composed of the stuff of sunrise and morning, of light trapped undecided between night and day . . .' His voice trailed off, and then he added, 'I will compose a poem in celebration of it one of these days.'

The bard shook his head in wonder as he walked out on to the delicate-seeming bridge. 'It is very beautiful.'

Something of sunset and evening was in the composition of the bridge, of light shafting through purple clouds, of the close silence that tells that the day is almost done. The bridge looked insubstantial, almost wraith-like, but it was hard and unyielding beneath his feet, and when he stamped his foot, he almost imagined he heard a dull echoing boom.

The bard walked side by side with the Yellow God across the bridge; they paused once and stood to one side as the Grey Lights – the semi-sentient creatures which are the precursors of the dawn – flitted by on wings of smoke. Paedur looked over the twisting rail and down to the tiny pockets floating in the mist on the multi-hued clouds: the domain of C'lte, the Lands of Life Eternal. For a moment, he forgot he had come here to steal from the god, he forgot the lies and the treachery and the greed that had brought him this far; now, he was just a man, staring at something which had never been seen by mortal man before.

The bard looked across at the Undying and there were tears in his eyes. 'We know nothing of all this,' he said simply. He gestured broadly, taking in the bridge, the clouds, the islands. 'Man is blind to the beauty, the complexity of it all.' He pointed back to where the Grey Lights drifted across the edge of the bridge. 'To us, dawn is just the beginning of a new day, dusk the ending.' He shook his head sadly. 'Few can appreciate the beauty of it all. We are blind.'

The Yellow God nodded agreement. 'You Little Ones barely live, inhabiting that zone between life and death where all is blurred and shadowed. All your colours are pastel shades, all your sounds are dull; and your lives are akin to that, they too are dull and muted. You strive and strive and in the end what do you achieve. . .? Naught. And why?' The Yellow God shrugged. Because you have no vision, no sight. You look ahead in spans of hours, days, weeks and sometimes years – but never centuries, millennia.' The god's voice rose, taking on a harsher note, and suddenly he didn't look so young. 'And yet in your arrogance you say, "That is the sun, an orb of fire, it has nothing to do with me." But without Nusas to light and heat and protect you, where would man be?

'You see the Broken Mountain in the tales and drawings of your fathers and you say, "God once lived atop that mountain," and then you laugh and mock the faith of your fathers, and yet without that faith, and the Life that burns atop the mountain, man would not – could not – exist. Man cannot see greatness, for he is petty-minded and ignorant. Ignorant!' C'lte laughed bitterly.

'But we believe,' Paedur said forcefully. 'We – I – had the faith to climb up the mountainside, fully expecting – knowing – that I would find the God of Life. I know the gods are real, and there are many like me who also believe.'

'Aye, but there are also many who do not believe,' C'lte interrupted, 'they mock the faithful, revile the sacrifices, offend the priests: some even worship false gods.'

'But that is your fault,' the bard snapped. 'The gods have not come forth in strength since my father's father was a young man, and even then it was but the momentary appearances of Oigne and Uide to bless a new city.'

The Yellow God was silent for a while, and when he eventually spoke, his voice was soft and distant. 'There are gods upon your plane even now; they come unexpected and go unheeded, but they are there. There is a change abroad upon your world, this we know; while some men openly question the Old Faith and are content with leaving it at that, there are others who are creating new, false gods. Human gods devoid of mystery and lacking in power – for the moment.' C'lte gazed into the distance and his yellow-gold eyes narrowed as if he were gazing into a future, a future the bard could not even guess at, but a future which he feared he might live to see.

'But surely a false base god cannot harm one such as you?' he asked quietly.

'Faith is a prerequisite for Substance,' the Yellow God said softly, 'and man is now playing with forces beyond his understanding, for he is creating gods in man's own image, and that is the most dangerous game of all.' His long slender fingers brushed the bard's shoulder and he pointed beyond the Lands of Life to a region of twisting shadow. 'There are many creatures lurking beyond the Threshold of Life who have not yet entered the gateway of the Silent Wood and who could provide a semblance of godhood to a gullible mankind. And, believe me, some have already been called!'

20

Paedur shivered suddenly, for there was a note almost of fear in the god's voice.

They crossed the remainder of the bridge in silence until they came to a series of broad shallow steps leading down into the clouds. The god gestured. 'But come bard, enter into my kingdom: the Lands of Life Eternal.'

Paedur stood on the top step and looked back along the Bridge of Twilight which was now tinged with amber as Dawn prepared to cross on dewed feet. And then he turned and looked down on to the fields of eternal youth, those unattainable, mystical lands sometimes glimpsed in fevered sickness or drug-induced delirium. From this height, they looked like tiny islands in a sea of coloured cloud, obscured and hazy in the distance. These were the islands of myth and legend, of faith and fancy. As the Yellow God led the bard down the steps which had been hewn from a white, almost translucent stone, he pointed out the various isles. Here was Tir na nOg, the Isle of the Blessed, and rocky Circondel; wooded Beliessa and beyond them haunted and sunken Lyonesse; golden tZlanta-tLeoto and Mu, twin islands with their similar tall bastions of glittering crystal stone. And there were more, many more, each one strange and different, and yet each one united in one thing – these were the lands where Death held no sway, basking forever in the reflected glory of the Yellow God of Life.

'My kingdom,' C'lte said proudly.

Paedur shook his head in wonder. 'I never realised that it was so . . . large.'

The god smiled. 'Oh my kingdom expands, it will never fill. It is said that each man carries his own immortality within him . . . all I know is that some men create their own immortality. However, you may wander here for a while,' he said in a different tone, 'here you may fill your poet's mind with images and your bard's imagination with tales and sagas. But a warning,' his hand brushed against the bard's shoulder and he pointed beyond the fields once again to the region of shadow. 'Do not stray beyond the Lands of Life Eternal, do not approach the region of the shadow, the Netherworld.'

Paedur squinted into the distance, but the black cloud wall was in constant motion and he suddenly felt dizzy and light-headed. His eyes watered and he blinked back tears as he turned back to the god.

'It is the Netherworld; it is neither mine nor Mannam's, belonging neither to life nor death. But it is inhabited by . . . creatures, the souls of men – and others – which have been cast out of the planes of existence to mouth and cry in silence for all eternity. And you would prove a tasty morsel for them, and it would not be just your corpse they would devour,' he added with a grin.

2 The Geasa

He walked the Lands of Life Eternal, planning deceit.
The Life of Paedur, the Bard

Paedur walked slowly along the bone-white sands bordering the
Aman, the White River, that flowed through the Yellow God's
kingdom. It was, he reckoned, early morning, since he had lately
seen the Bridge of Twilight blaze salmon and gold with the dawn.
A heavy silence hung over the scores of islands – even the river on
his right-hand side flowed without a sound and the crunch of his
booted feet on the sands sounded almost unnaturally loud.

Several days had passed – exactly how many, he had no way of
knowing, but he had watched the Bridge blaze and burn with
sunrise and sunset five or six times. In that time he had travelled
through most of the Lands of Life Eternal, crossing from field to
field, island to island, ferried by an ageless creature in rags who
acted as boatman. His sense of wonder had quickly dulled as he
conversed with the heroes of legend who had been granted eternal
life by the grateful gods; with the sages who had delved deep into
the hidden lore and therein found the path to the Lands, and with
the great kings of old who had attained immortality of a kind
through the power of their sorcerer-physicians.

He had learned many of the secrets of the past as the procession
of characters told their stories of the battles and migrations, of the
building of cities and the rise of empires, and of the races that
walked the world with men.

But although he learned much and discovered more, he learned
nothing of the Mandlethorn.

Paedur sat down on a smooth rounded boulder set deep into the
white sands. He felt as if time were running out; C'lte would not
allow him him to stay very much longer in the Lands of Life
Eternal. He needed more time . . .

'Time is meaningless here.'

Paedur looked up into the god's smiling face. C'lte was still
dressed in yellow leggings and a short jacket, and today he wore a

23

pair of soft velvet sandals embossed with gold thread. The Un-dying sank down on to his haunches by the bard's side and stared out across the broad slow river. He deliberately turned to look at the bard, and when he turned back to the river he continued on, his voice unusually solemn. 'But although Time's encompassing hand does not fall over my kingdom, he still holds sway on your plane.'

'You sound almost as if you fear Time,' Paedur said quietly, tossing a handful of white sand into the turgid water.

'Time,' C'lte said seriously, 'is greater than us all, even greater than the gods – and we can only maintain pockets of timelessness with great difficulty. Were you to remain a little longer in my domain, then you would find your world much changed when you finally returned, for the world as you knew it would be lost in the past.' The god stood and dusted off his hands. 'So, I fear you must go now. I trust you have seen everything . . .?'

The bard stood up and nodded silently.

The Yellow God led the bard along the banks of the Aman River, the white particles of sand rising and swirling in the still air before falling back on to the beach, erasing their footsteps.

C'lte prattled on in his high, thin, musical voice, pointing out some of the furthest, most distant isles: silent Zotichal and Paran-dale, wherein it is always morn; tUse-tUse, inhabited only by lovers; Valsengard with its icy cliffs and eternal covering of snow; Nsu, the paradoxical Land of Waves . . .

'My lord,' Paedur said suddenly, as they came in sight of the broad shallow steps leading upwards into the clouds.

The god paused and turned, and the bard thought he saw something like amusement in his yellow eyes.

'My lord, there is one thing I would like to see before I leave.'

'And that is?' C'lte whispered.

'The Mandlethorn,' Paedur began, and then hurried on when he saw the god's expression harden. 'It is said that you stole it from Mannam himself . . .'

The god smiled bleakly, and when he spoke his voice was cold and distant. 'Aaah, yes, the Mandlethorn, you must see that. You will want to construct a poem or tale from its history – and my part in its theft . . .' He paused and smiled with something of his usual good humour. 'Something suitable; something flattering and yet praising . . . and of course subtle, perhaps hinting at deeper mysteries.' He laughed briefly. 'But of course you bards are very good at that sort of thing, and I presume to teach you your craft. I will leave the Epic of the Mandlethorn to your own discretion. This way.' He stopped, looking at the bard, his strange yellow eyes dancing with some private amusement. 'There is something we have to do first, before we see the Mandlethorn; something important . . . indeed, crucial almost. You will bear with me – I'm sure you will find the diversion interesting.' He nodded quickly, 'Yes, very interesting, I'm sure.' C'lte touched the bard's shoulder and led him away from the banks of the river and along a thin, winding pathway that led up into the rocky highlands which, although they were part of the god's kingdom, were not a portion of the Lands of Life Eternal. The bard had attempted to explore them some days ago, but had been politely – but firmly – turned away by two warriors still wearing the ancient wood-and-leather armour of the Shemmatae. He had been told then that this was the god's own private garden.

Paedur walked behind the slight form of the god. He could feel the small hairs on the back of his neck rising: something was amiss, there was something about C'lte's attitude . . . something he just couldn't put a finger on. Did he know – or guess? He was a god – Paedur didn't even presume to guess at his abilities or powers – but yet for all his bluster, the bard hadn't actually seen any demonstration of power that was unusually startling. There had been the cloud, of course, but levitation was possible – he himself had seen some of the Shemmat fakirs levitate themselves some several lengths into the air. The spell the god had cast over him to make him see the visions on the barren mountainside was not that difficult either: every trained bard possessed it to some degree; it was the ability to make an audience see what was not, and imagine what had been, to translate the speaker's words into pictures. So just how powerful was this boy-god, and just what did he know?

'How did you steal the Mandlethorn?' Paedur asked boldly. 'I came across a mention of the feat in an ancient manuscript, but it didn't give any details,' he added hastily.

C'lte glanced over his shoulder, and Paedur shivered at the look in his eyes. 'Oh, it was very easy,' he said quietly. He took a turning off the track to the left and almost immediately the ground began to slope down, and smooth walls of polished stone rose on either side. The Undying's voice echoed off and was distorted by the stone and Paedur had to strain to catch every word.

'It was many years ago when I took the Mandlethorn, bard. Of

25

course, the people's belief in Life was much stronger then, and I too was strong.' His shoulders slumped. 'In these times man seems to live only for death – and I am not as strong as I once was. However,' he continued, 'I disguised myself as a corpse . . .' The bard blinked as he thought he saw the Yellow God's form flicker and take on the shape of a bloody and battered warrior from a bygone age. '. . . And I managed to creep past the wooded sentinels and the stone-bound guardians into the Silent Wood.' The god's shape flickered and wavered again and he reassumed his own youthful form. 'I was accompanied by Luid, the Fire Sprite, and for several days we wandered the length of the Silent Wood avoiding the savage beasts that Mannam keeps as pets and the bands of men – warriors who have died together but who find it difficult to accept their deaths and thus continue on as if they were still alive.'

The track branched and C'lte took the right-hand fork that continued to lead downwards into the shadows. The walls on either side rose higher and almost joined overhead. 'However, we eventually found the Woodsheart and the Secret Grove that runs the length of it, and there, growing on a small island, surrounded by filthy water, we found the Mandlethorn, the Bush of Life, the Thorn of Death.'

The track swung to the left and the bard saw a long oblong of light on the wall ahead. 'I took the twelve seeds that grew between the roots and I gave the rest of the bush to Luid . . .' He smiled grimly. 'It was a brief fire.' He paused, remembering, and then hurried on. 'I took the seeds back here with me where I had created a suitable . . . garden . . . for them. I then called together Quilda, the Goddess of Growth, and Huide, the Little God of Summer Rain; they both blessed the seeds – and the bush has flourished.'

C'lte led the bard out into a hollow and then into a grove of trees which blazed with liquid light. Paedur groaned aloud as the light burned his eyes and seemed to pierce right through to his skull. C'lte murmured an apology and the light abruptly dimmed. Paedur rubbed his streaming eyes with the corner of his cloak and when he looked at the trees again he found that they were not wooden, but rather had been constructed of rare metals: gold, whele, silver, orchilium and *juste*. The leaves shivered slightly in a breeze the bard couldn't feel, and their delicate, haunting music hung – almost vibrating – on the air. He moved, and he suddenly found himself reflected on every side, glittering and scintillating in countless shades and hues. The Undying cast no reflection.

C'lte led him through the metallic forest along a winding track that led out into a perfectly circular clearing. In the exact centre of the circle stood a tree, a tree of natural wood which looked almost drab in comparison with its metallic copies. And it was surrounded by a carpet of shifting, pulsing, coloured light.

The god stepped forward and the light on the ground swirled and eddied, pulsing and throbbing like a living thing; Paedur hesitated a moment, and then followed closely behind. He found it was like walking through water: there was a slight resistance but it was gentle and comfortable, and as they neared the tree, the drag lessened, and it became obvious that the light was seeping out from the ground about the base of the tree itself.

C'lte stood beneath the spreading branches and bowed low, and the bard saw his lips move slightly, in salutation or prayer, the bard was unsure which. The Undying then reached up and, bending a low branch, plucked a small red-gold fruit from beneath the leaves and handed it to the bard. 'Eat,' he commanded.

Paedur examined the fruit carefully: it was small and soft, the skin slightly furred. He looked warily at the god.

C'lte smiled gently. 'Eat it – it won't harm you . . . indeed, it has been known to grant men their heart's desire.'

The bard lifted his hook, preparing to cut into the soft skin, but the god's fingers closed on his arm, pushing it down. 'Eat it,' he commanded.

'Not until I know what I'm eating,' Paedur objected.

'This,' C'lte said coldly, 'is the Tree of Knowledge, and what is Life but Knowledge?'

'I don't understand,' Paedur said, truly puzzled now.

The god looked surprised and then he said, 'No, I really believe you don't. Trust me,' he said, taking the fruit from the bard's hand and biting into it, and then handing it back. The same look of sly amusement the bard had glimpsed earlier in the god's eyes was back once again. 'It will help you to appreciate the Mandlethorn all the more.'

The bard nodded doubtfully but bit into the fruit, immediately tasting the bitter-sweet tang on his tongue. He coughed and his eyes watered: the Yellow God, the tree, the metallic wood dissolved into an artist's palette of colours, constantly moving, constantly changing. He swallowed the fruit, and fire and lightning coursed through his body; his muscles locked and trembled as if he were fever-ridden, he felt his heart slow . . . slow . . . slow . . . stop – and then start again. And his left hand – his missing left hand – ached with an agonising pain.

Paedur opened his eyes. For a moment he thought his vision was still blurred and he brushed his hand across his eye – and then he saw the flickering aura that outlined his fingers. It took him a few moments to recognise it for what it was and then he realised that he was actually seeing his own life force. He looked about: everything had changed.

The trees and bushes, the blades of silvered grass, the golden rocks, the artificial stones, the shifting clouds overhead and even the very rivers and streams now throbbed and quivered with a burning aura of life. And the Tree of Knowledge – which had at first seemed so drab and colourless – now threw off streamers of fire which trembled on the still air, and the individual leaves now sparkled like gemstones.

The bard turned and looked towards the god, but C'lte raised his hand, his long fingers closing over the bard's face. 'Do not look directly at me,' the god warned. 'You can now see the visible aura of Life that surrounds every living thing. I am the very essence of Life . . . the sight of me would blast your senses.' The god moved around behind the bard and instructed him to close his eyes, and then Paedur felt a feather-light touch against his temples. 'Perhaps it would be better if I were to dull that part of your new-found perception – at least for the moment, until you have learned to control it yourself. You may look at me now,' the god said.

Paedur turned, half expecting to see a pillar of flaming life forces, but the god appeared unchanged. C'lte spread his hands and smiled. 'Don't look so disappointed,' he said. He put a hand on the bard's shoulder, and led him deeper into the mirrored wood.

The god led him down into a small stone-enclosed hollow and then stopped before a slight mound. Even before he saw it, Paedur felt his skin crawling, and the hair on his head beginning to rise in long wavering streamers.

'Behold the Mandlethorn!'

The bard blinked – and then cried out in pain at the vision that lanced his eyes: a vision of Life and Death inextricably entwined.

The Mandlethorn was a small stunted bush nestling against a huge boulder on the top of a tiny artificial mound . . . and it was familiar. Paedur could have named a score – or more – of bushes that it resembled – and yet it did differ from them, but only in small subtle ways. With his heightened senses he could see the very essence of life and growth covering the patina of death and decay, and the sweet smell of corruption mingled with the bitter perfume of growth.

'I can see the Life in it,' the bard whispered, awed, 'and at the same time the Death: both are present.'

'In all Life there is Death,' C'lte quoted, 'but of course here,' he encompassed his domain with a sweeping motion of his arm, 'here Death can gain no foothold, and only in the Mandlethorn are we reminded of Mannam and his drear kingdom.'

'Are there then creatures of life in the Silent Wood, reminders of this place?' the bard asked softly, still staring at the bush.

'There are some who shamble in a semblance of half-life in the Dark Lord's kingdom; a spark of life still burns within them, but it burns low, and they do not live in a way that you would comprehend.'

Paedur moved closer to the bush and gently stroked the long drooping leaves which were shaped like flattened spearheads. They felt like human skin, soft and sensuous, warm and smooth, trembling slightly. Then he swore and withdrew his hand, pain and puzzlement in his eyes, a bead of liquid crimson nestling delicately on his fingertips. He brought his fingers to his mouth, but the god stopped him.

'No, do not swallow the poisoned blood.' He took the bard's hand in his, breathed on the cut, and then gently brushed the blood from the wound . . . and, beneath, the jagged puncture had healed.

'Look,' C'lte said and, kneeling beside the bush, carefully pulled aside the quivering leaves revealing the thorns: long thin evil spikes which pulsed regularly. They were both hooked and barbed and each barb glistened with a tiny spot of dark liquid. They recoiled like writhing serpents from the Undead's hand. The god smiled. 'See how they cannot bear the touch of Life, for these are the Thorns of Death. It was a thorn from this bush which sent Artre the White King to his death and put Erta his brother on the throne.' He shook his head slowly, and then a sly smile spread across his thin face. 'But Alile the Judge Impartial sent Coulide Dream-Maker to haunt the murderer with memories from the Eternal Fields of Childhood, and the usurper never again slept without Nightmare and Terror, Coulide's pets, stalking his dreams.' The god's smile faded. 'And in the end Erta took his own life – and that was a terrible crime for which we are solely responsible – and you might learn from it, bard: though the gods are all-powerful, they are not wholly omnipotent. And now the soul of the suicide cries beyond the realm of Life and before that of Death in the Netherworld . . .'

'My lord,' Paedur said abruptly, 'there is something I have to tell you.'

C'lte rose to his feet and looked up into the bard's dark eyes – and for the first time Paedur realised how small the god was. 'You are going to tell me of the bargain you made with Mannam for the Lament of Lugas and the Harp of Auigne?'

C'lte laughed at the bard's expression, and taking him by the arm led him back through the wood and into a grove of trees which guarded a small black-and-gold marble pool. The Yellow God peered into the flat waters and moved his hand across the surface. Immediately the pool clouded and swirled with unseen currents, and as it settled fragments of images rippled across the surface. Suddenly the bard stiffened, for the pool had cleared and there, reflected in the waters, was not C'lte and the bard but rather the Dark Lord and the bard in his stone cell in the Forest of Euarthe, and he could hear with the sound of trickling water his conversation with Mannam.

'How long have you known?' he asked the Yellow God quietly.

'I suspected you were not all you purported to be from the very beginning, but I knew for certain shortly after I brought you here.' The god dipped his yellow-tinged hand in the placid pool and gently moved his fingers to and fro, creating fleeting patterns of sparkling colours that danced in the evening light. 'Faurug and Taisce came to me with a tale of conspiracy between man and Duaite, and the Dewspreader had recorded everything within his liquid pearls, and some he cast into this pool . . .'

Paedur looked over at the god. 'And if you knew that, did you also know that I intended to try and trick you into granting me eternal life?'

C'lte smiled. 'I guessed you might – and when you told me on the mountain that you were ill, and I could see that your aura burned bright and unblemished – that's when I began to suspect that something was amiss.' He paused and shook glistening water droplets from his long gold-tipped fingers. 'And so rather than allowing myself to be tricked, I took the precaution of giving it to you,' he added almost in a whisper.

It took a moment for the god's words to sink in . . . and then comprehension dawned. 'The fruit of the Tree of Knowledge!'

C'lte nodded. 'The Fruit of Life. You now have Life Eternal, Paedur – may you live long enough to enjoy it.'

'But why?' Paedur demanded. 'You knew I had lied to you; you knew I was coming up here to try and steal the Mandleseeds . . . and yet you gift me with . . . with . . .' he stammered, something he had not done since he had been a child.

The Yellow God smiled distantly. 'Do not thank me for your gift yet; perhaps there will come a day when you will curse me for it.'

'But why did you give it to me?' Paedur demanded.

'It is . . . necessary.'

'Necessary? I don't understand.'

'You will in time; suffice it to say that it is necessary to grant you Life Eternal.' He pulled a small satin purse from his belt and handed it to the bard. 'It is also necessary to give you these.'

Paedur pulled the drawstrings and opened the bag. The contents tumbled out on to the palm of his hand where they lay pulsing like six clots of fresh blood. They could only be one thing . . .

'The Mandleseeds,' C'lte said. 'There are only six there, but those you may bring to Mannam, and henceforth let there be peace between us, for are not the Spirits of Life and Death equal, opposite and yet alike?'

'My lord,' the bard protested, 'I cannot accept these.'

The god smiled grimly. 'You have no choice. You are oathbound to return the seeds to Mannam, and now you are also oathbound to repay me for my gifts to you . . .' he said, his voice hardening.

Paedur went ice-cold. 'Why do I suddenly feel as if I've just walked into a very well-laid web?'

C'lte shook his head. 'You have not been trapped; we are not about to force you to do anything against your will. Yes, you have been . . . persuaded to come here, but I think you have little to complain about. You have been well treated and have even obtained your heart's desire.'

'Granted; but you might also bear in mind that I almost died on your mountain.'

'*Nonsense*! Mannam watched over you the whole time. You

31

might have suffered some discomfort but you were never in any danger.'

Paedur wiped the blade of his hook across his legging. He controlled the sudden impulse to lunge at the god, use the sharpened edge and point of his hook to tear out his throat. 'Would you like to tell me why you have gone to all this trouble to bring me here then?' he asked tightly.

'You are angry,' C'lte said surprised. 'but you have no reason to be.'

'I think, Lord C'lte, you will find that no human likes to be tricked, to be moved about like a piece on a game-board. Now just what is it you want?' he demanded coldly.

C'lte sat on the edge of the pool and stared up at the bard. He found it difficult to accept the other's ill-humour, but then, man had always been difficult to comprehend. He looked away down the grove to where the last of the metallic trees blazed golden with the evening sunlight.

'You are aware,' he said, without turning his head, 'of the sudden resurgence of interest in the New Religion, that blasphemous, scurrilous, obscene travesty of a belief? It is not new, but lately it has grown in strength and there has been an unprecedented increase in its followers.'

'I know of it,' Paedur said quietly, 'but I don't see what this has to do . . .'

'Bard, for many generations of man the Gods of the Pantheon and the Old Faith have held sway through the Seven Nations and beyond. The great faith and belief of the people has lent us substance and their worship has made us strong. But now the people are beginning to drift away and follow the New Religion. They have created a god in their own image . . . and now a being has come forth from the Netherworld, a creature that was once a man – we think! – a being called Trialos, and he has assumed the mantle of godhood, and such is the people's belief in him – misguided belief it is true, but still powerful – that the New Religion, and especially their god, Trialos, now threatens the Old Faith.' He paused and his eyes grew clouded. 'Some of the older, wilder gods have already retreated to the more distant planes of existence where the faith of their followers still remains strong.' C'lte turned and stared up into the bard's dark eyes. 'Should the people cease to worship us, then we will return to the Void from whence we came.'

Paedur breathed deeply, unaware that he had been holding his breath. Fragments of the old myths and legends came back to him, the tales of men and women called by the gods in times of great danger and confusion. He felt his whole world slide and shift; perceptions changed, plans were abandoned, and he felt something die within him. 'What do you want me to do?' he asked numbly.

The Yellow God stood up. He placed his right hand on the bard's shoulder, and Paedur felt the tingling transference of power. He looked deep into the god's flat, cat-like eyes and saw something like pity mirrored there.

'This is your *geasa*. I charge you to wander the roads of the Nations and to uphold the Faith against the evil of the New Religion. And I charge you never to waver in your task.' The god's voice boomed and echoed about the little grove. The smooth water in the pool vibrated and thrashed and leaves broke from the branches overhead and floated down over the pair.

'Paedur, I charge you to be the Champion of the Old Faith!'

The bard opened his mouth, but the Yellow God smiled, and his aura expanded, dazzling him with painful brilliance. Spots of exploding colour shattered on his retina and ran in rainbow hues, dancing, whirling and fading in a glittering kaleidoscope of confusion . . .

. . . When he could see again, the bard found he was standing outside his cell of wood and stone in the Forest of Euarthe – with the six tiny clots of blood pulsing in the palm of his hand. He had the Mandleseeds.

In the days that followed, Paedur lived partly in a dream world as he tried, with quill and parchment, to fashion a record of his experiences in the Lands of Life Eternal. It would, he reasoned, be his monument. It would survive down through the ages: a true saga of the gods and their relationship with man, the true stories of the heroes and heroines and the first complete history of man . . . if he lived long enough to finish it.

If he had been chosen as the Champion of the Old Faith, then it was highly likely that the followers of the New Religion would soon get to know of it and it wouldn't take them long to find him. He could of course flee now, but he had never run away from anything in his life. Let them come, he was ready.

His small stone cell had been encircled and warded with the old

High Magic, and the one direct track that led to his grove had been *touched* with a spell of misdirection and delusion. A knowledge of the arcane arts was not common to every bard, but Bard Masters – in their further researches and delvings into the lost lore – almost unconsciously picked up a smattering of the rituals and incantations.

The season changed and so did the weather, and the bard began to think that the gods had forgotten him – or at least temporarily passed over him. The Forest of Euarthe remained quiet; his traps had not been sprung and his spells remained unbroken, and as the Month of the Wolf drew to a close, Paedur relaxed and began to consider gathering in supplies for the coming winter months.

The morning of the last day of the month – market day – dawned dull and overcast, with Faurug the Nightwind still lingering and the world covered beneath a mantle of white, evidence that Snaitle had been abroad during the night. Paedur abandoned his thoughts of going into the nearby town to the market and spent the day wrapped in his long dark cloak huddled over a small fire, attempting to finish the tale of Kutter Kin-Slayer which he had heard from Yuann the Wood Sprite in the Yellow God's kingdom. Yuann had been dead and had passed into legend almost five hundred years before the bard had been born.

The day remained dark and towards mid-afternoon it began to snow again. The only sound in the small cell was the muted crackling of the fire and the scratching of the bard's quill across the thick parchment.

'*Bard*!'

Paedur started and threw himself backwards, his hook flashing redly as it lashed out at the sudden sound. It struck something solid and the bard felt pain, quickly followed by numbness, shoot up his left arm. The shadow in the doorway moved . . . and Mannam stepped into the firelight.

Paedur struggled to his feet, nursing his trembling arm; it felt as if he had struck a tree-trunk. He swore when he saw the condition of his parchment, now sodden with ink where he had uspet the inkhorn when he had fallen. He held up the curling square and allowed the ink to run off. 'Ruined . . . ruined,' he groaned.

'It is a parchment,' Mannam whispered, 'it is nothing.'

'To me everything,' Paedur snapped, and angrily crumpled the stiff skin and tossed it into the fire. It caught immediately and blazed, the still-wet ink hissing loudly. The Dark Lord retreated back into the shadows.

'I am surprised you have returned,' Paedur snarled. 'After all, you tricked me . . .'

'I never forced you to go,' Mannam breathed. 'I did my best to persuade you .. . . but it was your own greed that decided you in the end.'

Paedur changed the subject. 'Have you got the Lament and the Harp?'

'Have you got the seeds?'

'I have – but let me see my reward first,' Paedur demanded.

The Duaiteoiri moved, the sound like withered leaves being crushed underfoot, and produced the relics bundled together in a twig-woven basket. The Dark Lord handed them across the fire and then withdrew into the deepest shadows.

Paedur gently lifted them out of the basket and unrolled the covering, bringing the ancient talismans to light. The Lament of Lugas was tightly sealed within a tube of engraved time-yellowed ivory, etched with the glyphs of the Culai, the First Race. It was stopped at both ends with caps of delicate white-gold, and it exuded an aura of peace and silence that was almost visible. He placed it carefully on his writing desk and then unwrapped the Harp of Auigne.

The dark polished wood of the instrument ran with liquid high-lights from the flames. It was sidhe wood, wood from the Sidhe Forest of the Far Isles of Ogygia, and it would neither rot nor warp, burn nor crack. Its strings were twined sun-wire, impossibly strong; once tuned, they would keep a note for all eternity. The soundbox was plain and unadorned save for a single black stone set flush with the wood: the *Clocauigne*, Auigne's stone, sometimes called the Heart of the Black Ibix. The air about the harp tingled with barely suppressed elemental forces and the bard with his heightened senses knew, although he did not know how he knew, that it had been blessed by both Maker and User, two of the earliest gods.

'The seeds, bard.' Mannam's voice jolted Paedur back to reality. He reluctantly put down the harp and produced a small carved quill box. With the point of his hook he pulled back the sliding lid – and instantly the small cell was bathed in a pulsating blood-light which painted everything in shades of liquid crimson.

'You know of course that there are only six here,' Paedur said quietly, trying to make out the Duaite's shape in the corner.

'Of course,' Mannam whispered, 'and for that reason I will take

35

the Harp and Lament back.' A skeletal stick-like hand reached out from the shadows.

The bard grinned wolfishly. 'You still owe me for the six seeds,' he reminded Mannam.

'C'lte has already gifted you,' the Dark Lord snapped.

Paedur nodded. 'He gifted me – you owe me payment for what I have brought back to you.'

The Lord of the Dead rustled angrily. 'I can see now why you have been chosen.' Leaves and dead wood rustled. 'Choose then.'

Without hesitation Paedur chose the Lament of Lugas; with only one hand, the Harp was useless to him.

Mannam's stick-like hand swept out – and the crimson light was swallowed up within it. Abruptly the Duaiteoiri laughed and the bard shivered with the sound. 'And thus is our bargain completed. And now your wandering begins. You must flee from here, bard; the followers of Trialos are almost upon you.' The god's voice faded to a muted whispering.

'Now you must begin the revival of the Old Faith. Use your tales, they are your greatest weapon. Take the road northwards; follow the King Road beyond Karfondal, and there seek an inn called the Coined Sword . . . the Faith is strong there . . . you must strengthen it even further . . .'

The wind moaned in through the cracks in the stonework and carried with them the last words of C'lte, the God of Life: *You are the Champion of the Old Faith*.

3   The Beginning

... This day: a bard, by name Paedur, tall of stature, sharp-visaged, and with but one hand ...

Register of the Coined Sword Tavern

Something was wrong. Carp, ex-mercenary and proprietor of the Coined Sword, immediately sensed the change in atmosphere as he climbed up from the cellar with another barrel of rofion. The long, low-ceilinged room was unusually quiet, the crackling of the log fire at the gable end of the house unnaturally loud and intrusive. At this hour, with the men heading home from the fields and forests, the tavern should be humming with conversation and laughter and the clink of glasses and tankards.

The huge innkeeper paused at the top of the stairs and shifted the cold sweating barrel into a more comfortable position, and then, before stepping out into the room, he loosened the knife he carried in a sheath in the small of his back. Silence in a tavern could only mean trouble. It could be bandits; there had been some trouble in the district recently, and only a month past four men had attempted to rob the customers and his day's meagre takings.

Carp smiled at the memory. Two of them had held the door with drawn swords while the others demanded coin and valuables. The old soldier had hesitated; it had been a long time since he had seen battle with the infamous Coined Sword Regiment, fighting the savage Chopts in the northern ice-fields, but he still knew how to fight.

Carp had impaled one of the bandits to the door frame with a crossbow bolt and almost severed another's head from his shoulders with a thrown axe. It had all happened so quickly that the others had had no time to react. One managed to shout a warning before the ex-mercenary dropped him with a thrown barrel. The last man turned to flee and had almost reached the door before another crossbow bolt split his spine. There had been no trouble since.

But there was certainly something amiss now.

The huge innkeeper squeezed up through the door from the cellar, the barrel of rofion held before him like a shield, and stepped out into the room. He stopped, poised on the balls of his feet, ready to run or fall as the situation demanded. The smoky atmosphere stung his eyes and he quickly blinked away the tears, and then frowned: everything seemed in order. The customers – most of them regulars, and nearly all farmers, woodcutters or charcoal-burners from the nearby forest towns – were all sitting quietly at their usual tables and chairs.

And then Carp realised what was wrong; they were sitting far too quietly. There was no shouting, no laughter, no coarse jesting. He padded across to the long wooden counter, moving surprisingly quietly for so large a man, but no-one was looking in his direction – all heads were turned towards the far end of the room.

He was reaching under the counter for the loaded crossbow he kept there when Bale, the pot-boy, suddenly emerged from the shadows and almost ran across to the wooden bar. His small dark eyes were wide and there was a pulse throbbing visibly in his throat.

'Did you see him?' Bale whispered urgently.

'Who? What's happened up here, boy?' Carp demanded.

'Him. The bard.' The boy glanced nervously over his shoulder towards the gable end of the room and the blazing fire.

Carp looked down the length of the smoky room. His eyes were not as sharp as they used to be and while the worn flagstones directly before the fireplace were bathed in warm red-gold light, and he could make out Amblad, one of the oldest men in the province, sitting in his usual seat beside the carved log-box, he could see no-one else.

'What bard?' he hissed.

'There!' the boy said, pointing, and his voice quavered and almost broke.

Carp squinted into the shadowy corners on either side of the fire – and then he started: there was someone there! And suddenly all his old warrior senses flared, as they had during his fighting days whenever they camped near one of the ancient Culai settlements. He was no sorcerer, no wizard, but he had a feel for Power. He had sensed the Power in some men before, but never so strongly as now; something was badly wrong.

He eased himself out from behind the counter and started down the room, squinting against the light from the fire, vainly attempting to make out the figure sitting back in the shadows to the right of the hearth.

'Now sir,' he blustered, walking into the circle of the firelight, 'what can I do for you?' He moved directly in front of the figure. 'A tankard of rofion perhaps?' he asked, edging closer to the shape, puzzled. It was a man certainly, but it was difficult, almost impossible, to make out the features clearly.

'Yes, that would be very welcome.' The voice was strong, clear and vibrant, and, as the man raised his head, Carp saw the distinctive triangular bardic sigil high on his left shoulder. The bard stood up and the innkeeper stepped back unconsciously as the darkness seemed to ripple and flow with him. The bard's right hand came up and the enveloping darkness rippled again, and then it fell away and Carp suddenly realised that it was nothing more than a long furred travelling cloak. He was tall and thin, almost unnaturally so; his face was angular, with high cheekbones and deep-sunk eyes. Carp was about to turn away when he caught a glimpse of the silver hook that took the place of the bard's left hand.

'I'm going to need your name for the register,' he said quietly, strangely disturbed by the gleaming half-circle. In his fighting days, he had come across many men who wore artificial claws or walked on wooden stumps, but he had never seen anything quite like the bard's hook. It was flat, shaped like a sickle, with a vicious-looking point and a blade that looked as if it had been recently sharpened; there also seemed to be script of some description etched into the flat of the blade.

'My name is Paedur.'

'I'm sorry,' he started, realising the bard was looking at him expectantly.

'I said my name is Paedur,' the stranger repeated with a smile.

Paedur. A bard, Paedur. Now where had he heard that name before? He fitted a spigot to the new barrel of the strong dark beer he brewed himself and poured a foaming tankard for the bard. He didn't frighten easily, but there was something about the stranger which chilled him to the bone. He had once fought the *quai* – soulless warriors – and he remembered feeling exactly the same.

He called Bale and gave him the drink and in the unnatural silence in the tavern he could even hear the pad of the boy's bare feet on the sawdust-covered earthen floor. He waited until the boy gave the tankard to the bard and saw him drink before he stepped into the back room. There was something about that bard . . .

Before Carp had purchased the run-down way-station which he had transformed into the Coined Sword, he had scratched a living collecting the bounties on escaped prisoners and slaves. And now, during the winter months, when trade was poor, he usually travelled south into Karfondal and collected the crude 'Wanted' posters: it didn't hurt to have them just in case someone wandered in . . .

He found it close to the end of the pile. There was no illustration and the print was dark and blotchy, even cruder than usual. Carp spelled slowly through the heavy black letters: *A Bard Paedur . . . single hand . . . blasphemy against the New Religion!*

The reward was substantial – far more so than simple blasphemy would have merited. Carp smiled. Well, if the bard followed the Old Faith, then he would find himself amongst friends here. He tore the thin yellow paper in half, crumpled it into a ball and threw it into the corner of the room.

'We have not seen a bard hereabouts for many years,' old Amblad was saying when Carp returned to the bar. 'Your kind are usually to be found in the palaces of kings now and not on the roads – where they belong.'

'Some of us still wander the roads,' Paedur said quietly. 'Not many, it is true, but don't forget, there are not as many of us as there used to be. The old ways are dying; young men are no longer interested in training to become bards and lore-masters.'

'Who will preserve the old ways then, the old tales, the legends?' Amblad wondered, his small, strangely smooth face creasing in a frown.

'The old ways are dying,' Paedur repeated, very softly, 'there is a new order rising.'

'An order in which there will be no place for you or your kin,' the old man said. His eyes were sharp and blue, watching the bard carefully, judging his every word and movement.

Carp came up behind the old man and touched his shoulder gently, almost respectfully. Amblad lifted his head, but his eyes never left the bard's face while the innkeeper whispered urgently to him. Amblad nodded and then turned back to Paedur, his gnarled hands playing with a small amulet on a leather thong about his neck. 'It seems you are a follower of the Faith,' he said, his voice dropping to a whisper.

'We worship the same gods, *Datar*,' Paedur said, using the title for a priest of the Faith. He glanced over at the innkeeper who had moved back to the wooden bar. 'But how did he know?'

Amblad shrugged. 'Carp makes it his business to . . . to keep in touch with persons wanted by the Imperials. Your name and description was on their last list.'

The bard sat forward suddenly, red firelight glancing off his hook, reflecting back on to his chest. 'I'm on the lists? Since when?'

'Since before the season turned; Carp would be able to tell you exactly when. You are wanted for blasphemy against the New Religion.'

The bard sat back into the shadows. 'But I've been on the road for most of the Cold Months – I haven't had the opportunity to blaspheme against the New Religion. I've stuck mainly to the back roads and avoided contact with men' – he raised his hook briefly – 'I am rather distinctive.'

'Be that as it may, there is still a price on your head.'

'Is the Religion that powerful already?' Paedur asked. 'I've been a little out of touch lately.'

'It grows stronger every day; in some towns the Faith is already openly frowned upon and the Religion has found many converts in the palace, and Geillard has spoken with the priests, and has even received the High Priest, Thanos. And you know what will happen if they convert him . . .'

Paedur nodded, startled. If the Emperor was converted, the New Religion would become the accepted belief and that would in effect prohibit the worshipping of the Old Faith. 'How does the Faith fare here?' he asked the old man, nodding to the rest of the tavern.

'My congregation shrinks almost daily. Most of the people here are of the Faith, but there are some with serious doubts . . .' The old man paused and added quietly, 'That is why you are here, isn't it?'

'How do you know?'

The old man smiled toothlessly. 'I have been a *Datar* of the Faith since my youth; I believe in the gods, I have spoken with them, asking for their help. I have known someone was coming since before the season changed.'

'That's even before I knew,' Paedur said wryly. He glanced around the room and then back to the old man. 'What would you have me do?'

41

'You must speak to them,' Amblad began. He paused as Carp came up and stood by his chair.

'The doors are locked, *Datar*.'

'Good.' He looked up at the innkeeper. 'You will ensure that we are not disturbed.'

'Of course.' Carp bowed slightly and disappeared back down the tavern. He stopped by the bar to lift a heavy hunting crossbow from beneath the counter, and then went to stand by the door.

Paedur shook his head. 'I'm not sure I know what to say to these people.'

'You are a bard, a storyteller; tell them a story.'

'But which story?'

The priest sat back in his high-backed chair, and his red-rimmed eyes turned towards the fire. 'A question which I am often asked concerns the Great Beginning of the Faith.' His sharp eyes darted back to the bard. 'You see, the Religion, its gods and their beginnings are well documented. If a people know where their gods come from, they somehow find them easier to worship. However, many do not know the Birthing of the Gods of the Pantheon, and so they are that much more remote, that much more distant, and that much harder to worship. The priests of the Religion use this, exploit it to their own ends.' The old man paused and his voice dropped to a whisper. 'Tell them of the Great Beginning.'

Paedur paused to consider and then he nodded.

Amblad raised his head and then he spoke loudly in the formal speech. 'Would you honour us with a tale, bard?'

'What would you have?'

There was silence in the tavern; several people moved uncomfortably, but no-one attempted to leave. To do so would be to invite the stranger's attention.

Paedur repeated the question.

'A tale of the Pantheon,' Amblad cackled finally, 'something we are not likely to have heard before.'

Heads nodded in agreement and there was a quick murmur of assent.

The bard nodded. 'Very well, and I'll make it short enough; I will tell of the Great Beginning,' he said in his strong commanding voice, 'I will tell of Creation.' He sipped some of the strong rofion and then placed the empty flagon on the floor beside his feet. His dark eyes closed and he sat back against the cold stone wall, and began his tale . . .

In the Beginning, before all things, there was the One and the Void and the Chrystallis, which was the wind that blew through the soul of the One into the Void.

And the One slept, for there was naught to do in the Beginning, and he dreamt – but his dreams were troubled.

Now the One was without presence and beyond imagining, and thus his dreams – although the One was without gender – were curious and novel. And in the swirling chaos that was the stuff of his dreams, there arose concepts strange and images alien, for he dreamt that he had Form and Shape and Substance, and these dreams were both exciting and bizarre to the One, for he had no Form and was without Shape or Substance. And thus he stored these dreams in his soul to ponder and comfort him in his boredom, for he was often bored.

But the Chrystallis, the wind that blows through the soul of the One, grasped the dreams in aeolian paws and scattered them out into the Void.

And thus Form and Shape and Substance came into being.

But still the One slept – and his sleep was not akin to that of mortal man, being of a duration beyond time, and his dreams lasted aeons. And as the Void gradually took on a Form and assumed a Shape and Substance, the One dreamed again, and now his dreams thrilled him, for he dreamed of an Essence. This too he stored with his soul to comfort him, but once again the Chrystallis swept through his soul and carried it out into the Void and the Essence joined the other three and fused into their core.

And now the sleep of the One was troubled and he grew restless and his dreams were no longer pleasing nor exciting for he was haunted by Identity, and this displeased him and he cast it out, and it went forth into the Void and henceforth Form and Shape and Substance had an Identity and the Essence was at the core of all.

Thus it was for a timeless while.

And Chrystallis the Soulwind grew bolder still, and gathering together the dreams of the One, which it had brought forth into the Void, it mixed them together in the cauldron of the soul of the One. And there the dreams boiled and seethed and there was created that which was akin to Life, but which was puny and weakling, and the Chrystallis was displeased with it and cast it out into the further reaches of the Void.

Still the One slept and still his dreams were disturbed by that which gibbered and jibed beyond his comprehension, and these were the Passions, and they were anathema to the One and he cast them out; and thus the Greater Passions of Love and Hate and their brood of Lesser Passions joined with Form and Shape and Substance and took on an Identity, and were linked together by the mysterious Essence.

And again the Chrystallis swept through the Void gathering

together all the elements of the dreams of the One and again it mixed them in the cauldron of the soul . . . with one addition – the merest drop of the Life of the One.

And when the heaving and rolling had ceased there had been created Life. It was strong and viable, with a form and a shape and created out of a substance; it was infused with the greater and lesser passions and it had an identity. And at the heart, the core of the newly-created Life, was that Essence akin to the One.

Then the Soulwind blew through the forgotten corners of the soul of the One, unearthing the old dreams and unrecalled nightmares, bringing them all out into the Void. Light there was and Darkness also; Chaos and Order and – greatest of all – Knowledge. And these settled into the Void and were infused into the Life.

And the One awoke.

And now a Lesser Passion held sway and grew, and this was Fear, and the Life attempted to hide. But when the One looked about, what he saw pleased him, and though he was unused to Creation, he delighted in it, and it amused him.

Thus he set about creating the very fabric of the Universe, fashioning it from the stuff of the Void. But it was empty and so he created the Galaxies and Suns, and Planets to circle the Suns and Moons to circle the Planets; and he scattered meteors and asteroids freely throughout the Universe. Now, on to some of the Planets he set the newly-created Life, and in places it thrived – albeit in strange and grotesque forms – and in others it did not flourish and died.

But the One soon tired of Creation and wished to sleep again, but still desired to keep that which had been created, and he pondered on how that might be. And so he took part of himself and enwrapped it with a Shape and gave it a Form and Substance and infused it with Identity and then he broke it in half and set one part to rule Order and the other part to watch over Chaos, and he called his creations Hanor and Hara, and then he slept and sleeps still.

And Hanor and Hara were the first Great Gods.

Now Hanor and Hara were full of the spirit of the One, and were powerful, but like all the gods, prone to boredom and, furthermore, were envious of the One's Creation, and thus in their envy and boredom they sought to emulate him. But they found that there was little left to create.

And so they found they must content themselves with Shadowworlds created on planes other than the one already in existence. And these new planes were like and yet unlike the Prime Plane in many respects. So the first Great Gods set Life upon these planes and it thrived.

But now Hanor and Hara had the Universe of the Prime Plane, created by the One, and their own multi-planed universe to rule, and they found it was vast – and they were but two, and thus they resolved to create others like themselves to ease the load of godhood.

Hanor and Hara then worked with the stuff of Chaos and Order, and brought forth the Old Gods, and these in turn tried their hands at creation and brought forth the lesser gods, the spirits and sprites, the demons and elementals, and set them up as the servants of the gods.

And in the Elder Days the gods walked upon the planes of existence and communed with the Life that swarmed upon it and finally brought forth their ultimate creation, the Culai, the First Race.

But that is a tale unto itself.

Thus endeth the tale of the Great Beginning, of the Creation of Life, of the fashioning of the Prime Plane and the lesser planes of existence, and of the greater and lesser gods . . .

The tavern remained silent long after the bard finished, drinks forgotten on the stained tables, the untended fire burned down to glowing embers. Paedur's dark eyes blinked and opened and a smile touched his lips as he looked around the darkened room. It was a great tribute to his storytelling. He dropped his voice to little more than a whisper and continued.

'In these days – modern, cultured days – there are those who no longer worship the Old Faith, nor call upon the Pantheon . . . and then they wonder why the gods do not answer their prayers. There is a magic in names – call upon the old gods by their true names and they will listen to your prayers.' He paused and added, 'In the naming of the New Gods, for example, there is little magic.'

'But the New Gods come,' a small, defiant voice muttered from the darkened corner of the room, 'the Old Gods no longer heed the people's pleas: they are dead, but the gods of the Religion live!'

Paedur leaned forward, his hard eyes piercing the gloom. 'Aye, and when you call a dog it comes. Are the gods of the New Religion lackeys to be called at your beck and whim? And when you call – are you really sure you know what comes?' The bard's silver hook flashed redly in the glowing firelight. 'Do you really know what you're worshipping?' he demanded.

The question hung on the still warm air, but no-one moved to reply.

The bard sat back into the darkness and continued quietly. 'I know there are those who argue that the Old Gods – ever fickle, ever wilful and disdainful – have deserted man; some will say that they have been overthrown by the New Gods. But know this,' and suddenly the bard's voice rose on a commanding note, 'the gods – your fathers' gods and their fathers' before them – are ever with us, and though they are often forgetful and heed not the prayers of man, they are there, and they will come again in power and glory. They will come again.'

And once again silence settled over the tavern and encompassed all within its heavy warmth.

A figure moved along the wall, the sound of cloth against the cold stones loud in the silence. The bard sat forward, his head tilted to one side, listening. 'Come out where I can see you,' he commanded. He leaned across and tossed a log on to the fire. Sparks shot upwards as the resin-rich wood burst into crackling flame. Shadows writhed across the floor and up the stone walls, nestling in the smoke-blackened rafters.

A young man stepped boldly out into the circle of light. He was tall and thin, his eyes sunken and burning feverishly in an almost chalk-white face. He was shivering as he stepped up close to the seated figure of the bard. 'Blasphemy,' he hissed. 'There is no god but Trialos, the True God.' He pointed accusingly at Paedur. '*Blasphemer!*'

The bard didn't move, and the young man turned and gestured to the crowd. 'Do not listen to this man; he is evil, a spreader of lies. The priests will deal with you,' he added turning back to the bard, 'I will make sure of it.'

'You have to leave here first, boy,' Carp said, stepping up behind the young man, the crossbow cradled loosely in his arms.

'My gods will protect me,' he said with absolute confidence.

'From this?' Carp held up the weapon, shifting it so the firelight ran like blood down the polished wood and the iron tip of the bolt which projected almost a finger-length beyond the crossbow.

'You cannot kill me; I an Xanazius, acolyte and soon to be priest in the New Religion.' The young man rubbed both hands briskly together and laughed mockingly. 'Unless you reconsider your foolish beliefs you will all burn in the fires of the unbelievers. Count Karfondal has embraced the True Faith, and in a very few days it will become the official belief. Of course, you will all have the chance to repent . . .' Xanazius' voice rose higher and higher, verging on hysteria, but suddenly it dropped and he turned to the bard. 'But you, of course, must die,' he said casually.

He was moving even before he had finished speaking, the stiletto in his hand almost invisible as he lunged for the bard's chest. Paedur's hook flashed, metal rang on metal, and the finger-slim blade snapped as it buried itself in the hard floor. Although disarmed, Xanazius' momentum carried him forward, and instinctively his fingers hooked and reached for Paedur's eyes. There was a thump, and then he suddenly stiffened as the bard's left arm came up and the metal hook bit deeply into the flesh of his jaw and cheek. Xanazius slumped to the ground – and then the bard saw the bolt protruding from his left shoulder.

Carp stepped forward, smiling ruefully. 'Sorry, I was aiming for his neck; I must be losing my touch.'

Amblad leaned forward in his chair. 'Will he live?' he asked quietly.

The bard knelt by the young man's side. He pulled the long, thick-bodied bolt from his shoulder and tossed it back to the innkeeper and then rolled Xanazius over and pulled open his jerkin. Blood welled from the ragged tear in the flesh. The half-circle which the bard's hook had cut into his face was also pumping blood and, if possible, the young man's skin was now even paler than before. Paedur sat back on his heels and slowly moved his left arm down the length of the youth's body. Shadows abruptly shivered along the length of the metal hook and tiny blue sparks danced in the runes. He paused when the hook rested over the wound in Xanazius' shoulder; a thin high-pitched humming trembled on the air, and the bleeding slowed to a trickle and then the wound visibly clotted. The bard moved his hand upwards and covered the facial wound with his hook; again the bleeding visibly clotted and stopped.

Paedur eased himself to his feet. His hook sparked and crackled as he moved and the runes seemed to etch themselves into the semi-darkness. He nudged the unconscious man with his foot. 'Take him far from here and release him; by the time he finds his way back, I shall be long gone.'

'But he can recognise you,' Carp protested. The firelight danced across the flesh of his face as he smiled. 'I doubt if he will ever forget you – he'll bear your mark to his grave.' And then the innkeeper sobered. 'He can also bring the guards and priests here.'

'It will be his word against yours,' Paedur said reasonably.

'They usually ask their questions with a rack and hot irons,' Carp said quietly. 'However, we will do what we can. But perhaps it would be better if you left now.'

The bard nodded, and gathered up his cloak.

'Must you leave?' Amblad asked. 'With you by my side, with your tales and knowledge, I could make the Faith strong again.'

'I must go, I have work to do.'

'Then is there nothing else you can tell us? I know we have a lot to thank you for already. You have reminded us of our youth, when we had gods we trusted, and a tradition followed by our fathers and their fathers before them back to the First Age of Man.' There was a low murmur of agreement from the tavern. 'You have awakened that which has slept: our Faith. For that we thank you again.'

Paedur swung his cloak on to his shoulders and bowed deeply. Even if the Old Faith had regained only one of its former adherents, then he was pleased. And then he looked at the young man lying in a pool of his own blood, and he realised that the first blow in his battle against the New Religion had been struck.

The bard Paedur bowed once again to the old priest and the innkeeper and then he slipped out into the night.

4   Kutter Kin-Slayer

And the bard took the north road to Baddalaur, the College of Bards.
Life of Paedur, the Bard
This day returned to us a brother, by name Paedur, called the Hookhand.
Register of Baddalaur, the College of Bards

There was a flash of crimson and gold as the riders in Count Karfondal's livery broke out from the shelter of the trees and into the wan sunlight. Tendrils of early morning mist eddied about their mounts' hooves, and the riders' leathern cloaks were slick with moisture.

The leader raised his hand and reined his mount to a halt, pulling it off the worn stone road on to the soft muddy margin. While he waited for his small group to gather around him, he allowed his eyes to wander back along the road to where it disappeared amongst the trees and then reappeared further up as a thin grey-white line that led to the sprawling pile of Baddalaur, the College of Bards. It had been a natural assumption that the renegade bard would return to his old school – especially since he seemed to be travelling northwards along the King Road.

And they should have caught him there! He was a man afoot, and seemingly in no hurry, and damnably distinctive with that butcher's hook in place of his left hand. But they had somehow missed him. It had been the same story for the past three months. In every tiny hamlet and village they passed, they had heard talk of him, and saw the renewed signs of the Old Faith springing up again – but no sign of the bard.

Keshian was a warrior, and he had been in the employ of Count Karfondal for close on twelve summers now, a fighting man with little time for religion or the affairs of gods. But the way this man stirred up the people's faith in the Old Gods and turned them against the New Religion was frightening. And, unless he were stopped, Keshian could see the province erupting into a holy war.

'Again?' He turned, suddenly aware that one of his officers was talking to him.

'I asked what your orders were, sir?'

Keshian dropped his reins and stood in the stirrups, pressing his hands into the small of his back. He was a short, rather stout man, muscles beginning to run to fat – and getting far too old for this sort of thing. He sat back into the saddle gingerly. 'We have two choices,' he began slowly. 'We can return to the count, with the news that we have somehow missed this bard . . .'

'But I still can't see how – he is afoot.'

Keshian pushed back his mail hood and shook his head. 'I don't know. We've been told that he is afoot, but we don't know that for certain.'

'We found no horse tracks,' his sergeant reminded him.

'Nor did we find any mantracks,' Keshian snapped, 'and you also know that he was in Lechfair, although the town was cut off by floods for most of the time he was there. No-one answering his description came through Badaur, and yet we find traces of him in Baddalaur, which, you may recall, is accessible only through the town.'

Keshian and his troops had missed the bard by what must have been barely an hour in the College of Bards. He couldn't understand it – he had had men stationed at the gates day and night, checking the description of everyone entering or leaving. Baddalaur was Culai-built, one of the ancient artifacts that littered the Nations of Man, relics of their god-like ancestors. It was a sprawling building, surrounded by a wall of solid stone, with neither seam nor crack in it, and the only entrance was through a massive teal-wood, iron-studded gate. Since time out of legend, the bards, scribes, scholars and poets had occupied the massive rooms, and thus it was one of the better-preserved Culai sites.

Over the years a small but thriving township had grown up actually around the college's gates. The town housed mainly scholars, historians, priests or magicians who had come to use Baddalaur's enormous library, and it also helped to cater in some part towards the needs of those bards and scribes living and training within the college. The main street of Badaur ended up at the college gates and it was thus impossible to enter the college except by passing through the town.

'Our second choice is to continue on into the Northlands,' Keshian continued. 'From the little we know of this Paedur, he seems intent on pushing northwards all the time. The college records last place him south in the Forest of Euarthe. We next hear of him in the Coined Sword, close to Karfondal, and then in almost every village running north after that.' The captain pulled a short thick parchment tube from his saddle-bags and, giving one edge to his sergeant, pulled it open. His blunt fingernail traced the bard's route. 'If he continues on this road, he will eventually reach Castle Nevin along the Mion River, and the next stop after that is Thusal – which has a bardhouse!'

The sergeant grunted in satisfaction. 'His eventual destination perhaps . . .'

'Perhaps . . .' Keshian allowed the parchment chart to roll closed of its own accord, and slipped it back into his saddle bag. 'We travel north then.' He urged his mount back on to the road, and waited for his small company to fall in behind him. 'We're heading north,' he said gruffly. 'Our next stop will be Castle Nevin, which we'll try to make before nightfall since I'm sure none of you want to spend a night on the Wastelands. And remember, between Baddalaur and Castle Nevin, there is nothing but open country, inhabited only by beasts and bandits – so stay alert.'

Keshian urged his roan mount to a trot and, with his company strung out single file behind him, they continued down the King Road in search of the bard.

Behind them and beneath the trees, a tall cloaked figure watched them ride away. On his left shoulder gleamed the eye and triangle of the bardic college, and in place of his left hand was a gleaming silver hook.

There was a shrill keening sound and then a crossbow bolt sank up to its feathers in the scout's chest, punching through a hauberk of banded mail and leather and driving him up and out of the saddle.

Keshian was already dropping to the ground when the sudden screaming flurry of bolts scythed through his men. No, not men, he realised bitterly, boys; most of them had never seen any actual combat . . . most of them never would now.

He lay on the ground, unmoving, listening to the death-shrill of the quarrels as they spun through the air. He recognised the sound of old; Wastelanders cut tiny holes in the heads of their crossbow bolts so that the air, passing through them, shrilled like a cat in agony.

A horse bolted past him, its iron-shod hooves sparking from the hard road barely a handspan from his head; there was another brief flurry of whistles and then the horse crashed to the ground with an almost human-like scream. There was no movement from the rider.

The scarred battle-captain lay on the road listening to the pounding of his own heartbeat. The sun was warm on his face and beads of sweat were gathering just under his hairline and running down the back of his neck. There was a long burning scrape along one cheek, and blood from a split lip dripped on to the ground.

If the Wastelanders followed their usual procedure they would pillage the dead, stripping them of everything, clothing, armour and weapons and leave the naked corpses to rot in the sun or as food for the scavengers.

There was a sudden scrape of metal off stone and then the slow rasp of a sword being withdrawn. Booted feet walked the pitted road off to one side, and there was more movement ahead of him.

'Karfondal's colours.' The voice was rough, and strongly accented.

'Aye, and I wonder what they were doing this far north.' The second voice came from behind Keshian; it was softer and the accent was cultured.

'Eight men,' the first voice remarked, 'travelling light. Chain and banded mail, no heavy armour, pressed provisions.'

The voices came closer and a pair of scuffed leather boots stopped barely a finger's breadth from the captain's face. 'Are there any message tubes?'

There was a brief pause, and then the first voice called back. 'None.'

'Then they must have been hunting someone,' the second voice, which carried an unmistakable air of authority, said quietly, almost to himself.

'We cannot linger, sir.'

'Aye. Call the men down and let them take what they will. Are there any left alive?'

'Just one!'

Metal rasped on metal and then a long slender dagger bit deeply into Keshian's leather-gauntleted hand. He winced and then his head was pulled back while a foot was pressed into the small of his back. His back arched and his spine threatened to snap. A cold sliver of steel touched his outstretched throat.

'This one still lives . . . for the moment.'

Keshian found himself looking up into the broad smiling face of the leader of the Wastelands brigands.

'Let him up.'

The foot was removed from the captain's back and he was roughly hauled to his feet, but the dagger never left his throat.

'Kutor the Renegade,' he gasped, suddenly recognising the man before him.

The man bowed slightly. 'At your service.' He was a short, rather stocky man, slightly smaller than the captain. His hair – although he could not have yet reached his thirtieth winter – was iron grey, matching his sharp eyes. His features were broad, and there were tiny wrinkles around his eyes and mouth. He smiled and the wrinkles deepened into folds. 'Tell me now, where were you going and in such a hurry?'

Keshian stiffened, his eyes gazing straight ahead, over Kutor's right shoulder at the group of bandits stripping the bodies of his men and their mounts. He watched two men, wearing stained leather aprons, move from horse to horse and cut free the crossbow bolts. In the Wastelands, nothing was wasted.

'I asked you a question.' The voice was still mild, and the smile was still in place, but the eyes had turned hard and cold.

The captain knew a little of Kutor the Renegade; Kutor the Bastard; Kutor the Pretender. He was rumoured to be the Emperor's half brother, by Geillard's father and a country wench, and he often used the title of Prince. Some years ago, he had been persuaded by some disaffected nobles to attempt to enforce his claim to the throne by force of arms. With an army of mercenaries at his back, he had marched on the capital. His army had been welcomed as liberators in every village they passed through, and by the time he had come in sight of the capital, its numbers had doubled and redoubled. But they faced one of the most highly trained and well-equipped armies in the known world. The battle itself was brief – and his mismatched and ragged following had been slaughtered. Kutor and his few remaining followers had fled to the Wastelands, where they now preyed upon unwary travellers. It was a long way from attacking the capital, Keshian thought. He suddenly realised that they would not usually have attacked a group as heavily armed as his. . . .

A blow to the back of the head sent him sprawling at Kutor's feet. The cut on his face began to bleed again and he tasted the copper tang of blood in his mouth. A hand caught in his hair and hauled him to his feet.

'So, tell me.'

Keshian spat, spraying bloody saliva into Kutor's face.

Kutor smiled. 'We could have talked, you and I. We could have talked. You could have told me where you were going, and perhaps I would have let you go. But now . . .' he smiled almost sadly and shrugged, 'now, you will tell me and then I will have to kill you.'

There was a sharp whistle and Kutor's head snapped around. Keshian heard booted feet running across the cracked road-stones behind him and then pound on to the grass verge. The brigand looked at the captain and then at the man standing behind him. 'Take him, I'll deal with him later.' And then he turned and vanished into the undergrowth that lined the road. Keshian twisted around – in time to see a rounded dagger pommel flash down into his face . . .

There was meat roasting and the pine-fresh evening air was rich with its odours. Fire crackled and resin popped and spat, also lending its particular odours to the twilight. Keshian came awake with a pounding headache and no feeling in his hands or feet. There was also water running down on to his face, and when he looked up there was a coarse-featured peasant woman standing before him with a dripping bucket in her hands. She laughed when she saw he was awake and then walked away. Keshian shook his head, shaking out as much of the ice-cold water as he could, and then attempted to take stock of his surroundings.

He was sitting on one side of a small clearing of low, thick-boled trees. There was water bubbling behind him and a small muddy streamlet twisted by his side and across the encampment. He guessed that he must be in one of the small oases that dotted the Wastelands; small, fertile patches where life proliferated whilst all around the rocky Wastelands lay barren.

Centuries ago, when the Culai first built the King Road, they had chosen the small sheltered hollows as the sites for their Way Stations. These were long, low, strongly built buildings that served as resting posts for travellers. They were equipped with supplies of blankets and wood, dried provisions and simple medications, and travellers were expected to replace whatever they used. But as the years passed, inns had taken over from the Way Stations, and the routeways had changed, leaving many of the buildings isolated and abandoned. And then, of course, there were rumours that many of the Culai-built ruins were haunted. However, the Way Stations –

safe on account of their isolation and the stories surrounding them – were often used by bandits both as a base and a refuge.

Keshian twisted around and stared into the gloom, looking for the station. At first he could see nothing, but as his eyes adjusted to the twilight that had already gathered in the hollow, he could make out the outline of the small square building against the scrubby undergrowth and stunted trees.

The battle-captain shivered. The Wastelands brigands had stripped him of everything except his breeches, and the cold wind that ruffled the trees and bushes prickled his skin and bit into his bones. Keshian was into his fortieth year now; a tough warrior once but grown soft with city living. The only action he had seen in the past twelve years in Count Karfondal's guard had been hunting brigands – such as these – or doing escort duty on the taxes into the capital.

Time had changed him, weakened and softened him. In his youth he would have never thrown himself to the ground when Kutor and his brigands had attacked; he would have fought them, charging into their midst with a swinging sword – and would probably have been shot down. Age had taught him caution; but then, who ever heard of an old hero? These people would question him, and if they didn't get the answers they wanted, they would torture and then kill him. In fact, even if he did tell them what they wanted to know, they would probably kill him anyway – but at least it might be quick and painless. And when a man reached Keshian's age in his particular profession, the best he could hope for was a quick death.

It was close to midnight when they came for him. He had fallen into a fitful doze earlier on that night, although he had awoken briefly some time later to watch the stars beginning their slow dance across the clear skies, and tried to gauge his location.

The agony of returning circulation brought him awake again. Someone had cut the bonds on his legs, and his ankles and feet were afire with stabbing pains and cramps. Still only half-conscious, he was hauled to his feet and dragged across the clearing towards the Way Station.

The light inside the long, low, rectangular room was sharp and painful, driving slim daggers of pain into his throbbing head. The air was harsh and dry, foul with the stench of unwashed bodies, urine, vomit and burnt food, and he had to swallow hard to keep his gorge down. But it was warm; he was grateful for that. All conversation died to a dull murmur as he was dragged across the room towards the huge open fire to where Kutor sat alone and apart from the others.

The prince was seated before a small ornate table of polished wood, its delicate filigree work inset with flecks of dark gold and winking gemstones. The remains of a meal were still on the table and, although the fare might have been rough, the tableware was of the finest worked gold.

Keshian's stomach rumbled hungrily.

Kutor patted his lips with a white napkin and looked up into the captain's eyes. He remained silent for a long time, and then slowly and deliberately he poured a measure of deep red wine into a tall fluted glass. He held the glass in the fingers of both hands under his sharp nose and stared deep into the swirling depths. 'You are a very foolish man,' he said finally, without taking his eyes from the glass.

Behind him, Keshian was aware that the entire room had grown quiet, and he could almost feel the malicious smiles.

Kutor glanced up and smiled briefly. 'We can talk, you and I,' he said. 'You can tell me who you are, where you were going, and why.'

'And if I don't?' the older man asked quietly.

The younger man's smile deepened, and he shrugged. 'I can wait while my men . . . question . . . you, and then we can speak again. You will tell me then,' he said confidently.

Keshian nodded wearily, and his shoulders slumped. 'Aye, so you could.' He nodded at the vacant seat, and then at the wine. 'May I sit, and drink?'

News of the slaughtered scouting party was carried back to Baddalaur by an itinerant poet returning to the College. Custom and tradition decreed that those poets and bards who had received their training in the College of Bards must, at least once in every five-year cycle, return to the College and record their tales and epics in the library, so that the lore of the Seven Nations might never again be lost as it so nearly had in the past.

The scholars in Baddalaur relayed the message back to Karfondal through one of their number who had the power of Speech, and that same night, while Kutor was questioning Keshian, word was being relayed back to the capital that the bard Paedur had slaughtered a band of Karfondal's men with his Old Faith sorcery.

No mention was made of the crossbow wounds on either man or beast, nor was the fact that they had been stripped of their arms and armour even discussed.

'My name is Keshian, son of Keshen, a smith, and I am a captain in Count Karfondal's army,' the old warrior began, carefully sipping the heady ruby wine. He was sitting in a chair across the ornate table from Kutor, his hands unbound and a rough woollen cloak thrown across his shoulders. 'Some days ago, word came in that a dangerous criminal was on the loose, a bard by the name of Paedur . . .'

'What was his crime?' Kutor asked.

'Sedition against the New Religion.'

'Sedition against the New Religion!' Kutor spat into the fire. 'That's hardly a crime.'

'Aye, but the count has been received into that faith and he is enforcing his will on his court and subjects,' Keshian protested. 'The New Religion is now the official belief of this province.'

'The people will never follow the Religion,' the young man snapped, 'but continue.'

'This bard is immediately recognisable by the fact that he has but one hand and wears a silver hook in place of his left. The only other description we had was that he was tall and thin, sharp-featured and dark-eyed. I was told to bring him back to the count – alive.'

'And all because he was preaching against the New Religion?' Kutor asked with derision. 'It seems unlikely.'

'I am a soldier sir, I follow my orders.' Keshian paused and sipped his drink. 'Perhaps sir, I might add that this Paedur does not exactly preach against the Religion; he is a bard, and by all accounts a master of his craft, and so by using his tales he insidiously turns people back to the Old Faith.'

'But to what end?'

Keshian shrugged. 'I don't know.'

'I don't believe him,' one of the bandits, a huge ill-kempt southerner said, his accent thick, slurred from too much wine, his eyes bright and dangerous. 'Eight men to follow one bard . . .'

'There was some talk that he is not wholly a man,' the captain said quickly.

'You seem to know a little more about him now,' Kutor snapped. 'Perhaps if we were to pry a little more, we might find out what else you know about this bard, eh?'

'That's all I know . . .'

'Why don't you ask me?'

The voice was sharp and penetrating and cut through the thick atmosphere like a chill breeze.

In the stunned silence that followed, the crackling of the fire seemed unnaturally loud, and even the wind hissing against the thick stones of the walls was audible. A shadow moved at the back of the room and then a figure stepped out into the light.

Steel rasped as weapons were drawn.

The figure was that of a man, clad in a long dark cloak of fine hair that covered him from head to foot. His features were shadowed beneath the cloak's deep cowl, leaving only his eyes glowing in the reflected firelight.

One of the bandits stepped in front of the man, bringing a thick-bladed sabre up before the figure's face. 'Let's have a look at you, eh?'

There was a blur of silver, and metal sang – and the sabre was entrapped in a gleaming half-circle, a hook, that the figure was holding. The brigand attempted to pull his weapon free, but it was firmly lodged.

'The bard,' Keshian breathed, recognising the hook.

'You know this man?' Kutor snapped.

'It can only be the bard . . . the man we were sent to follow,' Keshian said quietly. 'But, how did he come here . . .?'

The bard twisted his arm and then the sabre blade snapped with a sharp ringing sound, leaving its owner looking stupidly at the stump of metal he held in his hand. 'Perhaps there was a flaw in the metal,' Paedur said quietly, his long-fingered right hand coming up and brushing back the hood of his cloak.

The bandits drew away from the bard then, touching amulets and relics, for there was something strange about him, something about the way his sharp eyes seemed to linger just a moment too long on each person that lent him an almost inhuman air.

He indicated the drawn swords and knives with a wave of his hand. 'Do you defy the King's Privilege, and draw steel on a bard?'

'We do no honour to any King's Privilege,' Kutor snapped.

The bard rounded on him, and the look in his eyes stopped anthing else the prince might have been going say. 'If you intend to rule some day,' Paedur said gently, as if speaking to a child, 'you must base your rule upon solid ground, a background founded in history and folklore. People trust what they know.'

Kutor stood up and moved away from the table, his hand falling to the knife in his belt. He took a step closer to the bard. 'What do you mean,' he hissed, '"if I intend to rule"?'

The stranger smiled and, with his right hand, undid the ornate ouroborus clasp near the throat of his cloak and swung it off his shoulders. He was clad in a black shirt of fine mail over a shirt of cotton dyed a deep purple. His leggings were a deep brown and he wore high black boots that had obviously seen much use. High on his left shoulder, the triangular bardic sigil winked blood-red in the firelight.

He tossed his cloak over Kutor's chair and sat back into it with a sigh of contentment. He looked up at the brigand, who was still standing, and indicated the chair opposite him. 'Please sit.'

Keshian scrambled up out of the seat and Kutor sat down slowly, his eyes never once leaving the bard's.

Paedur sat back into the chair and lowered his head into his shirt's high collar, until only his slightly prominent cheekbones and his burning eyes were visible.

'You want to rule,' he began quietly, his voice certainly not above a normal conversational tone and yet carrying to everyone in the room, 'you feel – and perhaps rightly so – that you have some claim on Geillard's throne.'

'I am the Emperor's son – albeit on the wrong side of the blanket. In the past, men have come to power who have had as little claim to the throne,' Kutor said almost defiantly.

The bard inclined his head slightly. 'Indeed, that is so. But to continue. Your attempt to take the crown by force of arms failed and so now you are forced to live out your days here in the Wastelands. You have harried the Emperor's forces, robbed the merchants, slain or held to ransom the unwary and unlucky travellers who have fallen into your hands. You have made your name a curse on men's lips and turned the Wastelands into a feared place.'

Kutor nodded, smiling slightly.

'And how long do you think you can continue?' Paedur asked mildly. He leaned forward and tapped the table with the point of his hook. 'There is a change abroad at court. So far, Geillard has left you alone – the gods themselves know why, but perhaps he does feel something for you, his . . . his half brother.' The bard shrugged and sat back into the chair. Above him on the wall a torch guttered and died, oily black smoke wending slowly upwards against the stained and blackened beams. No-one made any move to replace it and the area below the torch was touched with heavier shadows which rendered the bard almost invisible, only the gleaming half circle of his hook and the bardic sigil visible. 'If Geillard moves against you, he will crush you – totally.'

'But he won't move against us,' Kutor protested. 'He would be stretching his resources too far; Count Karfondal would never lend him the support needed for any lengthy campaign in the Wastelands.' He glanced up at the captain standing by his side, 'Is that not so?'

'My lord Karfondal does not see eye to eye with the Emperor in many things,' Keshian said carefully.

'Aye, but has not your lord been acting strangely of late?' the bard asked.

Keshian shifted uncomfortably from foot to foot. He shrugged. 'Perhaps he has not been himself recently . . .' he agreed cautiously.

'Perhaps since he adopted the New Religion?' the bard persisted, leaning forward, his eyes catching the firelight and blazing like red coals.

'Perhaps.'

'I don't see . . .' Kutor began.

The bard's hook rose. 'Wait; listen.' He turned back to Keshian. 'And what is his attitude towards Geillard now?'

The captain rolled his cup in his large hands, looking down into the swirling depths. When he looked up his eyes were troubled. 'He has changed towards the Emperor. In the past few moons many messengers have come and gone – and indeed, more so since we were ordered to seek you out. And Karfondal has even announced his intention to visit the Imperial Court in the near future – something which he has never done before, not since Geillard had his uncle put to death for treason.'

The bard turned back to Kutor. 'And tell me, what would happen if Karfondal were to make his peace with Geillard; how would that affect your position here in the Wastelands?'

Kutor shifted uncomfortably in his seat. 'If . . . and I say "if", mind, the Emperor decided to move against us, and he had the count's support, then it would make things difficult for us,' he agreed cautiously.

'They would wipe us out,' one of the men behind him suddenly shouted. 'The Wastelands are our refuge, but they would also make a fine trap.'

Keshian nodded. 'It would be an easy matter to bring in troops to encircle the south, west and eastward sides of the Wastelands, and then draw them in – driving you northwards at the same time. Soon you would be trapped between the encircling troops and the Seven Bastions along the River Mion. And even if you did manage to cross the river – which in the Cold Months is possible across the ice – the Chopts would surely get you.'

'Thank you,' Kutor said grimly. He turned back to the bard after a moment's consideration. 'But tell me, bard, why should the count suddenly resolve his differences with the Emperor?'

'You have heard no doubt about the New Religion that is sweeping across the land?'

'Rumours have trickled through to me – but I have little time for gods and their ilk; I pay them no heed.'

Paedur shook his head. 'Foolish, very foolish. A good leader ignores no rumours, no whispered tales, no scandal that might affect the higher echelons of power.' He sat forward suddenly and impaled Kutor with his hard dark stare. 'This New Religion is not just another fad, not just another passing fancy. It is a very real and dangerous threat to the Seven Nations.'

'I don't see how any religion . . .' the brigand began.

'But it is not just any religion,' Paedur snapped, his voice cracking through the room like a whip. 'It is a man-made and inspired faith, and its believers are dedicated to it with a frightening passion. And it is that faith alone which gives it strength and substance. But – and this is where it affects you – old enemies have now become friends, old rivalries forgotten, old feuds mended. Groups such as yours – bandits, thieves and brigands – have already been slaughterd in the south and east. There is a move abroad to wipe out anyone – *anyone* – who does not conform to the standards of the New Religion and worship its gods.'

'But why?' Kutor whispered.

Paedur shrugged. 'I don't know,' he confessed. 'But perhaps you represent a freedom of sorts, and the New Religion is not too keen on freedom.'

'And what is your part in all this?' Kutor asked suddenly.

'I have no part,' the bard said, smiling. 'I am merely a storyteller – in the traditional way,' he added, with a sly smile.

'Do many listen to your stories?'

'More and more.'

'And what do your tales accomplish?'

'They help to remind the people of the past, of the traditional ways, the old beliefs, the old gods. A lot of people out there believe, indeed, they find it easy to believe. But they need someone to form around, someone who will focus their energy – they need a leader.'

'What sort of a leader?' Kutor asked cautiously.

'Someone to rally behind.' He paused. 'My stories remind them of the past; I stress the importance of tradition and order. They need someone who would also stress the traditional ways; someone with an honourable ancestry, someone with a name. Perhaps someone with at least some sort of claim to the throne.'

There was silence in the Way Station for a long time then. The implications behind the bard's words were not lost on any of those present, and it was as if a chill breeze had blown through the room. And even though nothing had happened, everyone there felt as if something had changed. It was an invitation – and a challenge. In the course of a few heartbeats their lives might take on a new direction. But the final decision would be Kutor's.

'What are you, bard?' Kutor asked softly.

'A storyteller.'

'What else?'

The bard smiled easily, and shrugged. 'As I've said, nothing else.'

'Then tell me, storyteller,' the prince asked quietly, 'what would you do if our situations were reversed?'

'I don't have to make that decision, thank the gods.'

'But if you had . . . if the decision were yours to make?'

Paedur sat back into the chair and seemed to consider. 'I would move fast and by night, heading west to one of the ancient Culai settlements. Beyond the Wastelands many of the old forts are still in good order. With a little work they could be rendered inhabitable and virtually impregnable. As you know, they are usually well situated, solidly built, with their own water supply and often on a branch of the King Road. If I were going to conduct a campaign against the Imperial forces, I would certainly consider using one of the old forts.'

Kutor nodded slowly. 'And what then?'

'Then if a bard, let us say, were to continue on his travels and send anyone interested in the restoration of the old ways, the Old Faith, westwards to you, you would soon have a formidable force under your command.'

'But to what end?'

The bard tapped his silver hook against the wooden table emphasising his points. 'Overthrow the current court which has degenerated into a cesspit, and overthrow the New Religion. The Old Faith must be restored to its former position as the Empire's official religion – is that understood?' he demanded fiercely.

The brigand nodded, taken aback by the bard's vehemence. 'You talk as if it's a foregone conclusion.'

The bard smiled again. 'Ah, but I'm only a storyteller, I've no gift for prophecy.'

Kutor leaned back in the chair. 'So you say,' he mused. 'What you've said is interesting, but you've got to let me think on it . . .'

'You don't have much time left,' Paedur said quietly.

Kutor nodded. 'Aye, well . . . let me think.' What this bard was proposing was . . . incredible. A few years ago he would have said yes immediately, and bedamn the consequences, but now . . . but now he had to think. Once he had started on this course, there was no turning back. He had to think.

He looked around the room, at the ragged men and women, brigands, outlaws, thieves, a few ex-soldiers. They would follow him, he knew, but had he any right to lead them away from here into what might be almost certain death? But if what this bard said were true, then their days here in the Wastelands were numbered. He needed to buy some time to think.

Kutor turned back to Paedur. 'Well, sir bard, why don't you give us an example of your craft; why don't you let us have a tale, eh?' Behind him, the company shouted their approval, tension evaporating like the morning dew under the sun.

'Aye, a tale.'

The bard ran his hook down along his jaw, his face serious but his eyes were bright with amusement. 'A tale. Well then, what would you have?' He looked across at Kutor. 'Choose . . .'

The brigand smiled. 'Give us a tale of my namesake: Kutor Kin-Slayer. It was a story I learned at my mother's knee. Give me your version.'

Paedur nodded. 'A strange choice . . .'

'Do you know it?'

The bard smiled. 'I know all the tales and legends of our land.' He tucked his hook into his sleeve and leaned back in the chair, and the shadows clustered about him, leaving only his eyes burning in the paleness of his face. There was a brief pause as he

63

looked around the room, claiming everyone's attention, and then he began . . .

In the time of Churon the Onelord and Deslirda his lady, there was peace over the land for the first time in many years.

But it had not always been so, for when the invaders had come, the first decade of the Onelord's reign had been one of war and famine. But Churon had sworn to free his land, and to this end had cunningly oathbound the Brothers, the six kings of the neighbouring lands, and, gathering his allies together on the Sand Plain close to where the invaders from the Land of the Sun had beached their metal craft, he waged war upon them. And in a great battle lasting a day and a night, his army utterly vanquished the Shemmatae. From that time he ruled with an iron hand from his place in the Silver City of Shansalow, acknowledged by the Brothers as their overlord, the Onelord.

But the land was vast and still untamed, and there were large tracts which were claimed only by the beasts. Thus the Onelord, recognising that he could not rule alone, and, realising the dangers of even attempting to do so, therefore appointed his most trusted retainers to oversee the provinces on his behalf. The Onelord remained in the capital and his regents were answerable only to him.

And Churon ordered his loyal and trusted friend Kutor the Strong to invest the Castle of Oakin, and from there to rule the western seaboard on his behalf.

Thus Kutor, called the Strong, for he was a man of great physical strength, made preparations for the journey. And when his servants, warriors and retainers had gathered together their belongings and possessions they set out along the King Road to the West, and Gallowan Province.

For many days Kutor and his retainers rode, travelling westwards all the while. The year was drawing to a close and the days were long and heavy with time losing all meaning. They rode past the Twin Cities of Foara and Faora upon the Heights, past ancient Palsaor, and then on to Broar where they stopped with Prince Huiet, feasting and making merry with their jovial host.

They continued on, and the Lady Lussa rode in her full finery thrice across the skies. And then, on that morning dedicated to Cam, the God of Bridges, they came to the Gluaddon Wood, and they rode through the ancient wood with their arms and accoutrements clattering and twinkling in the dappled sunlight, and their voices were raised in song and laughter.

And thus Kutor, in his haste to reach his new domain, failed to pay tribute to the Wood Folk that abode deep in the leafy fastness, and furthermore, did not preserve the Wood Silence, that ancient law which enjoined all travellers to *"raise not a voice in joy nor anger, nor carry sparkling metal within the fields of the Crinnfaoich, the Wood Folk."*

And the Wood Folk were greatly angered, but decided to grant unto the new Lord of Oakin the opportunity to redress his omission, and thus they sent to him Yuann, the Wood Sprite.

Fair she was to look upon; her hair dark as the moss upon the bark, soft and shining, her skin tanned as dark as the great toor trees. Her features were delicate, yet sharp, and her eyes were naught but dappled pools of light amidst shadow. She flitted amongst the trees clad in a shift of feathery mostle leaves which clung glovelike to her skin.

She came to Kutor in the evening twilight as he sat beneath a gnarled toor tree looking down upon his camp which lay spread out over the Dale of Duil. When she spoke, her voice was like a summer breeze whispering through soft leaves.

'Lord Kutor . . . Lord Kutor,' she called, 'why dost thou not pay tribute to the Old Folk who have lived amidst these trees since time immemorial, and why dost thou not honour the Wood Silence?'

Kutor started and his hand reached for his great broadsword before he realised that that maid who had crept up so silently upon him was alone and unarmed. 'Fair maid,' the lord replied quietly, although he was nigh struck dumb with wonderment at the sight of such beauty and grace, 'I know not what you mean.'

'You have not acknowledged the Crinnfaoich as Lords of the Forest, my lord,' said the maid.

'Child of the Woods,' Kutor said roughly, 'you must know that I am called Kutor the Strong, and I acknowledge no man my lord, saving my lord Churon.' He paused and added in a gentler voice, 'So you see, I will acknowledge no tree dwellers my superior, be they either gods or men.'

The Wood Sprite fell silent, for the man's fearlessness – and foolishness – appalled her. 'Surely you must acknowledge your gods as your superiors?' she wondered.

'Why should I?' Kutor demanded. 'The gods have little respect for a snivelling man; they have fought to reach their present position in the Pantheon, and thus they respect a fighter. I am a fighter, and I therefore acknowledge the gods as my equals.' He paused and added quietly, 'Of course, the followers of Churon are expected to pay homage to the Pantheon, it is part of Churon's attempt to unify the Seven Nations: One Faith, One Land, One People.' Kutor shook his head and laughed bitterly. 'Aye, well he'll never see it, nor will I.'

'A godless man,' the Wood Sprite whispered, 'surely thou art lonely and afraid?'

But Kutor misunderstood her question. 'I have friends in plenty. I am alone only in that I have no wife.' The warrior's meaning was clear.

'Then you will not honour the Crinnfaoich?' the blushing maid said quickly.

'No, I will not; I cannot for honour's sake,' Kutor said harshly.

'Then I prophesy that there will be little peace between you and yours and the Wood Folk . . . and I would wish that it were not so.' A single tear slipped down her cheek, but Kutor brushed it aside with a gentle hand and drew the maid close to him.

'I do not even know your name,' he murmured softly, brushing the maid's green-tinged silken hair.

'I am Yuann, a Wood Maid, a *fraoicht*, in the Slé tongue.'

And Yuann and Kutor walked into the wood and spoke of many things and when night drew on they lay together in a little bower beside a clear pool and took pleasure in each other's bodies. But in the morning, Yuann was gone, leaving Kutor puzzled and frightened, although he did not know what he feared, and as the day wore on he came to believe that perhaps he had dreamt of the *fraoicht*.

But she came again that night, and every night thereafter while the Lord of Oakin passed through the ancient wood, and she always vanished with the advent of morning.

Now on the last day of their passage through the Gluaddon Wood, when the crenellated turrets of Castle Oakin rose tall and misty above the greenery, the Wood Sprite did not come. And though Kutor searched the deep forests and silent woods all that day and for many days thereafter, he never again found Yuann the *fraoicht*.

And the Wood Folk never forgave Kutor, and thereafter neither wood nor anything fashioned thereof survived in the Castle of Oakin. Doors warped, tables and chairs collapsed, storm shutters split and cracked, wooden platforms and fencing rotted overnight and neither bows nor arrows could be fashioned from the wood of the forest. Even the usually indestructible brukwood rotted and powdered once within the castle walls.

And thus all men knew that the Lord of Oakin had been cursed by the Crinnfaoich.

That first winter of Kutor's rule was a hard one, and the castle was cut off from the surrounding countryside by deep drifts of snow and packed ice. Even the castle's well had frozen over and fuel was running dangerously low.

One night, nigh on one year since he had invested the castle,

Kutor found he could not sleep and walked the battlements as night's midnight hour was drawing on. It was in the very depths of the year, when Faurug the Nightwind with Fiarle and Snaitle the Cold God were abroad and dark clouds scudded across the face of the Lady Lussa, the Moon Goddess, like clumsy beast-like paws attempting to grasp a single pearl. The wind howled through the leafless trees, rent by the sentinel branches and Kutor shivered, for he fancied he heard voices whispering and conspiring together within the cloaking darkness of the forest.

Then a sudden movement below stopped the lord in his tracks. A shadow had slipped from the mocking darkness and flitted swiftly along the ground, ominous and furtive, seeking every clump of darkened shelter and gradually drawing nearer to the castle. Then the night creature had reached the walls and crept along them to the postern gate. It hesitated a moment before stooping down and slipping a bulky object in the shadow of the gate; then the creature turned and vanished back into the hard chill night.

Kutor followed its movements until he could see it no more, then raced down the battlements to the small gate, calling forth the watch as he did so.

And upon the step, deep in the shadows, they found a blanket woven from the branches of the toor tree and lined with mostle leaves . . . and lying wrapped within, they found a baby, a boy-child and not yet one hour old.

Now the years passed and the babe grew into boyhood and thence to manhood and he was called Kutter. He was tall and strong like his father, but unlike Kutor, his looks were somewhat sharp and pointed and his skin was smooth like a woman's. He was wise in the ways of the wood and the lore of the forests and he had great skill in the working of wood.

But of his birth and finding Kutor told his son nothing, and instilled into the boy a deep and burning hatred for the Crinnfaoich, for the Lord of Oakin held the Wood Folk responsible for the loss of his love.

Now as Kutor reached middle years he became more and more distracted, and often disappeared for many days into the fastness of the woods, obsessed with his search for Yuann, the *fraoicht*.

His followers wondered at this, and they feared, and their fear turned to anger, for the Lord was neglecting his duties, and at last, in desperation, they made representation to Churon the Onelord.

When Churon heard of the matter, he was greatly troubled and saddened, for he counted Kutor a good and loyal friend and it pained him to lose a friend to the Nameless God of Delusion and Madness.

But if the lord were unfit to rule . . .

So Churon pondered on the matter, seeking someone to replace Kutor even though he was loath to dishonour his friend by passing the regency of the province on to a stranger. And so, to settle the matter, he made Kutter vice-regent of Gallowan.

And thus it was for many years.

Now, when Kutor reached his eightieth year he grew ill, having contracted marsh fever while wandering through the damp woods. And age, which heretofore had but lightly touched the lord, now lay heavily upon him, shortening his breath, enfeebling his gait, dimming his sight and dulling his hearing.

And he knew he was dying.

So on the evening of the fourteenth day of his illness and his last in this life, he dismissed his servants and called his son to him. His old eyes filled with tears when Kutter came and knelt by the bed, for he saw in him a shadow of his own youth. Tall and proud he stood with great strength of limb; his hair was a burnished copper and his skin deeply tanned, but even if one had not guessed it from his features, his eyes told of his mixed parentage, for they were pools of deep unreadable mystery.

And it suddenly saddened the old man that his son knew nothing of his mother, whom he so closely resembled.

They talked late into the night on many subjects, for the lord knew his end was near and wished to advise his son, and Kutter listened and remembered.

But one promise Kutor extracted from his son, a promise born out of a terrible anger: a promise that he would search out the woods and forests of Gallowan for the Crinnfaoich and put them to the sword, and the old man convinced his son that they were evil and had sought to usurp his rule and conquer the land.

But Kutter demurred, for although he feared the Wood Folk with a superstitious awe, he did not hate them with his father's violence.

But Kutor bound him with a thrice-sworn oath and sealed it with a *geasa* . . . and Kutter had no choice but to swear.

And as the dawn rose over the tree tops that were turning ochre and bronze with the turning of the year, and Nusas flooded the room with a fragile light, the old lord passed into the Silent Wood, the domain of Mannam, the Lord of the Dead.

On the morning of the following day – once called Ellamas Day, but thereafter called Kutormas – the lord was laid to rest with all due pomp in a simple grave which stood in sight of the forest – for that had been one of his last wishes.

And many came to pay homage to Kutor, for he had been a good ruler in his prime, his justice had been stern and swift, but fair also, he had laboured hard for his province and left behind a legacy of roads, bridges and aqueducts.

Now some weeks after the death of Kutor, an emissary came from the Onelord, for Churon, having heard of the death of his friend, had sent his son Chural to Gallowan, to place on the grave of the dead lord a broken spear, inscribed with the runes of the Onelord and hung with tattered pennants. It was the highest military honour, and a sign that Churon had lost a loyal and true friend who had served him faithfully to the end.

On the morning following the prince's arrival, Kutter and Chural, with a small company of guards, rode out towards Gluaddon Wood and Kutor's grave.

As they drew near to the spot they noticed a young woman kneeling by the graveside and there was an air of strangeness – of wildness – about her. Kutter was puzzled, for he had never seen her before and he was familiar with all the maids in the nearby villages and surrounding countryside. They were almost upon her before she stood up and faced them – and both Kutter and Chural were amazed, for hers was an almost frightening beauty. Though not above middle height, she exuded a presence, an aura, that lent her stature. Her hair was long and dark and rustled in a silken wave down her back, so dark indeed that it seemed to gleam darkly green and moss-like in the morning light. Her skin was clear and deeply tanned as if she had spent all her days in the open under the sun and her eyes . . . her eyes were deep and mysterious, and Kutter somehow found them almost frighteningly familiar. But as he dismounted, he saw that she was clad in a shift of feathery mostle leaves, and that there was dirt on her hands . . .

Fear and anger flashed through his brain with blinding comprehension, his sight darkened and his head began to pound. Here was a Crinnfaoich, a Duaiteoiri, come to despoil his father's grave!

Mindful of his oath and now filled with a loathing of this beautiful creature, he pulled his sword free with a cry of rage and in one movement plunged it into the woman's breast.

Prince Chural leaped from his horse with a cry of horror and ran to the stricken maid, clasping her in his arms as he tried to staunch the blood that flowed from her wound and dropped on to the heaped earth of the grave.

'Kutter, what have you done?' he demanded.

'She . . . she is of the Crinnfaoich,' shouted Kutter, 'come to torment my father's shade and befoul his grave.' The young lord turned away, for now the anger and hatred had drained away and he was sickened and shamed and repented his hasty action.

But had he not sworn an oath to his dying father, and was she not of the Wood Folk and . . .? Slowly he returned to the graveside and crouched by the prince and the dying woman. 'Forgive me,' he whispered, 'forgive me.'

The woman shuddered in Chural's arms and her head lifted and her eyes looked up into his . . . looking at him . . . through him . . . with eyes that reminded him of . . .

And then he fell back, understanding coursing through him like a levin bolt, shattering the night of ignorance. But as he reached for the small, delicate figure, she shivered and passed unto Mannam, to Death.

Chural turned to look at the stricken lord, and there were tears in his eyes. 'She said she was called Yuann,' he whispered. 'Yuann, beloved of . . . Kutor the Strong . . .'

The bard's voice trailed off to a whisper that seemed to linger on the heavy air of the Way Station long after it should. Even when the last tendrils of sound had disappeared, no-one moved or spoke, still enwrapped as they were within the bard's tale. Some of the bandits' drabs were weeping openly, and even the men's eyes were suspiciously bright and glittering.

A taper suddenly guttered and died, and the oily smoke coiled around the room, and the rancid bitter-sweet odour made someone sneeze, and suddenly the spell was broken. People moved, conscious of numb feet or hands, and reached for drinks that had grown warm and flat while the bard had worked his own particular magic.

Only Kutor remained unmoving in his chair, his eyes closed, his face curiously blank and almost childlike. When he opened his eyes, they seemed almost lost. 'Tell me, bard, was there ever a Churon, a Kutor and Kutter?'

When Paedur began to speak again, the Way Station fell silent. 'History confirms that there was a Chur'an, called the One or the Overlord, who ruled from Shansalow, some sixteen generations ago, and that he did appoint a Kutnor – who was called the Strong – Lord of the Province of Gallowan. There is also some evidence that Kutnor's successor was his bastard son, Kutear.'

Another taper failed and died and Paedur paused until the smoke had dispersed. 'Kutnor died insane and indeed Kuttear did pursue a policy of land reclamation and cleared many forest tracts and woodland areas, putting those inhabitants who refused to leave the forest and quit their hereditary occupations – charcoal-burners, wood-bearers, moss-gatherers – to the sword. The land was then settled with refugees from the decimated Whale Coast.'

'What happened there?' someone asked from the heavily shadowed room.

'A series of natural disasters which culminated with either the rising of the sea or the sinking of the land. It was probably a tidal wave,' Paedur added, and then continued. 'However, some years later, all settlement ceased in Gallowan, and there was mass emigration from the region. Those fleeing the province told of unnatural growth; of trees sprouting overnight, and growing into horrific shapes, of cleared fields suddenly sprouting rank weeds and shrubs in a matter of hours, of pathways and roads abruptly covered in impassable growth.

'The whole region quickly returned to forest, and this area may correspond with the present location of the Great Guadne Forest, which lies to the north and west of here,' he finished.

'And Kutter,' Kutor said quietly, 'how did he die, do you know?'

The bard shook his head, the movement almost lost in the shadows. 'Not for certain, but Cambris, in his *Heraldic Genealogies*, states that a Kuttear, Lord of the Province of Gallowan, ruled for seven years following the death of his father Kutnor, son of Katar, son of Kata. Kuttear himself died when he fell from his horse and was impaled through the chest by a branch of a toor tree.'

Kutor nodded. 'So I've heard, bard; so I've heard.'

Another taper sputtered and died – for they had not been attended to while the bard told his tale – leaving only one smoking sconce lighting the room from above the door.

When the prince opened his eyes again, there was a look of absolute weariness in them. 'So Kutor did not act soon enough, and Kutter acted too soon. What should I do, bard?' he asked simply.

'But, remember, Kutor did not heed the advice of the *fraoicht*. However, if you want my advice – head west; take one of the old Culai fortresses; gather together an army – a proper army this time, and prepare yourself for the coming battle.'

'And I?' Keshian spoke for the first time, startling Kutor, who had almost forgotten him.

'Perhaps Prince Kutor will have need for a good officer, familiar with the Imperial Forces,' came the bard's voice from the shadows. 'I will send others of a similar mind to you, Kutor; in time you will have your army.'

'How will I know them?'

'They will carry my mark – the sign of the hook.'

'And what now, bard?' Kutor asked.

But there was no reply; the bard had gone.

71

5   The Weapon Master*

And the bard met many on the road to the north and swayed them to his mission.

Life of Paedur, the Bard

A Man without Soul; a Man without Heart; a Man without Conscience. He seemed to me a man not of this world; he seemed to me a dead man.

from . . . *The Warrior, the Life of Owen, Weapon Master*

Owen spent the winter in Palentian Province that year, resting and recovering from his wounds which, although many, were not serious. When he was fit, he took employment with Count Palent, instructing his son in matters of weapon-craft and the Way of the Warrior.

However, as the days lengthened, the Master grew restless and longed to be on his way, but he found it difficult to extract payment from the count, for the old man maintained that his son's education was as yet incomplete. But the boy was slow, and far too fond of his cups and his cronies to pay the Master much heed, and seemed to forget everything he learned almost immediately.

So, one evening, close to the Yearchange, as the sun was sinking below the castle walls and the night chill was closing in, Owen came for me. I was seated in my room in the small outhouse behind the stables, cleaning his shield with fine sand. It was dim and dark and smelt of horses, but a room in the castle had not been considered proper for the Weapon Master's servant.

Owen entered the small room suddenly. He pushed the door shut behind him and moved to the hide-covered window and peered out into the gathering night. Although the Master was dressed in his stained travelling cloak and the guttering taper on the straw beside me did not shed much light across the room, I immediately noticed that he seemed bulkier than usual.

I guessed what was happening and was already bundling my gear together when he moved across the room and knelt beside me, gathering up his longsword and shield. In the light I could

* from . . .*The Warrior, the Life of Owen, Weapon Master.*

see that he was wearing his battle gear beneath his cloak: a hauberk of thick yet supple leather and mail designed to turn an arrow or knife blade. He strapped his longsword across his back, with the hilt projecting above the left shoulder, and slipped his small shield high up on his left arm. He tossed a cloth-wrapped bundle onto the straw pallet.

'We're going Tien, leave nothing behind.' He moved about the room gathering up his few pieces of body armour while I arranged a bundle of straw beneath a blanket on the pallet. To the casual observer, it would look as if I still slept there. I then strapped my two axes on to my belt and slung my gear across my other arm and I was ready.

The Master extinguished the taper, and then we waited until our eyes had adjusted to the darkness; it was with such precautions that we survived as long as we did in our dangerous trade. And then we silently slipped from the outhouse, Owen in the lead, his left hand cupped in such a way that I knew he carried a blade hidden up his sleeve.

We moved from shadow to shadow, neither hurrying nor acting furtively, doing nothing that would attract the attention of the patrolling guards on the rooftops above our heads. We encountered no-one until we reached the postern gate. A single guard stood watch, leaning back against the wall, head nodding, a halberd cradled in his arms. He started awake as Owen drew out of the shadows, fumbled for his weapon and then levelled it at the Master's chest.

'Who goes there?' he called, but his voice was low and soft; he was young, inexperienced and tired. He stood uneasily, off-balance, the point of his halberd wavering between the Master's chest and throat.

'Who goes there?' he repeated, his voice rising slightly, and then cracking, his wide eyes darting from side to side.

'There is no cause for alarm,' Owen said, stepping forward into the light, and as the guard recognised him and relaxed, the Master grabbed the halberd behind its hooked and pointed head, jerking the man forward. He stumbled and Owen deftly cut his throat as he fell; he died without a sound.

I then drove the halberd point first into the soft earth and held him while the Master tied the body by the hair and belt to the staff. From the distance, it looked as if the guard had dozed limply at his post; it was a ruse we had used on several occasions, buying time.

While Owen put the finishing touches to the guard, I probed the lock on the gate. It was old and heavy, of the double key type, but I had served a locksmith in my youth and had picked up much of the trade, and so with a little probing with the point of my dagger, I soon had it open. Owen made me lock the door after us; it would help delay and confuse any pursuit.

We travelled hard and fast that night, until we struck the Seme which we followed upriver until it was bridged by the old King Road. We camped for what remained of the night on the fishing ledge under the bridge and there Owen explained why we had fled Count Palent's castle in such a hasty fashion.

'It seems the count had no intention of ever paying our wage,' he said, drawing his cloak tighter about his shoulders. 'I had served my purpose and trained his son to a degree of weaponmanship he would never otherwise have attained – although, Tien,' he added, 'he lacks all feeling for his weapons, they are mere killing tools. He will always remain a butcher, he will never be a killer.'

'How did you learn of their plans?' I wondered.

'I overheard him boasting that the good count wished his son and a company of guards to try some of their new-found skills on me,' he laughed softly, shaking his head.

It was not the first time this had happened and undoubtedly it would happen again. The services of a Weapon Master do not come cheap, and the better they are, the more expensive they become – and Owen was one of the best. Thrice before he had been hired by unscrupulous lords who thought that they might have him disposed of before they actually had to pay him.

But it is difficult to kill a Weapon Master.

We took to the road as the first grey tinges of dawn lightened the eastern horizon. We made good time, for the King Road was in a fair condition even after the recent flooding and storms, although in places the ground tended to be soft and muddy beneath a thin covering of ice.

About mid-morning we passed through the town of Badaur which lies under the shadow of Baddalaur, the College of Bards, an ancient pile of time-worn masonry built, Owen told me, by the Culai, the First Race of Men. For generations the bards and minstrels, poets and scribes who roam the Nations have been trained there; all knowledge passes through Baddalaur, for its pupils are everywhere.

The town was buzzing with the news that a crack battalon of

Count Karfondal's troops had been found slaughtered either by bandits or a hideous hooded demon – there were two versions – just inside the Wastelands. The small town was packed with the count's men in their red and gold, and as we arrived some Imperial troops in their more sombre blue and black rode in, so we hurried on.

We ate our midday meal as we marched – luckily we hadn't stopped for any reason, because the gates were closed shortly after we left, and the soldiers began systematically to search and question everyone there. We continued pushing northwards, for we wished to put as much distance between ourselves and Count Palent as possible.

Once beyond the town, the character of the landscape – which was rough at the best of times – became even more desolate, and the King Road knifed arrow-straight and coal-black through it, rising and falling in long slow waves with nothing but grey, barren rock on either side. The road was deserted, no-one braving the crisp weather and roving wolves and the recent bandit atrocity. But we were in good spirits, and chanted a soldier's marching song as we trekked northwards, heading for one of the Seven Bastions of the North, where a warrior was sure to find work.

Owen was in high good humour. Earlier I had remarked that the count had cheated us of our wage, but the Master had laughed gently and tapped the bundle he had given me back in the castle. When I opened it I found it contained cloth-wrapped gold plate stamped with the count's crest, which he had taken in lieu of payment. 'He would have cheated me, slain us, but I was too quick for him, and struck first. Remember that, Tien, always strike first.'

About mid-afternoon the sky clouded over and we began to think about seeking shelter for the coming night, for a blizzard was brewing and to be caught in the open would almost certainly mean death.

However, the ground on either side of the King Road was flat and unbroken and we continued on, looking out for a suitable hollow, or windbreak. As we crested a slight rise in the road we spotted the lone figure in the distance, moving northwards. We immediately grew wary, for in these wild lands a single traveller was often used as a decoy, live bait for the marauding outlaws, escaped slaves, prisoners and the like who have made the Wastelands their home. What further increased our suspicions, was the fact that the figure didn't seem to be moving at any great speed, and no-one lingers on the King Road after dark, and though it was but mid-afternoon, night comes early to the Wastelands this far north.

I saw Owen unsheathing his short curved sword, and I carefully unhitched my belt-axe, but kept it concealed beneath my cloak. As far as we could see, the figure was alone, and the ground seemed far too flat and barren to afford shelter to anyone or anything, but . . .

We hurried on, and soon caught up with the lone traveller and, although dusk had not yet fallen, the figure – a man by his height and build – remained strangely shadowed. I shivered, for who knew what strange creatures roamed abroad in this desolate land? Owen too, was disturbed by this strange apparition which glided silently and seemingly unconcerned before us.

Now, there is no-one who can dispute my Master's bravery – no-one alive that is – but I thought I heard his voice quaver as he called out to the figure. 'Hold! You there, stop!' His voice sounded shockingly loud in the silence, and his sword came up threateningly, the burnished metal glowing wanly in the fast-fading light, and I could see that his thumb rested on the bone relic set into the hilt.

The figure stopped and turned slowly, eyeing us seemingly without surprise. He was tall, very tall, topping even Owen who was accounted a tall man, and he was thin, and his height made him seem skeletal. His face – from what I could see of it – was long and thin, and his eyes large and dominating, but most of his head and the fine details of his features were shadowed by the cowl of a long travelling cloak he wore.

He spoke, his voice soft, controlled and cultured. 'Yes, what do you want?' His coolness surprised us, for he had displayed no emotion upon being confronted by us . . . and I must admit we did not present a comforting spectacle. Owen, tall and well-built, his harsh features scarred and tanned, brandishing a wickedly curved short-sword; myself, short, fur-clad, and – why should I not be truthful? – my features and yellow-tinged skin must surely have seemed sinister and alien to him.

'Tien, a light!' The Master's voice was harsh, a trifle high, as it was when he was unsure of himself. I knelt down and struggled with flint and tinder as the stranger approached Owen.

'You have no need of your sword,' he said to the Master and then he laughed, and it was the most frightening sound I have ever heard, 'I will not harm you.' And truly, I could not tell whether he jested or not. The flint sparked and the tinder caught; I uncovered the small travel-lantern, lit the oiled wick and slid the polished metal plate behind the flame, bathing the stranger in a ghostly milk-light. In the light he seemed even larger and more disturbing, for night had swiftly fallen, absorbing him into the blackness, and it was as if a disembodied face floated in the night before us.

'Who are you?' Owen snapped, waving his sword past the stranger's face in a move designed to draw his gaze, but the sinister figure never even blinked.

'I am Paedur,' he replied, and then a glowing silver hook flashed in the light and a corner of his cloak was pulled back, revealing a sparkling eye and triangle device high on his left shoulder. 'I am a bard.'

'A bard! I . . . I beg your forgiveness, bard.' The Master had been taken off guard and was disturbed and shaken, for no-one accosts or draws a weapon on a bard, for they, like minstrels, priests and pilgrims, are accorded the King's Privilege and it is death to harm or obstruct them in any way. 'I did not know, I feared . . .' he finished lamely.

The bard smiled then, and I have yet to see a smile so change a man. Although he still radiated an air of power and assurance, the aura of menace fell away. 'I know and I understand and you are right to be wary, for this is a wild and dangerous place, inhabited by men who are little better than beasts and beasts which are in turn imbued with the intelligence of men. Aye, a dangerous land.' He turned and stared into the moonless, starless night as if he could penetrate that utter darkness. His unnerving gaze returned to Owen. 'But not too dangerous for one such as you . . .' His voice was gentle and held just a trace of amusement.

The Master swelled with pride. 'No, I think not. I am Owen, Weapon Master, and this is Tien tZo, my slave-companion.'

The bard bowed slightly to us both. 'Your name, Owen Weapon Master, is of course familiar to me; the south is full of your glories and deeds and you are hero and villain both.'

The Master laughed, pleased, for though he was a great man, vanity was always one of his failings.

The bard then turned and addressed me directly. 'You I have not heard of . . . but then few remember slaves. What land do you hail from, Tien tZo?'

It is a question I have often been asked, for my yellow skin and jade-green up-tilted eyes attract attention wherever I go. 'I am descended from the Shemmatae, who are called the Invaders by your historians,' I replied. 'My forebears were taken as slaves on the Sand Plain, but I am of pure blood and can trace my lineage back to there and beyond to my homeland, and thus it might be said that I hail from the Land of the Sun, to the east.'

The bard nodded. 'Strange . . . strange,' he murmured, almost to himself, 'I can see the hand of the gods in this.' He glanced back to me. 'I have but lately recounted the tale of Churon and his vassal Kutor; Churon defeated the Shemmat Invaders on the Sand Plain, and it is curious coincidence to meet one of their descendants.'

It was now getting on for the forenight, and a sharp breeze had struck up, whipping across the Wastelands and carrying flurries of snow and ice. Paedur adjusted his cloak about his shoulders. 'We must find shelter soon; Faurug, Fiarle and Snaitle are abroad tonight.' I didn't understand the references, but I noticed the Master's startled look.

'And where are we going to find shelter around here?' Owen asked.

'This way.' The enigmatic figure turned around and headed off the road. We hesitated a few moments before finally following him. We struck off due east from our original path, cutting away from the road and on to a thin, barely visible animal run. The ground was soft at first, for the day had been mild and the earth had thawed somewhat, but it was now beginning to freeze again. Pools of ice cracked and splintered beneath our boots and we found ourselves sinking up to our ankles in freezing mud. We stumbled through patches of irongrass, frozen as solid as its name, and it rattled and clacked horribly together, sounding like the finger-bones that the shamans of the south use for divination.

I had been counting – almost unconsciously – and we had walked perhaps a thousand or more paces when suddenly the path crumbled beneath my feet and I fell and crashed headlong down a slight incline into a copse of withered bushes. They collapsed around me with a noise like that of a score of sap-filled logs burning and sparking. I dropped the lantern as I fell and the light died and the night closed in, swallowing everything in its maw. I thrashed about, scattering branches and twigs in an effort to free myself, but I only succeeded in becoming thoroughly entangled in the claw-like core of the bush. I could not even cry out, for my face was pressed into the chill damp earth.

Suddenly something cold and sharp and metallic touched my cheek. My heart almost stopped. A voice hissed close to my ear. 'Don't move; I will free you.' It was the bard.

I couldn't move, even if I had wanted to, but with the bard's chill warning ringing in my head even my breathing stilled. Then above the gathering wind, I heard whistling – such as a sword makes upon the downward stroke – followed by a deep crackling report beside me. Again and again the bard chopped into the tough dry wood, cutting me free from the entangling branches. A hand gripped my collar and then I was pulled out and hauled to my feet. Something cold and metallic was pressed back into my hand almost making me scream with fright, but I recognised the shape as the lantern.

And only then did I realise that the bard had cut me free in absolute darkness.

Paedur's hand then sought mine. It felt cool and dry, the skin rough and hard; it felt like the skin of a reptile. 'This way,' he said, and led me up the incline and back on to the path. He then took my hand and put it on Owen's shoulder and he placed the Master's hand on his own and thus we marched along behind him, blind-beggar fashion.

We continued on for what seemed like an eternity, when Owen suddenly stopped; I stumbled into him and I heard the bard walk on a few steps before stopping. 'Where are you taking us?' Owen demanded. 'There doesn't seem to be anything in this direction.'

'There is shelter,' Paedur replied shortly.

'Where – and when?'

'Nearby – and soon. Come now, we daren't linger; some of the night creatures will soon be abroad.'

He must have reached out and taken the Master's arm, because I felt the Master stiffen and then his hand caught mine and placed it on his own shoulder. We trudged on a while longer, heads tucked down into our cloaks, for the wind had quickened and it was snowing heavily now – great soft, silent flakes that touched like chill fingers. A wisp of moon showed through the racing clouds and I could suddenly see Owen in front of me. He was silhouetted against the night as the snowflakes painted his left side white, whilst his right remained in darkness, and I could just make out the ghostly image of the bard ahead of him.

'I think you'd better tell us where this shelter is now, bard,' Owen said loudly above the wind, and his voice was harsh with suspicion.

The bard stopped. 'There!' He raised his arm and pointed, his hook flashing ice-silver.

I peered into the darkness, but I could see nothing save the dimly phosphorescent flakes whirling and dancing before my eyes. And I wondered then – and not for the first time – how this Paedur could see in the absolute night, how he could move so confidently, how he could point out a direction with such assurance and wield a blade with such certainty. It was unnatural – and terrifying – and if I had not been bonded to Owen, I would have turned and fled and taken my chances that night in the Wastelands.

'Let's go,' Paedur said, and then we were moving again, this time slightly north of our previous direction, and we must have topped a rise for we were now descending, slipping and sliding on loose rocks and hard, dry earth. Once we found ourselves below ground level the wind immediately dropped, and the night became still and silent.

'Perhaps you should light your lantern now,' the bard said quietly. For a moment I didn't understand what he was talking about, and then I realised I was still clutching the travel-lantern in my frozen hand. I knelt on the ground and fumbled with my flint box, but my fingers were numb and it took several attempts to even open the box. I stooped low over the lantern, covering the wick with my cloak, striking the flint, blinking as the sparks flashed and exploded in the darkness. The oiled wick caught and the dim half-light soaked into the air.

We were standing in a deep round hollow, one of many hundreds which pock part of the northlands. Above us the snow-laden wind whipped along in a white sheet, but very little actually drifted into the hollow and we were almost totally protected from the wind, and even the ground underfoot was dry.

The bard walked forward a few steps and we hurried after him, more fearful now, I think, of becoming lost than of him. Again the silver hook flashed and pointed and I lifted the lantern in that direction. Owen grunted in surprise and the light shook in my hand: there was a building in front of us. And in the north – and especially in the Wastelands – every building was inhabited, and not always by men.

But the bard moved forward without hesitation, and there was little we could do but follow him. As we drew near to the building,

I could see that it was a Way Station, one of the countless that litter the countryside along the length of the King Road . . . except that this station was nowhere near the road and had obviously not been used for many seasons. The moon slipped free from the racing clouds and briefly washed the building in stark bone-white light. It was long and low, seeming smaller than usual, little more than a squat rectangle built into the ground in a style long out of fashion.

And with the shadows edging in around it, it resembled nothing so much as a great beast about to spring.

The closer we came to the station, the more conscious I became of an air of great age that hung about the place. I have stayed in Way Stations in many lands, and whilst they have always been spartan, comfortless places none of them seemed as old and as forbidding as this. I remembered stories I had heard about the creatures that inhabited the more isolated stations, that preyed on unwary travellers, feeding on their blood.

'I can't say I've ever seen a Way Station like this one,' Owen said loudly, and I could tell that he too was disturbed.

'It was one of the original Way Stations, said to have been built by the Culai themselves,' Paedur said quietly. 'Most of the stations you would be familiar with are usually modern copies.'

'How modern?' the Master wondered.

'A thousand years old, perhaps younger.'

We stopped and I held the lantern high, looking cautiously at the building. The stones were smooth and rounded, polished and shaped by countless seasons of wind and rain, ice and heat. The door leaned drunkenly to one side, held to the rotted frame by encrusted hinges; the shutter on the window nearest me was cracked and blackened where it had once been set afire and a large rounded hole gaped under the window, with the bricks and stones pressing outwards as if they had been struck from within by some great force or power. I wondered what had happened here – and then I decided I didn't want to know.

I looked from the station to the Master; surely he, with all his superstitions, would see that this deserted and ruined Way Station, so far from any track or road, was a place of ill omen.

The bard descended the few steps that led down to the shattered door, and then he stopped and listened. He then silently retraced his steps and whispered softly to Owen, 'I do not think anyone or anything is within, but . . .' he paused, his lips pulled back from his teeth in a smile that I found disturbing, almost mocking.

The Master nodded. He pulled off his heavy cloak and tossed it to the bard and then slipped both sword and dagger from their scabbards. I passed the lantern to the bard and unhitched both belt-axes, and then I took up my position behind and to the left of the Master.

The bard lifted the lantern, and the pale oval of light threw the doorway into sharp relief. Owen raised the tip of his sword slightly, the signal to prepare and then he dipped it . . .

We leaped into the darkness, Owen moving to the right, I to the left. We stood poised, ready to move in any direction, but all was quiet, save for the drip-drip-drip of water somewhere to my left. We stood in silence, holding our breaths, almost half expecting to hear the scuffle of feet or the click of claws on the hard-packed earth. But nothing moved. Finally, when it became clear that the Way Station was indeed empty, Owen's sword clicked into its scabbard and then a softer metallic whisper told me that his knife had followed. Slowly, I relaxed.

I heard Owen move across the littered floor towards the doorway. 'Bard, you may enter.'

There was no reply.

The Master waited and then he tried again, now sliding his sword free. I pressed back against the chill stone wall, staring towards the paler rectangle of the doorway against the utter blackness of the interior of the station.

And then something sparked behind me!

I whirled about, one axe snapping out on its leather thong towards the sound. There was a sparking flash of metal on metal, a sharp high-pitched ringing and my arm went numb as the axe was deflected to one side. I swung around my other axe, and then I was suddenly blinded by a light that ripped through the station. I dropped to the floor and rolled away to one side, eyes streaming, allowing the Master a clear field of vision.

But there was no flurry of combat, no shouts or screams, and only Owen's voice asking a question. 'How?'

For a moment I thought he was questioning me, but when I had brushed away the streaming tears and was able to see again, I found the bard standing before me!

'How did you get in? No-one entered through that door.' Owen's voice was tight and controlled, and I could see that he was angry and confused. 'You couldn't have got past me.'

Paedur just smiled and shook his head. 'But there is only one way in.'

The light that had blinded me turned out to come from two small battered light bowls that still hung from the ceiling, which the bard had lit, thus throwing the room – and everyone in it – into sharp relief. Even in the harsh light the bard lost none of his mystery. Indeed, his dark fine-haired travelling cloak seemed to absorb the light and, save for his face and silver hook, he resembled nothing so much as a shadow, animated by some foul sorcery.

Owen turned from the bard, and I thought I saw him shudder slightly. He reached out and pulled me to my feet. 'You had better bring our stuff in.'

I nodded and slipped outside to where our cloaks and few belongings lay piled beside the door. It was snowing again, more heavily this time, and the world was gradually losing all shape and definition. With one last glance into the night, I re-entered the ruined Way Station.

Later that night – or it might have been early the following morning – after a tasteless meal of hard bread and dried meat, washed down with sour wine, we sat around the fire I had built in the shattered grate, staring into the glowing embers, listening to the wind howl around the building.

For all its great age, the station was in surprisingly good repair, except for the damage to the upper end of the building. The single room was on two levels, with the lower end cut deep into the ground, windowless and with but a single door. In the past travellers used the lower section, while their mounts were stabled above them, both for protection and for the heat they provided. The room was bare, except for a single stout wooden chest set into a niche close by the fire. In the past it would have held dried food and blankets but the box was empty now, except for twigs and a score of tiny feathers, the remains of a bird's nest.

Thinking of the Way Station brought me back to the bard, this Paedur.

He exerted a curious fascination for me, his mystery, aloofness, detachment and . . . power. He radiated an aura of almost tangible force, of power, although I doubted that he actually was a sorcerer or magician. I was inclined to believe that he was in truth, a bard, and I had little doubt that he would prove to be a terrifying storyteller.

Owen once said my curiosity would prove my undoing. But I wanted to know about this man, this creature, who professed to be a bard. Did bards usually wander the lonely and dangerous wild northern roads? Where were his students, his servants, his possessions? Where did he come from, and more important, where was he going, for there was little to attract a storyteller in the Wastelands?

His hook also intrigued me. It was of exquisite workmanship; I wondered who had crafted it – no ordinary silversmith, I'd wager. It seemed to be of solid silver, inlaid with a delicate filigree of angular etchings that resembled nothing so much as some of the barbarous scripts I have seen in the Seven Nations. I don't know how it was joined to his wrist, but I got the impression that it was set directly into the bone. Along the edge of the hook, a thin band of darker metal ran from point to wrist. It would make a fearsome weapon – and then I realised just how the bard had cut me free from the bush earlier on.

I glanced across at the Master, and found that he too was watching the bard while trying not to appear to. Unconsciously, his left hand fingered the hilt of his dagger.

A burning log fell into the grate and rolled on to the flagstones, scattering sparks and blackened chips across the earthen floor. Owen reached out and grabbed it at one end and flipped it back into the fire. As he did so, the sleeve of his jerkin slipped back, revealing the Iron Band of Kloor which covered his forearm.

Suddenly the bard's hook flashed in the firelight and encircled the thick iron bracelet in its silver grip. 'Kloor?' he whispered, his eyebrows raised in question.

Owen angrily pulled his arm free.

'Kloor,' repeated the bard, 'I didn't think a Weapon Master would honour such.'

Owen tensed. 'Surely it is of little interest to you whom I worship? But yes, I worship Kloor, the Warrior's God. I am a warrior, he suffices.'

Paedur was silent for a moment, and when he spoke again his voice held a trace of puzzlement. 'You are a Weapon Master, therefore your father must have been a Weapon Master . . .' It was a statement rather than a question, but Owen nodded. 'But surely your father would have honoured Buiva, the Old God of War and Warriors and not . . .'

'What are you getting at bard?' Owen snapped.

'I am merely wondering why one who once worshipped Buiva now wears the Band of Kloor,' Paedur said softly, curiously.

Anger flared in the Master's eyes, and I saw his face tighten. A muscle began to twitch in his clenched jaw. But when he spoke, his voice was soft and controlled. 'I drew a weapon on you earlier, but that was in ignorance for I did not know your status. But unless you want to find my knife in your belly you will leave off this questioning. Here, bard, no-one will find your corpse, and when they do it will be assumed that you were slain by bandits. My religion, aye, and my father's also, are none of your concern.'

The bard laughed gently, almost mockingly. 'You would not kill me, Weapon Master; you could not, you are too honourable for cold-blooded murder.' He paused, and then added in a different tone. 'And I think you would fear the retribution that would follow it if you did, eh? Consider what would happen when Mannam brought me before Alile the Judge Impartial to plead my case; surely he would send Coulide Dream-Maker to haunt you. Consider, Weapon Master, never to know a night's sleep again . . . to have the Nameless God hovering by your bedside . . .'

'*STOP!*' the Master shouted pressing both hands to his ears and beginning to rock to and fro like a child. 'Stop – no more. Stop!'

It had happened so suddenly; I wasn't sure how this Duaiteoiri had reduced my Master to this state with just a few words, but it could only be one thing – sorcery.

The Master had been ensorcelled. But how? Those who think a mage can weave a spell without the usual trappings of the craft know little of how such things work. No, the bard had said something to frighten – no, to terrify the Master. I would stop it – even if I had to kill the bard. Unhooking an axe, I rose to my feet.

I allowed the heavy war axe to slip down low into my hand, until I was holding it by the thong. I spun it around once, twice, preparing to throw it at the creature – and at this range I could not miss. But then he looked up and his eyes caught mine – and held them. They took the light from the fire and began to burn with something like an inner fire of their own; it was as if something behind them now gazed out at me. They looked at me, through me, beyond me. I was caught in a whirling pool of exploding dust motes, of blackened stars in lighted darkness . . . falling, falling, revolving, spinning faster and faster . . .

'*S-S-S-i-i-i-T-T-T.*' The shout – or was it a whisper? – blossomed and exploded within my skull and I lost all control of my body. My legs jerked and twitched of their own accord, my axe fell ringingly to the floor from nerveless fingers . . . and I was sitting frozen and paralysed – useless, although aware.

'You would kill me,' the bard repeated, turning back to the Master as if nothing had happened. Owen still rocked to and fro, now crooning softly to himself, lost within some inner recesses of his mind. It was as if something had snapped, or a gate had suddenly opened and released . . .released what?

But whatever it was, whatever had happened – the bard was to blame, and I swore I would be revenged on him for it.

He spoke again, his voice rising and falling as if he spoke to a child. 'Peace, peace. Do not upset yourself. No, you need not tell me of your faith, nor of your father's either. I know. I know.' He paused and said, very gently, 'He worshipped the Old Gods, did he not?'

The Master nodded silently.

'And you follow the New?'

Again that silent nod.

'You must have disappointed him greatly when you converted.'

Owen stopped his rocking and raised his head; and his eyes were sparkling with moisture. 'He never forgave me,' he whispered.

'Tell me,' Paedur continued, 'when were you converted? You must have been very young, impressionable . . .?'

'In my seventeenth year, in the last month of my training,' the Master said, and then he suddenly sobbed, and there was nothing but pure anguish in his eyes. 'But they tricked me,' he suddenly shouted. 'Tricked me. They entangled me in webs of words, confused and confounded me until I did not know what to believe; and then they pushed and pushed . . . and lied . . . but I believed them. They extracted an oath from me, thrice-sworn and *geasa*-bound, and then what could I do? I had sworn, I was trapped,' he added bitterly.

The bard leaned forward, and the firelight took his face, deepening the shadows, ageing it. 'Aaah gently, gently, Owen. You are greatly troubled, and you have been deeply hurt. But now let us see what can be done to salve that pain.'

'I am not in pain,' Owen muttered.

'There are wounds that are not of the body,' Paedur said.

'There is nothing you can do. There is nothing anyone can do,' the Master said fiercely, his eyes beginning to sparkle with tears again.

It shamed me to see Owen reduced to this, and I wondered just how this bard had frightened him. And yet I could also see that it was not the bard who had frightened the Master, but in some strange way, himself. There was something buried deep within him, something which the bard had consciously or unconsciously – I wasn't sure – triggered off. And then, dimly, I felt that here might be the answer to something which had troubled me for many years: the Master's belief in the supernatural.

Owen was a brave warrior, fearless and cunning in battle, usually victorious and always generous in defeat, and there was neither man nor beast that troubled him in the least. In many respects he was the perfect warrior. But if there were omens on the morning of the battle, or signs in the night sky, or if there had been foretellings and forecastings that had proved inauspicious, or if his dreams had been troubled – then he would not fight, and no amount of threats or bribes could force him against his will. He shunned the ruins that men said had been Culai built, and wherein the gods of his people once lived. He detoured around bridges blessed in the name of Cam, and often cut across fields to avoid an unlucky gallows-road. He fought with his sword in his right hand and his knife in his left, for he held to the belief that a knife was an assassin's tool and thus not worthy of the right hand. He favoured amulets and talismans, and he even had a relic, the finger-bone of some ancient seer, set into the hilt of his sword.

There were times when I even believed that he kept me because he thought I was lucky.

I have never made the Weapon Master out to be perfect, and he had many failings, and of those failings superstition was his worst, and now it seemed the bard had – accidentally, deliberately? – invoked the core of that fault, bringing it to the surface, terrifying the man.

Paedur reached out and touched Owen on the shoulder; then I suddenly felt the almost palatable aura of peace and tranquillity that emanated from him and enfolded the Master, soothing him, calming his fears.

'Come now, you are a Weapon Master, a warrior. It is not fitting that you should fear this. If you would exorcise this demon, then face it. Now begin your tale, and who knows, perhaps I can help . . .?'

'I don't know . . .' the Master said uncertainly. The lines on his broad, rather ugly face had softened, the muscles relaxed, so that he looked like a young man once more. Even when he spoke, his voice lacked the harshness, the authority, it usually carried.

Paedur leaned back, moving away from the firelight. 'Start thus,' he said; 'you worshipped the Old Gods, you and your family. You had brothers . . . sisters?'

The Master ran his fingers through his hair and then sat back against the wall, his head tilted forward and almost resting on his knees, which he had drawn up to his chest. 'Yes, yes, my family worshipped the Old Gods. My father was an Elder of the Faith, and my mother had served in the Temple in her youth. Thus ever since we – my brother and sister – could talk and understand, we were so deeply infused with the Faith and it was such a part of our lives, that we knew nothing else.

'We could recite the entire Pantheon before we could walk; we could list the Roll of Minor Spirits before we had learned our letters and could enumerate the Virtues of the Gods before we could count.' He grinned mirthlessly. 'We never missed a Sabbath, and always kept the Purification prior to the Holy Days or Hallowed Nights. The Four Great Eves were always days and nights of feasting and merrymaking in our home. The fattest bothe was always slaughtered, the tenderest *cuine* sacrificed, and the purest wool, the strongest crops, and the clearest water were always dedicated to the gods.

'We couldn't be stronger in our faith.

'As we grew older, my father decided our futures. I, as the eldest son would, like himself, become a Weapon Master; my brother would be trained for the religious life, and my sister would be dedicated to the Order of the Lady Lussa, where she would become a priestess of the Moon and versed in the magic of the tides of life and growth, birth and motherhood.

'And we were all satisfied. Including me.

'However, as I approached manhood, I began to question my faith.' He shook his head, his eyes dim and distant as he looked into the past. 'My father spoke of the gods as if they existed in a corporeal body; and while they might have been real to him, to me they became little more than abstractions. All the pomp and ceremony of the Faith's festivals suddenly seemed shallow and worthless.

'Like a fool, I kept my doubts to myself, and they, like a hideous disease, grew dark and monstrous. Should I have discussed them with my father? Should I?' He looked across at the bard like a lost child, but Paedur gave him no answer.

'In the last year of my training these fears and doubts came to a head, and in the last month of my training in weapon-craft, a priest of Trialos came to our town. He was not unlike you, bard; he was tall and thin and his very dedication to his beliefs was almost frightening. He spoke of the New Religion in a field outside the town, for the town fathers would not allow him to preach within the walls. We were, of course, forbidden to attend.

'But I attended. And as I listened to the preacher, I found that he made sense and his words had meaning. Perhaps I wanted to find a meaning in his words – I don't know; I was searching for something, and the Religion seemed to give me what I was looking for. When he was finished speaking, he walked through the small crowd that had gathered to listen, stopping now and again, speaking quietly with a man here, a woman there . . . and then he came to me. He stood before me and said nothing, and then he took my arm and led me to one side. Perhaps he sensed my uncertainty and doubts, I don't know. He talked long and cleverly, oh, so cleverly, I know that now. He told me how his belief was the One True Religion; of how the Old Gods had been defeated by the New, and how the Old Faith was dying. Most of the Old Gods were dead, he said, and this was why they no longer appeared to man as they had in times past. But the New Gods came and inhabited the bodies of their priests and thus were ever with us.

'And then the preacher told me of Kloor, the Warrior's God, and how he had defeated Buiva, the Old God of War and Warriors, in single combat, thus symbolising the defeat of the entire Pantheon of the Old Faith . . .

'And I believed him. I believed him, and then and there I foreswore the Old Faith and embraced the New. My word, my bond, was given and the bargain – for my soul – was sealed with a thrice-sworn oath, and thus unbreakable.

'That same day I was initiated into the band of Kloor, a select group of warriors dedicated to the War God and whose function was to fight and die in defence of the New Religion. And this,' – he touched the iron band on his forearm – 'was locked on to my wrist, sealed there by a light which burned without heat and which the priests said was a sign of my acceptance by Kloor . . . and of course, Trialos, Lord of the New Religion.' He looked at the iron wristlet with dead eyes. 'It is a band proclaiming my allegiance to the New Religion.' The Master sighed and remained silent for a long time then.

'Your father,' prompted the bard, 'what did he say?'

'He was angry, terribly angry.' Owen continued, his voice wooden. 'I thought he would kill me – and he would have too had not my mother intervened, crying and begging him to spare me, her first son. And then my brother and sister entered, he in his robes of a Guardian of the Faith, and she in the gown of the priestess. They were shocked and sickened by what my brother called my foul desertion. And then there were words spoken – angry words, violent words, words I regretted even as I spoke them; words I regret now.

'But now it is too late.'

'What happened?' Paedur asked.

'They challenged me to prove that my new-found gods even existed; they mocked them, but I said my gods would be revenged for their blasphemies.' His face tightened and his voice dropped to a dull whisper. 'And they laughed. They laughed.

'Two days later, a strange fever raged through the town. My brother and sister died, and it crippled my father.

'I fled then; I have never returned.' Owen buried his head in his hands, and his shoulders shook. He raised a frightened face and gazed imploringly at the bard. 'I wasn't responsible for their deaths – was I?'

Paedur smiled gently, and placed his hand on Owen's shoulder, his long fingers biting into the flesh. 'No, no, of course not. Their time – foredained beyond the reckoning of man – had come. Mannam, the Dark Lord, had taken them to himself. But you must not believe that they were taken through any intercession of the New Religion and its feeble deities.' The bard's voice fell and he stared into Owen's eyes and began to whisper urgently to him. 'You were tricked, you know that; tricked by those more versed in oratory than in religion.'

The Master shook his head and squeezed his eyes shut, but Paedur gripped his chin, and forced him to look into his terrifying eyes. 'You were tricked by clever, merciless men. Merciless, yes, merciless. Consider: they took a boy who, though strong in his faith, nevertheless wavered and questioned as the young are wont to do. They tricked and trapped him with webs of words, and bound him in threads of invisible honour, and turned him into a guilt-haunted man, doomed to search for the truth, and forced to regret his decision.'

Owen pulled himself free from the bard's grip. He sat back against the chill wall and stared deep into the fire. 'They said Kloor was the stronger god, and that he had defeated Buiva,' he said, his voice almost defiant, 'I didn't know . . . I still don't know.' He looked over at the bard, 'What is the truth?' he cried.

'Truth. Truth,' the bard's voice rose on a commanding note.

'Let me tell you the truth; let me tell you of the battle between Buiva and Kloor, the Old and the New, the Faith and the Religion. Let me tell you that part of the Battles of the Gods . . .'

The bard sat back into the shadows and folded his arms into his long sleeves and then, bowing his head, he began . . .

In the third hour of battle – though it was no common time-piece that measured the aeon-long hours – Buiva, the aged God of War and Warriors, blood-stained and weary, for he had fought long and hard, came upon Kloor the Usurper and self-styled god as he skulked behind the battle-lines directing his minions.

And when Kloor saw Buiva he felt the wind of fear blow across him and called forth his legion of *quai* – which are those souls claimed neither by C'lte nor Mannam and thus are neither of Life nor Death. The legion of *quai* positioned themselves before their lord, protecting him from the single ancient warrior.

But Buiva remained dauntless, and called out for Kloor to attend him in single combat to decide the day. And Kloor heeded him not and directed his *quai* to attack the lone god, and his laughter was terrible, for he felt assured of victory.

Now as the *quai* legion advanced upon Buiva, their lacquered armour rasping, swords gleaming in the light of no known star, the tramp of their booted feet heavy upon the chequered plain, the War God raised his nocked and blood-stained broadsword and cried aloud in the language of the gods, '*A w'Mhannaimm 'a w'bainte*.' Immediately the air about him darkened and there was a sound like that of a thousand leafless trees rustling and clattering together, and suddenly the air was filled with a myriad of furred winged and taloned creatures.

And these were the *bainte*, the messengers of Mannam, the Dark Lord.

They circled above the chequered plain in heedless confusion, and then as one they wheeled and settled in a vast ebon blanket about the feet of the Warrior God. Now each *bainte* clutched within its razor talons a tiny spark of indeterminate hue, and each spark throbbed and pulsed with an independent life, now flaring into an eye-searing brilliance, now dying into slumbering quiescence.

And Buiva pointed with his sword and wordlessly commanded – and the *bainte* rose over the advancing *quai* and, hovering there, released their miniature cinders. The sparks floated downward in an intricate spiralling dance, and Kloor cried out a warning and tried to recall his undead legion – but it was too late. Each spark dropped atop a legionnaire, and instantly disappeared.

The legion of *quai* stopped.

Kloor, suddenly realising what was about to happen, retreated and called forth his six great sheol, which are kin to those ice-entombed feline remains which oft come to light in the frozen north. And he ordered these cat-like monsters to guard him – from his own *quai*!

And even Buiva, who feared neither God nor Duaite, man nor beast, moved back, away from the *quai* and the sheol.

The vacant stare of the *quai* had now been replaced by the first glimmerings of dawning intelligence; their mouths no longer hung slack and open and their gait – which had been shambling and beast-like – was now erect in the manner of men. They looked around in confusion, like dreamers awakening from a vivid nightmare.

And then realisation dawned, and the eyes of the former *quai* glazed with sudden insanity – for this, all of this, was beyond their comprehension. Had they not died? Were not their last memories of death, some of violent deaths, in drunken brawls or dishonourable battle, and some by their own hands? Had not their souls been taken to the Silent Wood, and there been judged by Alile, the Judge Impartial?

Did they not remember a time then, a time of terror and confusion when they seemed to wander through an interminable gorge or a crevasse with towering walls of slimed rock on either side. And then . . .? And then . . .? And then what?

How came they here?

And what was this before them, spattered with gore and reeking blood, like the very personification of War? And behind them, in armour of gleaming iridescent scales, armed with weapons of gleaming light and surrounded by creatures out of their nightmare? Where were they?

Was this the Afterlife?

And then the souls rebelled in shrieking terror – for that was what the *bainte* had returned to the *quai* – their living souls. They had been men before they had become *quai*, and they knew now that this was *WRONG* – and who knows, perhaps the Nameless God of Madness and Delusion had breathed upon the living sparks before the *bainte* had returned them, and thus each man – for they were men again – went totally insane.

They turned upon their companions, seeing in each one an enemy, cutting and slashing, chopping through fine lacquered armour, tearing chain-mail with sword and axe, mace and spear. Bloodless they fell, dismembered limbs twitching in a hideous semblance of life, bone glinting through ragged wounds, gaping mouths crying silently, wordlessly, and their eyes glazed in a second death with a terrible truth frozen therein.

Through the brief and bloody struggle Kloor raged and screamed, threatened and mouthed behind the six huge sheol. And the God of Warriors of the New Religion felt fear then, for he had seen his personal guard, his indestructible legion destroyed by their own hand.

Once again he faced Buiva.

And once again the War God of the Old Faith called forth his challenge, but Kloor disdained to reply and released a sheol - a giant ebon cat-like creature.

Taller than the god it stood, thighs as thick as his waist and tipped with claws as long as his hand. Its eyes burned with a crimson fire, radiating pure hate, its one instinct to kill, to destroy. It opened its maw, revealing a double row of needle-pointed teeth, and it roared. Low that terrible cry began, almost inaudible, but it quickly rose to a skull-shattering scream that threatened to freeze Buiva where he stood.

The old man shook his head, angrily shrugging off the creeping numbness and gripped his great broadsword – the *Clef Fuin* of legend – and prepared to meet the sheol's charge. Carefully, he studied the play of muscles along the creature's haunches, watched them ripple and flow with every movement. Then the muscles bunched and the sheol was flying through the air, bristling claws and fur, its mouth agape in anticipation, dripping scalding saliva.

The warrior dived forward under the creature, slashing upwards with his sword, disembowelling the sheol in one swift movement. But still it lived. As it fell, Buiva came to his feet and chopped down on to its massive corded neck and almost severed the head. Again and again *Clef Fuin* bit into the still-living feline until it finally quivered and stiffened.

And now Kloor in a paroxysm of fury released the five remaining sheol, and Buiva despaired when he saw them, for he could not hope to defeat them all. So, in desperation he called upon the Lady Adur, the Goddess of Nature, sister to Quilda, the Goddess of Growth and cousin to the Triad of Life.

'*A nAdur ea pl'ea,*' he cried forth in a strong voice that echoed across the battlefield. And the huge sheol slackened in their headlong run, for though their inner natures had been warped by Kloor, a part of them – a tiny part which all creatures of Life possess – recognised the name of Adur, their mistress.

But Kloor urged them on.

Suddenly a tiny insect fluttered before the Warrior God, spinning in the complicated rhythm of a dance, and as it weaved its pattern about the god, it grew, and then flickered in a startling metamorphosis, from an insect, black on gold, to a delicate patterned butterfly . . . a fragile rainbow-coloured humming bird . . . a shining evil-eyed raven . . . a sharp-featured hawk . . . a golden-winged eagle . . . a monstrous harpy – and finally, a woman.

She was tall, taller even than Buiva, who looked down on most of the Gods of the Pantheon, and very beautiful in a strange haunting way that is almost beyond description. Her beauty was akin to that which is sometimes glimpsed in nature on a summer's eve across a mirrored lake.

And about her – as there is in nature – there was constant change; her hair and eyes flickering with multitudinous colours and varied hues and her skin rippling in ever-differing tints.

Now she was cold, hair white and snow soft, her eyes like blue chipped ice and her skin a translucent alabaster; and now her skin was a delicate russet with eyes of startling green, and then her skin became a darker hue, and her figure fuller. And now she smiled and there was the touch of summer in her smile, her eyes – sparkling brown – danced with merriment, her hair of rich ochre and skin deeply tanned.

And she was all shades, colours, moods and seasons in between. She was Adur, the Goddess of Nature.

The sheol froze when she appeared, and their roars and savage cries turned to whimpers as they lay belly down on the chequered battlefield.

Buiva bowed to the Lady Adur, for he had a soldier's appreciation of nature, and then he pointed to the cowering creatures. The goddess turned, and anger flashed in her blue-green eyes, for were these felines not a travesty of nature? An abomination. They should not exist, they had no right to existence, and so . . .

Adur raised one pale white hand and pointed, her long vermilion-tipped nails splayed. Her steel-grey eyes hardened as she began to close her hand.

The sheol began to turn and twist upon themselves; they ran in tight circles, snapping, clawing and tearing at each other in anger, confusion and pain. And then they began to dwindle, to shrink in upon themselves . . . smaller . . .smaller and then . . . gone!

Adur closed her hand. In her domain there was no room, no place for the unnatural. She turned and bowed to the bloodied warrior, and then closed her eyes – and disappeared.

Buiva rested on his sword. 'Face me now Kloor in single combat and let there be an end to this foolishness.'

But Kloor was still afraid, for Buiva was the most powerful of the gods and had he not fought against many gods and godlets and the worship of many sects to reach his present position as the accepted God of War and Warriors?

But as Kloor looked at the Old God, something began to change his mind. 'The Old God is tired,' he murmured to himself, 'he has fought long and hard and has put many to the sword this day. I am fresh, my weapons are sharp and well honed; he is set in his ways and is bound to fight with honour and courtesy, whilst I have many tricks and am not hidebound by such morals.'

'I will fight you, Buiva,' he called. 'Soon, Old God, you will be a dead god.'

But Buiva the Warrior laughed, and such is the mirth of the gods that, far beyond the Void in that place between the worlds, out where none will ever venture, elsewhere and otherwhen, a small planet winked fiery red in the heavens, and those who saw it, wondered and accounted it a portent.

Then Kloor took the living sword *Sant*, and ran at Buiva, for he had a mind to take the Old God by surprise, and *Sant* keened and moaned with pleasure at the prospect of drinking blood.

And elsewhen and otherwhere, a tiny incandescent comet streaked its fiery trail across the night sky . . . and directly in its path lay the Red Planet; and astrologers nodded sagely and withdrew to consult their charts and make their calculations.

The *Clef Fuin* met the *Sant*'s wild swing with a clangour that rippled through the Void, and the swords burned with a blinding light so that it was as if the two gods fought with staves of light. Back and forth across the chequered plain they fought, their weapons hissing and sparking with the violence of their battle.

And as the sparks from their weapons fell into the Void, they supplemented those numerous shapeless asteroids that were created by the One and which litter the heavens. And the blood of the gods – and it was spilt on both sides – became those crimson suns which glow on dead worlds.

Now, although Buiva was tired and weakened, he fought hard against the Usurper. And Kloor, young, untried and inexperienced, retreated before the Old God's onslaught. Buiva laughed aloud, for he could see that this would-be war-god was no warrior. And this was true, for Kloor had gained his position as the War God of the New Religion through cunning and the skilful manipulation of a weak and frightened priesthood, and he had once been but a minor spirit babbling beyond the Gorge until he had broken through the barriers of the mind of a heretic. The spirit that was Kloor had then used this heretic to spread his gospel of hate and violence, and then exhorted the people to pray for succour to the god Kloor, for even then, he had been styling himself a god.

Some folk prayed. And Faith lends Substance.

Soon the Cult of Kloor had taken hold, and the priests of Trialos had accepted the new god into their Pantheon of New Gods – a

Usurper amongst Usurpers. They created the Band of Kloor, a group of warriors, all believers in the New Religion, and used them as the Guardians of their Religion. Then the priests of Kloor set forth on their mission: to entice more and more young warriors into the Band, and they chained these youths with an Iron Band, a physical reminder of their chains to the New God.

And this New God was now terrified, for should he be defeated, then that spark of soul which animates both Gods and men would be consigned back to the absolute depths of the Gorge for all eternity, never to rise again. So he fell back, further and yet further still, defenceless against Buiva's great sweeping blows. At last the Usurper reached the mound on which he had stood in the early stages of the Battle of the Gods, and then his questing hand gripped the haft of his great war spear – the *cle bor* – which stood there. It was a fearsome weapon, a relic even amongst the gods, which Kloor had stolen from the Tomb of Bor, the Man God. It was fashioned from the wood of the Sidhe Forest of the Far Isles by Hanor, the first of the Gods. Twice the height of Kloor it stood, its length engraved with glyphs of power, unutterable in any human tongue. Its massive head – as long as the god's arm – was of the purest diamond, and it had been honed and pointed in some unknown manner.

Kloor grasped the weapon desperately, and, leaping back, swung it around to face Buiva. To do this he had to turn to one side and drop *Sant* to grip the *cle bor*, and here the Old God's honour was almost to prove his undoing, for he did not strike the Usurper while he was momentarily defenceless.

But there is little doubt that the New God would not have acted in a like manner had the positions been reversed.

Kloor held the spear tightly in both hands and jabbed at Buiva. He was safe behind its prodigious length and now strength poured into him – for such was the nature of the weapon – and he felt for the first time that he could even defeat Buiva.

He struck out with his new-found strength again and again, jabbing with the spear. But each time Buiva managed to turn the point with his sword, though each time by a narrower margin. Now it skimmed within a hair's breadth of his face, now actually brushing his throat, pricking his arm, nicking his side. His sword leapt and darted, turning the point here, deflecting it, now stopping it – but all at a price.

For each time the *cle bor* struck the *Clef Fuin* the sword chipped and dented, even though it had been forged by Shaon the Smith using only the purest materials in his forge in the Woodsheart.

Suddenly the sword snapped; the battered blade shattering under the impact of the spear's diamond head, leaving Buiva defenceless against Kloor's attack. The New God immediately plunged the spear into the god's chest, driving him back and pinning him to the ground, the terrible wound spurting blood and ichor.

This ichor scattered into the Void and became that which men call the Core of the Universe, wherein there is but one light, and that is the light of a million million suns – drops of blood from the veins of the War God. And there are some that think that these suns are living, growing, expanding in an ever-increasing torrent – like blood seeping from some cut.

Kloor moved in to kill the stricken god, for though gravely wounded Buiva still lived. But he grasped the hilt of his shattered sword and flung it full in the face of the advancing, gloating usurper. The broken edge struck him across the bridge of his nose, and flakes of the enchanted metal entered his eyes, blinding him. Kloor screamed and screamed again, and great pools of empty dissolution opened in the Void as the very fabric of space was torn by his cries.

Then Kloor the Usurper turned and fled, and in the distant reaches of timelessness his cries are still heard, for there is none to succour him.

But in the temples and churches of the Old Faith there was a terrible emptiness and the priests felt as if their altars had been forsaken, as if all the Gods of the Pantheon had left this world. The sun disappeared below the horizon and didn't reappear, and even the Lady Lussa failed to ride across the night skies.

Thus it was for seven days. Then on the morning of the eighth day, Nusas shone forth with all his accustomed brilliance, and by this sign men knew that the gods had returned; and many wondered at their absence.

Now when Buiva had fallen, the shock of his wounding had torn through all creation and thus the entire Pantheon knew that their brother was sorely wounded. They quit their temples and palaces, gardens, dales and glades to come to render aid to the stricken god, and soon the chequered battlefield was dark with their glittering shadowless forms. Then from that gathering came forth an aged man, thin and stooped and with hair of purest silver, and he knelt by Buiva and ministered to him, for he was Ochrann, God of Medicine and Healing.

And for six days Buiva lay thus, and the assembled gods feared for their brother. Even Ochrann finally admitted that he could do nothing further, and so the gods – the great and little, the minor and major deities – took council together, but they could reach no decision and Buiva weakened further.

At last Huide – who is the Little God of Summer Rain – spoke. 'My lords, it is my thought that there had been laid a Darkness upon us, for is not the solution to our problem plain for all to see? Let us send for the Triad of Life; for surely it is within their power to save the Warrior.'

Thus the three Gods of Life were sent for, and Sa'lte, Qua'lte and C'lte came, riding on clouds of purest ebon, cobalt and saffron, and they laid their hands upon the dying god and poured Life into him.

And he lived.

And when the gods would have rewarded Huide – for it had been his idea – he would have nothing. But thereafter, whenever Huide scattered his fine mist-like droplets upon the parched summer earth, there was seen emblazoned across the skies an arch of seven hues, in tribute and recognition to that tiny god's intelligence.

But the tale does not end here.

It was put about by the priests of Kloor and Trialos that the Usurper had defeated Buiva, and, to those who have the Hearing, they described the screams of the blind god as his cries of victory. Enough people still pray to Kloor to keep him in existence – but that existence is one of eternal torment.

But know this, Owen, Weapon Master – Buiva, God of War and Warriors, lives!'

The bard ended on a triumphant note. The Master's eyes were shining, but with what emotion I could not tell. What I do know is that, although it was a fanciful tale, it both moved and impressed me deeply, and to such an extent that although many events and happenings in my long life now fade and grow dim, the tale of the bard Paedur still burns bright in my memory.

'Then Buiva lives; he defeated Kloor, snatching his victory from defeat?' the Master asked quickly, stumbling over his words in excitement.

'Yes, he lives. You were tricked, lied to. And not only you, but others like you: all young, impressionable men. And the Religion is continuing to do the same today, continuing to corrupt your people.' He paused and added softly, 'And that is why it has to be stopped.'

The Master nodded. 'Aye, it has to be stopped,' he agreed. 'But how?'

Paedur leaned foward, the dying firelight washing his face in red. 'The present order must be overthrown. There is a move abroad to do just that.'

'Revolution?'

The bard smiled thinly. 'Call it a Holy War, if you will. South and west of here, Prince Kutor has just set off on a journey into

the west, to one of the ancient Culai forts which he intends to use
as a base to wage war on the Emperor's forces.'

'Kutor – Geillard's bastard brother; but his last attempt on the
throne ended in a bloody massacre.'

Paedur smiled. 'He hadn't a cause then, even he didn't really
believe that he could win. He was defeated before he had even
begun. Now, he has that cause, and he is putting together an
army – a proper army – but they will need training and
equipping, and for that he needs a man of experience.' He
paused and added, 'I am advising those interested in fighting for
the Faith to go to him . . .'

Owen smiled grimly. 'Yes, it might be good to fight for a cause
again.'

'I don't think there'll be much coin in it – not unless it's
successful,' the bard warned.

'Oh, Tien and I have often worked for meagre wages.' Owen
nodded again, and then the smile faded and he held up his arm,
looking at the ugly metal band.

'It will be a good cause,' Paedur said, 'you will be fighting for
the Old Faith.'

'An atonement,' Owen said softly, fingering the metal band.

'Perhaps, but remember, you were tricked, lied to, and your
promise was extracted under false pretences, so you were never
bound in fact. But now you can return to the Faith. You have
obviously felt lost without it, and so you fell back on petty
superstitions, pretty baubles and crude amulets as a crutch to
ease your troubled mind.'

The bard suddenly reached over and tapped Owen's wristlet
with his silver hook. Immediately a tiny network of cracks ran
along the band; they widened and thickened, covering the band
in a darkening web. Then the Iron Band of Kloor dissolved in a
fine powder which hung momentarily on the still air, then disappeared. It was gone and the only outward sign of its existence
was a swath of pale skin encircling the Master's wrist and
forearm.

'I thank you,' Owen said simply, and then he tore the bone
amulets from about his neck and prised the charm loose from the
hilt of his sword. 'We'll head south and west with the dawn,' he
said then, 'and find this Prince Kutor.'

'You'll need this then,' the bard said, and, leaning forward, he
slid Owen's knife free and etched a half circle on to the metal of

the blade with the point of his hook. 'This is how they will know you. It is the sign of the hook, the mark of the bard.'

We slept then, and when we awoke the bard Paedur had gone. But of his going I could find no trace, for the snow piled high outside the door was clean and unmarked.

6   Gered and Leal

And he was master of all tales and had great skill in their telling.
Life of Paedur, the Bard

Aeal, the Captain of Bowmen, leaned over the edge of the walkway and looked down into the courtyard. The smells of man and horseflesh mingled with the resinous torches and other more pungent odours wafted up to him, and he felt his eyes sting and water.

Another carriage had arrived, and there was a brief flurry of confusion as the horses and men settled into the already over-crowded square. Steps were brought as the door of the carriage opened and a servant helped an ancient withered woman to the ground. Aeal was about to turn away, when he saw the second person alighting from the carriage; she was young, pretty and dressed in the latest court fashion that left the neck and shoulders bare. She stopped on the bottom step of the entrance hall and looked around, and the sharp-eyed bowman saw a flicker of disdain cross her heavily made-up, too-pretty face. He suddenly lost all interest in the woman; Castle Nevin might not be much to look at, but it was one of the Seven Bastions of the North, one of the forts which allowed the young woman to sleep peacefully in her bed without fear of being savaged and eaten by the Chopts.

Aeal turned back to the miserable-looking scribe standing on the battlements beside him. 'Well?'

Danel consulted the parchment scroll in his hands and then nodded. 'That was the Countess Devesci and her daughter; now all the invited guests have arrived – though some of their servants are still on the road.'

'We'll keep the Waytorch burning awhile longer then.' The bowman stared out across the moors. 'There's a fog coming in – Chopt weather, we call it.'

'Will they come?' The scribe looked anxiously across the Wastelands towards the black line that marked the Mion River. The bowman saw the look and smiled, 'For a learned man, you know remarkably little,' he said.

101

'This is my first appointment as a professional scribe – and the first time I've ever been in the Northlands,' Danel said quietly.

'It shows.'

Danel was completely out of his depth – and he knew it. He was a third-degree apprentice, with another year's training to do before he had the experience, the etiquette and the knowledge to perform the duties of a scribe. But when Count Nevin had announced the betrothal of his daughter to Adare, the son of Count Adare, and had sent to Baddalaur for the services of a scribe, the only person available had been Danel, since most of the senior scribes had been called to the capital to assist in the recent census.

Danel didn't like Castle Nevin; it was small, cold and miserable. The people were distrustful of strangers, and the fact that he was an educated man only served to increase their suspicions and distrust. And Castle Nevin was far too close to the Chopts for Danel's comfort.

'There's no moon,' Aeal said.

'I beg your pardon?' Danel asked, looking at the tall thin bowman in confusion.

'I said, there's no moon, and the Chopts will only attack when there's a moon. They believe that it guides their spirits to the Otherlife.'

Danel nodded quickly in relief.

'It was one of the reasons the Betrothal was timed for the dark of the month . . .' Aeal stopped abruptly and leaned across the merlons, staring down along the length of the broad road that led to the castle.

'What's wrong?' Danel asked, his voice rising and cracking.

The Captain of Bowmen waved him silent. 'I thought I saw something on the road.'

'Where? I saw nothing.' The small stout young man squinted over the edge of the battlements and down on to the road. He could just about make out the paler colour of the roadway itself, and the distant bulk of the Watchtower, but aside from that he could see nothing. 'There's nothing there . . .' he began, but Aeal abruptly turned from the battlements, brushed past him and raced down the steps. A few moments later Danel saw two score men hurrying down along the road, with every second man carrying a travel-lantern.

The scribe watched the balls of light bob down the road, until they had passed the Watchtower. Then they stopped and milled around, and Danel thought he heard a muffled shout. With mounting excitement, he watched the lanterns form into two flanking lines – like that of a guard of honour – and then they turned and slowly began to retrace their way to the Castle.

But surely all the important guests had arrived? Obviously, someone of importance was arriving, and the scribe was just about to re-check his scroll of names when a young boy in a page's livery came panting up the steps and stopped before him. 'My lord the count wishes to see you,' he said breathlessly.

'Me?' Danel whispered.

The boy nodded silently, and then bowed and turned away. Danel followed him slowly.

Count Nevin was standing on the top step that led into the entrance hall waiting for the scribe. He was a tall, bulky warrior, looking very uncomfortable in court silks and satins, and the broad-bladed shortsword on his hip looked decidedly out of place. He glared at the young man as he paused on the bottom step and bowed.

'Who comes?' he demanded.

'I don't know, my lord.' He held up the scroll of invited guests. 'There are only servants left to arrive.'

Count Nevin nodded. 'That's what I thought,' he murmured. He fingered the plain leather patch that covered his left eye-socket, and then, with a warrior's decisiveness, dismissed the matter. 'Well, my guards seem to consider whoever it is to be someone of importance. Make ready for a new guest,' he called out across the courtyard, and as the servants hurried to lay new rushes across the polished flagstones the old count turned back to the scribe. 'You – stay by me until we find out who's coming.'

Danel bowed and then stepped back away from the count, into the shadows, trying to become as inconspicuous as possible.

The wooden drawbridge thundered and roared as the squad returned, and the sound of their boots echoed off the high walls of the defensive entrance. Tension increased almost perceptibly in the courtyard, and the scribe saw movement high on the battlements as bowmen and archers moved into position.

The guards stamped to halt in the centre of the courtyard, facing the steps and Count Nevin. Aeal stepped out from their ranks and shouted a command and the men snapped to attention.

'Captain . . .?' Nevin asked.

'A guest, my lord . . .' Aeal began, and then stopped suddenly as a figure stepped out from amongst the warriors.

It was a man; a tall, thin, almost sinister figure clad from head to foot in a long dark travelling cloak. The figure walked to the foot of the steps and bowed slightly to the count. He pushed back the hood of his cloak, and the torchlight touched his long thin face with yellow light, giving it a faintly demonic cast. 'My lord Nevin,' he murmured softly, although his voice carried to everyone in the silent courtyard.

The count glanced from the stranger to Aeal, and frowned, his hand falling to his sword. He opened his mouth to speak, when the stranger reached up and undid the ornate clasp that held his cloak at the throat. Nevin stared – first at the silver hook that took the place of the man's left hand and then at the eye and triangle symbol of a bard high on the man's left shoulder – and then the old warrior smiled.

'You are a bard?' Nevin said, a statement more than a question.

'I am Paedur, Bard Master, once of the Imperial Court at Karfondal, although now without position.'

Nevin nodded. 'Aye, I saw you once, and heard you speak there – but that was some years ago.'

Paedur smiled slightly. 'It would have been.'

The old man walked down the few remaining steps and stood by the bard – although the count was by no means a small man, Paedur topped him by a head and more. The count's voice dropped to a whisper. 'What brings you here – and now?'

'Chance,' the bard murmured, 'and the will of the gods.'

'The will of the gods,' the old man said, smiling. And then he threw back his head and laughed. 'Aye, the will of the gods. But come bard, you must hunger and thirst after your journey. I will have a guesting room prepared and you may rest awhile, and then you will join us; this night my daughter is to be betrothed to one of my neighbour's sons. Perhaps you would do us the honour to speak for us . . .' Nevin threw his arm around the bard's shoulder and led him up the steps and into the hall.

The Captain of Bowmen was about to turn away, when he spotted the scribe in the shadows. He walked over to him. 'Do you know this bard?' he asked, nodding up the steps.

Danel nodded. 'I've heard of him,' he said cautiously.

'What about him?'

'His name is almost legendary in Baddalaur. He threw away a fine position in the Imperial Court and went to settle in some forest so he could work without distractions.'

'And what's wrong with that?' Aeal asked, hearing the disapproval in the scribe's voice.

'Well . . .' Danel said slowly.

'Well?'

'I did hear a rumour that he was wanted by the Imperial Court.'

'On what charge?' Aeal asked quickly.

'Blasphemy against the New Religion,' Danel said, a little breathlessly.

The bowman smiled. 'Since when has that been an offence?'

'Since the Emperor Geillard began studying the Religion.'

'Well, in the Wastelands we judge a man by more than the gods he worships,' Aeal said turning away.

The Great Hall of Castle Nevin had been newly decorated for the betrothal. The tall fluted pillars had been washed in shades of light brown and cream, making them look like trees, and the high vaulted ceiling had been painted a pale eggshell blue, giving it the appearance and effect of the sky.

Paedur the bard walked slowly down the empty hall. He looked around, nodding slightly, and then turned back to Count Nevin who had remained standing by the door. 'Master Eldesan's work, I think.'

Nevin folded his arms and began to rock back and forth on his heels. 'Aye, I brought in craftsmen from the Outland Guilds, but they were under the direction of the Emperor's own mastercraftsman.'

Paedur nodded. 'I recognise his touch.' He wandered down to the end of the hall, running the fingers of his right hand against the golden-bronze of the long guesting table that took up most of the room. 'This has a tale to tell, I shouldn't wonder,' he murmured.

Nevin nodded, obviously pleased. 'Aye; my ancestor, Nevin Ironhand, commissioned it on the occasion of his handfasting to Maggan, the daughter of Thurle of the Two Forests. He was the ancestor of Adare – whose son my daughter is to be betrothed to this night. The legends say it was the source of the interbinding between the two families which continues to this day.'

The bard rested the palm of his hand flat against the table and the old count imagined he saw something spark between the flesh and the polished wood. 'It's carved from a single piece of wood,' the bard said, almost in wonder.

Nevin stepped away from the doorway and walked to the table.

He rested the tips of his fingers almost delicately against the wood. 'It was carved by Chriocht the Carpenter, the Crinnfaoich.'

Paedur glanced down the length of the table at the count and shook his head. 'He was not pure-blooded Crinnfaoich; he was part human. He originally hailed from the Sidhe Forests of Ogygia, but he set out as a young man to wander the known world. His workmanship can still be found in the most surprising places.'

'Well, this is my family's most prized possession. In all that time, it has neither cracked nor warped and, although wood quickly rots in this cold and damp northern clime, this has remained as fresh today as it was when it was first hewn from the tree.'

The bard nodded. 'There is a little of the Old High Magic in it.' He looked sharply at the old count. 'Is there a wizard you trust . . .?'

Nevin was caught off guard by the sudden question. 'Well . . . well yes, I suppose there is. Why?'

Paedur smiled. 'Have him fire the table. Oh, don't look so alarmed – I don't mean burn it. He will know what you mean.' He lifted his left arm with the hook and held it at chest height above the polished wood. A sudden bright blue spark leapt from one to the other. 'There is Power in this wood; everything that has happened in this room is caught – trapped – by that Power. If your sorcerer fires that Power you will be able to see what happened here since the day Chriocht etched the final glyph into the wood when his work was complete.'

'That . . . that might be interesting,' Nevin said slowly, and then he added, 'perhaps even more interesting following tonight's events.'

Paedur walked to the head of the table and rested his hand and hook on the back of the ornate High Chair that Nevin would occupy later that night during the festivities. 'Perhaps you would like to tell me why you've brought me here.'

The count looked around and spread his hands. 'Because it's the quietest room in the castle at the moment. We're not likely to be disturbed . . .' He glanced over at the thick-bodied red-ringed time-candle set in a tall holder in a corner, '. . . well not for a little while longer.' He turned back to the bard. 'Your coming here is a gift, an answer to an old man's prayers. Tonight, I want you to tell the company here a story . . .' he stared down the length of the table at the bard. 'I want you to tell a story that will terrify my daughter!'

106

The bard's long face remained expressionless, but he lowered his head, allowing the shadows to fall across his face, leaving only his mirror-bright eyes visible, reflecting the warm gold of the polished wood.

'My daughter Suila is a witch,' Nevin said quickly, 'not a full sorceress, nor bonded to any religion. We have a fine library here and she has used some of the ancient texts to . . . dabble. She has mastered a few of the minor incantations, but I'm terrified her meddling will soon come to the notice of . . . something powerful.'

'I've seen it happen.'

'I want you to tell her a tale that will warn her off from meddling with those forces.' He paused, and then asked, 'Can you do it?'

'Tell me why I should?' the bard said quietly.

'Because you are a bard, a follower of the traditional ways, and by your own laws you cannot refuse a request for a story.' He stopped, looking into the crackling fire, and then added, 'And because you might save a girl's soul.'

The bard turned away from the chair and began the long walk down one side of the table. 'I can tell the tale, but I cannot guarantee that she will listen, much less take heed.'

The old count smiled broadly. 'When a Bard Master tells a tale, then everyone listens.'

The meal was a long slow affair, the food plentiful, and the wines, meads, ports and beers even more so. There were some speeches, followed by entertainments: actors, jugglers, harlequins, tricksters and dancers who had been brought in under special escort for the occasion.

Towards midnight, Count Nevin finally called for silence. He attempted to stand up, but he shifted and swayed and his speech was slurred and broken. 'We . . . we are to be honoured on this . . . this happy occasion . . .' he began. He sat down suddenly, amidst a burst of drunken laughter, and continued his speech from his chair. 'We are to be honoured by a bard – a wandering Bard Master in the grand tradition – who chanced upon the castle earlier this forenight, and he has agreed . . . he has agreed to tell us a tale of our choosing.'

A sudden burst of applause drowned out the rest of the count's words, but they died just as quickly as the long room's double doors were thrown wide and the bard made his entrance in a gust of frigid air which guttered many of the candles and tapers.

Paedur walked the length of the hall in complete silence, all too conscious of the frightened stares he was receiving and aware of the half-concealed signs that were made as he passed. The northern folk were superstitious people, he reminded himself, and their fears and beliefs were a double-edged dagger – to be used either way.

He stopped before the tall main table and bowed slightly to the counts Nevin and Adare and their wives. He turned slightly and bowed to the young man and woman sitting apart in the brightly-flowered wuuwreath decked chairs: Suila, daughter of Nevin, and Adare, son of Adare.

'A tale, bard,' Nevin said quickly, glancing at his daughter and then turning back to the bard.

'And what would you have?' Paedur asked, his voice low and soft and yet carrying to every corner of the hall.

Nevin smiled curiously over the rim of his goblet. 'Why . . .' He paused, looking drunkenly down the table. 'Well, this is my daughter's night. I think she should choose, don't you?'

The bard nodded slightly and then looked over at Suila. 'And what is your pleasure?'

Suila looked from her father to the tall bard. As the head of the household, only the count had the right to ask a bard to speak, and now she instinctively felt that something was wrong. Suila was a tall thin young woman, with copper-red hair and dull green eyes. Her face was long, and seemed almost flattened, and while she was no great beauty she was witty and intelligent, spoke four languages fluently, and could read almost as many more again. She looked at her betrothed, Adare. 'What would you like to hear?' she murmured.

Adare was now more than a little drunk. He was a warrior, stationed in one of the border outposts beyond Thusal; a short, stocky man, a soldier in his ways and manners. Suila made him uncomfortable and, in some vague way, frightened him. He grunted, 'Your choice.'

Suila looked back at the bard. 'My choice,' she said, her hard eyes narrowing. 'Can you tell me a tale of lovers,' she asked slowly, 'but yet, let it have a little spice to it, let there be war and death – and sorcery. Can you tell me a tale like that?'

'I can.' The bard turned to Nevin. 'With your permission then . . .?'

The count waved his hand. 'Of course – but first a chair.' He half-turned and called back over his shoulder. 'A chair for the bard.'

While two pages struggled to manoeuvre a heavy chair up the hall to the centre of the floor, Paedur turned to look at Suila. She held his gaze – and then she shivered, for she felt as if he were looking through her, into her very soul. Finally, she blushed and looked away, busying herself with her goblet.

Paedur sat back into the high-backed ornate wooden chair and in the dim half-light of the hall the shadows seemed to cluster and gather thickly around him, leaving only the gleaming half-circle of his hook and the triangular bardic sigil visible.

Suddenly, he rapped his hook against the arm of the chair and a thin high musical note hung on the air, stilling all sounds. 'This is the tale of Gered and Leal,' he began . . .

Before the Cataclysm that destroyed the Second Age of Man, when the Southern Kingdoms were but a single continent, a new faith came into being – the unholy worship of Lutann, one of the Demon Gods. The Demon Lords were wholly alien creatures, not of this universe, but they gained access to it through the rents in the fabric of space which were created by the howling of Kloor, the defeated War God of the New Religion.

The worship of Lutann centred in the western city of Osteltos, the so-called White City. However, time and the smoke of countless sacrifices had blackened its squat marbled walls, and its ivory towers – which were literally sheathed in ivory – had tarnished and stained, giving the city a yellowed, diseased appearance from the distance.

Beton, the Blind King, ruled at this time, and he actively encouraged the worship of the Demon God.

Now to the north of Osteltos, although separated from it by the ancient Mathin Woods, rose Solestel, the City of Spires. It had been built in the centre of a broad, gently sloping plain, with one side to the sea, and its back to the Tirim Mountains. And, although it had been built using the same marble from the Mathin Quarries which had been used in the construction of Osteltos, while the latter had darkened, Solestel's walls still blazed golden with reflected sunlight on bright summer days.

Mechlor ruled in Solestol. He was Beton's twin brother, and they were the sons of Madran the Saviour who fell at Cellen Field, in battle with the Shemat, who were the ancestors of the Shemmatae, who were in turn defeated by Churon the Onelord in later generations.

Although they were twins and in their youth had been indistinguishable, time had changed that. Beton's strange worship had

109

taken its toll and had warped his tall frame, scarring his flesh and robbing him of his sight. But Mechlor, who followed the Old Faith, retained his youth and vigour, and could almost have been taken for Beton's son.

But although the two brothers were now separated by a divide that was greater than any ocean, their lives still followed a strangely similar pattern. And so at the time when Hanuiba, Beton's concubine, gave him a daughter, Mechlor's wife Iaiale, bore him a son.

In the time of celebrations that followed, both kings swore to their differing gods to bring up their children according to their respective faiths. Beton named his daughter Leal, and she was dedicated to Lutann and, almost from the time she could talk, she was trained in the mysteries and workings of his magic.

And Mechlor, following the traditions of his race and family, named his son Gered, after his grandfather – Gered the White King – and he was raised in the Old Faith, and taught the ways of healing and kinghood.

Now many years passed, and the emnity between Osteltos and Solestel grew, and soon a bloody sectarian war raged between the two cities. And when the mortal armies had clashed again and again, but with little effect, the cities fought with magic and sorcery. Creatures and beings – some called from the furthest plains of existence and others wholly created by the magicians – stalked the Mathin Wood and the huge marble quarry which it enclosed. These in turn disturbed some of the older forest dwellers and the quarry stone folk, and in the skirmishes many of the magical creatures native to this plane died.

Soon, the cities became isolated, while their creations roamed the lands between, destroying everything in their path. And Mannam claimed many – and they were the lucky ones – for there were countless others who were slain by the creatures, and whose spirits were claimed neither by Mannam of the Faith, Libellius of the Religion nor the Demon Lords, nor were they consigned beyond the Gorge, but continued to walk the land as spectres – but spectres with a taste for blood.

The war dragged on, and neither side gained the advantage. The priests and magicians on both sides began to research the elder lore of their race, and they began to call up ever more terrifying creations. Finally, in desperation, both sides, in their different ways, turned to their gods for help.

The priests of Maker and User and the priestesses of the Lady Dannu gathered in conclave in the holy place deep in the heart of the Shining City, and prayed for guidance.

And the Lady Dannu, the Mother Goddess, attended by her twelve handmaidens, appeared to the conclave and spoke to them.

She told them many things; of how the Demon God's priests were even now attempting to grant Lutann a physical form upon this plane and, if successful, the creature would be almost invincible.

And she also told them that the Gods of Pantheon would not be able to assist their followers, for the gods themselves were under attack. There were others – creatures of the Gorge – who wished to usurp the gods of the Old Faith, and had thrown in their lot with the Demons and now made war upon the chequered fields of Ab-Apsalom, the Battleground of the Gods. The Lady Dannu added that if the Old Gods were ever defeated then the planes of existence would be divided between the Demons and the Usurpers, and cleansed of the followers of the Faith. Lutann must not be allowed to incarnate on this plane, for in time, by his very nature, he would destroy all life, and not only on the Prime Plane but on all the minor planes also.

But the Demon Lord had been summoned and was very near, hovering just beyond the Ghost Worlds, biding his time, awaiting a suitable host for his spirit. Also, his activities were restricted by the Old Gods, but they were hard pressed by the Usurpers.

The Lady Dannu reminded the priests and priestesses that a god's strength was in direct proportion to the number and faith of his followers, and thus, if the followers of Lutann and the Usurpers could be slain, then their gods would weaken and the Old Gods triumph.

Mechlor listened to his priests' report and called a full council, and after little argument they decided they had little choice but to carry the war to Osteltos and attempt to raze it to the ground. Only by destroying the city and its inhabitants and by wiping out the belief could they destroy the opposing gods and demons.

Raiding parties from Solestel attacked Osteltos, but with limited success. However, they did prevent the evil miasma that cloaked Osteltos from spreading and the numbers of the creatures roaming the woods – which men said sometimes resembled lizards and sometimes great birds – did not increase.

Famine raged across the land and struck equally at the Twin Cities, and in a very short space of time killed almost twice as many as had died in the war. The cities gradually became isolated from the rest of the continent, and became almost completely independent, leaving the Mathin Woods to whatever were-creatures that had survived.

And on Ab-Apsalom, the Battleground of the Gods, war raged unceasingly between the Gods of the Faith and the Usurpers, and there were many outward signs of the Great War. By day the skies were darkened with showers of meteors, which the philosophers said were the spirits of the defeated lesser gods and demons winging

111

their way to the Gorge. Nusas the Sun was shadowed again and again as he battled with the Mist-Demon, and a great fiery ball of deepest bronze rode across the heavens and challenged Nusas. When this appeared, the priests of the New Religion and the Worshippers of the Demons rejoiced, for the Mist Demon was Sinn and the bronze sun Quatatal, the Sun God of the Religion.

By night the skies burned with leaden colours, and the light of the stars was befouled with rolling fogs and clouds that flickered with pulsating lights. The Lady Lussa bravely rode through the heavens, but even her pure light was trapped and dissipated by the Usurpers and coloured by the Demons.

And those both beloved and cursed by the Moon Lady – the fool and the changeling – screamed and writhed in invisible agony; coastal towns were swamped and none dared put to sea for the tides were treacherous and unpredictable. Children and animals were born before their time, unformed and dead, and there were those that were never born but lingered long past their term in the womb until mother and child died in torment.

Then there came a lull in the battle, when it seemed as if the Old Gods had triumphed and some semblance of normality returned, and the clouds of evil that had covered Osteltos dispersed, and the creatures that had haunted the fields and woods surrounding the town vanished as mysteriously as they had come . . .

Gered, son of Mechlor, was two-and-twenty when the Old Gods held sway in Ab-Apsalom. He was a strange youth, tall and thin like his mother, although with his father's darker colouring. There was probably some fey blood in him – his mother's people were not pure human – and he preferred the wilds of the domain of the Lady Adur to the restrictions of town and city. When the land became safe again, he spent much of his time roaming the Mathin Woods, wandering amongst the towering groves and hidden bowers and bathing in its secret streams. He developed an interest in the ancient healing and herbal lore, and when he returned each evening his saddle-bags were usually bulging with rare herbs and strange plants.

One day in late summer his wanderings through the wood took him further than he had ever ventured before, almost to the southernmost edge. The blackened towers of Osteltos were visible through the trees, and evidence of the creatures that had once roamed this part of the wood was visible everywhere. There were great swatches cut deep into the heart of the forest and most of the trees bore wounds and scars of some kind.

However, almost as if the forest were trying to make up for the damage that had been done to the trees, the floor was carpeted with scores of plants – many of them unseasonal, and most of which were very rare. It was a herbalist's paradise.

Gered swung his leg over the high pommel of his saddle and slid to the ground, pulling his satchel from his shoulder. He knelt on the soft spongy turf to pluck a herb of healing when he heard the metallic trickle of water and, looking up, spotted the glittering sparkle through the undergrowth. The sound suddenly made him realise just how hot and thirsty he was. He skirted the entangled trees and shrubs, and made his way around to what he realised must be a small pool. He was just about to pull apart the drooping branches of a Moss Maiden Tree when he stopped in astonishment, his heart beginning to pound; there was a naked young woman bathing in the pool!

From where he was standing Gered could see only her back, as she swam slowly across the pool. Her pale skin had been recently tanned by the sun, and he could see tiny spots of skin beginning to peel away, exposing the pink flesh underneath. And strangely, the sight of the young woman's sunburn made him forget his fear, and the fact that he was so near Osteltos' walls. He crouched behind the drooping branches of the tree and watched her. There was something about the dark-haired young woman swimming in a hidden pool in the depths of the wood that fascinated and attracted him.

The swimmer made her way to the far side of the pool and slowly emerged from the rippling water, her long-fingered hands squeezing out her thick black hair. She then bent for a towel – and spotted Gered. Colour rose to her cheeks but she made no attempt to cover her nakedness. She straightened up and pointed to the youth.

'And how long have you been there? Long enough I'll wager. Well, shame on you. No honest man would spy on a lady as you have done.'

Gered blushed in turn. He scrambled to his feet and bowed low. 'My lady, I beg your pardon. I've only just arrived . . .' He glanced up to find the look of disbelief on her face. 'It's true, I swear it . . .' He looked away, and he heard cloth rustle, and when he glanced up again he found she was now dressed in a shift of rich cloth, stiff with gold thread and heavy with lace.

'I believe you,' she said finally. 'But you still haven't explained what you're doing here in this part of the wood.'

'I've been wandering in the woods since early morning,' Gered said quickly, and then he shook his head and took a deep breath. He was all too aware that his hands were sweating and his heart was pounding painfully in his chest. 'I am a herbalist,' he said slowly, 'and I range the forest in search of the rare and unusual herbs and flowers. Look!' He dug into the deep cloth satchel that hung around his neck and pulled out a tiny blue-petalled star-shaped flower. 'I found this earlier this afternoon. It is commonly called "Lover's Eye", but it also has the singular property of healing head pains and muscular aches when it is properly prepared and applied.'

The young woman rose on her toes and stared across the still water. 'It is very lovely,' she said, 'I have never seen its like before.'

'It is yours then,' Gered said quickly. He stooped down and placed the blue star on a water pad, and then pushed it out across the pool. The maid leaned out and plucked the flower from the broad leaf and held it to her face. 'Aaaah, it is beautiful and such a fragrance . . . delicate, familiar and yet strange.'

'It will be stronger at night,' Gered said, almost absently, staring at the young woman's face. 'I am sorry . . .' he began again.

She raised a slim hand. 'There's no need; I am convinced you meant no harm. Anyway,' she laughed, 'when I first saw you, there was a look on your face as if you had seen a vision.'

'Oh, but I thought I had,' Gered protested. 'At first I thought you were a forest sprite, some creature of the Crinnfaoich, but now I see . . .' He paused and coloured.

'What do you see?' the young woman asked with a smile.

'I see a maiden of flesh and blood, and a very beautiful maiden at that.'

And the Princess Leal, Beton's daughter, smiled and curtsied. 'You are very kind sir . . . what is your name?' she asked.

'I am . . .' Gered paused, and something made him hold back from giving his true identity. 'I am Dereg, a wandering herbalist. And you?'

Leal smiled, and her inbred caution and sorcerous training prevented her from giving him her true name. 'I am called Lean,' she said, 'I am a ladies' maid in the palace.'

There was a pause while they looked – almost shyly – at each other. Then Leal glanced up at the darkening sky. 'I must go. My . . . mistress will be waiting for me.'

'Will I see you again?' Gered asked.

'If you would like to.'

'I would.'

Leal smiled, her eyes softening. 'Do you know the ruined Fane of Bleis the Unbeliever . . .?' Gered nodded, and she continued. 'Tomorrow then, at noon.'

'I'll be there,' Gered promised.

On the chequered fields of Ab-Apsalom the war between the gods renewed, and once again the elements were thrown into turmoil and the sky – which is but the canvas of the gods – boiled with the fury of battle. But now war had turned in favour of the Old Gods and they began to prevail against the Usurpers and Demons, and so in desperation the priests of Lutann decided that it was now time to incarnate the Demon God on this plane. With his terrifying powers, they would defeat the city of Solestel and kill the followers of the Old Faith. With no worshippers to support them, the gods would soon be defeated. So they looked around for a suitable body for Lutann, for the Demon God was due only the best.

It was Andulin, High Priest of Lutann, who suggested that a Great Examination should be carried out to find that person most fitted to house the Demon's essence.

Weeks passed in the Great Examination, but in the end the priests had to admit that they had failed to find a suitable sacrifice – for the body of the host would have to be slain to allow the essence of the Demon to enter. So the priests of Lutann gathered together once again, and they performed the Rite of Questioning.

Andulin took seven night-black ravens and sacrificed them in the Demon God's name and their blood was collected in a white porcelain bowl. A sheet of whitest linen was spread upon the chill stone floor and the still hot blood was cast upon it. As it struck the cloth it boiled and hissed as if it were molten, but the blood did not dry into the linen. It began to shift and twist about like a nest of serpents, while Andulin and his priests chanted to their Demon God for guidance.

There was a stirring in the air above the cloth and the liquid blood rose, as if straining to reach the disturbance. The air thickened, darkening all the while, and then suddenly something flickered from the darkness on to the cloth in a bolt of intense white light.

When the priests could see again, they found the linen cloth crisped and blackened, and the blood had dried to rusty streaks on the stone flags. Andulin bent over the marks, his thin lips moving as he spelled out a word in the Old Tongue, the word *Bleis*.

The High Priest returned to Beton and told him of their Questioning and the strange reply. The Blind King was silent for a time, his sightless eyes staring in the direction of the fire which, even in the heart of summer, was always blazing. When he spoke his voice was harsh and strange.

'My daughter Leal has taken to visiting the Temple of Bleis in the Mathin Wood lately. She says she feels a waxing of her powers in the ruined fane . . .' The Blind King fell silent again.

'Interesting,' Andulin nodded slowly.

Beton nodded. 'Yes, interesting.' His scarred face turned up to the High Priests. 'But I thought she was Examined?'

'She was – and found to be unsuitable.'

'Well then, perhaps she goes there to meet someone – someone suitable.'

'What time does she leave for the fane?' Andulin asked.

'About an hour before noon,' the king said softly. 'Perhaps, if you were to be there before her . . .?'

At first light, Andulin, accompanied by a decade of the King's Own, Beton's personal guard, set out for the Temple of Bleis. Now, little is known of Bleis, who is sometimes called the Unbeliever. He paid homage neither to god nor spirit, demon nor elemental, and furthermore he believed each man had the seeds of godhood within himself. He preached that each man should pay homage to himself and direct his devotions inwardly. And for this heresy his spirit is claimed neither by the Faith, the Religion nor the Demon-worshippers, nor does it wander in the Gorge nor the Netherworld. And the spirit of Bleis the Unbeliever, forever outcast, wanders the planes in search of faith, in search of a god, in search of rest.

The temple was nothing more than a tall cylinder in a ragged clearing close to a tiny stream. Its door was long gone but Andulin noticed that the growth that had once obviously rioted its way across the entrance had been cleared away. The priest and guards entered and following the scuffed footmarks on the dusty stone floor and steps, made their way to the top floor, where they found the remains of fruit and some empty casks of wine. Then they waited.

It was almost exactly noon when there was movement in the woods below, and then footsteps were heard on the crumbling steps. The guards tensed as the sounds approached, and then – almost abruptly – the rotten trapdoor was thrown back and a figure climbed up on to the flat roof.

Two of the guards leaped forward, a weighted net in their hands. The struggle was brief, but in that time the man killed one with his knife and crippled another and had actually managed to cut himself free when he was struck unconscious. But only Andulin recognised Prince Gered, son of Mechlor, King of Solestel.

And to prevent a search for the missing prince, the High Priest sent a merchant to Solestel, with a tale of having found Prince Gered's clothing by the side of a pool in the heart of the Mathin Wood.

As the day of sacrifice drew near, there arose the problem of who would actually sacrifice the body of Gered to the Demon God. In its way, it would be a great honour, and advancement in the priest-hood would be sure to follow. But then Andulin discovered that the young man was still a virgin and therefore could only be slain by a virgin . . . and it suddenly became much more difficult to find someone to kill the young man. However, there was one candidate . . .

On *Nathanaday*, which was the day of sacrifice, Gered was taken from his cell under the Temple of Lutann and brought in an enclosed cage to the Great Henge that nestled just beyond Osteltos' walls on the seaward side of the city. There he was stripped naked and chained upon the altar stone, there to await his executioner.

The stone gateways were ancient, dating back even beyond the First Age, back to the time when the gods had not yet perfected the creature that would become man. Nothing is known of its builders, for the Henge was old even when the Culai first walked this world. And in those elder days, when the gods walked this world, and the great lizards roamed free, the Culai worshipped within the gaunt and forbidding stone circle, invoking their dark deities with blood and sacrifices. So much evil had been done within the Great Henge that even the stones themselves seemed to have absorbed it into themselves. They were grimed and decayed, streaked with phosphorescent mosses which glittered dully, even in the light of day, although within the Henge it was always dusk, for the circle was forever shadowed within a twilight pall, and always – even on the warmest days – radiated a subtle chill.

Legend tells of other circles scattered through the planes, connected in some occult way, but their locations and use have been lost and the stones themselves have been tumbled and scattered.

And as they chained Gered to the flat slab, the sound of the wind moaning through the standing stones took on a different almost human sound. Gered strained his neck upwards to look around, and for a single instant he thought he saw images of different times and strange alien places flicker between the Henge stones.

Then the worshippers began to arrive; singly and in small groups. Soon they thronged in a vast multitude beyond the stone circle, murmuring like the sound of the sea . . . and yet, even they, who were all too familiar with the horrors that haunted the streets of Osteltos, even they feared to approach too closely to the stones.

Then came the priests in their robes of grey, led by Andulin, who was clothed in white and Leal, who wore the crimson executioner's garb. The priests stopped just inside the Henge and spread around it, until they encircled the altar stone, but even they were still some distance from it, and the sacrifice, lying flat against the stone, was barely distinguishable.

The King's Own arrived next, surrounding Beton's ornate litter, and he was seated in pride of place beyond the First Door Stone, and beside him sat Arak, the Eye of Beyon, a small withered old shaman from the northern icelands, who reported all he saw to the blind king.

And the ceremony began.

The rituals were long and the day was hot, but Leal stood as if carved from stone, not moving a muscle, clasping the sacrificial knife – the Talon of Lutann – before her in both hands. The rites lasted throughout the day and it was evening, as the last rays of the sinking sun were striking through the perpetual twilight of the circle, bathing the altar stone and the sacrifice in dark ruddy hues, when Leal was called forward to consummate the ceremony.

She moved forward slowly, murmuring the Rite of the Talon, as she paced to the beating of a single throbbing drum, and then a pulse pounding in her temples took up the rhythm, lulling her into a daze.

Closer to the altar she moved . . . closer . . . closer still. She was only a few paces from the altar stone before she realised just who was chained there. She stopped, confused, and looked at Andulin who stood by Gered's head.

'Who . . .?' she murmured.

'Gered, son of Mechlor, a most fitting sacrifice,' he said smugly.

'No,' Leal whispered, shaking her head from side to side, 'I cannot sacrifice this man. I love him.'

'Aaah, but you must, you must,' Andulin gloated, 'you have very little choice now you know he is the son of your father's most hated enemy, Mechlor of Solestel.'

Gered raised his head from the chill stone and looked up into the woman's face. 'You are Leal, the daughter of Beton?'

Leal nodded silently, not trusting herself to speak.

But Andulin continued. 'Consider this; if your father, indeed, any of the people, should hear that you have violated your holy vows of chastity and consorted with this . . . this . . .' words failed the priest. 'They would tear you limb from limb.'

'My vows remain intact,' Leal protested. 'I am still a virgin.'

Andulin nodded. 'Oh, I know that. But would they believe you?'

'But Dereg . . . Gered is my betrothed, I love him!' Leal pleaded.

'So? Consider this if you will. Sacrifice him, and in the sight of Lutann you will be doubly blessed. It would be as if you had given one of your own family to the god. He would reward you greatly for the gift.'

'Leal, if you truly love me, lay down the knife and announce your love openly, and if we must die then let us die together. I do not fear death,' Gered said suddenly.

'Remember, Leal, what power will be yours,' whispered Andulin persuasively.

'Remember our vows, Leal, those promises we made together in the secret places of the wood, pledged beneath the noon sun.'

'Remember the holy vows, Leal, which you made before you met this youth,' Andulin urged. 'You cannot throw your life away for this creature. Yes, you will feel the pain of parting, but you are young, you will soon recover from your loss. There will be many youths only too eager to help ease the pain. Yes, there will be many, I promise you.' The priest's eyes glittered strangely, and his gaze drifted to where his own son stood amidst the ranks of the lesser priests. 'But the choice is yours, and yours alone. And you would be wise to think carefully before answering, but choose now and, for your sake in this life and the next, choose correctly.'

By now the dim rays of the diffused sun were slipping off the altar stone and the congregation were whispering urgently amongst themselves, wondering at the delay.

'The people grow agitated,' the High Priest hissed. 'The sun is sinking; you must give me your answer now. What is it to be? Your life and the power and glory that are yours by right of birth and acclaim, or the life of this wretch – who will die in any case?' he added with an icy smile.

Gered saw the distant look come into Leal's wide eyes, and it terrified him. 'Leal, it is I, Gered, whom you knew and loved as Dereg . . . remember?'

'Be quiet,' she snapped, 'I must think.' She was struck by strange and conflicting emotions, but there were two that bubbled to the top of this seething cauldron and cried out for attention. And truly the matter was simple. A simple choice; her love for Der . . . Gered, balanced against her lust for power . . . and life.

Which was the stronger?

There had been little love in her life before Gered. Her father had been a distant terrifying figure and, although she knew her mother's name and could point her out in the crowded harem, Leal had no feeling for her. She had been infused with the dictates and laws of Lutann almost before her birth, for she had been dedicated to the Demon God while still in her mother's womb. The priesthood was her life and it was a hard and brutal way of life, with little love or beauty about it.

And it has been said that those who traffic in evil sacrifice a little of the gentler emotions in return for the baser powers.

She glanced back over her shoulder at the people crowding beyond the Gates. She saw their empty staring faces, their slack mouths and dull eyes, panting in their blood lust. Did she want to rule this?

And the answer turned out to be very simply, yes. Here, she would be worshipped as a goddess, with limitless and untold power to exercise. She would have wealth beyond her wildest imaginings, the coffers of one of the richest nations of the Southern Kingdoms would be hers to use as she would. She was born to rule. From earliest childhood this had been held up as her ultimate destiny. Would she – could she – toss this away for a youth?

119

And what of the youth?

She looked down at Gered lying bound upon the stained altar stone. He had lied to her – and she to him, but that was forgotten – he worshipped not her gods, nor she his. Could there ever be true love between them?

But somewhere deep, deep within her, a small voice, a voice almost smothered under fear and uncertainty, perhaps the voice of the Leal that might have been, murmured, '*You love him . . . you love him . . . you love . . . save him . . . save him . . . save . . .*'

And then the voice of fear and ignorance spoke: 'How? How can I save him and yet retain all that I possess, the power, wealth, position – and my life. How?'

'*Save him . . . save him . . . his life . . . his life is in your hands.*'

'How?'

There was a moment in which she stood undecided, torn between the two voices, and then the crowd began to shout. And suddenly the decision was made. She stepped up to the altar, the black-handled knife in her hands burning like a single flame in the last rays of shadowed sunlight.

'Leal . . .?' Gered whispered.

'Silence, fool!'

'I thought we meant . . .'

'You meant nothing to me,' and her voice was harsh and flat and strangely alien. 'You were but an amusement.'

She raised the knife high.

'I love you *Leaaaaaaa . . .*'

As Gered screamed his farewell, Leal plunged the Talon of Lutann up to the hilt in his breast, and as he died, with his blood upon the hands of his betrothed, he whispered softly, for her ears only, 'I forgive you, my love . . .'

'Thus died Gered, son of Mechlor, King of Solestel, by the hand of Leal, daughter of Beton, King of Osteltos.'

The bard's voice faded in the vastness of the hall, and in the silence that followed many turned to look at Suila. Colour rose to her cheeks but she couldn't ignore the hard stares. 'Why do you look at me? I am neither witch nor sorceress. I am not like the Leal of the tale.'

Adare, her betrothed, suddenly looked up from the goblet in his hand and turned towards Suila's father. 'I think there was a reason in the telling of this tale, and I think its contents were not unknown to you. Would this be so?'

Count Nevin nodded solemnly. 'It is so. I asked the bard to tell a tale such as you have heard.' He looked from Adare to Suila. 'We all know my daughter has had leanings towards the darker knowledge of the ancients and I feared, not only for her spirit, but for those close to her. I didn't know what story Paedur would tell, but he has chosen uncannily well. Thus, for those with a mind to listen, there is a warning here.'

The bard's voice suddenly cut across the count's. 'There is a little more – my tale is not yet complete.'

Nevin bowed. 'My apologies . . .'

Paedur continued.

But the truth reached Solestel, for the spirit of Gered had been wrested from the grasp of Lutann by the Lady Dannu and her Maidens and now abode in the Silent Woods in peace and safety, though his body remained in unhallowed ground. And Coulide Dream-Maker visited Mechlor in a vivid nightmare to show him how his son had died.

And Mechlor, rallying his people behind him, overran Osteltos and razed it to the ground, killing everyone there, man, woman and child, for they were all tainted with the evil of the place.

Andulin, the High Priest, attempted to oppose Mechlor's army with spells and sendings, but the priests and priestesses of the Lady Dannu and the Old Faith successfully protected the army from sorcerous attack, and Mechlor's sendings came back on Osteltos. And it was Mechlor who plunged his sword into the priest, and took his head and set it up on a spire of the Temple of Lutann, where it gibbered and mewled with a hideous life of its own until the temple itself dissolved in flames.

Beton, the Blind King of Osteltos, fell to his death while trying to escape from the Solestelians, for his slaves had deserted him and he knew true blindness then for the first time. His body was taken and tossed to the dogs, but it is said that even they refused it.

And the Cult of Lutann died that day also, for its followers were completely destroyed, and without faith there is no substance, and the weakened Demons were defeated with ease by the Old Gods.

But of Leal little trace was found, save charred ashes and chipped bones in a tower by the outskirts of the city, where it was rumoured she practised her evil craft. It was said that she had tried to raise the shade of Gered and had been blasted by her own foul sorcery or perhaps the Demon Gods took her because they had lost Gered to the Old Gods.

Although the Southern Kingdoms vanished beneath the seas in the Cataclysm that destroyed the Second Age of Man, the Great Henge survives on one of the Arrow Isles that are the last remnants of the once huge land.

But on winter nights, when the Wingstar shines to the north, it is said that shadow-creatures perform strange rites within the standing stones, and strange landscapes can be seen through the gates, and the shades of a hundred thousand sacrifices pace silently around the circle.

And on such occasions the wind whispers, Gereddddd . . . Leallll . . .

'Thus ends the tale of Gered the Prince who was destroyed by his love for the sorceress Leal.' Paedur sat back into the chair, and was lost in the shadows.

The count turned to his daughter Suila, who was now weeping openly, while Adare tried uncomfortably to comfort her. 'I asked for a tale such as this as a warning to you,' he repeated. 'Heed it.'

The old man rose stiffly, thus signifying that the festivities were at an end. He walked around the ancient table and approached the bard's chair, pulling a heavy purse from his belt. He stopped in front of the heavily shadowed chair. 'You have done me a great service . . .' he began softly and then suddenly stopped.

For the chair was empty. The bard was gone.

7 The Legend of the Shanaqui

The legend grew, making him a Duaiteoiri, a demon, a god, but in truth he was none of these things – he was still a man and, for all his powers, he was a puppet of the gods.

Life of Paedur, the Bard

There had been a time, when he was still fully human, when he slept and ate and his bodily functions were like those of normal men. He had feelings then, he knew love and hate, anger, rage and pity. He had been able to weep.

All that was gone now.

He had lost that part of himself when the Old Gods had chosen him as their champion and gifted him with immortal life. Now, sleep was unnecessary, and he needed only the simplest food to survive. His emotions had also suffered; they had been dulled, muted, and he was no longer capable of the extremes of feeling, and love and hate had become almost abstractions. A dull satisfaction was all that was left to him. Even his tales, which had been his greatest joy and pleasure, were now little more than studies, picked and told for the greatest effect, chosen to excite a set of responses from his audience. Usually, it didn't bother him overmuch, but tonight . . . tonight had been different.

The bard leaned back against the tall pillar of rock and looked back down the long road, past the black line of the Mion River to where he could still see the lights of Castle Nevin. And he wondered at the morality of what he had just done. He didn't know Suila, nor did he owe anything to the old count, and yet, on Nevin's word, he had succeeded in ruining what should have been one of the happiest days of a girl's life.

Perhaps his tale would have some effect, and he might have deterred her from further delvings into the ancient lore, but somehow he doubted it. He had the Sight to a minor extent, and the only future he saw for Suila was a bloody fire-filled death. And he knew that she would remember the bard for the rest of her life – and hate him.

Shaking his head, Paedur the Bard turned around and continued on the road that led into the icy Northlands.

Paedur reached the coast in the still silent hour just before dawn. The darkness was absolute, with low clouds covering the stars and the Lady Lussa, but with his enhanced sight the night held no secrets from him. He allowed the rest of his senses to come to the fore, and the pre-dawn came vibrantly alive. The on-shore breeze was fresh and chill, carrying with it the promise of sleet from the Northlands, but he was also able to distinguish the odours of humanity nearby – smoke, cooked and burnt food, sweat and urine . . . and fish. He wrinkled his nose in distaste; the stench of rotting fish was almost overpowering. He looked down the winding length of the road, and found it branched further on, one turning leading down towards the pebbled beach to a small fishing village, the other leading upwards towards an obviously ancient yet still formidable fortress perched on the clifftop almost directly across from his present position.

Paedur frowned, trying to place the spot, working out its position in relation to Castle Nevin and the River Mion, and then he realised he was looking at the northernmost community of the blue-robed monks of the Order of Ectoraige, the God of Learning and Teaching.

The monastery was built in two distinct parts and styles, with one higher than the other. The older building was constructed of rough-hewn blocks, cunningly set into each other without mortar, with a slightly sloping wood-and-lacquer roof. The two massive gates were solid brukwood, thick with characteristic square-headed rivets that were the trademark of the Culai carpenters and which were never known to rust. By contrast, the sprawling school, huddled at the foot of the monastery building, was built entirely of plain cordwood, and though it was an impressive structure in itself it seemed almost shabby and insubstantial against the older building.

Grey light flared far out to sea, startling the bard, but when he looked he found it was merely the dawn breaking the horizon. He turned back to the monastery and school; it would be a good place to stop for a time, Paedur decided, it would give him time to make some plans and consider his future. It was sometimes difficult to remember that it had been barely half a year since he had left the Forest of Euarthe, and in that time he had walked almost half the length of the Nations, telling his tales, spreading the Old Faith. Yes, it would be good to rest.

His decision made, he was just about to move when he felt heat surge through the metal hook that was set into the bone of his left arm. He acted instinctively, dropping to the ground and rolling to one side into the twisted bushes that lined the track. He had been attacked on his journey on three previous occasions; twice by humans, and the last time by Tixs, the Bat God of the New Religion. And each time his hook had warmed and warned him.

He parted the bushes and looked around, now tasting a harsh metallic tartness in the air that overlay the salt tang of the sea. Light had seeped across the sky and in the twilight greyness he could see that a spot directly above the track he had been following was shimmering, sparkling with scores of tiny coloured dust-motes.

And then a tree appeared on the pathway. A tall thin blasted tree, with tendrils of leaves and ragged mosses clinging to it. The bard's metal hook turned ice-cold – it was a sending, and a powerful one at that.

Paedur pressed his hook to his lips, silently calling on the Pantheon for help, as he quickly ran through the gods and demons of the New Religion, trying to place the sending, trying to remember which one used a withered tree as a symbol . . .

The tree moved. It straightened, its branches twisting and curling, and what Paedur had at first taken to be leaves and mosses now formed and re-formed into a long cloak of withened leaves . . . and the bard suddenly recognised the figure.

'Mannam,' he murmured.

The Lord of the Dead moved rustlingly forward and stopped and then its head turned to where Paedur still lay. The figure bowed slightly, 'Bard.'

'Surely my time has not come yet?' Paedur asked quietly, standing up and brushing dirt from his cloak and tunic. He peered up at the Duaiteoiri. The last time he had seen the Lord of the Dead it had been dark, and the creature's features had been shadowed behind the long cowl of his cloak. However, even now, with his enhanced sight, he still couldn't make out the Dark Lord's features.

'Not yet, not yet,' Mannam whispered sibilantly, 'you have no need to see my features yet. When you do you will have passed from this world, and will be in my domain.'

'I thought you were one of the Religion's minions coming for me,' Paedur said.

The Dark Lord nodded, his cloak whispering and hissing softly. 'Aye, you must take great care now; their attention is fully on you, and I fear their attacks will become more frequent. But you have done well.' Mannam drew a slightly gasping breath and continued, 'Where you have been there is a swing back towards the Old Faith, people are beginning to question the New Religion openly and in some cases even defying its priests.'

'There will be war,' Paedur promised.

Mannam nodded, his leafed cloak rustling harshly together. 'In all probability. Prince Kutor is already putting together a sizable army in the west, and the Weapon Master will soon join him. A little while longer and this army of the Old Faith will be a force to be reckoned with. Perhaps it might be wise to send you back to them, allow you to weave your own particular magic on them . . .' the god's sibilant, breathless voice died away. 'But all that in time.' The god paused, and the bard thought he heard a note of hesitancy creep into his voice. 'But now there is something you must do for us, something important . . .'

'More! You want me to do more! Have I not done enough already?' the bard snapped, brushing past the Duaiteoiri and striding down the roadway.

'Your task has only just begun,' Mannam whispered, falling into step beside him. 'It will be complete only when the New Religion is destroyed.'

'I may be dead then.'

'If I do not take you, then you will not die,' the Dark Lord said.

'And what will I become then? A *quai*, a mindless thing?' Paedur snapped.

'I will not allow that to happen,' Mannam promised.

'That gives me little comfort.'

Mannam glided around in front of the bard and stopped, forcing the bard to a halt. 'Something is troubling you,' the Duaiteoiri said.

'Tonight I told a story – the tale of Gered and Leal – to a young woman at her betrothal; I told the story with the sole intention to frighten her.'

Mannam nodded. 'I am aware of the circumstances.'

Paedur ran his fingers through his hair, dragging it back from his face. 'I told that story without stopping to think of the consequences; without thinking how the young woman would take it; I told the story because I was asked to.' He stopped, and then added in a softer voice, 'I'm beginning to wonder.'

'About what?'

The bard shrugged. 'If I'm doing the same thing. If my tales are only frightening people back to the Faith. Why am I doing this?'

'You are reminding people of their Faith, of the belief their fathers held and their fathers before them. And their belief makes the gods stronger, and in turn we protect them. When we asked you to be the Champion . . .'

'Asked?'

'Decided then, that you should be the Champion of the Old Faith, we did not lay down any rules for you. You were gifted with certain powers and then allowed to choose your own path. For reasons of your own, that path led northwards . . .'

'You told me to come north!'

'I merely suggested it,' Mannam hissed, 'but you chose it.'

'I'm not even sure myself why I came north – perhaps I was just trying to stay out of trouble.' With his single hand he pulled his cloak close around his throat. Although he was usually impervious to the weather, the Duaiteoiri radiated an insidious chill. 'You know the Religion has offered a reward for my capture – dead or alive?' he asked.

Mannam nodded. 'Yes; and a special arm of the Iron Band of Kloor have been assigned to track you down – their orders are not to return without your head and hook.' The Dark Lord suddenly reached out and tapped the bard's chest with his long stick-like arm. 'They fear you now – already the people speak of the *shanaqui*, the Tale-Spinner. You have become a symbol of the Old Faith – a symbol the priests of the New Religion must destroy if they are to keep the people's belief.'

Paedur shrugged. 'Well, I should be safe enough here . . .'

'If you continue into the Northlands they will find you. They are already watching the bardhouse at Thusal.' The arm moved, pointing across to the monastery. 'A scholar has recently joined the brothers to study in their library. He is one of the Iron Band.'

'How do I know if you're telling me the truth?'

There was a sound of crackling, snapping branches that Paedur remembered as the Duaiteoiri's laughter. 'You don't. You must trust me – I have no need to lie to you.'

Paedur nodded and sighed. 'What's this important task you want me to perform?'

Mannam turned to face the spreading dawn, and the bard who was looking up into the darkened cavern of Mannam's cowl

127

suddenly caught a glimpse of the Duaiteoiri's face – a face like a slab of rotten wood, wormed and eaten with mould, with patches of scabrous moss clinging tightly to it. Paedur blinked – and the image faded.

'The gods of the New Religion have been busy of late, but to what ends we have been unable to fathom – until today. We knew for example that Hercosis the Dreamlord had visited most of the high-ranking priests and even the Emperor himself, and that Hirwas of the Far-Seeing, who is second only to Trialos himself, had ranged the length and breadth of this plane . . .'

'What were they looking for?' Paedur asked, interested now for although he had lost much when he had gained immortal life he still retained his bard's curiosity and inquisitiveness.

'They were seeking a small sealed vessel, of the kind that are commonly found in the ruins of the Culai settlements.'

'What's so special about this one?'

'It contains a fragment of the Soulwind,' Mannam whispered.

It took a moment for the god's words to sink in. 'The Soulwind,' he asked, 'the wind that blew through the soul of the One in the Beginning?'

Mannam rustled. 'The same.'

'But where is it, and what do they want it for?' Paedur asked quickly.

'It took us some time, but we finally located it; it lies beyond the Straits of Pinacloe, across the Sea of Galae, on the Blessed Isle of the Culai. The vessel itself is kept in the Inner City, enclosed within the Circle of Keys.'

'What do they want it for?'

In the long silence that followed, the sound of wind rustling through leaves and shaking branches was clearly audible. 'They intend to open it.'

'But will that not destroy . . .?' Paedur began.

'They believe that the Soulwind will sweep away the Old Gods into the nothingness from whence we came, leaving only the Gods of the New Religion.'

'Will it?'

'The Soulwind will wipe everything clean. When they open it, this plane, and every other plane of existence, will vanish.'

'And you want me to try and stop them?' Paedur asked incredulously.

Branches snapped and crackled. 'You must stop them, bard.'

8 The Taourg Pirates

This day: a merchantman taken and sunk off the coast of Adare, in sight of Mion Bay; a curious prisoner taken, a hookhanded warrior who professes to be a storyteller . . .

> . . . *from the log of the Taourg pirateman, Duneson*

'Sink it – leave no trace.' Duaize, Captain of the *Duneson*, a Taourg corsair, turned to his First Mate. 'No trace, mind, we don't want the Imperial warships knowing we're in the area.'

Tuan, the first mate, nodded briefly. 'Of course,' he said quietly, looking down on the captain, 'of course.' He was a tall mountain warrior, a native of Moghir, a province of Gallowan on the rocky north-western coastland, pale-haired and pale-eyed in the manner of his people, and completely in contrast to the short swarthy Taourg.

Duaize nodded and moved down the ship, leaving the first mate standing by the rail of the *Duneson* to supervise the rest of the crew as they systematically sacked the sinking merchantman.

Although the squat coastal trawler was hooked and grappled to the pirate ship's side it was listing badly to port, and the storm that had driven the craft from its customary safe shore route was blowing up again. Both ships were rocking on the growing swell and Tuan glanced into the northern sky, his grey eyes reflecting the metal colour of the sky. 'Hurry it up there! Storm coming.'

There was a shout from the merchantman and then the *Duneson*'s cargo net was hauled across the short divide separating the two ships. Tuan watched the huge bundle thump to the deck, where it was opened and each item quickly recorded by two of the ship's officers under Duaize's greedy eye. As they worked they set apart a one-hundredth part of the spoils which would be weighted and cast overboard immediately, dedicated to Sewad, the Nasgociban Lord of the Waves.

Suo-Ti, the Shemmat navigator and tillerman, joined Tuan by the rail. The small man nodded to the growing pile which was destined to be cast overboard. 'I have sailed with some strange crews in my time, but these Taourg are the most superstitious,' he said softly, in his sibilant accent. 'Such a waste.'

Tuan nodded. 'Aye, but if you've a mind to look closely, you'll find our captain's only disposing of the defective, spoiled or damaged goods.' He looked down at Suo-Ti and winked. 'Profit before religion, eh?'

The sallow-skinned man laughed – and then turned it into a cough when he saw Duaize glaring at him. He turned around and leaned on the rail, looking over at the sinking ship. 'I have decided to leave at the next sizable port,' he said quietly to Tuan. 'If you have any sense, you might think about doing the same.'

Tuan ran his fingers through his salt-stiffened hair and beard. He glanced briefly at the Shemmat. 'I have.'

'Good; perhaps we will find a berth together. I find these Taourg disgust me.' He spat into the water. 'They should have stayed in their desert.'

Still watching the captain sorting through the merchantman's cargo, Tuan asked, 'How many dead?'

'We have lost six. We were lucky; the storm hid us, and the Taourg corsairs are not expected this far north.'

'And the merchantman?'

The navigator shrugged. 'They lost many before they even knew what was happening, the rest died in the fighting, and the wounded were despatched. There was one female on board, but she slew herself . . .'

'Rather that than be sold on the slave block at Londre,' Tuan finished. He was about to continue when a shout from the merchantman made him turn. The pirates were finished, all the cargo had been transferred and the pirates had begun to swing back aboard the *Duneson*. 'There was a prisoner,' he said suddenly, 'what happened to him?'

'Below, and in chains; unconscious when I last saw him.'

'I wonder why Duaize wants him alive,' Tuan murmured.

Suo-Ti spat into the water again. 'Why wonder,' he said, moving away from the rail, heading back towards the huge tiller.

With the crew back on board, the navigator set the men to the oars and manoeuvred the *Duneson* off the merchantman, using the motion of the waves to wrench free the metal-shod ram. She then stood off from the ship and sunk it completely with a shot from her ballista. The first mate then ordered the skiffs into the water to collect up as much of the broken wood and shattered spars as they could find, thus leaving no trace that the Taourg were in these waters. Even as they worked, the dark waters boiled with the frenzy of the *ise* and *rize*, the finger-sized scavengers of the northern waters; no bodies would be washed ashore.

Suo-Ti then brought the *Duneson* around into the wind and the Taourg corsairs headed south, running before the storm, seeking a safe harbour for the night.

Tuan joined Duaize amidships. The captain was examining part of the cache of weapons the merchantman had been carrying. Duaize was a small swarthy man, with coal-black eyes and a sharply hooked nose. When Tuan had first sailed with him, a little more than three years previously, he had been going bald, but lately he had taken to shaving his head completely. His beard was thin and sparse. He looked up as Tuan stopped before him. 'What do you make of this?' He tossed the mate a long, broad-bladed knife.

The sudden weight of the weapon surprised him and he almost dropped it. It was heavy, far heavier than a knife should be, but then the blade was almost twice the normal width of a knife and as long as his arm. 'It's a Chopt knife, I'll wager. Aye, look at the hilt.' The broad flat hilt was a dull, slightly furred, brownish colour. 'That's Snowbeast horn. It's a Chopt knife right enough.'

Duaize smiled nervously, rubbing his hand to his bald head. 'I have never seen one of these Chopts.'

'In my homeland, there is a saying which goes, "The only Chopt you ever see is the one which kills you."'

Duaize reached for the knife, and Tuan passed it down to him, hilt first. 'If this is the knife, what then must the sword be like?'

Tuan smiled broadly. 'Big,' he said.

The captain had looked up, his dark eyes sparkling. 'And what would a merchantman, carrying nothing else but ales and cloth, and some fancy metal-work, want with a cargo of knives? Eh?'

'Smuggling?' Tuan suggested.

Duaize looked almost insulted. 'Unlikely. However, we can find out. Bring the prisoner,' he called. He slammed the lid of the weapons chest and then stood on it.

Tuan covered a smile with his hand; the captain – like most of the Taourg – was a small man, and the mate noticed that he was always careful to position himself where he could look down on those he was dealing with.

Two of the corsairs hustled the prisoner up from the hold and pushed him over to the captain. The crew formed a semi-circle around him, while Tuan folded his arms and took up position behind and to the left of the captain. Suo-Ti sidled up beside the mate. 'What is he?' Tuan murmured.

The navigator shrugged, shaking his head slightly.

The prisoner was tall, though not so tall as Tuan, and though thin was well muscled. He was clean-shaven and unscarred, and his limbs were sound save for his left hand which was missing and had been replaced by a hook. Tuan frowned; he had seen many mariners with hooks or claws in place of hands, but this was not a common sailor's hook: it was a broad, rune-etched half-moon, seemingly of silver though edged with some darker metal. Its sheen was dulled and darkened with rust-brown stains. He was wearing a shabby black-and-purple leather jerkin and close-fitting leather breeches. His boots were scuffed and worn and had obviously seen much travel. When he had been captured he had been wearing a long hooded cloak of coarse fur.

The prisoner had not entered the fighting until it became obvious that the Taourg intended killing all on board the merchantman, and even then he had not sought combat but rather had waited until it had come to him. He had slain six of the Taourg before he had been taken. Three had died with their throats opened as neatly as a priest guts a sacrifice. The almost casual killings had brought two more of the corsairs and they had attacked together, but he had pulled one into the other and then deftly cut open both their leathern jerkins in one smooth fluid movement. Another had attempted to spit him with a short harpoon, but he had easily eluded the barbed head and, pulling the man forward and down, had driven the point of his hook into his eye.

With his back to the mast, he had faced the ever-growing circle of Taourg without flinching, and when the archers would have cut him down Duaize had intervened. With a score of spears and harpoons at his throat, he had been netted, struck unconscious, chained and dragged to the *Duneson*.

'You fought well, Hookhand,' Duaize said suddenly. 'Killed six of my men; good men too.'

The prisoner didn't react.

'What is your name?' Duaize snapped.

'I am called Paedur,' the prisoner said quietly, looking up at the captain for the first time. His voice was soft and cultured, and without fear.

'You are a warrior?' Duaize asked, 'I have need of warriors, particularly now with six of my best dead,' he added with a grin, some of the crew joining him.

'I am a bard.'

There was silence. Some of the crew began to edge away from the man, and those of the Seven Nations and the Old Faith made the Horned Sign of protection, for they all knew the penalties exacted by the gods for drawing a weapon on a bard. But the captain was a Nasgociban and cared little for the superstitions of the effete northern nations.

'I do not think you are a bard, Hookhand. I think you are a warrior, a Weapon Master perhaps? In the employ of some northern noble, heading south on a secret mission?' He hefted one of the heavy Chopt knives in his hand. 'Yes, a spy. Now just why are you travelling on a merchantman at this time of year, eh, with a cargo of weapons? Your mission must be of great importance,' he added.

'I am a bard, nothing more.'

'Your destination then, where is your destination?' Duaize demanded.

'The Sea of Galae, and ultimately, the Blessed Isle.'

There was a quick murmur of surprise and superstition that rippled through the crew. They moved away from the prisoner, touching amulets and relics. The Blessed Isle was a myth, one of the universal legends common to every religion and faith. The very name was a mockery. Every belief described the Isle with loathing as the last home of the Culai, the First Race. It was a haunted place, close to the Abyss, the Gorge and the Netherworld, and where the damned roamed freely. It was said that beneath its sculpted glass cliffs lurked the sea deities of every belief, forever warring for the supremacy of the seas. The very mention of the Isle aboard a ship at sea was forbidden lest one of the gods – Sewad, Vorance, Paisod, Truil, Vi, Doge or one of the lesser sealords – be angered, and rise to vent that anger.

'No lies now – I asked you your destination,' Duaize said quickly, visibly shaken by the bard's reply.

Paedur stared at him, his eyes hard. 'You have my answer, and my destination.'

Duaize dismissed the answer with a wave of the Chopt knife, and then he changed the subject. 'You are on a mission then, something of great importance I'll wager.'

'Something of great importance, I'll grant you that,' Paedur agreed, with a thin smile.

'*HAH*! I thought so. What is it, eh?'

'That is not your concern,' the bard said quietly, looking around at the crew. He glanced back up at Duaize. 'And now, if you have finished . . .'

In the sudden silence that followed, the slapping of the waves against the tarred sides of the ship seemed very loud indeed.

Tuan's admiration for the bard increased. For a man facing torture and certain death, he was cool enough. Suo-Ti caught his eye. 'He's either crazed or dangerous,' the Shemmat whispered.

The first mate shook his head slightly. 'Not crazed, no, definitely, not crazed.'

Duaize jumped down from the weapons chest. Standing, the difference in height between the two men became very obvious. 'I have not yet finished with you, though there will come a time when you wish I were. You should watch your tongue Hookhand – lest you lose it. And,' Duaize continued, stepping closer to the bard, his deeply tanned face flushed, 'everything – everything – on board this craft is my concern. Now, answer me. What are you seeking?'

Paedur folded his arms, the chains about his wrists rattling, and smiled down at Duaize.

The captain suddenly struck at him, but before his open hand could connect it stopped, frozen in mid-air, not a finger's length from the bard's jaw. Paedur smiled curiously, but with his mouth only; his eyes remained pitiless. 'You will now order these chains removed,' he said softly, staring into Duaize's startled eyes. 'Release me.'

The captain tried to stab upwards with the Chopt knife in his left hand – but the broad thick blade snapped before it touched Paedur's stomach.

Duaize suddenly screamed as his right hand twitched and convulsed and then leaped to his own throat, fingers digging deeply into the soft flesh.

Suo-Ti reached for his dagger but Tuan gripped his shoulder, his fingers digging deep into the muscle, numbing the navigator's arm. 'Let it be.'

Duaize fell to his knees as his face began to darken, his eyes bulging, his tongue protruding. Saliva began to trickle in bloody lines down his jaw where he had bitten through his lips and the soft flesh of his cheeks. He dropped the hilt of the shattered knife and the fingers of his left hand tore bloody strips of flesh from the right in an effort to pull it from his throat.

The bard turned to the crew, his gaze seeming to linger on each one in turn, chilling them. 'Release me now, or he will surely die.'

'Do it,' Tuan said, turning away.

The atmosphere aboard the *Duneson* was tense and uneasy in the days following the bard's release. The Taourg avoided him, and he, in turn, seemed to prefer his own company, spending most of his time leaning against the ship's figurehead, a teel-wood carving of Sewad in the Third Aspect, the Water Seeker.

Duaize stamped about the decks in a foul temper, fingering his throwing axe and closely watching the bard, who was neither prisoner nor passenger. The entire crew had seen him humiliated and the presence of the bard was a constant reminder of that humiliation. Yet he could not dispose of the Hookhand, for the crew would surely mutiny; the bard having taken on an almost supernatural aspect, and even Duaize himself wondered whether the black-and-purple-clad stranger was a *deiz*, a spirit creature from the sands beyond the Fire Hills of his native Nasgociba.

The *Duneson* continued on its southward course and though the weather became warmer and the days longer, the seas grew progressively heavier and the wind stiffer. Seven days after the sinking of the merchantman, they hove in sight of the first of the Arrow Rocks, the chain of islands which run compass-straight from north to south off the eastern shores of the Seven Nations. On Suo-Ti's advice, Duaize decided that they should lie up off the first island they came to and wait out the growing storm that loomed dark and menacing on their port side. It would be the third storm in as many days, and the *Duneson*, already in need of repair, might not survive another.

They dropped anchor in the small natural harbour of a barren clump of rock inhabited by birds that rose in raucous demonstration at the ship's appearance. The harbour, however, was in the lee of the island's jagged cliffs and they were sheltered from the gale that gusted now with ever increasing frequency across the waves.

The evening meal was prepared while Tuan and Suo-Ti listed the most urgent repairs. Spirits were low, the presence of the bard having cast a shadow over the usually good-humoured crew, and Duaize ordered a ration of rofion to be dealt out. A fire-bowl was lit and the pirates huddled around it in their cloaks, warming their hands about the steaming mugs, for a thick, chill sea-fog was rising, carpeting the waves with billowing white banks that brought with them the icy breath of the northern seas.

As the night drew on, the men grew sullen and quiet and the half-hearted attempts at songs or chanties fell flat. Now and again, eyes would flicker across to the stranger as he leaned against the rigging, almost invisible save for the silver hook shining like a new moon in the lantern's wan light. If any eyes caught the bard's cold gaze, they were quickly averted and an amulet clutched or a Warding Sign made.

At last Duaize spoke, realising that if this situation were to continue then his authority would be irreparably undermined; a ship's crew should fear only the ship's captain. 'What is it you want Hookha . . . bard?' he called, his voice louder than was necessary. 'Let us have an end to this waiting. Name what you want and if it is within our power to grant it then it is yours, yes, and gladly too.'

The bard stepped into the wavering circle of light, although his dark clothes, and particularly the hooded cloak he wore, almost seemed to absorb the light. 'Take me south,' he said in his strong quiet voice, 'south to Maante at the tip of the Aangle Peninsula, that is all I ask. I cannot pay for this journey with coin, but I am a Bard Master and well versed in the ancient lore of the sea, in the tales of the great mariners and in information – both ancient and modern,' he added, with a thin smile.

'Information,' Duaize mused, and then, grasping an opportunity to regain some of his self-respect, said, 'Yes, that might be payment enough – if the information were of the proper quality. Perhaps we can work something out.' He laughed and rubbed his hands quickly together. 'Come – sit by me.' He patted the deck and moved a little to one side, nodding to Tuan and Suo-Ti to join him. The rest of the crew quickly moved away, giving the four men a semblance of privacy.

'This is Tuan, my first mate,' he said, 'and this is Suo-Ti, my navigator.' The three men sat cross-legged, facing the bard. 'Now,' the captain continued, 'bear with me awhile. You are a learned man; name for me the towns upon the Arrow Rocks, north to south.'

Paedur smiled briefly. 'You still doubt me, eh? But you must know that a bard is also a trained cartographer – it is a relic of the days when this world was first mapped by the wandering bards.

136

However, the larger towns are Smos, Torg, Cossi, Vosge, Musen and Forme. These are also the names of the larger islands, but there are of course countless fishing villages along the Arrows. Indeed, it is unusual to find an uninhabited isle,' he inclined his head slightly in the direction of the night-hidden island across the bay.

'Now,' Duaize said slowly, 'of these islands, which is the wealthiest?'

The bard did not answer immediately, and Tuan glanced across at the captain, wondering where this line of questioning was leading. Musen was the wealthiest of the islands, and the Musensi silver mines were renowned through the Seven Nations and beyond for the quality and purity of their metal.

'You already know the answer to that, captain,' Paedur said softly.

Duaize nodded. 'Yes, I know. But I want to hear your answer. You may take it that the information that you supply will pay your passage in part – for no man, be he bard or mage, warrior or merchant, takes passage aboard my ship without first having paid. You may pay your way with information and news.'

'But why information, why news?' the bard persisted. 'What need have you for such?'

Duaize smiled broadly, showing his gold teeth, and then shrugged. 'We have been at sea this half year and more, and in that time we have stopped at no port – no civilised port that is. Many years ago I learned the value of fresh news. Even now, the merest snippet can lead me to a fat cargo. Now I have heard rumours – little more than whispers – concerning the Arrows. Mysterious comings and goings by unlicensed slavers, the disappearance of ships in calm weather, one isle raiding another, or cutting off contact with the outside world . . . but only whispers, whispers.' Duaize shrugged again. 'But even such whispers are interesting. In my land we have a saying: "the cloud on the horizon forewarns the wise." It is obvious that something is happening on the Arrows. Perhaps plague has destroyed Forme's harvest, or Musen's silver mines have failed?' He smiled. 'So, I listen to these whispers, and I say to myself, perhaps these whispers might have some basis in fact, and if they were true, what do they mean? And then, when I find a bard-warrior coming south on a merchantman, I wonder afresh.'

Paedur laughed softly. 'I see now what you're leading up to;

you're wondering whether I was making my way to the Arrows, but I've already told you my destination – believe it, if you will. I leave the Arrows to you. However . . . as to information, and your question as to the richest of the isles, well then, Musen is accounted the richest of the islands, the Silver Rock it is sometimes called.' He paused and added with a sly smile, 'But . . .'

'But what?' Duaize whispered, leaning forward.

Paedur leaned back, out of the light. He brought his hook to his lips and said, almost absently, 'I could make you take me to Maante,' and then he smiled, 'but that is not my way and it would probably leave me drained . . .' He suddenly pointed with his hook at Duaize, who drew back. 'Attend me then. On Vosge – which has always been one of the poorest of the islands, with a small population of stoneworkers, weavers and fishermen – great pools of stinking black water have burst forth from the earth, as they once did in ages past.

'Now this is not as ordinary liquid, for when placed on water it floats . . .' he caught Tuan's startled look and nodded, 'Aye, it is lighter than water, and furthermore, it burns – even on water. Now the Vosgeans have been purchasing slaves by the score, and paying for them with small glittering black stones, the like of which exist only in the most ancient relics.'

'All this is very interesting; the black water could prove to be of some value . . .' Duaize said doubtfully, 'and the black stones of course, if they are precious . . .'

'To continue,' Paedur said, ignoring the interruption, 'and if I may digress for a moment,' he added. 'Ramm, the city atop the Wailing Cliffs, and not many leagues north of Maante – my destination – is besieged by a Count Palent with an army of mercenaries.'

'I have not heard of this Palent,' Duaize said. 'Has he campaigned before?'

'No, the count has but lately ridden forth from the marshes of Palentian, where he had his son trained in all manner of weaponcraft, and no doubt the count wishes to make some use of his son's new-found skills.

'However, Ramm is, as I have said, atop the Wailing Cliffs, and furthermore, it is built on a spur, which means it is unapproachable on the landward side save along a narrow road which winds its way up the cavernous cliffs, with a sheer drop to the crags below on one side, and the sheer wall of the cliffs on the other. This road is held by a small force of the Rammans, and thus the count, try as he might, cannot reach the city, and he has lost many men on the cliff road. But the count and his son hold the lower reaches of the road, and while he cannot get in, the Rammans cannot get out.'

'Then starve them out,' Duaize said quickly.

Paedur nodded. 'That is the obvious course, but Ramm has a reasonable supply of foodstuffs and is blessed with a freshwater lake in the caverns beneath the city.'

'It would seem it cannot be taken,' Suo-Ti said quietly. 'The Rammans have but to wait for the coming of the Cold Months, and then this count will be forced to flee with his tail between his legs.'

The bard shook his head slightly. 'Ramm, remember, is a stone city atop a barren cliff . . .'

'Fuel!' Tuan interrupted.

Paedur nodded again. 'Yes, fuel is certain to be in short supply, and the seasons are beginning to change. Surely the Rammans would pay good coin for . . .'

'The black water!' the captain shouted, rubbing his hands together. 'Bard,' he continued sincerely, 'sail with us, forget this mythical isle you seek, sail with us and your fortune, aye and several more besides, shall be made. You have that ability, rare even in the most seasoned commanders on land or sea, the ability to connect seemingly unconnected information, and weld it into a coherent whole.'

'The work of a bard is often to collect seemingly disparate tales and weave them into an ordered mythos,' Paedur said, unmoved by the captain's wild enthusiasm.

'Aye,' Duaize murmured, 'it must be so.' He turned to the mate. 'Tuan, rouse the crew, inform them that the bard has conceived a plan that will make our fortunes. Tell them to prepare for a raid on the morrow. Now, where are my charts? We need a small fishing village. My charts!' he suddenly roared, 'bring me my charts.'

'I will bring them.' Suo-Ti rose smoothly to his feet and moved silently down the craft. When he reappeared, he was holding a pile of ill-cured vellum charts against his thin chest.

Duaize snatched them eagerly, his hands trembling as he un-rolled them, spreading them on the deck and moving the light-bowl closer. 'Now, where are we . . .?' Suo-Ti tapped the chart with a long-nailed finger. Duaize nodded and continued. 'Here. Now we will raid . . . Tobb! Aye Tobb,' he went on, seeing the bard's inquisitive look. 'For barrels, casks, skins, urns, containers of every description. Then on to Vosge, the black water, and wealth.'

'A warning,' Paedur advised, 'the Vosgeans guard their black lakes jealously, for they worship them as being formed from the blood of Sleed, the Maker of Mountains. They call the black water Sleedor, and furthermore, I have heard tell that not all their guardians are human.'

'*HAH*!' Duaize roared, afire with visions of wealth, 'be they human or demon, beast or sprite, they will not stand between us and fortune, eh Tuan?'

'No captain,' Tuan said quietly, although his lack of enthusiasm was evident.

'And then,' Duaize continued, 'when we have filled as many containers – even the cooking pots if need be – with this Sleedor, then on to Ramm.' He stopped and looked across at Paedur. 'Is Ramm a rich city, bard?'

'It is built of common white smoat stone, but it is faced with red-veined black marble, and its temples are of rare red smoat and faced with ivory, and the roof of the Temple of Dannu is said to be made from thin sheets of worked gold.'

'Good, good.' The captain rubbed his small hands together furiously. 'The nights grow cold in these waters, do they not? That too is good, for a cold Ramm will pay more for the magic black fuel, eh bard? The rich cold Ramm will soon be a poor, warm Ramm,' he laughed loudly, almost drunkenly. 'Go now, go leave me. I have work to do. Navigator, stay awhile.'

Tuan bid the bard good rest as they both rose and moved away from Duaize who was now rocking back and forth on his heels, still studying the charts. 'I can't say I like this,' the first mate said quietly, glancing across at the bard.

Paedur looked back at Duaize and nodded. 'It's a risky enough venture.'

'But profitable?' Tuan asked with a smile.

'"There is no gain without loss, and oft much loss without gain,"' Paedur quoted.

The Taourg raided the island designated on the charts as Tobb just before dawn two days later. But, although they entered the natural harbour under cover of darkness, with oars shipped and all lights doused, merely drifting in on the morning tide, the village which clustered around a crude freshwater well just off the shore was deserted.

Duaize ordered the island searched, but the scouting parties that were sent into the interior all returned empty-handed. It was as if the villagers had disappeared, and Duaize had to content himself with ordering the entire village to be levelled, but not burnt, for he did not wish a tell-tale plume of smoke rising to the heavens and perhaps attracting the curious.

Also, the village was not particularly rich in barrels and casks and the Taourg had to content themselves with four large wooden barrels, which smelt strongly of fish, and two score small clay jars, which reeked of vinegar, sour wine and cheese.

Back on board the *Duneson*, the captain had raged and threatened to raid another island on the morrow, and another the day following that – as many as he needed to until they had gathered enough containers for the Sleedor.

However, Paedur had pointed out that the more islands they raided the more certain it was that the presence of the Taourg would be made known, with the result that Imperial warships would soon infest these waters. The bard suggested that the ship's main hold, which ran almost the entire length of the *Duneson*, be emptied, and its interior tarred, turning it into one huge watertight container. Thus the Sleedor could be carried from Vosge in whatever containers they already had and emptied into the hold. He added they were almost certain to find more casks on Vosge itself.

Duaize had grudgingly agreed, and the *Duneson* put in off one of the smaller Arrows for two days while the hold was emptied, the contents taken inland and concealed in a large cave, and the cave mouth sealed. When the Taourg had completed their business with Vosge and Ramm, they would return for their cargo.

Tarring the *Duneson* was a dirty, messy job, and soon the entire crew reeked of sulphur and pitch, and few escaped burns and scalds. However, when the mammoth task was complete, even Tuan, who had thought the idea unworkable, had to agree that it was the ideal solution to their problem, and that perhaps it just might work.

The *Duneson* then crept down the Arrows under cover of darkness; by day, they lay up in the sheltered bays of the smaller islets. Now that they were so close to their target, Duaize feared that a chance sighting of the distinctive Taourg ship with its triangular sail and snarling figurehead would bring the Imperial warships down on their heads.

And so, seventeen days after the sinking of the merchantman and the capture of the bard, the *Duneson* hove in sight of Vosge.

Dawn was breaking as the longboat beached on the rough Vosgean beach. The *Duneson* bobbed offshore, almost invisible against the night-dark sea and sky, stars still winking over its masts. Paedur, sitting in the bow of the longboat, gazed at the heavens where night was reluctantly giving way to day; the distinction was so sharp, he could almost trace the dividing line between the two. To the east the sky was ochre and gold, and the day promised to be both hot and dry.

There was a scraping of sand and gravel and the longboat shuddered. The four Taourg who had accompanied Tuan and himself jumped into the shallows and dragged the light craft up the shingle beach, stones and grit echoing against its sides, the sound shockingly loud in the dawn silence. Two of the Taourg then moved silently about the thin strip of beach, obliterating their own tracks and the gouge marks left by the boat in the shingle, while the others cut fronds from the encroaching forest to drape across their craft.

Paedur walked to the forest's edge and stared into the darkness. Dawn might be breaking behind them, but night still lingered within the fastness of the trees, and he doubted if the forest floor ever saw the full light of day.

The vegetation was subtropical for the most part, for the southern Arrows benefited from the 's Landa Drift out of the Itican Gulf. The two great islands further south, the Arrow Gates, Musen and Forme, the Silver Rock and the Grain Bowl, were completely tropical both in climate and vegetation. However, the middle and upper Arrows grew progressively temperate the further north they went.

The forest growth stopped barely one man-length from the water's edge, and consisted mainly of the small thick alm trees, which clustered about the perimeter of the beach, while behind them were the great laide trees that towered scores and sometimes hundreds of man-lengths into the sky, their thin stick-like trunks suddenly sprouting thick fluffy heads as they broke into the sunlight.

Dense matted undergrowth grew through the alm trees, an almost impassable barrier growing thickly back into the forest for about one man-length with wire-thin blood-vines and finger blossoms to the fore where they could catch the rays of the life-giving sun that penetrated the forest edge. Further in, however, the forest floor was devoid of vegetation save for the faded albino creepers that struggled upwards along the laide trunks and looped across from tree to tree, creating a vast network of criss-crossing vines, web-like in its complexity.

Tuan joined the bard at the forest's edge. He was swinging one of the large-bladed Chopt knives. 'I thought this might be handy,' he said. 'Which way?'

The bard pointed with his hook. 'Straight on; the going gets easier a little further in.'

Once they had hacked their way through the undergrowth with the Chopt knives, and the forest floor opened out, Tuan became aware of the absolute silence that hung over the forest. No birds sang, nor were there any of the red-furred apes that usually infested the southern Arrows. All the normal cries of the life and death hunt of the forest beasts were absent, and even the crashing of the waves was muted, as if they had passed through some veil that deadened all sound.

The Taourg, too, sensed the unnatural silence and grew restive and nervous, whispering uneasily amongst themselves, drawing closer together, fingering their short-swords and crossbows. When they reached a clearing, they stopped and looked to Tuan for direction and he in turn looked to the bard.

Paedur silently raised his left arm and, hook flashing dully in the light, pointed to the ground. 'There's a track here; it's an animal run, but an old one.'

The track meandered through the forest, but keeping roughly to a northerly direction. Once, they sank to their ankles in soft green-brown muck that lay over the forest floor. It sucked noisily at their feet, exuding a foul choking miasma with each step they took. The muck clung to their boots, drying and hardening swiftly to a rock-like compound that weighted down each step, until they finally stopped and scraped it off. But, ominously, the thousands of miniature insects that should have fed on this rotting soup were absent.

It was as if the entire forest were dead.

Suddenly the vague trail they had been following broke out into a broad uncluttered track – a road almost – that crossed their present route at right angles. Gesturing to the Taourg to remain where they were, Paedur stepped on to the road, and then knelt to examine the surface. Tuan joined him. 'What is it?' he asked, gesturing to the flat almost glass-like smoothness of the surface of the trail.

The bard tapped it with his hook. 'It's compressed earth. Look, you can make out the leaves and twigs – it's as if some great weight had passed over it. And see here, where the road curves upwards at the edge of the forest . . .' He pointed upwards. 'There also . . .' The trees on either side of the pathway curved away from the road, interlocking branches overhead cut through with the same cylindrical design. Those closest to the road looked unhealthy, bare of both bark and leaves. The bard stood and gazed down the roadway, and he suddenly got the impression of a great tunnel. He beckoned to Tuan. 'What do you think?' He nodded to the strange roadway.

The first mate looked down the length of the road and turned to look back along it, and then he called over Shode, who had been born and raised in the jungles of Rrank.

'Do you know what made this?' he asked, and was troubled to find his voice shook as he spoke.

The small pale-haired Rrankish tribesman swelled with his own importance, and began to bob back and forth on his heels. 'I like it not, sir, I'll tell you straight. To me – and I am experienced in these matters, as much as you or the captain is in matters of the sea – well, to me this has the look of a beast run. And I'll tell you further, I've yet to see the beast that could make a run that allows three men to stand abreast on it. And I'll tell you further, I don't think I'd like to meet that beast.' He shook his head violently, 'No sir, I would not.'

'Say nothing of this to the others,' Tuan warned the strutting Shode as he dismissed him, and then he turned back to the bard, his eyebrows raised in question. But Paedur just shrugged and no word passed between them. Tuan called the Taourg from the forest and put them in formation along the track, two men on either side, close to the forest, with himself and the bard in the lead, in the centre of the trail.

The mate joined the bard at the head of the group and then waited until they had moved a little away from the Taourg. 'Is it wise to follow this path; we could not hope to combat the beast that made this?'

'I do not think it is a beast,' the bard said quietly. 'There is no beast odour.'

'I can only smell the rotting vegetation,' Tuan spat, 'Ach, I can taste the filth.'

'It's strange,' Paedur mused; 'there is . . . there is not only an absence of odour, but also of vibration, there is no lingering aura as there normally would be.'

Tuan looked askance at the bard, his finger and thumb automatically meeting in a circle to ward off evil.

Paedur laughed softly. 'You need not fear me, I am not evil; you fear me because I am not as you, because I am different. Perhaps you hate me; "Hate and Fear are brothers in blood," as the proverb goes. But know this, Tuan, I am not the Duaiteoiri you think me, nor am I *quai* either. It is true that I am not fully of the world of man, but nor am I yet fully beyond the call of man . . .'

'What are you then?' Tuan whispered, feeling the chill sweat trickle down the back of his neck, even though it was stifling in the forest.

'I truly don't know,' Paedur said, sounding almost surprised. 'I inhabit the twilight world between god and man; I am a little of both, and yet I am neither.'

'Why do you tell me this?' Tuan asked.

The bard smiled slightly. 'Because . . . because I feel you will understand, because I think you are not fully in accord with the Taourg, and because I urge you to consider what you are now, and what you might become.'

Tuan nodded slowly. 'I have already considered that, but I will think about what you have said. And you can see what men cannot?' he asked, pointing to the trees.

'Aye, I can see beyond the physical,' the bard explained. 'All my senses are more highly attuned than those of man. You see – but I perceive.'

Tuan nodded slowly. He was unsure just how far to trust the bard, how much to believe what he said. They knew not what awaited them on the island, they were facing the unknown, but Paedur was an unknown quantity also. And he wondered which was the more dangerous; the island or the bard.

'What do you see here?' he asked finally.

'I see nothing. No, that's not true. I can see a lack of life. This is a dead area; furthermore, it has but lately died. Something passed by, probably that which created the pathway and leached the life from this part of the forest. And not only the life but the very essence of life, therefore preventing any hope of further growth.

145

Nothing will ever grow upon this path, the forest will never reclaim this wound through its heart.'

Paedur stooped suddenly and, with his hook, cut a thin sliver of the compressed leaves and twigs that composed their path. He crumbled the hard earth between the finger and thumb of his right hand, and then licked the dry, gritty dust.

Tuan stared, appalled.

'This land is poisoned,' Paedur spat, 'doubtless the rivers also. In time the entire island will die and become a barren waste. Warn your men not to eat any fruit they may find nor drink from any stream; should they be wounded, or even be scratched by a thorn for that matter, ensure that the wound is cleaned immediately, and that no dirt enters the cut.' He brushed his hand on his cloak and then, as if chilled, drew the cloak in around his shoulders. 'The sooner we leave this island, the better.'

As the mate passed on the bard's instructions, Paedur continued on down the trail, pausing every hundred paces or so to test the soil, still seeking some tiny pulse of life. But there was none.

The trail abruptly opened into a small circular clearing, surrounded on three sides by the forest and on the fourth by a slight rocky incline leading up to the slopes of the smouldering volcano that dominated the centre of the island.

Deserted tumbledown reed huts and the remnants of a log palisade littered the clearing. The forest had made some effort to reclaim the clearing, and the huts on its periphery were little more than shapeless mounds of dried grass pierced through by thin shoots of a dull leprous yellow growth. The huts in the centre of the clearing that clustered about the blackened remains of what must once have been the communal fire were larger and in better condition.

The pathway they were following cleaved right through the village, through two of the huts and out again into the forest beyond in a straight line. The two huts were flattened into the ground, the only evidence of their existence were the gaps in the circle of huts and the lighter coloration of the ground beneath where the pale straw had been crushed.

Tuan called Shode over. 'How long ago was this village abandoned?'

The Rrankish tribesman bobbed back and forth on his heels, twirling his long moustaches. 'Well now, I really couldn't be sure. Six moons certainly but no more, I'll wager. And I wouldn't say it was abandoned, no, not abandoned. More likely deserted, suddenly like. You see those stakes,' he pointed to the listing palisade that at one time had encircled the village, 'stakes like those; now they're not easy to come by. Blunt plenty of knives and axes in the sharpening of them. Now back home, when we moved camp, we took our stakes with us; when we got to a new place – rich pasture and the like – we just banged them down. These folk, though, they were in a hurry, else they would have been sure to take them with them. Strange, now I come to think of it,' he added, looking around, 'strange they didn't come back for them. Unless, of course, there were none left alive to come back.'

Tuan nodded. 'Aye, my thoughts too. Remember, say nothing to the men,' the mate's voice was flat and emotionless. He turned to the bard. 'I don't think we should go any further, Paedur. I fear neither man nor beast, but we've no idea what sort of creature we're chasing.'

The bard stared across the island, his eyes dark and hooded. 'I don't know either,' he murmured, 'but whatever it is, it is destroying this island.' He looked over his shoulder at Tuan. 'And when Vosge can no longer support it, where will it go then? No,' he shook his head, 'it must be destroyed.'

'How?' Tuan protested. 'It must be enormous, but beyond that we know nothing at all about it.'

'I think it must be connected in some way with the Sleedor pools. There are traces of Sleedor along this track; perhaps if the pools were destroyed, then the creature would die also.'

'Did you know about this creature when you suggested that we came here?' the mate asked suddenly, 'did you come here for a purpose . . .?'

Paedur smiled. 'No. But the gods move men such as myself to their bidding, as you would move the stones on a gaming board. It may be that they ordained that the *Duneson* should sink that merchantman, and thus capture me, therefore precipitating this venture.'

Tuan looked uncomfortable. 'I don't know,' he said finally, 'but it's true that I've never known the captain to spare an obviously poor prisoner before – no male prisoner, that is. If we're not within a day's sail of a slave market, then they're usually slain out of hand. And he went along with your plan with little objection; a plan which, in my opinion, is foolhardy in the extreme.' He suddenly shivered. 'It chills me to think that, even now, the gods may be watching us, directing our actions, and all to some obscure purpose of their own.'

But the bard shook his head. 'No, never to their own purpose – but man's. Their duty is to us, their worshippers. Should we cease to exist, so too would they. For remember the old commandment, "*Faith lends Substance*". So, you can rest assured, our mission on this island can only be for the greater good of man.'

Two crewmen who had scouted the deserted village returned and stood before Paedur and the mate. 'What did you find?' Tuan asked.

'The pathway continues off into the forest and thence downwards into a depression. We did not follow it there,' one said, and then the second man took up the report in the same expressionless monotone. 'There is another path leading upwards, there,' he pointed back towards the incline. 'It is overgrown and has not seen recent use. It leads to the mountain.'

Tuan looked to the bard. 'Which way?'

Without hesitation, Paedur chose the left-hand path, leading upwards.

The track wound up through entangled undergrowth, interwoven with stout vines, and Tuan had to caution the men against using their knives on the creepers, after the bard had severed one with a swing of his hook only to result in the earth beneath shifting and crumbling away. It seemed as if the creepers were actually holding the dry flaking rocks and soil together. Further up the slope, the vegetation thinned out and the going became easier. Soon they found themselves on a rocky trail winding up the mountainside. The forest on their right-hand side gradually fell away, until they were level with the heads of the feathery laide trees, and even these in time fell below them. To their left, the black volcanic mountain rose dark and threatening, pitted and scored with thousands of tiny cracks and rough-edged holes. Here and there hardy rock plants struggled for existence in some soil-covered corner.

The trail they were following gradually thinned down to a cinder ledge which crumbled in places, and this gave way to a thin strip of soft cinder rock and gravel barely a handspan across. Ahead, the ledge narrowed and rounded a bend in the rock.

They could go no further.

Paedur, who was leading, turned back to Tuan. 'I will go on. Around that bend the path broadens out on to a ledge from which I can look down on to the Sleedor pools.'

'How do you kno . . . No,' he raised one hand, 'I believe you. Will the path support my weight?' he asked, looking doubtfully at the crumbling strip of blackened cinders.

'I think not. However, you might climb around to the ledge.' He pointed. 'Up there and across. It would be difficult, but I think Duaize would like to have one of his own men report back to him. I am sure it would be better received than just my word.' Paedur looked up along the rough rockface, sparkling with many-faceted crystals. 'It would be a difficult climb; would you make it?'

'Bard,' Tuan laughed, 'I was born in Moghir, to the north and west of here, in Gallowan. I climbed cliffs like these before I was weaned.'

'Aye, perhaps.' The bard sounded doubtful. 'Well I will meet you on the ledge on the far side. Try to make as little noise as possible. Although this forest looks dead and deserted, I'm sure our presence here has already been noted. Be careful.'

Paedur turned and moved forward, swiftly, almost carelessly, cinders of blackened rock crumbling under his boots to fall hundreds of man-lengths into the trees below. The ledge almost disappeared as it rounded the corner on to the far side. Paedur placed one foot on to the path, sliding it gently along the strip, his long fingers almost delicately seeking a hold in the gritty rockface. He edged forward, pressed flat against the cliff, his face turned away from Tuan.

There was a crack, and then suddenly the ledge crumbled into fine black dust. Tuan cried a warning but it was drowned in the echoing roar of the rockslide as a whole section of the cliff face fell. The Taourg cowered back, coughing and choking on the fine grit. The bard had disappeared into a maelstrom of flying rocks and billowing dust. Boulders tore down into the forest below, crushing through the trees to bury themselves in the soft ground beneath.

As swiftly as it had begun, the rockslide stopped, the final rocks seeming to take forever to clatter off into the distance.

The black volcanic cinders gradually settled back on to the remains of the ledge, but the thin path on which the bard had been standing had disappeared.

And of the bard Paedur there was no sign.

9 *Quisleedor*

Daily this cursed hookhanded bard grows more dangerous. The crew fear him or respect him – it is one and the same. I would kill him, if I could afford to, but we need him for a little while longer . . .

Journal of Duaize, Captain of the Duneson, Taourg Corsair

The bard was dead!

Tuan breathed deeply, consciously loosening his grip which had tightened in shock on the rockface. He blinked dust from his eyes and spat, clearing his mouth and throat of the sharp gritty cinders. Looking down over the edge of the track, he could see a billowing cloud of dust in the forest below, marking the bard's grave.

The bard was gone – no-one could have survived that rockslide – and though he regretted his passing, Tuan had long ago learned not to mourn the dead. He would however send his men into the forest below to search for the body and give it a proper burial. He felt in some way as if he owed the enigmatic bard that much.

The small Rrankish tribesman stepped up beside him. He was brushing dust from his hair and there was a swelling under his right eye.

Tuan glanced at him, and then nodded to the bruise. 'Anyone else hurt?'

'Cuts and bruises, sir, cuts and bruises. Nothing serious. The bard . . .?'

Tuan shook his head.

'What do we do now?' Shode asked.

Tuan ran his fingers through his hair and beard. 'Duaize will want a report,' he said, tilting his head back and looking up along the cliff, 'and the bard did say that there was a ledge on the other side which looked down on the black pools . . .'

Shode looked up, and then glanced down into the forest below. 'It's a long climb – and an even longer fall,' he remarked.

'I know. Shode, take the men back down the trail and search the forest there,' he pointed to where the pall of dust still hung in the air, 'and try to find the body of the bard. Bury it and then wait for

150

me in that deserted village. Conceal yourselves and make no contact with the islanders. I will go back up the path and attempt to climb over to the ledge mentioned by the bard.'

'How long should I wait?'

'Until nightfall; if I'm not back by then, well then . . . then head back for the *Duneson*, and tell Duaize what happened here.'

Tuan waited on the path while the Rrankish tribesman led the three Taourg back down into the forest, and then he turned to face the black volcanic mountain once again. He shivered, for though it was drawing on for mid-morning and the sun rode high in a cloudless sky, this side of the mountain was still in shadow and harboured the early morning chill, and the bleak face of the volcano only served to enforce that chill.

He started back up the path to the point where the bard had disappeared. He would have to climb up two or three lengths, and then crawl across the rockface for another three lengths; then he would have to manoeuvre around the sharp angle to bring himself out on to the far side. Shaking his head slightly, Tuan spat on to his hands, found footholds and fingerholds and levered himself up.

Though he had boasted to the bard of his climbing prowess, his ascent up the rockface proved more difficult than he had imagined. The volcanic rock should have presented no difficulty to an experienced climber; the countless fissures and breaks in the cliff face were ideal handholds and footholds. However the rock was, for the most part, blanketed beneath a thick layer of powdered black ash that soon coated his hands and boots with a slippery gritty skin that prevented a sure grip. The rock was also diamond sharp in places, and fire-hardened splinters of stone gouged and tore at his fingers and hands. Several times the rock crumbled beneath his feet, leaving him pressed desperately against the jagged cliff face while dust and rocks rained down all around him. By the time he reached the bend in the cliff, he was coated in ash and blood, his shoulders and arms ached and the open wounds on his hands stung with every hold he took. Tuan dimly recalled Paedur's warning about getting dirt or dust in a wound. He looked at his hands, and then at the streaks of thickened blood that marked his path up and across the cliff face. 'Too bloody late now,' he muttered.

As he rounded the bend in the cliff, the sun's rays struck him full in the face, blinding him. Desperately he squeezed his eyes shut, still seeing the orange disc through his clenched lids. And then the rock shifted. He froze to the cliff face, knowing that any movement could send him flying back off the mountainside to the forest below.

When the dancing lights in his skull dimmed, he opened his eyes, blinking away the tears, and taking care only to look at the rocks under his lacerated hands he began to move again. He shifted his handholds to chunks of the darker, harder rock, wincing as they cut into his raw flesh and then he gently eased his way over the bend in the rock. Every movement sent stones and gravel rattling off the rockface beneath his feet. With the sun now warming his back, he climbed down the remaining man-length on to the broad ledge below. His questing foot found the reassuring width of rock and he collapsed exhausted on to the ledge, gently cradling his torn hands across his body, sobbing with relief.

But he knew he would never be able to make the climb back over to the other side.

He cursed the bard then for a fool, a madman, a crazed tale-spinner. He cursed the captain for listening to such crazed advice; he cursed himself for following it. They must have been bewitched, ensorcelled by that bard, that Duaiteoiri . . . Tuan's head began to nod and, as his vision darkened, his thoughts became more and more confused, dream and nightmare running together, with the bard flickering wildly in and out of both . . . he was a creature of Alile the Judge Impartial, come to pass judgement on the Taourg in general and himself in particular . . . was he a minion of the Destroyer, Maurug, or was he just Mannam, Death, in one of his many guises . . .? Finally he drifted off into a feverish troubled sleep.

Tuan felt the shadow that fell over him while still sleeping. The nightmares shifted and twisted, and now an immense furred black creature swung a huge scythe closer and closer to his face . . .

He awoke, his heart pounding raggedly, echoing the pulse in his throat and at his temples . . . and he focused on a pair of scuffed boots before his face. His heart almost stopped. Forcing himself to remain still, he took stock of his situation. He was alone on a broad shelf of rock, facing an unknown number of potential foes. He was armed with short-sword – no, he had left that behind in a cleft in the rock on the far side of the cliff, as it had proved too cumbersome. He was armed then only with one of the broad-bladed Chopt knives. Against that, his hands were cut and torn, and they had now stiffened; he doubted he would be able even to hold a knife. His shoulder muscles had locked and there was no feeling in his legs, for he had fallen asleep with them tucked under him. He wasn't sure if they would support him . . . perhaps he could suddenly push the figure off the ledge, but even if he rolled against the legs . . .

He stopped, realising he was contemplating suicide.

He opened his eyes a fraction again and peered between gummed lashes. Black boots, scuffed and torn as if they had climbed rock; brown trousers tucked into the boots, and a purple-lined furred cloak fluttering between the legs . . .

And Tuan knew of only one . . .

Abruptly he pushed himself to his feet and found he was staring into Paedur's hooded face! And then with a cry he pitched forward as his numbed legs refused to support him. The bard caught him under the arms and eased him to the ground.

'Gently, gently now,' he murmured, 'you've been hurt.'

Tuan shook his head, trying to clear it, then groaned aloud and pain lanced about his eyes and into his skull.

'I'll wager you never climbed a mountain like that before you were weaned,' Paedur said with a sly smile, taking both the mate's torn hands in his right hand and examining them closely.

Tuan groaned again and licked his dried lips with a tongue that felt twice its normal size and was coated with foul grit. 'I thought you were dead,' he croaked.

'Aaah no,' Paedur smiled wistfully, 'the god-sought, god-bought do not die so easily. Besides, Mannam and I do not care overmuch for each other's company.'

The mate shivered. Paedur spoke of the gods with an all too easy familiarity, as if they were real and he had met them. And what was even more frightening was that it was very easy to believe he had. Perhaps he was mad, but if he were mad and touched by the Nameless God of Madness, then surely that self-same god was even now enfolding the mate within his gelatinous paws.

'You're cold?' Paedur asked, unclasping his cloak.

Tuan shook his head vigorously, even though he felt as if his skull were about to burst with each movement. He didn't want the bard to bring his furred cloak anywhere near him; his nightmare image of a furred, scythe-wielding creature was still fresh.

Paedur looked from the man to the cloak and laughed softly, almost chidingly. 'You still fear me, you think me either devil or madman, or both. But I am neither.' His voice dropped and he seemed to look beyond the man lying on the rock. 'At one stage I feared that I was both; but I little realised what I had become then and what I was destined to become.' He shook his head, dismissing the memories. 'Now, your hands.' He took Tuan's right hand in his and stared intently at the wounds. There was a stab of pain and the mate tried to jerk his hand back, but the bard's long fingers tightened, holding it firm, his strength surprising. 'No, leave it.' His hard gaze caught and held Tuan's eyes. 'If your hand is not cleaned and healed, you will not make it back to the *Duneson*.' Tuan looked at his lacerated hands, encrusted with grit and volcanic ash. Already a pale fluid was seeping along the edges of the wounds.

'Do whatever you have to,' he muttered.

Paedur produced a handful of leaves, plucked from the few bushes that clustered about the sun-warmed ledge, and proceeded to wipe off the encrusted blood and dirt that covered the mate's hands.

He then spat on to the edge of his cloak and cleaned the wounds themselves, forcing them to bleed, wiping off the blood and dirt with his cloak. Then, holding the mate's right hand in his, he gently ran his hook over the open cuts. As the tip of the silver half-moon scraped along the wounds the skin burned, and then it seemed to flow, to melt. Tuan squeezed his eyes shut and clenched his teeth to keep from crying aloud as cold slivers of pain shot through his arm and chest. With an effort he forced his hand to remain in the bard's. Then the pain began to lessen, gradually dying off to a dull throbbing. When he opened his eyes, he found that the skin of his palm was criss-crossed with thick white lines, like half-healed scars.

'You must brace yourself now,' Paedur said calmly, placing his hook flat across the mate's open palm. Tuan nodded, and then felt the hook grow warm, pleasantly so at first, and then gradually becoming hotter and hotter, until it was almost unbearable. Sweat ran down his face, and he tasted blood in his mouth where he had bitten into the soft skin of his inner cheek. Suddenly the hook blazed intolerably, and he almost screamed aloud with the pain.

He took a shuddering breath, almost expecting to taste scorched flesh on the air, and opened his eyes, expecting to see his skin seared and crisped. But the air remained clean and when he looked at his hand again, it was whole, complete even down to the callouses that ridged the base of his fingers and the ball of his thumb. All traces of his wounds were gone.

Silently, Paedur took Tuan's left hand, and began the process again, first cleansing the wound, then drawing the skin together and healing the scars. But this time, Tuan thought the hook didn't burn his flesh so strongly. Even so, it was agonisingly painful. But once again his hand was whole. His breathing was ragged and he wiped sweat from his face, but when he began to thank the bard, Paedur raised his hook, stopping him.

'You have seen a measure of my power – word of which I would not like to have bandied about this ship. You will say nothing of this . . .' It could have been a plea or a threat.

Tuan nodded holding both hands up to his face, examining the flesh, and he assured Paedur of his silence. He was about to stand up when Paedur pushed him back. 'We will remain here for a short while. Stay alert; watch the skies for anything unusual. A cloud, a bird, aught that you consider . . . unnatural.'

'What am I looking for?' Tuan asked.

'I'm not sure.'

'What . . . what could come?' Tuan persisted, 'and where would it come from?'

Paedur stared out over the forest, looking into the sky. 'It would be one of the Trialdone, a sending of Trialos, the Usurper. They might come, if they caught the disturbance.'

'Disturbance?'

'I healed your hands by using the natural power from the place-between-the-planes, the Shadowlands, the Ghost Worlds. Any use of the Power, even such a minor draining of the Ghost Worlds, disturbs them with ripples, like a stone dropped into a pool. For those of human-kind with the Sight and Hearing, such uses of Power are noticeable, recognisable as a momentary chill, a shudder, or an overwhelming sensation that someone is looking over your shoulder. However, the non-humans, the gods and demons, lesser gods and spirits are very sensitive to the changes in the Shadowlands, and if they are curious, they might decide to investigate.' He rose on one knee and scanned the skies. 'I hope not. A Sending might warn whatever lurks below of our presence.'

'You mean because you used your power to heal me, that could have warned these others of our presence here?' Tuan asked.

'Yes.'

'But what are these others, these Trialdone, and why should they seek you out?'

'Oh, they would investigate any major use of Power, but it would be an added bonus for them if they could find me.'

'What would they do?' Tuan asked quietly.

'Kill me – or try to.'

'I'll fight for you,' Tuan said quickly.

Paedur laughed. 'Well, let's hope it doesn't come to that. What power I drew off was small, it would barely register in the Ghost Worlds, and hardly worth the effort on their part to trace it.'

'But how would they go about doing that?'

'First they would have to assure themselves that it is not one of their own people working; then they would have to quest through the rough and shifting greyness of the Shadowlands to track the disturbance to its source. Then they would have to open a window to this place and only then might they act.'

'What will we do if something comes?' Tuan asked anxiously.

'If something should come . . .' he shrugged. 'Well, although I might be hard put to defend myself, I should survive, I think. But you . . .' he shook his head slowly, 'I think not.'

Tuan drew his knife. 'Any lizard-winged Duaiteoiri that tries . . .' He stopped as Paedur began laughing.

'Sit, Tuan, sit. If they send anything, then rest assured that it will not try to take us by force of arms. You will not find yourself fighting a creature of flesh and blood. Probably the volcano will erupt, or this ledge will disappear in a landslide into the forest below; a storm will sweep us off the ledge or we shall be struck by lightning – or something equally unlikely.'

'That's not very reassuring,' Tuan said, with a wry smile.

'But it's the truth,' Paedur said gravely.

Tuan crouched down again, looking up at the cone above their heads, watching the sky for any hint of cloud and the sea for any creature or disturbance – anything that might herald the coming of the Trialdone.

But the volcano remained quiet and the sky retained its bleached metallic white-blue appearance, completely devoid of cloud, and the sea was calm, the waves broken by nothing other than the reflection of the sun's rays.

Gradually, he relaxed. 'Will anything come?'

Paedur shook his head. 'Not now. If they were coming they

would have been here by now. Perhaps the Trialdone have other things to think of and tracking through the Ghost Worlds is exhausting, both mentally and physically,' he added, almost to himself.

They sat in silence for a while, the bard with his back to the warm stone, his head bent, while Tuan knelt and examined his healed hands in fascination. Finally Paedur, rousing himself from his reverie, looked up, catching the mate's eye, and nodded to the edge of the cliff. He dropped down flat and crawled to the edge of the outcropping of stone. Lying full length on the rock, he parted the stunted thorn bushes that grew in the soft earth at the edge and pointed to the forest below. Tuan joined him.

'The Sleedor pools of Vosge,' the bard whispered.

There was a dry withered scrubland at the base of the cliff; diseased leprous bushes and trees that had rotted where they stood ringed a long deep bowl-shaped depression. In the centre of this bowl lay a vast shimmering black pool, surrounded by four smaller pools. Strange lights glinted within the pools and rainbow colours swirled lazily in wide swaths through the blackness. Otherwise, there was no movement, and the pools neither eddied nor rippled in the stiff offshore breeze. A strange vapour, like a heat shimmer, hung over the main pool, and this, too, seemed to be unaffected by the breeze. It was visible only in its distortion of the forest beyond. The four minor pools were connected to the larger pool by thin tendrils of the black Sleedor, which ran like shadows across the ground in short thin canals. The sun, now at its zenith, burned almost at the centre of the main pool, reflecting back in a strange, blue-green-white colour that dazzled the eyes – and lending the pool the appearance of a huge staring eye.

Grouped about the black pools were the ruins of a once sizable town, built in what must have been a series of concentric circles. With the main pool at the centre, the lines of the streets and remains of the encircling buildings were still clearly visible. In places whole sections of houses and streets remained standing, which managed to convey an impression of its former grandeur. As far as Tuan could see there were no signs that the town had been either attacked or sacked, and he got the impression that it had just been allowed to fall into ruin.

One building, however, larger than the rest, appeared to be in better repair. It stood almost on the edge of the main pool, a tall greenstone building, its massive blocks and mortar-less construction betraying its Culai origin, unlike the rest of the buildings which had been built some time later. However, it was surmounted by an elegant spiral, the top of which had been sheared off. That must have been a later addition, Tuan reflected, since the architecture of the First Race had no room for useless ornamentation. He also noted that a rough door and two equally crude windows had been broken into the side of the building, which led him to speculate whether the building – a temple obviously – was occupied or not.

The bard gestured with his hook towards the building. 'See there; that was once Culai-hewn, but the additions were made by the Vosgeans. The spire, that was never Culai built . . . but even so, it is old, crafted when the pools first made their appearance in the distant past, back when there were still craftsmen in the world. The Cult of Sleed were the first to settle on the island when they heard of the pools; they commissioned the spire from the native islanders.'

'The door and windows are even more recent,' Tuan said. 'There are still blocks of greenstone about the pools. But one thing is puzzling me. Where are the original doors and windows?'

Paedur parted the bushes and pointed to a cube of blank stonework. 'Look closely. Almost at ground level you can just about see the top of the lintel. See where the blocks are shaped . . .'

The mate nodded. 'The buildings are sinking!'

'Aye, and the main temple more swiftly than the others because of its proximity to the pool. The Vosgeans have broken open the doors and windows for whoever plays priests to the . . . to that which lives in the pools.'

Tuan pointed to the blackened streaks that covered the greenstone walls of the buildings. 'It looks as if the pools covered the building at one stage,' he said.

The bard nodded. 'Perhaps; and there is something rather unusual about this place – the buildings are older than the island.'

'That's impossible!'

Paedur smiled. 'Not really. You will find examples of Culai architecture on nearly every one of the Arrows. And if you should examine the seas about some of the larger islands, you may be able to see the outline of stone walls and roads on the sea bed. What is now sea was once dry land. The Culai built on it; then the land sank and was covered by the seas. Then, some thousands of years ago, during the Upheaval caused by the Demon Wars in the Southern Kingdoms, the shock waves rippled through the planes of life. On most planes there was wholesale destruction, but on others the land rose – such as it did here, creating the Arrow Isles. Some of them still had the Culai-built temples and roads which went down with them in the Cataclysm. Indeed, I have heard it said that the Arrows run along the site of an ancient road, the remains of which can be seen from the Musen Causeway. When the islands were settled by the fanatics, the fools and the gutter-scrapings of the Seven Nations, they either used the ancient buildings themselves, or took the dressed stones to build dwellings of their own.'

'I've often wondered about the massive stone temples and fortresses that stand isolated and forlorn on islands scattered among the oceans of the world,' Tuan mused, 'and of those mariners' tales which tell of cities and lights beneath the waves, and of bells that toll in the night far out at sea.'

'Aye,' Paedur said, 'the Culai left us many strange and terrible relics of their time. "The Culai Heritage", I've heard it called by some . . .'

'*Their day is done, their time is passed, let none mourn their passing,*' quoted Tuan from an ancient proverb of his homeland.

'No,' Paedur whispered, 'It is not finished yet; the age of the Culai still lingers. But soon . . . soon, it will end,' he prophesied. His eyes suddenly blazed and the air about him seemed to chill. He looked at Tuan, and his expression was hard and frightening, and he opened his mouth as if he were about to speak, but then he turned away in silence. He pointed down to the temple by the pool. 'See there, they worship dangerously.'

Tuan looked over the ledge. Above the rough wooden door of the temple, set into a rusted sword scabbard, a reed torch burned, the flame sputtering smokily, yellow, blue and green, glowing sparks spiralling to the heavens. 'What's wrong?' he wondered.

'On no account bring fire near to the pools.' He gripped the mate's arm for emphasis. 'The liquid burns far stronger than fish-oil.' Tuan nodded and rubbed his arm where the bard's iron-hard fingers had bitten into it, bruising the flesh.

Then, faint in the distance, a low murmuring began, rising and falling like the waves on the seashore, an ebb and flow of sound. It had the cadence of a chant, such as is sometimes sung in the great cathedrals of the Nations, but it was wordless, a mere droning on

159

two levels. It drew nearer, and Tuan and the bard were able to make out other sounds – low whistles and gutterul cries – that ran through the chant.

'It's coming from over there,' Tuan said, pointing off to the right, the east, to where the diseased scrub had been pushed back to form a path. He loosened his knife in its sheath.

There was a hoarse shout, and the chanting suddenly stopped, and silence once more fell over the forest. Paedur gripped the mate's arm again and whispered. 'No matter what happens, remain hidden. They must not know they are being watched.'

There was movement along the track, and then four white-robed figures stepped into the clearing. They were small dark-skinned men, and although their features were almost indistinguishable from that distance, Tuan thought they were Formenai, from the southernmost Arrows. Their robes had once been white, but were now soiled, encrusted with thick deposits of matted filth, and streaked with what looked like Sleedor stains. They moved slowly through the ruins of the Culai settlement, threading their way around the shattered remnants of the once massive palaces and temples along a pillar-lined route. When they reached the main building with its shattered spire, they stopped and bowed thrice to the guttering flame, and bowed again as they faced each of the four smaller pools, before turning back to the great pool in front of the large building.

Behind the priests came a small band of warriors. These were native Vosgeans, being taller, more robust than the priests, with lighter skin and straight hair. They were heavily armed with short spears and throwing clubs, and some had metal knives and axes. They wore armour of overlapping scales of lacquered wood, which gleamed with the same shimmer as the pools. Tuan quickly counted six of the warriors, and wondered why they needed weapons in this seemingly deserted place.

Then another larger group came down the withered track. Tuan suddenly swore and had begun to move when the bard pressed him flat, holding him down seemingly with no effort. 'Stay down,' he hissed, and then Tuan felt a strange dizziness sweep over him, and a tingling in his limbs. When the bard released him, Tuan attempted to rise, but he found his arms and legs were numb and useless. He could only watch in anguish as the four Taourg from the *Duneson* were dragged forward. They must have been captured in the village, he realised, and by trickery, too, since they seemed uninjured. He should have sent Shode and the others back to the ship but it was too late now.

The Taourg were herded forward by six more warriors. They had been shackled with manacles of what looked like stone, and were led forward by leashes of heavy metal links about their necks. Like *cuine* to the slaughter, Tuan shivered. They were separated when they reached the periphery of the pools, where the twelve guards broke up into four groups of three, each group taking one of the Taourg pirates to stand by the edge of the smaller pools.

When the prisoners were positioned before the Sleedor pools, the robed priests moved forward and, with arms raised high, began to chant in a shrill whistling tongue, totally unlike their earlier chanting. Simultaneously, one warrior from each of the four groups stepped up to the black water and dipped a spear into its glittering, glistening depths. They moved the spears back and forth in a deliberate weaving pattern, setting up a spectacular display of shifting lights beneath the surface. When they lifted their spears, they held them poised over the pools until the priests hurried over to them, each with a curiously worked metallic vessel, which they held under the spear points in order to catch the droplets of the precious liquid.

The four priests then turned and faced the temple, bowing deeply, the metal bowls held high in both hands. Something moved in the darkness of the crude doorway. The flame in the scabbard above the door flickered wildly as if torn by a strong breeze. Then a figure stepped out. He was tall, inhumanly so, and had to stoop almost double coming through the door. His skin was black, though not with the warm browns or soft blacks of the southern Arrows nor with the deeper shades of the Teouteuchalai further south but in a deep matt black almost the same colour as the Sleedor. His features were indistinguishable, though Tuan had the impression that they were sharp and angular, and when he opened his mouth to speak his teeth shone long and glistening white in the blackness of his face. His voice was slightly sibilant but sharp and piercing, the tongue that of the priests. When he raised his arms, his robe – a long white garment interwoven with black, silver and gold thread – slipped down his forearms, revealing a series of long sinuous tattooed curves that winked and sparkled in the sun, as if they had been worked in metal rather than ink. His fingers were tipped with long pointed nails, painted like a courtesan's with a black lacquer.

While the High Priest had been reciting, an absolute stillness had fallen over the priests, warriors and prisoners alike. They stood as if carved from stone, and Tuan wondered if they had been frozen by some magic, similar to that which the bard had worked on him.

The bard glanced over at him. 'Our power is similar, and yet dissimilar,' he whispered, 'for his aura is etched with evil. He controls a far darker power than mine, in keeping with his Gorge-spawned gods. Watch!' he hissed.

Below, the High Priest had finished his incantation.

Almost at once the pools became agitated, the disturbance starting with the main pool, and spreading outwards in slow languid waves. Large rainbow-hued bubbles rose to the surface of the pools, bursting with a noxious rotting odour. It was as if some great creature stirred and awoke in the depths.

And then the High Priest screamed a single word, bringing his hands together in an explosive clap. Immediately, those warriors whose spears still glistened with steaming Sleedor, stepped forward, bowed to the High Priest, then stabbed the four Taourg through the back, pushing until the spear-points protruded through their breasts. Then the Taourg, still impaled on the spears, were pushed into the pools.

The black liquid boiled furiously, the disturbance flowing in towards the main pool this time. Light exploded in cascading streamers within the pools, flaring and then dying slowly, and there was the sudden stench of charred meat. The slow waves gradually subsided as they rolled inwards, swirling as they entered the larger pool, as if caught in a whirlpool – but then this too, quietened.

The priests and warriors bowed to the smiling High Priest, and began to make their way through the ruins back into the forest. The High Priest remained in the doorway for a while longer, his head bent as if in prayer, then he turned and ducked into his tumbledown temple. Curls of weed and leaves gusted across the surface of the pools, but there was no other movement.

And silence returned to the island.

The fish-oil lamp swayed gently to and fro, illuminating the captain's cabin with moving shadows that leapt from wall to wall, giving them an eerie semblance of life. Tuan recited the day's events tiredly, reporting only what he had seen and omitting any mention of his own injuries or the bard's magic.

He drank deeply from a mug of rofion, and his speech was slurred though not with drunkenness. He was exhausted, a mind-numbing physical exhaustion that stemmed from what he had seen and experienced that day.

Following the sacrifice of the Taourg, and the disappearance of the priests and warriors, Paedur and the mate had remained on the ledge until the shadows had lengthened across the ruins below. The bard had held Tuan bound with his magic for a long time, fearing that the mate would have run amok below; he couldn't forget the almost casual sacrifice of the Taourg and the delighted smile of the High Priest. He had raged at the bard, cursing him in every tongue he knew, damning him to the Netherworld, Gorge and Abyss and every torment he could think of. But through it all, Paedur had merely smiled, until finally a mocking voice had spoken deep within the mate's head, commanding sleep. When Tuan had woken it was already mid-afternoon and a chill breeze blew across the ledge, bringing with it the promise of rain. The bard had at some time pulled him back from the bushes until he was in the shadow of the cliffs and had lifted the binding spell, so he was able to move again.

The climb back over the rough jagged cliffs had not been as difficult as the mate had expected. He was refreshed by his enforced sleep, and the bard had the knack of finding natural handholds and footholds in the cliff face, and at times it seemed as if they almost walked over to the other side. When they started the climb, Tuan wondered how Paedur would fare with only one hand, but the bard used his hook adroitly, cutting handholds in the sharp cinder rocks with great skill. 'You're good with that,' Tuan said at one stage, when Paedur had stopped on a tiny outcropping to allow the mate to catch up. 'And you've climbed before, I'll wager.'

The bard held up his left arm and allowed the half-moon to catch the light. 'Aye, I've grown accustomed to it – it's part of me now. And yes – I've climbed mountains before,' he added, with a faintly mocking smile.

However, it was a hard exhausting climb, and when they had reached the other side Tuan's strength left him and he would have fallen had not the bard caught him. Paedur had supported him down the barren track through the village back to the beach.

They had been met on the shore by a boatload of Taourg that had sailed with orders from Duaize to search the island and bring back the crew of the first boat – or their bodies. Tuan had fallen

163

into a fitful sleep as the Taourg rowed back to the *Duneson* through roughening seas. His mind had wandered in that half world between sleep and wakefulness, and he cried out more than once in terror at some waking nightmare that stalked him across the waves, until the bard had gently touched his forehead with his hook, and he had fallen into a deep dreamless sleep.

When the boat reached the *Duneson*, Tuan had awoken feeling refreshed, though he guessed that the bard had somehow bolstered his exhaustion with some reserves of strength, and he guessed he would pay for it later with complete collapse.

Duaize had been silent upon seeing only the two return, but had ordered them to be taken to his cabin, and food and drink brought. As Tuan gave his report, Duaize only broke the mate's monotone with the occasional question, and though the captain drank a great deal from a delicately spun crystal goblet, he betrayed no dulling of his awareness, and his questions were always succinct and to the point.

When Tuan finished, Duaize remained silent for a time, and the mate had dozed off in the heat of the cabin. At length the captain raised his head and looked at the bard, who had remained still and silent neither drinking nor eating, sitting swathed in his hooded cloak, as one with the shadows.

'You're costing me dearly in men, bard. What happened on that island?' he said almost gently, though his eyes were hard.

'Something that has not occurred on this island for a long time. A blood-sacrifice to Quisleedor, the Life Child of Sleed.'

The captain's knuckles whitened on the stem of his glass. 'Explain yourself, bard.'

'Quisleedor is the creature of the black pools, perhaps it even *is* the black water. It demands blood sacrifice else it rises from the pools to ravage . . . *Aaah*,' he hissed in satisfaction, 'that would account for the lifeless track through the forest. So, the creature has already risen . . .' his voice trailed off in contemplation.

'Bard, if I thought you knew of this Quis . . . Quis, Quisleedor, and did not tell me . . .' The stem of the goblet snapped between the captain's fingers.

'I knew of the pools, but not of the creature.'

'Then how do you know of this Life Child?' Duaize snapped triumphantly.

'I am a bard,' Paedur said simply. 'And the creation of the Life Child is recounted in many of my tales. Listen, and I will tell you of the birthing of Quisleedor.'

'Be brief then, for dawn fast approaches, and I intend to raid that island with first light, no matter what tale you tell, if for no other reason than to avenge my men. Sacrificed!' he spat. 'No pirate will be sacrificed and lie unavenged while the Taourg still sail.'

'Briefly then,' Paedur said, 'the tale of Quisleedor. A thousand years ago, in the Southern Kingdoms, there were those who contrived to worship neither the Old Faith nor the New Religion, but rather took as their gods those we call today the Demon Gods. Now these were not of this plane of existence, and their fashioning was neither by the One, nor the first Great Gods.' He looked from under his cowl at the captain. 'You understand these references?'

'Many men sail with the Taourg; many men and many faiths. I have sailed with the Taourg for almost thirty years, bard, and though I do not question a man's faith, as captain I must know a little of my crew's beliefs, for if they have served with honour, then, when their time comes, they should be hastened to their gods with all due ceremony. Aye, I know the legend of the Beginning and the creation of the Gods of the Pantheon. Continue.'

Paedur nodded. 'The Demon Wars were fought on two levels, that of gods and men. And the fields of Ab-Apsalom ran with the ichor of the gods as the fields of men ran with blood. Now there was one of the Elder Gods of the Old Faith, by name Sleed, and he was the Maker of Mountains, and his day was done, for nearly all his work had been carried out in the early days of this plane.

'And so now he rested.

'Now there came a time when the battle went against the Pantheon, and they called upon all the Elder Gods for aid, and Sleed was one of these. But in the battle that followed, Sleed took a mortal wound and even the ministrations of Ochrann could not heal his wound, for the blade had been poisoned.

'Thus the dying Sleed came to the Arrows, which had risen up during the Upheavals, and spent the rest of his days in solitude before he died here. And when men came to Vosge they saw that his blood had poured forth over a rocky wasteland in large black pools – for the blood of the gods was not like that of men, and differs in texture and colour.

'And those pools came to be worshipped as the blood of Sleed.

'However there came a time, not long after the island was settled, when a beast roamed Vosge, destroying all in its wake, and where it had been was marked by total desolation and naught would grow there until the area had been cleansed with fire, and the soil replaced.

'And the Vosgeans traced the beast back to the Sleedor pools, and thus they reasoned that whatever lived in the black water must be the Child of Sleed, a child perhaps created by the death of the god, thus the Life Child of Sleed: Quisleedor.

'Furthermore, they found that if a sacrifice, a blood sacrifice were offered regularly to the creature, it did not rise. And so the priesthood of Quisleedor came into being, but the High Priest was invariably of the Susuru, for they are not wholly of the race of man and can commune with the beasts without harm to themselves, and their special gift is the taming of all creatures, be they flesh and blood – or otherwise.'

'The tall one, with the blackened skin and tattoos; he is of the Susuru?' Duaize interrupted.

'Aye,' muttered the bard, and his voice sounded troubled. 'He is Susurun; I had not thought any of that cursed race still lived. But to continue. Five or six generations ago the Sleedor pools disappeared almost overnight, and with them the Life Child also. The Cult of Sleed went the way of all godless faiths, and the native Vosgeans returned to their primitive animalistic beliefs. Now, during the time of Quisleedor, the priests had not allowed anyone to leave the island but only those duly approved by the High Priest, and even then they were chained to the island by the priests with bonds of *geasa* far stronger than iron. Thus the island regressed and the people inbred almost to barbarism and imbecility.'

'And nothing more was heard of this Quisleedor?'

'Nothing. It was as if he had never been. But now it seems, with the re-emergence of the pools, the Life Child has awoken and with it the Cult . . .' the bard's voice trailed off. 'But there is one thing I would like to know. Where did the Susurun come from?'

Duaize shrugged. 'Who knows? Perhaps he is somehow linked to the creature in the pools. When it sleeps, he sleeps. Maybe we'll find out later.' He paused and breathed deeply. 'So, it seems there is a creature in the pool with a liking for flesh and blood that leaves a trail of desolation in its wake whenever it emerges from its hold, and all this is watched over by an inhuman High Priest?' Duaize summed up.

Paedur nodded absently.

'Somehow, bard, I do not think draining the pool is such a good idea. Ramm can wait a while longer. We must withdraw and draw up a plan. The creature must be lured from the pools. We'll need a . . . a . . . a net of some sort. No, not a net, a great cave perhaps . . . aye, and we'll coat the insides with pitch, and we'll trap the creature, and then toss a torch inside.' He nodded. 'Aye, we'll sail for . . .'

'No!' The bard rose to his full height and glared down at the captain. 'I have wasted enough time on this affair for you. I have but one moon to reach Maante, I cannot afford to delay any longer. Either you raid Vosge on the morrow or you sail for the Aangle Peninsula. It's a simple choice.'

'Damn you,' Duaize shouted, leaping to his feet and hurling the glass goblet at the bard. 'No-one tells me what I do on my ship.'

The glass shattered on the bard's hook, the sound bringing Tuan awake. Still not fully conscious, he seemed to hear the bard's voice rumble around the room like distantly heard thunder, echoing within his head, powerful and commanding. 'You, captain, will do as I say. And you will raid that island on the morrow because I wish to get another look at those pools, and the Susurun – particularly the Susurun. Then you will take me to Maante, and then – and only then – will you return to Ramm where you may sell your Sleedor – if you get any in the first place. Whether you get the black liquid tomorrow or not matters little to me; we are to sail from here on the evening tide. My mission is of the utmost importance. And should I fail, well then, Ramm will never need its fuel and you will have lost nothing. Have I made myself clear?' he demanded.

'We will raid Vosge for the Sleedor on the morrow, and we will sail for Maante with the late tide,' Duaize replied woodenly.

'Just so,' Paedur smiled, 'just so.'

10   The Burning of Vosge

Four more men dead; perhaps the bard is a *deiz* – what the westerners call a Duaiteoiri . . .

Journal of Duaize, Captain of the Duneson, Taourg Corsair

Paedur parted the dead undergrowth and pointed across towards the ruins surrounding the shimmering black pools. 'That is the main temple and as such is to be avoided. The guards will enter along the path yonder and then take up positions about the four smaller pools. So if you . . .'

'You need not tell me my job, Hookhand,' the captain snapped, though he was careful not to meet the bard's eyes. He felt uncomfortable being so close to the bard; his memories of the previous night were hazy and indistinct, and their very unreality made him nervous, convincing him that he had been spellbound. He could recall talking with the bard following Tuan's report, but then . . .

When he had awoken the following morning, he had apparently given orders that Vosge was to be raided with the full complement of the *Duneson*'s fighting men. He had also given Suo-Ti instructions to plot a course to Maante, following the raid – no matter how it turned out. He could not, however, remember giving those orders.

What could he do? He could not say he had been ensorcelled by the bard again. No crew would respect a weak-willed man, and a strong will, he imagined, should be able to resist any spell, so he was trapped into following his own orders . . .

Duaize turned to Tuan. 'Divide the men into five groups, one to each of the four smaller pools, the other to guard this trail. Conceal the barrels and skins in the ruins, and then wait for my command.' Tuan nodded briefly and disappeared back along the track.

The *Duneson* had beached under cover of darkness and Duaize had led the crew ashore, carrying the casks and barrels with them. Tuan and the bard had then led them along the path they had cut through the forest the previous morning. When they reached the strange dead track they paused while Paedur tested the ground. He looked up at the captain. 'Men have passed this way late last night.'

Duaize nodded silently, feeling the hairs at the base of his neck rising. He didn't know how the bard knew – nor did he want to.

When they came to the village, the captain had ordered the tumbledown huts searched. They were all empty, save one. It held the skeletons of two children; in both cases the skull had been shattered and the spinal cord snapped across. The bones gleamed as if they had been polished, displaying not the yellow ivory of age but rather a bleached almost chalk-like appearance; like chalk also, they crumbled at a touch.

The bard had then led them down the second of the two tracks leading out of the village, the right-hand path, following it to a curve in the forest, where the vegetation began to sicken and die. Soon the great trees were gone, and those that remained were spindly and diseased. The undergrowth paled, the rich greens of the deeper forest giving way to a pale yellow-green, and thence to a dried and seared grass-like weed that waved gently above their heads.

Soon, they came to the first half-buried blocks of the Culai buildings that even in ruin towered above their heads. At one time the forest must have completely claimed them, hiding them beneath a thick carpet, but the vines and creepers were now dead and hung like old ropes from the walls. As they walked through the dead ruins, Paedur took Tuan by the arm and pointed to the side of one massive edifice. 'Remember what I told you yesterday . . .' he said softly. Along one mortarless seam clustered the rocklike remains of barnacles and sea urchins – proof that these buildings had once rested beneath the waves.

They continued on deeper into the ruins, moving towards the shattered spire of the temple.

The vegetation finally gave out as they neared the Sleedor pools, and now even the stones began to take on a scaled, flaky appearance, as if they too were rotting away. And while those buildings closest to the forest were still recognisable as having once been dwellings, those bordering the pools were merely chunks of ragged, misshapen stone.

Duaize began to mutter orders, and his men slipped away singly and in groups, taking up position around the pools. Paedur and the mate crept nearer to the main temple, seeking shelter where they could behind the great huge tumbled blocks, flitting from shadow to shadow across the open spaces, until they were almost directly opposite the temple door.

'Will the Susurun not sense us?' Tuan asked, peering over the rim of a shattered column of dressed stone.

Paedur pulled him back and the mate heard something like anger touch his usually calm voice. 'Stay low; we cannot afford to be caught now.' He looked back across the desolate ruins, seeking any sign of the concealed men. 'No,' he replied finally, 'the priest will not know we are here. He should still be concentrating on the creature and yesterday's sacrifices. Aye,' he continued, seeing the mate's puzzled stare, 'he draws on the departing life essence of the sacrificed, taking it to himself, and thus prolonging his own life.'

'Undead!' Tuan shuddered. '*Vampire*; we have them in my homeland.'

'Undead yes, but not *vampire* of the blood-sucking type. He feeds upon emotional energy.'

'I'll kill him,' Tuan spat, 'leeching the living like a damned parasite.'

The bard laughed softly, almost mockingly. 'You? Impossible!'

Tuan opened his mouth to reply, but the bard raised his hand. 'No, Tuan, don't even think of it. The Susurun would blast you before you had even neared him. And,' he continued ominously, 'he would feed upon your essence, your emotions, your soul, if you will. You would then be condemned to the Gorge to wander and howl with the damned.' His eyes caught and held the mate's. 'No, don't even think of it. The Susurun, I think, is beyond even my power, for we are evenly matched, and neither he nor I could defeat the other. His doom is yet to come, and the doom of a Duaiteoiri is not pleasant to contemplate,' he shook his head slowly.

'He is a Duaiteoiri then, a minion of the Duaite, the Evil Ones?' Tuan asked.

'Aye, those of the Auithe do not pervert their powers. We do not need to steal the life essence of others to prolong our lives.'

'What of his gods . . .?'

The bard grinned mirthlessly. 'His gods are long since dead. When the Susuru died out, their gods died with them. There is a saying in the Northlands, "*There is no Substance without Faith*" – you must have heard it?' Tuan nodded. 'Gods need the worship of man; should the faith be questioned and the worship slacken, then the gods weaken and will eventually die. Thus it was with the gods of the Susuru; with no-one to worship them, they died out. No; I think the priest worships some of the primeval gods that still roam the darker corners of man's faith. Perhaps he worships even Quisleedor itself,' he added softly.

Tuan shivered although the sun was already baking the stones; this talk of gods and devils chilled him. The bard spoke so convincingly of their existence . . .

'Forever doubting,' Paedur chided, 'yet fearful of the truth.'

The mate said nothing.

They waited in silence while the sun slowly crept towards its zenith. The air was thick and heavy, redolent of the sharp odour from the pools that caught at the throat and stung the eyes. The rock basin, trapped between the cliff and surrounded on three sides by the forest, contained the heat, the stones soaking up the sunshine until they were almost unbearable to the touch, radiating it forth in wave upon suffocating wave until even the Taourg, accustomed as they were to heat, were bathed in sweat and every water skin was empty.

Tuan awoke from his doze with a start. How long had he slept? Where was the bard? The crunch of gravel made him turn suddenly, whipping out his knife.

It was the bard. 'You're awake then. I've just been rousing several of your crewmates,' he answered the mate's unasked question. 'Hah! The fearsome Taourg pirates sleeping on a raid.' His eyes twinkled with mischief.

Tuan grinned. 'We're not all demi-gods. Some of us need to eat and sleep; you know – the normal things of life.'

Paedur was suddenly very serious. 'Aye, the normal things of life.' He glanced up into the sky, and then peered over the edge of the stone, towards the temple. 'It's almost time.'

Even as he was speaking the murmuring became audible, thrumming faint in the distance. The deep silence that blanketed the island seemed to thicken with the sound, as if the noise added an extra dimension to the silence. The chanting grew, deepened, assuming an almost pulse-like beat, broken by the same deep-chanted growl and raucous cries that they had heard yesterday. As it grew nearer, the cries became clearer, beginning to sound almost bestial.

Tuan felt the bard stiffen by his side. 'What are they saying?' he asked.

'They are calling upon the Duaite of a thousand faiths, bidding them come forth to serve Quisleedor,' the bard whispered, aghast. 'Careful now, the priests are coming!'

The priests emerged from the forest, into the ruins.

Tuan flattened himself against the rock, his knife slipping in his sweat-dampened hands, his heart pounding like a youth on his first raid. The bard had pulled his cloak tighter about himself, and even in the full light of the blistering sun overhead, he resembled no more than a shadow.

The mate briefly glimpsed the four Formenai priests winding their way through the ruins following an obviously ritual path, their harsh shouts contrasting with the low mumbled chant of their followers. Abruptly all sound ceased, and Tuan guessed that they had reached the pools. The bard had stood up and was crouching over the stone, peering across the open square. Tuan slowly raised himself up and joined him.

To their right stood the main temple, the scabbard-held torchlight flickering wildly although the air was still. Before them lay the four Sleedor pools, arranged in a rough circle about the main pool, and before each pool a dark priest stood and bowed repeatedly to the main temple. The Vosgean guards stood behind them, staring blankly ahead, their eyes dead in their heads. And chained and manacled by the pools were the sacrifices – four young women.

Tuan gripped the bard's arm. Paedur nodded slowly. 'We have come just in time. They're virgins, I'll wager, and a virgin sacrifice would surely rouse the Life Child as nothing else would. The essence of the Unsullied would grant it power beyond imagining,' he whispered urgently. 'The sacrifice must not take place. Duaize must attack now.'

'He will give the command as soon as the Susurun appears,' the mate replied. 'Where did they get those girls from,' he wondered, 'they are neither Vosgean nor Formenai?'

The four girls were tall and slender, taller than the Formenai priests, topping even their guards. Their skin was pale, almost translucent, and their white-gold hair reflected the black water. Their features were small and delicate, their eyes wide and blue, but they showed no fear. They faced the pools calmly, heads erect, proudly accepting their fate. Their robes had once been pale blue though now they were soiled and torn, but the girls wore them as if they were robes of ceremony. About the neck of each hung an intricate amulet depicting a stylised hand clutching a flame.

'Priestesses of the Mother Dannu!' Paedur whispered.

'From Thusal,' Tuan added, 'probably shipwrecked, though what they should be doing so far south is beyond me.'

The bard's voice was cold. 'I don't think they were shipwrecked; I imagine they were kidnapped for this very purpose. Taken from the Northlands and brought south so they could not mindcall their sisters. Probably held in thrall to prevent them calling on their mother, the Lady Dannu. Had they been unprofessed girls, it would have been bad enough, but these are trained priestesses of the Mother.' He turned to Tuan, 'I can see the hands of the gods in this.'

'You see the hand of the gods in everything,' Tuan snapped. Then he shook his head and sighed. 'I can see that it would be too much of a coincidence,' he agreed. 'I don't think I like being manipulated, Paedur,' he added.

'You get used to it,' Paedur said with a tight humourless smile, 'and it is for your own good.'

'And that of the gods too, I'll wager.'

'That too, always that.'

The chanting died and the priests in their soiled robes faced the door expectantly, awaiting their master. Suddenly the flame above the door leapt as if fed with some volatile liquid, drawing all eyes. When the flame had died down the Susurun High Priest stood in the doorway. Tuan could see him clearly now and he felt his blood run chill, for the Susurun was undoubtedly inhuman. He recalled tales he had heard of the strange races that lived beyond the Land of the Sun.

Tales told by mariners who had sailed to the very rim of the world, and repeated in taverns for a jack of ale. Tales of the Starlorn, non-humans belonging neither to the seed of the gods nor the race of man, and belonging neither to the Star Folk, that are as gods but not gods, but rather of both. It is said that the Lorn inhabited the vast seas beyond Shemmat sailing forever in ships of purest gold and silver, crafts the size of islands. They had come . . .

'He is not of the *frai-forde*, the Starlorn,' Paedur whispered softly, breaking into his thoughts.

'How did you . . .? No! What then?' he demanded angrily. Was he to have no privacy? Were his thoughts to be open to this strange, frightening storyteller?

'I do not deliberately search for your thoughts, rather you send them about you in waves. I felt them because you were near me, and concentrating deeply upon the legends of the Lorn.' Paedur broke off as the Susurun began to chant in a high-pitched shrill tongue, the Formenai priests chanting the replies.

'But the Susurun,' he continued, 'is not of their race. His is an older, darker folk. The Susuru were akin to the Culai – some say they were even created by the Culai, the results of the sorcerous mixing of the essence of both base humans and beasts. And while the Culai could be wilful and thoughtless, they were not totally evil – unlike their creations. The Susuru worshipped the darker aspects of the Faith and delighted in evil, taking pleasure from senseless killing and torture. And through their arts they lived on for a while after the Culai died, though many died in the various cataclysms that warped the planes of life when the gods cleansed them of evil. Their gods were the darker side of the Pantheon; the true Duaite, vile bloated things that fed on the blood and violated life essences of sacrifices. But the Susuru were a fickle race and worshipped only those who could grant them the power they craved. When the Duaite's powers seemed to wane, they turned to other, wilder gods. It is said that behind every foul belief can be found the hand of a Susurun,' he finished bitterly.

'They are not human?' Tuan asked.

'No. Once perhaps, but over the centuries they have bred with the Gorge-spawn. Look!' he hissed.

The High Priest had moved out from the wall of the temple and was now standing not six manlengths from the Mate and the bard. His great height was added to by his extreme thinness, and his black skin – pure pitch in colour – seemed to absorb the light. He was completely hairless and his features were thin and angular, his nose sharp and jutting, eyes slanted like those of the Shemmatae and seemingly colourless, and his ears were without lobes. His teeth were filed sharp, like those of the island cannibals to the south or the northern Chopts. When he raised his hands in exhortation to whatever foul gods he now worshipped, his sleeves slid down his arms, revealing the strange metallic tattoos on his forearms. His long thin hands opened, his nails clawed the air, and he opened his lipless mouth to speak . . .

There was a sudden shrill piercing whistle and then the Taourg appeared in groups of twos from the ruins, bows and crossbows ready. There was another whistle – and they fired. Arrows and crossbow bolts screamed through the air, their irontips and barbs punching through the guards' lacquered wooden armour. Some fell forward into the pools and were pulled down by the weight of their armour and weapons, sinking with neither ripple nor bubble in the viscous liquid.

One of the Taourg dashed from cover across the shattered courtyard and grabbed the nearest priestess. She struggled until the realisation of what had happened sank in and then the four women turned and fled towards the forest.

Abruptly the minor pools erupted upwards in a huge gelatinous mass, their shapes vaguely bearlike. They seemed to claw the air and then the four waving black pools suddenly fell in towards the main pool, splashing across the ground. They fell short and immediately began to heave snail-like across the barren soil, trailing a shimmering rainbow-hued ichor. They slid – almost simultaneously – into the larger pool without a ripple. Initially nothing happened, and then, just below the surface, lights and spots of colour began to dance and shift. A ripple disturbed the surface of the pool, the thick, glutinous liquid shuddering like flesh.

The Susurun screamed, a single bone-chilling mind-numbing word that trembled on the air. Arrows buzzed about him, bursting into flame when they came too close, but he ignored them, his attention caught between the fleeing priestesses and the troubled Sleedor.

And then the pool rose.

It lurched up in a vast sinuous curve, resembling nothing so much as a giant serpent. Light and colour rippled down its length, pulsing and throbbing like internal organs. Its body was as thick as the *Duneson*, tapering slightly towards the 'head', but there were no features. It swayed above the pits that had once held it, then dipped down and nudged the bodies of the fallen Vosgean guards and Formenai priests alike, and when it had passed the bodies had been stripped of all flesh, leaving naught but gleaming polished bones in its wake.

'Quisleedor!' Paedur gasped.

The Taourg commenced firing on the creature, but their arrows had no effect – merely passing through its skin to hang, still clearly visible, within the body of the Life Child. Several of the pirates who had run forward intent on filling their containers with the black water, now stood frozen in shock. Duaize, standing at the edge of the ruins, with the four priestesses about him, shouted for his men to return.

But too late. The great head of the creature swung down,

seemingly to merely brush the men, but when it had passed the Taourg were little more than skeletons, their flesh stripped off the bone. Tuan saw one man, his arm nothing more than bones and strings of muscle but otherwise untouched, scream and scream again, until someone mercifully put an arrow into his throat.

The Susurun began to chant again, his voice rising and falling urgently. A pale white fire began to flicker about his head and extended arms, pulsing in rhythm with the light within the Life Child.

Paedur suddenly gripped Tuan by the arm. 'We can destroy the Susurun now, while his attention is elsewhere. Come!' He leaped from his hiding place and ran swiftly towards the High Priest. Tuan was up and running after him almost before he knew what he was doing. When he understood what he had done, he suddenly realised that he had just made a commitment to the bard in this and in all things – should he survive.

A ripple ran through Quisleedor and the Susurun began to tremble visibly; the creature's 'head' shifted towards the High Priest, and slowly he began to turn to face his attackers. The bard was nearer now, his long black cloak flapping behind him like wings, his feet seeming barely to touch the rocky ground, neither stumbling nor slipping on the loose soil.

And then the High Priest's eyes flickered open and he smiled hideously. The white fire suddenly blazed about his head, lending it a skull-like appearance. He extended one arm and the white fire snaked along it, trembling at the tips of his long black nails. A bolt of light spat towards the bard. Paedur allowed himself to fall to the ground, and the light sizzled over his head. It narrowly missed Tuan, but the heat alone as it passed was enough to singe his hair and beard. It finally splashed against a listing wall which immediately collapsed, and the fire continued to burn on the bare stones for a long time afterwards.

The Susurun raised his arm again, this time holding his palm cupped. A ball of white fire began to form there. Then the fire wavered, suddenly becoming veined with bright blue threads. The Susurun screamed as the white fire about his head was shot through with blue sparks, then long tendrils of the blue fire suddenly engulfed the white, turning it a pale blue colour. Now the fire no longer burned about his head, it was actually stuck to his skin, burning. The High Priest opened his mouth to scream, but then Paedur was on him. Seemingly oblivious to the heat the bard

176

raised his hook, shouted at Tuan to go, and then brought his silver hook down upon the Susurun. The hook sparked on making contact with the blue-fire but the fire was abruptly extinguished in the blood of the last of the Susuru.

With the death of the High Priest, Quisleedor was masterless. It hovered about the vast bottomless pits that it had inhabited, nosing the bodies of the slain. Then, as if it had made a decision, it lurched in the direction of the captain and the four priestesses. They turned and ran.

Paedur turned and grabbed Tuan by the arm, dragging him in the direction of the forest, calling on the Taourg nearest him to follow. They plunged through the seared undergrowth, the bard leading the way, angling away towards where the captain, the priestesses and the remainder of the crew must emerge. They burst on to the path used by the creature just in time to meet Duaize and the others round the bend in the path.

'To the shore,' Duaize gasped.

'We must leave this path,' Paedur said urgently. 'This is its run.' Without waiting for a reply, the bard led them across the path and into the depths of the forest, his hook flashing in the twilight, clearing the vines and creepers that barred their way. Without question the four priestesses of the Mother followed him; Tuan paused a moment, then he too followed the bard. The remaining crew looked at the captain. A tearing crash back along the track decided them, and they followed the bard into the forest.

Just as the last man dived off the track, the creature lurched into view, a vast undulating black column gliding swiftly along the track. It paused when it reached the point where the bard had led the others off the track, and swayed to and fro indecisively. A violent shudder ran down its body, and then it fluidly divided in two, one column continuing on down the track, the other smashing into the forest, following the fleeing Taourg.

Duaize called for a halt when they reached a small sundappled clearing in the woods. He was breathing heavily, as were the rest of the crew, and the priestesses looked close to collapse. The bard alone remained untroubled, his breathing even. 'We must continue, Quisleedor will come.'

Tuan began to count the stragglers as they came in.

'We can go no further, bard,' Duaize gasped, 'we must rest.'

'Nearly two thirds missing,' Tuan reported to the bard. 'They may turn up on the beach, but . . .' he left the sentence unfinished. They both knew the missing men would not be turning up on the beach.

Duaize rounded angrily on the bard. The Taourg was pale and shivering, and there was a bloody froth on his lips where he had bitten into the soft flesh of his cheeks. 'I hold you responsible,' he screamed. 'My crew lost, and all for what? Nothing . . .' A high- pitched scream – abruptly silenced – suddenly tore through the forest. In the silence that followed, Paedur turned to the priestesses. 'We must go. I know you're exhausted, but Quisleedor approaches, and you must call upon the Mother for strength.' He called Tuan over. 'We'll move again; we'll try and circle around to the beach. I am entrusting the priestesses to your care. Should any one of them fall behind, then you must kill her.' He caught the mate's jaw in his right hand and turned his head, so Tuan was staring directly into the bard's eyes, and continued, 'You must. They cannot be allowed to fall into the hands of the Life Child.'

'I cannot,' Tuan whispered.

'You must,' the elder priestess said. 'For our sakes, do not let the creature take us. Promise me this.'

Tuan looked from the four young women to the bard. 'I have learned to trust you, Paedur,' he said. 'If you say this must be done, then I will do it.' He bowed to the priestess.

Paedur turned and ran into the forest, followed by the priestesses and Tuan. Without waiting for any command, the Taourg followed him.

The captain pulled his sword free. 'Come back; we'll fight it here. Come back. This is mutiny. I'll kill you Paedur!'

And then, with a crash the Life Child broke into the clearing, its head reared high, its underside stained crimson. Duaize took one look, then he too turned and ran.

The forest began to thin out as their path led them uphill. Soon they were stumbling over small rocks and boulders set into the undergrowth, and a sea breeze began to ruffle the leaves. After the cloying stench of the Sleedor pools and the thick forest odour, it smelt like incense. The crash of the surf grew louder and the tang of the salt sharper while the incline became steeper and the climbing more difficult, though they were still in the forest and the ground underfoot was soft.

The forest ended abruptly, and the ground levelled out in a wide green swath of gently waving grass. But the grass was barely four man-lengths wide – for they were on a clifftop overlooking the sea.

Tuan looked helplessly at the bard. He had come to think of him as almost godlike, and now he had led them here to the cliff edge where there was no way down, and no way back save through the forest in which Quisleedor roamed.

They were trapped.

Paedur began to arrange the men in a semi-circle about the four priestesses, placing them as far away from the forest as possible. The Taourg were pitifully few, Tuan realised, too few to stand against the Life Child, but he doubted even if the full complement of the ship's crew would stop the creature. He walked to the edge of the cliff and looked down. It was at least sixty man-lengths – and more – down to the sea. To his left, the *Duneson* bobbed gently at anchor, toy-like in the distance. Directly below, the shore was broken with jagged remnants of a rockslide. The waves foamed and crashed about spears of rock which rose like pointing fingers and numerous eddies swirled about sunken rocks. Anyone jumping off the cliff would be dashed to pieces; there was no escape.

There was movement in the forest behind them, and then trees began swaying and falling, crushed by the weight of the creature, stripped down to the pith where its flesh touched them. A shadow moved within the cover of the trees where Quisleedor, smaller now, waited . . .

Duaize panted up to them and collapsed on the ground. Then he suddenly jumped to his feet and pointed. 'Look!' His voice was a shriek. In the distance, trees were swaying and falling in a long snaking trail that was headed in the direction of the gleaming blackness of the serpent creature below.

Paedur nodded. 'I see it,' he said softly, sounding almost pleased. He glanced around as Tuan joined him. 'The creature divided, it will soon re-join,' the bard said, and Tuan once again realised his question had been anticipated.

The rending crash of falling trees grew nearer as the second creature closed in. Then the trees at the periphery of the forest fell and the second Life Child appeared briefly. Within the cover of the forest, the two shudderingly melted into one. Quisleedor was complete once more.

Paedur passed from archer to archer, giving instructions.

The captain shouted at him. 'What's the use? Arrows have no

effect on it. Better to leap from the cliff than to die by that.' He pointed a trembling hand at the shape within the forest. Suddenly he turned and began to run towards the cliff. One of the priestess screamed and Tuan turned, striking out at him as he passed, catching him in the small of the back. Duaize fell moaning to the ground. One of the young women knelt by his side. 'Do not waste your life thus. Better for you that a shipmate slay you than you take your own life.'

Duaize looked up at the mate standing over him. 'Kill me, Tuan. Please kill me. Don't let that thing take me,' he pleaded.

Tuan looked helplessly at the bard, but Paedur shook his head briefly. The mate looked down at the captain. 'I'm sorry. I cannot kill you.' He walked over to the bard. 'I think he may be right; better we all leap off the cliff,' he muttered.

'All is not quite finished,' Paedur smiled. 'Wait.'

Quisleedor burst from the forest, branches and leaves showering off its back, some of them sinking into its flesh. It began to undulate up the slope. Behind it vegetation rotted and blackened, rocks crumbled to fine powder and a foul miasma floated up the slope.

The first row of archers fired and immediately pulled back. Although their arrows struck home they had no effect. The second line of archers also fired, and then they too pulled back. The third line was level with the bard. 'Fire on my command only,' Paedur ordered. The bard then took a flint from his belt pouch and kneeling, struck sparks from it with his hook on to a small pile of leaves. The leaves began to smoulder; gently he blew on them, coaxing them to a flame.

And Quisleedor approached.

Suddenly the leaves burst into flame. The archer nearest the bard stooped and snapped the iron head off his arrow, dipped the wooden end of the shaft into the flame, gently coaxing the broken head to burn.

Quisleedor reared, huge and black in the sunlight.

The rest of the archers turned and ran back up the slope, surrounding the four priestesses. Tuan loosened his knife in its sheath and wondered whether he would be able to kill the four young women. Duaize cowered, whimpering, on the ground.

The massive head began to descend.

Paedur touched the archer's shoulder and the young man raised his bow, the arrow tip sparking brightly, a thin tendril of smoke drifting almost lazily up from it.

Paedur looked back over his shoulder. 'Everyone down,' he roared. And the archer fired.

Those who didn't fall to the ground quickly enough were thrown down by the sudden blast that ripped across the clifftop. Three men were swept off the cliff with the force of the explosion down onto the rocks below.

Flames swept back into the forest in a vast sinuous curve; trees exploded as their barks cracked and their sap boiled. The creature was gone, consumed in a vast conflagration of oily black smoke and blue-white flames. Where it had once been an inferno now raged, even the rocks bubbling with the heat. Quisleedor was no more. The forest, however, was only beginning to burn.

'Come,' Paedur shouted, 'we must make for the ship now. Soon the entire island will be ablaze.' Obediently, the Taourg arose and, skirting the edge of the blaze, made their way down through the forest to the beach and the ship. All save one. Duaize, captain of the *Duneson*, remained on the clifftop, his face contorted in death, blood trickling from his mouth and nose. He had died of fright.

The four priestesses stood by the rail of the *Duneson* gazing back at the high plume of smoke that rose to the heavens, marking the site of the isle of Vosge.

'Will the entire island burn?' one asked.

'Aye,' Tuan muttered, as he and the bard joined them. 'Soon Vosge will be no more than a blackened ruin.'

'There is a lot we still don't know,' the priestesses said, turning to face the bard.

Paedur looked at the four young women and smiled. 'Perhaps it's just as well. There was an evil on the island. It is gone; that is enough for you to know. But I thank you; you saved me from the Susurun. May the blue fire of the Mother burn brightly within you all.'

The four women bowed slightly. 'But where did you come from?' one persisted.

The bard glanced briefly at Tuan. 'I imagine the gods had a hand in it somewhere,' he smiled.

'By the Mother?'

'Perhaps,' Paedur smiled, 'aye, perhaps by the Lady Dannu.'

'And where do you go now?'

'South,' Paedur said shortly.

'To the Sea of Galae, to the Blessed Isle,' the youngest of the four whispered, her voice sounding lost and frightened.

'You are Sighted,' Paedur said, looking into her pale distant gaze.

'You are one of the god-sought, god-taught,' she whispered, 'I pity you.'

'Spare me your pity – I don't need that – but rather grant me your prayers. Pray that the Lady Dannu will aid me in the coming battle with the evil ones.'

'Our prayers will be for you,' the older woman said.

'The priests of Trialos seek to open the vessel of the Chrystallis,' the youngest one said, her eyes wide with fear. 'But there is another danger – a far greater danger.' Her voice cracked and became harsher, sounding almost masculine. 'You will use the Magician's Law – the force of equals.'

'Can you see an ending . . .?' Paedur asked softly.

Her voice changed again, returning to normal. 'I can see the sun, hot and blinding . . . I see you . . . you approaching one who holds the vessel high . . . he raises it . . . All is blackness.' She crumpled over and began sobbing bitterly.

11   The Priestess

And in the early days of his travels there were two companions.
                                        Life of Paedur, the Bard
. . . a seafarer late of the sea, and a sorceress, both priestess and witch –
these were the companions of the bard.

                                        Tales of the Bard

Smoke coiled about the massive pillars in the ruined temple; grasping tendrils snaking about the scattered congregation, catching the torch lights, flickering in pale shades that hinted at deeper colours within. The torches spat and hissed as droplets of rain began to fall through the broken roof. Shadows wavered and writhed upon the lichened walls, disclosing the chipped remnants of once glorious murals now defaced by time, the elements and vandals. Sparks, spiralling to the ceiling, died against the fire-blackened crossbeams that had once lain concealed above a canopy of azure plaster.

A sudden gust of wind scattered the coals in the large censer in the middle of the floor, blowing them into flames which illuminated the pitifully few believers come to pay homage to the Old Faith this chill night. Without exception they were aged, for almost all the younger generation had been enticed away to the revels that had come to pass for the worship of the gods of the New Religion in recent years. Nor were they wealthy, for the rich would not risk being caught at such a service. The poor had nothing to lose save their lives, and they were of little value.

Beside the shattered remnants of the altar stone the High Priestess intoned the litany. With arms upraised and head bowed she invoked the Gods of the Pantheon to come and have pity upon 'your people; a people strong in faith and devotion; a people who have honoured the traditions and kept the holy days, and who but await the return of the gods of their youth; the gods of their fathers and grandfathers.' Softly the congregation muttered the responses, 'We await your return . . . we have remained faithful . . . we will remain faithful . . .'

The responses lingered on the still air in the ruined temple while beyond the shattered walls the storm that had been threatening all day broke over the ruined city. Lightning briefly lit up the interior of the fane, illuminating the High Priestess in bone-white light. Her jet-black hair burned almost indigo in the harsh light and her eyes were bottomless pits in the starkness of her delicate fine-boned face. The simple, ceremonial robes of office ruffled about her slender form as the breeze began to howl outside the temple, darting quick icy fingers through the gaping walls and tumbled doors.

The High Priestess raised her arms once again, her long slender fingers splayed, drawing from the Mother the strength necessary to continue and complete the service. She opened her mouth to speak, and lightning flared again. And then her breath caught in her throat in a strangled scream. Something had moved in the doorway. Something large and shapeless. Lightning flared again, but there was nothing there now. The congregation began to move restlessly, and she slowly raised her arms for the invocation once again . . . perhaps it had just been a trick of the light . . .

The priestess began to call upon the Pantheon to '. . . enlighten and protect and direct and govern us this day in the name . . .' The sky was rent as night was turned into day with the next levin bolt.

She screamed.

All heads turned towards the door. There were muffled shouts and curses and the rasp of steel as swords and knives were drawn. A creature stood framed in the doorway. Tall, thin and shapeless, it radiated an aura of power that was almost palpable. Then the light was gone and they were in darkness, save for the sputtering torches and the censer's smoky hissing.

The priestess was calmer now. She called the people to her and set them in a circle about the cracked altar stone. She took a deep breath and set about concentrating on constructing a protective circle. Then, taking a long peeled wand from the bundle that was to be used in the final sacrifice, she began to trace a circle about the huddled people. She knew not what lurked without the door; if it were men, then they were caught and she would soon be dead, but if it was a Duaiteoiri or some creature of the Gorge, the circle would at least afford her small congregation some measure of protection against it. The torches sputtered once again, and then died as rain began to fall steadily through the roof. The censer lasted a few heartbeats longer, but then, with a final hiss, it too died. In the darkness the unseen terror immediately magnified, and the temple that had once seemed so restful and secure now throbbed with unseen menace.

Lightning flared once again and all eyes turned towards the entrance, but the doorway was empty, and the brief light had only served to redouble the priestess's fears, for the shadows about the walls were darker, more intense in the harsh storm light. Anyone – or anything – could be lurking there.

Grasping the wand in both hands she began to concentrate, calling on Dannu and her daughter Lussa to grant her strength and the power to accomplish what she willed. The wand in her hands began to grow warm and the faintest nimbus of blue light flickered along the staff. So intent was her concentration that she failed to hear the soft footsteps which crunched up the dusty aisle to the altar.

'Dannu, aid me now,' she gasped, straining to make the staff burn.

'Let me help you.' The voice was masculine, though soft and gentle, and came from almost directly before her. Something rubbed against the staff and it suddenly blazed with the cold blue fox-fire of the goddess. The congregation cried out, and one or two swords were raised to strike at the figure revealed in the eerie light.

'No,' the priestess gasped, raising her hand, pushing down the swords by her side. She looked over her shoulder at her congregation, using the opportunity to regain her composure. 'No, he must be one of us.'

She turned back and coolly appraised the stranger. It was a man, of that she was certain, although the long, black, hooded travelling cloak almost completely concealed his face and most of his body. He was tall, for he topped her by a head and she was standing on the altar steps, and though the wand blazed with stark light the stranger was still partially in shadow, almost as if he absorbed the luminescence. And she knew that it was he who had activated the wand. She looked down at the rod she still held in one hand and gasped: there wasn't another hand above hers on the length of wood, but rather a flat silver hook, intricate runes and delicate tracery winking in the pulsing light.

'Who are you?' she asked finally.

'I am Paedur, a bard,' the stranger replied softly. 'You?'

'I am Cliona, High Priestess of the Old Faith,' she replied

185

proudly. 'You are of the Old Faith,' she said, more a statement than a question.

'If he is truly the bard Paedur, then he is of the Faith,' an old man stepped up to Cliona's side and murmured, peering over at the tall figure. He looked at the hook and nodded. 'This is the bard. You are of the east, Cliona, perhaps the tales of the bard have not reached the Isles of Monatome.'

Cliona shook her head, but then the bard spoke from beneath his cowl. 'I am of the Old Faith, priestess.'

'What are you doing here,' she asked, 'and how did you find us?'

The cowled figure bowed slightly. 'I am but passing through the city on my way . . . south. Earlier this evening, I felt a disturbance rippling through the Ghost Worlds, and knew that the Old Gods were being invoked, and I found I was curious.' He gently disengaged his hook from the wand, and it slowly dimmed, until only the faintest glimmerings of the blue fire lingered about its tip.

'Are you the one called the *shanaqui*?' a voice from the darkness behind the High Priestess asked.

The bard laughed gently and said, almost shyly, 'I am.'

Hurried whispers ran through the congregation, and Cliona could feel the sudden tension and excitement.

'I was about to invoke the Pantheon and beg their blessing,' she said, conscious that the night was drawing on and the service was still uncompleted. 'Will you join us?'

'I would be honoured.'

The congregation quickly found their places and Cliona relit the tall censer and then took up her position by the altar stone. She could just about make out the kneeling figure of the bard in the foreground, though in the flickering light he resembled some night-spawned wight.

Cliona raised her arms and crossed her wrists, palms outward. 'By the power and mercy of Hanor and Hara, and with the blessing of the Lady Dannu, I call upon the Pantheon to enlighten and protect, direct and govern us this day; to grant us the physical, mental and spiritual strength to bear our burdens lightly, to labour cheerfully and toil diligently. I ask this for my charges in the name of . . . of . . .' she faltered. Then another voice took up the chant, the strong powerful trained voice of a professional storyteller, a bard.

'In the name of the One who may not be worshipped, and of the Children of the One, Hanor and Hara, and of the Triad that are of

Life, and Mannam that is of Death, for there should be a balance. Be with us.'

'*Be ever with us.*'

The priestess took up the chant again. 'I ask of the Mother, the Lady Dannu, to send her daughters to our succour; may the Ladies Lussa and Quilida and Adur be ever above and below and about us. Be with us.'

'*Be ever with us.*'

And again the bard spoke, his powerful voice echoing off the chill walls. 'In the names of Maker and User, who were amongst the First, and of Huide who is amongst the least, and of Nusas who is Master of the Day, and Uimfe who had the Night for his domain, may the Lords of the Pantheon be ever with us.'

And now the voice of the priestess joined with that of the bard's. 'Be with us.'

'*Be with us now and always.*'

As the final response settled over the ruined temple, the storm which had lulled throughout the ceremony finally broke in full fury. Icy rain gusted through the broken roof and walls on to the shivering congregation. Grit hissed against the stone walls, for the wind sweeping off from the sea was contained by the high cliffs surrounding the city and so redoubled in force. Lightning cracked once more, and a long jagged spear leapt from the heavens down into the city. Close upon the lightning came the thunder, long booming rolls upon some heavenly drum.

Cliona felt a presence by her side, and a voice spoke in her ear, making her jump. 'We must be going; Uimfe plays host to the Stormlord this night. Come, let us go before the revels begin in earnest . . .'

'And this is Tuan, late of the Taourg; he has recently decided to accompany me.'

Tuan stood, his head almost brushing the low ceiling of the inn on the outskirts of the New City. He bowed slightly, showing the shivering priestess to one of the three chairs in the curtained alcove he had hired earlier that night.

'Tuan, will you get the priestess something to drink; and bring a firepot also, the chill of the night still lingers.' Paedur slipped off his cloak as the mate pushed through the leather curtain into the inn proper. He gently draped it around Cliona's shoulders, drawing her away from the curtain and the ears of any listeners. 'Here, sit here. Tuan will return soon, we can talk then.'

Paedur leaned against the rough stone wall, arms folded, and watched the priestess with hooded eyes. She was tall and slender, her face oval, the bones rounded, her cheekbones prominent. Her eyes were large, slightly tilted, a pale green in colour, and perhaps set too far apart to be called beautiful. Her most attractive feature was her hair – which flowed in a thick ebon mane down her back to the small of her knees. She wore a simple tunic, sandals and no jewellery.

She, in turn, watched the bard, seeing him for the first time without the enveloping, concealing cloak. She already knew that he was tall, perhaps a head taller than herself, and finely featured, clean shaven, unscarred and unblemished. His hair was fine and dark, almost invisible in the light of the flickering taper, and his eyes were just shadowed pits. Indeed, with his dark clothing it was difficult to make out details in the dull light. High atop his left shoulder a bardic sigil gleamed and his silver hook shone like a new moon across the night of his chest. She then lowered her gaze and allowed her eyes to unfocus, staring at her hands until she saw the warm gold outline of her own aura. When it was clearly visible, she looked back to the bard . . .

Two fingers touched her eyelids, closing her eyes. 'Do not look at me in that way,' Paedur whispered, 'it would blast your sight.'

And she, who had once dabbled in the darker arts, knew that he was not wholly of the race of man, although neither was he a god. Nor was he evil, for only those untainted with the essence of evil could invoke the Dannu-fire.

And if not Duaite, what then? Surely not Auithe; for the Auithe were of light and the bard was undoubtedly of the night and darkness.

The heavy curtain rustled and Tuan re-entered carrying two steaming mugs of potent rofion, and cradling a firepot in his arms. He put the mugs on the small knife-scarred table and then unstoppered the pot and blew gently on the red coals. A small flame flickered then flared as he dropped some rofion on to the coal. The warm glow that suffused the tiny cubicle immediately warmed the priestess.

Cliona and Tuan sipped the bitter brew and huddled about the firepot, while the bard sat back in the shadows, neither needing the drink nor the warmth of the fire.

The priestess watched the mate across the rim of her mug. His dark weathered skin and pale bleached hair reminded her that the bard had said he had lately sailed with the Taourg. But he had not the looks of one of the fearsome pirates. Indeed, his features were almost soft and his eyes and smile were gentle. However, she did not doubt he would prove to be an awesome opponent. For all his height, he seemed almost squat; muscles rippled and corded with his every movement. The earthenware mug of rofion was almost lost in his large hands, which, she imagined, could easily crush it to powder.

'There is something I must know,' the priestess said, turning to the bard. 'How did you find me tonight? Outside the few that still pay homage to the Pantheon, no-one knows the location of the Temple of the Mother in the Old City. And the route to the Temple is guarded with many cunning traps. And yet you found us without tripping any of the alarms or snares. How?' she wondered.

'I told you how I found you; I followed the ripples set up by your devotions in the fabric of the Ghost Worlds. And as for your traps . . . well, I didn't see them,' Paedur said almost absently.

'And what do you want?' she asked, looking from the bard to Tuan.

The mate caught her worried stare and turned to Paedur. 'I will go . . .'

'No, my friend, stay with us. What do I want? I want nothing, and yet . . .' he paused. 'Tell me, do you believe in the will of the gods, that the gods use and move men like pieces on a board?' Cliona nodded and nodded again.

'It is central to my belief,' she said, frowning, wondering where the bard was leading.

Paedur was silent for a moment, the fingers of his right hand rubbing against the runes cut into his hook, and then he said, 'Tell me a little about yourself – you are not native to Maante . . .?'

The sudden question caught her unawares. 'Well . . . but why do you want to know about me . . .?'

'I too believe that the gods move men, and I'm curious to discover why we have encountered one another. Why have the gods brought us together, eh? Answer me that! No, there was a reason, I'm sure of it. So . . .' he sat forward, moving into the light, his smile warm and encouraging. 'Tell me a little about yourself,' he repeated, 'how are you called . . .?'

The priestess smiled shyly. 'That depends who is calling me. My full name is Cliona Ravenshair Duringlaid, but in this city I am called priestess by those who know me. I come from the Isles of

Monatome, in the east. Why I came here, I cannot say, save that I think I was called. I dreamt . . .' She shook her head abruptly; the heavy fumes of the rofion were making her drowsy. 'I dreamt that the Mother called me, called me as if from a height and pointed out the headland of Aangle, and the town of Maante. And in my dream she said, *Wait, you will be needed.*' Cliona looked into the bard's shadowed eyes. 'But you should know that I am not worthy to serve the Mother; I am not pure, I cannot invoke the Dannu-fire.'

'Why?' Paedur whispered.

'I . . . my mother was of the Nightfolk, the dwellers in caves that come forth during the night to work their magics across the Islands. They shun the light of day, and it is said that the light of Nusas is deadly to them.

'My father was one of the princes of Monatome, and although third in line for the throne he only ruled a minor province on one of the lesser isles, for it was rumoured that the blood of the Duringlaid clan was not pure. Mayhap it was so, for my father liked to hunt by night, to work after dark; he was uncomfortable in the light of the sun. He made a point to conduct all his business with outsiders during the twilight.

'It was my father's passion to hunt the white stags that run by the light of the moon, for it is said that they are the steeds of the Lady Lussa, though I doubt that for my father once brought one home and it dripped blood and was of flesh as any mortal beast. He said it was merely an albino strain, and was probably sensitive to the harsh sunlight.

'But one summer night, and this was before I was born, while he hunted as usual, he disappeared. The servants scoured the forests for days thereafter, but they found no trace save for a scrap of cloth, the colour of which matched my father's cloak, not far from the Nigh Gates; the cave entrance to the dwellings of the Night-folk.

'My father re-appeared one morning the following spring, wandering alone through the forests, dressed in that same clothing he had worn before he went missing, and armed with the same weapons. He was paler and his sight, which had never been good during the day, was now much worse, so that he stumbled almost blind along the forest tracks.

'He was shivering with a marsh fever, and he raved during the first few days of his return, and those who visited him came away disturbed with what they had heard. In time, his sense returned and, save for a strange air that seemed to cling to him, he was much the same as before. But he never said where he had been for over half a year, although everyone supposed he had been with the Nightfolk.

'Then one morning, quite suddenly, he announced that arrangements were to be made for his wedding, but he did not name his bride and although there were several suitable maidens of noble birth on the neighbouring isles no representations had been made to their fathers. Speculation was rife as the day neared, but on the eve of the wedding there was still no sign of the bride's name. The guests muttered and said that his brain had turned; he had obviously been ensorcelled by the Nightfolk.

'The day of the wedding came and went, and still no bride appeared, but as dusk hung across the skies and night was falling there came forth from the forest one clothed in rock hues of grey and slate. It was a maiden, fairer than even the fabled Caia. She boldly walked to the altar stone of the fane of the Pantheon and announced herself my father's bride-to-be. In the silence that followed some of the guests left, refusing to attend the ceremony, some because she was of the Nightfolk and others because she was heavy with child.

'And she was Uaidara, my mother.

'I was born not long afterwards and named Cliona Ravenshair Duringlaid, "Ravenshair" because even at birth my hair was as black as you see it now.

'My father was of the Old Faith and worshipped regularly at the temples of the gods, but my mother worshipped the darker gods than those of the Pantheon and was versed in the Ancient Lore that is part of the Culai learning that still survives. And often, on those nights when the moon hid her face and even the stars seemed to shine less brightly, my mother would call me to her, and we would walk in the rock garden that my father had had made for my mother, and there she would instruct me in the dark magic of her people.

'I was enrolled in the Temple of the Mother when I reached my twelfth year and there I remained until I was professed. But on account of my dark knowledge I was told I would never attain the Higher Mysteries, and would never be more than a priestess. Although,' she added with a wry smile, 'the people here call me High Priestess.

'Then, as I have said, I dreamt that the Mother called me to her. In my dream she was seated upon the Throne of Heaven, she was all aspects of woman, yet none; maiden, mother, crone – ever-changing. And it was as if the land was spread out like a vast tapestry, rolling gently beneath my feet. And here was Aangle and here Maante, and the Mother rose from her throne and pointed out this town, and then it was as if a voice spoke from within my head. "*Go; wait; you will be needed.*" Then she was gone and I awoke cold and shivering in the dawn.

'And thus I came here on the first available ship,' she finished.

'Why do you conduct your services in secret,' Paedur asked, 'surely the Faith is not banned in Maante?'

'No,' she said, her eyes heavy with sleep. 'No, the Faith is not banned here; Maante is very tolerant. There are temples and fanes to a hundred gods and spirits here; though I have noticed that the scholars and learned men who flock here to use the libraries have little time for religion or gods.' She laughed bitterly. 'They are too busy denying the very existence of god; why, some even doubt the existence of man.'

'But you still haven't told me why you hold your services in secret,' the bard persisted.

Cliona held out her flagon and Tuan refilled it. She sipped cautiously. 'When I came here some four or five moons ago, the Pantheon was worshipped in the Great Temple of Hanor and Hara in the main square of the New City. A flourishing priesthood served the gods and the services were well attended. Since then I have seen all the priests die in mysterious circumstances – accidents – and the most prominent worshippers attacked, reviled and slandered, and in two cases killed. It did not take long for the message to sink in, and the congregation soon dwindled almost as fast as the priests.' She coughed as the rofion took her breath away. 'Hah, but the Faith does not need those who flee at the first sign of trouble!'

'Where do you come in?' Tuan asked suddenly.

'There is an Order House of the Mother here in Maante . . .' Cliona began.

'We know,' Tuan grinned, 'we escorted four of your sisters there not three days ago.' Paedur waved him silent and turned back to the puzzled priestess. 'Please continue.'

'I had heard of the death of the priests and slowly the realisation began to dawn that perhaps this was why I had been called to

Maante. When I learned that there were no more priests left to carry on the Faith, I went to the Mother Abbess and asked her if I might be granted special dispensation to minister amongst the people. The Abbess knew I was unhappy in the confines of the House; knew that I longed to be doing something – anything – except waiting. She knew that the Mother had guided me to Maante, and she too wondered whether I had been called here for this very purpose.'

'So you went amongst the people, knowing that your predecessors had all met their deaths. Was that not a foolish thing to do?' Paedur asked, curiously.

'I knew the Mother would protect me,' the priestess said simply. 'I was not afraid.'

'You were tonight,' the bard said softly.

'I panicked,' Cliona snapped. 'It will not happen again.' She drank deeply and then continued. 'I have been watched these past few days; my rooms have been searched. I did everything I could this evening to lose the men who were following me; I knew if they found the ruined temple, there would be a massacre. When I saw the shape in the doorway I thought you . . .'

'Have you any idea who is behind all this?' Tuan wondered.

'The priests of Trialos are in Maante,' she said softly.

'Aaah,' Paedur breathed. 'How many? Have they been here long?' he asked urgently.

'They are many,' Cliona said slowly, 'and though they have not been here these many moons they have gained many converts, for their doctrine is attractive and welcoming, and gives the people quick and easy answers. But . . .' she paused indecisively.

'But . . .' the bard prompted.

'I don't think that's the real reason all the priests of Trialos are here.'

'What are they here for, then?' Paedur asked.

'They seem to be waiting.'

'Waiting?'

'There is always a priest on the road by the Towers, yet he never accosts any of the travellers with offers of money or food, as is their custom. And there is always a priest by the harbour and yet again he never stops the mariners; and they are usually easy fodder for the smooth-talking priests.' She shook her long dark hair. 'No, I think they are waiting for something – or someone.'

'But for whom, I wonder,' the bard mused, 'someone important, I'll wager.'

193

'Important enough for them to pass over possible converts,' Tuan added.

Cliona put down her glass and, placing her hands flat on the stained wood, she stared over at the bard. 'Now, I have answered all your questions. Tell me, what are you doing in Maante?'

Paedur replied slowly. 'I am but passing through the city, nothing more.'

'Where are you going?'

'The Sea of Galae, the Blessed Isle,' Paedur said, almost absently, ignoring the priestess's sudden pallor.

'Why . . . why there?' she whispered, slowly rising to her feet.

Tuan stood and gently pushed the priestess back into her chair. He cupped her chin in one of his hands and said softly, 'The priests of Trialos seek to open a vessel holding a fragment of the Chrystallis; we are trying to stop them.'

Cliona sat still, only the sudden pounding of her heart audible in her head, though whether from the shock of the revelation or from the drink she couldn't tell.

Paedur moved suddenly, pulling back the leathern curtain. The thick yellow light of the inn spilled into the darkened alcove. One or two faces raised themselves from their flagons and looked curiously at the tall commanding figure who glared about the room; when they met his eyes they looked away. Tuan was behind him, the broad-bladed Chopt knife gleaming redly in the reflected glow of the firepot. 'What is it?' he murmured.

'There was someone outside, listening; I'm sure of it,' Paedur replied. He turned back to the priestess. 'Come, we must leave here. Where are you staying?'

'I have the old priest's quarters behind the Temple of Hanor and Hara,' she said, looking bemused. 'What's happened?'

Paedur slipped his cloak from Cliona and swung it about his shoulders, pulling the cowl up over his head. In the shadows, he was almost invisible.

Tuan pulled his heavy woollen jerkin over his head and made the priestess put it on. The thick wool enveloped her from throat to knee, disguising her female figure in its folds. Beneath his jerkin, Tuan wore a vest of blackened ring mail. He loosened his knife in its sheath and looked at the bard.

'What's happening?' Cliona asked again, a note of desperation creeping into her voice.

'We're leaving,' Paedur said shortly. 'You are coming with us.'

He turned to the mate. 'You go first and ensure that our way is clear; Cliona – you and I will follow. We will return to our quarters; yours are, in all probability, a death-trap.'

He nodded to Tuan, who slipped quickly through the curtain. Paedur moved to the thick leather and, with his hook, carefully nicked a piece from it. He put his eye to the hole and followed the mate's progress through the crowded inn. Several heads turned to follow him and, as he closed the thick studded door behind him, two men rose and wove their way – seemingly drunkenly – after him. Paedur turned to the priestess. 'He was followed.'

'What will we do?' she asked, her voice cracking.

The bard smiled thinly, and the glow from the firepot turned it bloody. 'We will wait for Tuan to clear our way . . .'

'But you said that there were two of them,' she whispered; 'should we not help him, call for help or something?' she finished lamely.

'Tuan can take care of himself; there are only two of them.'

The bard capped the firepot and they waited in the darkness. Paedur watched the inn through the tiny hole in the leathern curtain; everyone had resumed drinking and no-one seemed to be paying undue attention to the curtained alcove.

'Ready now?'

The priestess nodded in the darkness.

Paedur gripped Cliona by the arm and pulled her through the curtain. He led her quickly through the maze of tables. One or two coarse jests were flung in their wake, but they ignored them, concentrating on reaching the door. The bard's senses were tingling, alert to every movement in the room. Cliona stared straight ahead, looking neither right nor left, concentrating on the door, half expecting a knife in the back. Two men, the bard had said. Had they come to kill her, as they had the others? The Mother would protect her . . . wouldn't she?

The raw night air streamed in through the open door and she suddenly realised they were out into the street. She breathed deeply, cleansing her lungs of the smoke and stench of the inn with the sharp sea breeze that swept up from the harbour.

The mate. Where was Tuan? The street was deserted and in utter darkness. In the distance a pale spark bobbed as some late reveller made his way homeward, preceded by his lantern-bearer and no doubt surrounded by his guards.

Paedur took Cliona's arm again and pulled her off down the

195

street to their left, moving confidently through the blackness. He suddenly stopped and hissed softly. Something moved in the darkness and Cliona almost screamed as someone took hold of her other hand.

'One outside, two following,' came the mate's low whisper.

'And?'

'They sleep; one will not wake in this world, I think.'

Cliona shuddered as she realised that Tuan had just killed a man. She vainly attempted to pull her hand free from his, but he gripped her more firmly and muttered angrily, 'Be still, girl, or all is lost.'

They made their way through the darkened streets, cutting through echoing alleyways and across four plazas, each one more foul-smelling than the last. Once they climbed steps and Cliona guessed that they were climbing past the Quarter Wall into the Upper City. They stopped twice and waited in the shadows while the Watch made their rounds, stamping past with a jingling of mail, their lanterns held high, casting yellow pools of light about their bearers. They hurried on, splashing through pools of noisome liquid that leaked from the sewers which ran down the centre of the streets. Then the bard led them off the main streets and down a dank filth-strewn lane. They paused while the mate struck a light from his tinder pouch, transferring the flame to a single candle enclosed behind thin slivers of horn. A pale yellow-white glow lit up the dripping alley walls. They were outside a door set deeply into the wall; the door was stained and scorched and its base was rotten and reeked of urine and vomit.

Tuan stooped and put the guttering flame close to the lock. Tiny points of light winked back at them from the rusted keyhole and handle. He bent and ran the light over the ground under the keyhole. Spots of rust littered the rotted wooden step. Tuan turned to the bard and silently drew his knife from its sheath. No word passed between them, but Cliona knew: there was someone inside.

Tuan blew the candle out while the bard carefully slipped the long key into the lock, pushing Cliona behind him. Tuan pushed the door open. It squeaked, the slight noise like a scream in the night silence. The mate stood to one side while the bard preceded him into the blackness. There was a brief – almost noiseless – scuffle, then silence.

Paedur re-appeared as Tuan relit the candle, and in the yellow light they could see that the tip of his hook was dark and dripping.

'Just one,' he said.

Tuan pushed the priestess into the small hallway, then pulled the door closed. The flickering lantern shone wetly on the long black stain that trickled slowly down the wall. Under the stain a figure slumped, head tilted back to reveal the gaping slash across the throat that was still pumping blood. A long stiletto lay buried point-first in the hard-packed floor where it had dropped from his hand; blood pooled about it. Tuan nudged the corpse with his boot, and then he stooped down and pushed back his sleeve; a thick metal band encircled his wrist.

'The Iron Band of Kloor,' Paedur muttered.

'You know it?' Tuan asked.

'Aye, I know of it; and of how youths are tricked into joining it, forswearing their gods, their families, heritage, past . . . everything. For what? Nothing!' He looked down at the corpse; it was a boy of no more than eight and ten summers. Suddenly he knelt by the body and placed his hook across forehead, then breast. 'Rest in peace,' he whispered. 'Mannam, accept his spirit; Alile have mercy on him and do not judge him harshly.' He looked up at the priestess who was staring at him in sick horror. 'Do not condemn me, nor this youth either. We each have our reasons for doing what we do.' He seemed about to say more, but then he stood up abruptly and walked up the corridor, feet gliding noiselessly over the earthen floor.

'I think we should leave here,' Tuan said as they entered the tiny room at the back of the building.

'Aye, you're right; the priests of Trialos move swiftly.'

'I'm sorry I got you into this,' Cliona said quietly.

Tuan was swiftly by her side. 'Priestess, we were in this long before we came here. The bard has been sought by the priests of Trialos and the Trialdone across the Seven Nations. This is not new to him.'

'What will we do?' she asked.

'My destination is the Blessed Isle,' the bard said. 'But first I would like to know more about the priests of Trialos and, more particularly, why they're waiting here. Consider,' he said, holding up his hand, 'to open the vessel containing the Chrystallis is not a task given to any ordinary priest. Therefore it must be someone powerful, someone well versed in the lore of both the Old Faith and the New Religion.' His hand closed into a fist. 'Thanos,' he whispered. 'Thanos.'

Cliona shuddered. 'Thanos, the Hand of God.'

'Trialos' High Priest? Tuan asked. 'Surely not.'

197

'He's the only one it could be. No-one else has the power to open the vessel. And he will not come alone, half the High Priests of the false gods will accompany him.'

'And you would go against him alone?' Cliona asked.

'I have to,' Paedur said simply.

'There's movement outside,' Tuan said, peering through a slit in the warped wooden shutters barring the windows.

'This way.' The bard prised the shutters off the rear window that looked out into a squalid courtyard. A short drop below the window, a neighbouring roof jutted out until it was only half a span from the wall of their building. The mate went first, landing easily and coming to his feet in one smooth roll. He stood and stretched full length to receive the priestess as the bard lowered her down. 'I've got her,' Tuan hissed, 'now come on!'

'A moment,' Paedur snapped, and then he ducked back into the room. Cliona and Tuan stood and waited for the bard to reappear, faces raised anxiously to the gaping window.

Paedur meanwhile was slashing the rough mattress, his razor sharp hook cutting through the thin fabric to expose the straw beneath. He doused it with the remainder of a flagon of raw mountain spirit which Tuan had been drinking earlier, then he quickly spread the straw out around the door. He placed the lighted candle just inside the door – which opened inwards.

He ran to the window and leapt out, cloak flapping like wings, and landed noiselessly beside the startled pair. In the room above there was a crash, followed by a dull whoomp, and the window lit up with flames.

Paedur allowed himself a slight smile. 'Shall we go?'

12   The Hand of God

And Thanos, the Hand of God, the High Priest of the New Religion, sent his finest warriors to slay them . . .

Life of Paedur, the Bard

They reached the Old City as the dawn was breaking in from the east. The sun rose shortly afterwards, the ruined buildings etching long shadows about them. Cliona led them through the mazy paths, overgrown and sprouting small shrubs in the cracks in the stonework, past columns which had once supported vaulted roofs or held stairways, but which were now only shattered steps. The long snaking lines of walls were everywhere, gaps showing where the dressed stone had been taken down through the ages by the city dwellers for their own dwellings.

As the morning brightened and they saw movement on the outskirts of the ruins, they sought shelter in a squat two-storied ruin that had once been a massive sprawling house. The ruins of the outer wings had been torched at some stage and surrounded the main building in a crude and seemingly unbroken wall, looking harsh and ugly in the morning light. But the priestess led them through the tumbled stones and fire-blackened spars to the central rooms of the building – which was in surprisingly good repair. 'This was once the house of the Chief Magistrate,' she said, pointing to the crest depicting two crossed swords and a length of chain above the doorway.

'What happened?' Tuan asked, looking around at the desolation.

'I asked myself the same question, but all I could find out was that he hanged two fishermen for fishing without a licence. At the hanging there was a scene involving one of the men's wives, and she attacked the magistrate with a fish hook. She was cut down before she even got close to the man. The magistrate then ordered the families of the two fishermen all slain – as a warning I suppose.' She indicated the tumbled walls. 'Before the order could be carried out, the townspeople attacked his house . . . They

199

killed everyone. Since then, the house has been more or less avoided.'

'Why?' Tuan wondered.

Cliona smiled. 'It's supposed to be haunted.'

'Well, it's empty enough now,' Paedur said, squeezing through the half-open door. Tuan and the priestess followed him inside. 'I'm going to go back to the New City,' the bard said, his voice echoing slightly in the dim hallway. 'I want to see about hiring a boat, and I'll bring some food back with me.' He turned back to the door, and then stopped and looked over at the priestess. 'I can contact the Abbess of the Order House and have them come and pick you up . . .'

The priestess shook her head, the strands of her long hair whispering sibilantly together. 'There's no need. I'm sure the Order House is being watched; you daren't go there . . .' The bard silently nodded and then left, disappearing rapidly into the ruins.

Tuan looked at the priestess – and then he yawned hugely. 'I think we should try and get some sleep; it looks like it's going to be a long day . . .'

Tuan awoke suddenly, not knowing what had disturbed him. The house was deathly silent, the noonday stillness the Taourg called it. Without moving he opened his eyes – and then squeezed them shut again as the sunlight reflected back off the white rock and dressed stone of the hallway. But in that single instant he had noted that the priestess was missing.

He had fallen asleep in a niche behind the main door, and he was confident that nothing could have come past without awakening him. He had left her sleeping in a small room just below the main staircase, where he had been able to see her, but now the thin sheet she had wrapped herself in lay balled by the foot of the pallet. He quickly checked through the lower rooms, but they were all empty and the dust on the floor was unmarked. Panic gripped him now, and he ran up the crumbling stairs, taking them two at a time. He began systematically checking the rooms on the second floor but they too were all empty and caution prevented him from calling her name.

Tuan came back on to the landing and stood by the stairs, looking around. He felt Cliona was still within the house, anyone leaving – or entering for that matter – would have had to step over him. He was about to take the small staircase that led up to the third floor when he heard a small noise, the clink of metal on stone. It came from a room he had just passed; a room devoid of furnishing and with no possible place of concealment. He moved quietly down the hall, his knife gripped tightly in his left hand, his breath coming short and fast. He was conscious that he was more frightened now than he could ever remember being – even on his first raid, or even when Quisleedor had chased them through the forest.

He peered in through the open door. The room was still empty. The shutters were open and the sunlight, reflecting off the stones of the neighbouring buildings, painted the cracked walls in harsh colours that only served to highlight its bareness. Tuan eased the door open with his right hand. It protested loudly on rusted hinges. He suddenly pushed himself through the opening, diving to the left, rolling to his feet with his knife upraised and his back against the cracked wall.

And again he heard the noise. It came from outside and a shadow moved across the sunlight behind the shutter. Tuan threw himself across the room and hit the rotting shutters at a run, sending them crashing over the waist-high wall that encircled the balcony beyond.

And Cliona screamed. She had been standing by the wall.

'Where in the God's holy name were you?' Tuan demanded, fear and anger thickening his voice. He slammed his knife into its sheath, and then winced as darts of pain shot through his arm muscle. Long splinters of wood from the shutters had stuck into his left arm. Clumsily, he began to pluck them out.

'Here, let me,' Cliona said, taking Tuan's arm in her cool hands and gently plucking the long slivers of wood from his forearm and shoulder. 'That was a stupid thing to do,' she snapped. 'You could have been badly hurt; suppose you got a splinter in your eye?'

'I thought you were in danger,' Tuan muttered in embarrassment.

Cliona bent her head, seemingly concentrating on her task, but her long thick hair hid the deep blush that burned her cheeks. 'Thank you; but I was in no danger. I awoke a little while ago and . . . well you were sleeping and I didn't want to wake you. I came up here to get a breath of fresh air . . . and to think.'

'What about?' Tuan asked absently.

'Myself . . . the bard . . . you,' she replied shyly.

'Me!' He laughed. 'I'm nothing. A farmer's son who ran away

from home because I couldn't bear the thought of being a farmer. Since then I've been a wandering warrior and a sailor by trade. I've sailed with the Taourg these past years; and you know what the Taourg are,' he stated flatly.

'I know. The scum of the seas; killers, thieves, cannibals and . . . other things.' She blushed. 'Why did you leave them?'

'Paedur talked to me one day, gave me a glimpse of what I was and what I might become; told me a little of his mission – and saved my life.'

'He is a strange man, he frightens me,' Cliona said, leaning against the balustrade, staring out over the ruined city.

Tuan joined her, uncomfortably aware of her presence. 'You need have no fear of the bard; he is not evil.'

'No, he is not evil, but he seems so . . . so inhuman.'

'Perhaps he is. He is more – and less – than a man. He speaks with a frightening familiarity of the gods, and he also said that he was one of the "*god-sought, god-taught*."' He turned to face the priestess. 'What are they?'

'They are human souls, chosen by the gods to perform a task. Gifted by them, they wander through the land almost as living extensions of the gods' will. Sometimes a god will actually inhabit the body, then the host becomes a *quai*, a mindless thing directed solely by the gods' will. That is the way of Trialos. The Gods of the Pantheon merely direct their servants, sometimes subtly and on occasion with an order. But the bard seems to be neither directed nor ordered . . .' Cliona shook her head slightly, the wind coming in off the bay whipping her raven locks about her face. 'He is a mystery. Black and purple . . . are they the traditional colours of the bards?' she asked suddenly.

Tuan thought for a moment, then shook her head in puzzlement. 'I haven't seen many bards, and although they all wore dark colours, purples, browns, greys, I've never known them to wear black. Why do you ask?'

She frowned. 'In my land, black is the traditional colour of the dead. What of your land?'

'Aye, in Moghir we clothe our dead in black winding sheets, for we associate the colour with Mannam, the Dark Lord.'

They stood in silence, immersed in their own thoughts, gazing out over the Old City. Far off in the distance, the New City gleamed white against the blue of the ocean.

Cliona shivered suddenly. 'It's grown cold.'

Tuan nodded, glancing at the sky. 'Aye, and it's not much past midday; there's a storm brewing.' He stepped closer to the priestess and slipped his arm about her shoulders. He felt her tense and then relax.

'What about you and the bard,' she asked, keeping her voice light and casual, 'will you continue on with him?'

'I will, I have to.' He shook his head. 'It's hard to explain, but I feel I must.'

'But you don't even know what he is!' Cliona protested.

'No,' Tuan agreed, 'but I know he is not evil. You know what he seeks to prevent; and I will aid him, if I can.'

'I too,' the priestess murmured.

'What!'

Cliona smiled. 'Don't you see, this was what I was called to Maante for? When you sail the haunted Galae Sea to the Blessed Isle, I will be with you.'

Tuan gripped her shoulders with both hands and turned to stare down into her face. 'There will be danger. The priests of Trialos and the Trialdone are the least of our worries. The Blessed Isle is reputed to be . . . inhabited with much that no longer exists. The bard calls it a place out of time, between the planes of man. It may be death for us just to land there . . .' He stopped; Cliona was smiling at him. 'We may die,' he almost shouted.

'I do not fear death; do you?'

'No . . . yes! Yes, I fear death; only a fool does not fear death, but I have faced it often; we are no strangers.'

'I am still going,' she said firmly.

'Priestess . . . Cliona, I do not fear for myself. I fear for you. I would not see you slain – or worse – on the Isle.'

Cliona raised one finger and placed it across his lips, silencing him. 'And what if we are to die, then we will die together, in the cause of the Old Faith.'

'Much good will that do us,' Tuan said bitterly.

The priestess shook her head, her eyes bright and mocking. 'Why; shall we not enter the Silent Wood together, to wander hand in hand through the still graves . . .'

Abruptly, Tuan tightened his grip on her shoulders, and then he fell to one side, pulling her to the ground, his hand pressed over her mouth, bruising her lips, smothering her horrified cries. She bit his finger, and as he snatched his hand away she screamed, 'What do you think you're doing . . . you filthy Taourg! Take your hands off me lest I blast you . . .'

Tuan gripped Cliona's slender white throat and squeezed. The priestess choked and began to claw at his eyes. 'Quiet,' he hissed, 'there's someone moving in the ruins below.'

Cliona went limp beneath him and ceased struggling, the loathing in her eyes replaced with fear. Tuan rolled off her, and carefully raised his head above the edge of the balcony, his eyes seeking the spot of movement he had caught from the corner of his eye a moment earlier. The gathering wind moaned through the desolate remains of the once proud city; dust whirled and leaves circled in a smoothly intricate dance and tumbleweed rolled quickly down the deserted streets.

There!

He froze, his eyes never leaving the spot a little to his left, beside a shattered column. It could have been a shadow . . . and yet. It moved again. A figure ran from one clump of stone to another. Sunlight glinted off armour and a broad-bladed boar-sword. And then a second figure slipped from a doorway and joined the first. He raised his arm and several more figures appeared, running crouched from cover to cover, working their way steadily towards the magistrate's building. The leader raised his arm again, calling in more men, and Tuan stiffened and swore: a broad metal band encircled the man's wrist. He looked down at the priestess. 'The Iron Band of Kloor,' he mouthed.

Tuan pushed Cliona before him into the shelter of the empty room, then dragged her to her feet and hurried out on to the landing. They had to be out of the house before it was completely surrounded and they were trapped by the Band. They ran down the decaying stairs, sending chunks of rotten wood crashing to the floor below. At the foot of the stairs, Tuan paused, indecisively. To leave through the main door was out of the question, and he felt sure that any back exit was also watched.

A shadow crossed the half-open door. Quickly he pulled the priestess into the darkened alcove under the stairs, pressing her back against the mouldering wall. Again the shadow crossed the doorway, and an armoured figure darted through the opening, light flashing off the short-sword he held poised across his body. The warrior stood just inside the door, silhouetted against the light. He was close enough for Tuan to see the whites of his eyes as they darted about, seeking movement, and he could hear the soft quick hiss of his breath. He gave a short sharp whistle and several more of the Band joined him. No words were spoken, but they separated and systematically began a thorough search of the ground-floor rooms. However, one remained blocking the door and another guarded the bottom of the stairs, so close that Tuan could have reached out and touched him. There were sounds from above and a door slammed, the noise echoing and re-echoing through the house. The search ended, the warriors returned and reported to the officer waiting at the foot of the stairs. He listened to their reports in silence, then, leaving one warrior to guard the door, ordered the rest to follow him upstairs. The Captain of the Band had decided that the fugitives must be hiding on the top floor.

Now, Tuan realised, was the best – and possibly the only – chance they would have to make good their escape. Once the Band realised that they were not in the upper rooms, they would conduct a more thorough search, or possibly even fire the building. He measured the distance between himself and the guard at the door. It was too great a distance for a rush; the warrior would have cried out before Tuan had even taken a few paces.

Tuan weighed the Chopt knife in his hand. It was not a throwing knife and the weight and balance were wrong, but . . .

He reversed the knife until he was holding it almost at the point, drew his arm back, calculated the distance, allowing for the weight and balance of the blade – and threw!

He was moving even before the knife struck home, counting on his speed and reflexes to evade the guard's sword should the heavy hunting knife miss. The warrior opened his mouth to cry out – and then the knife struck him in the throat, pinning him momentarily to the door, and then he pitched forward, his eyes forever frozen in that last astonishment. The mate caught him as he fell, easing him gently to the ground, retrieving his knife and taking the guard's sword. Blood pooled about his feet and he cursed silently as he attempted to wipe the thick stickiness from his heels on the warrior's leggings. He beckoned to the priestess.

Cliona paused by the fallen guard and her fingers fluttered briefly in the Sign of Peace above his head . . . and then Tuan, all too aware how horribly exposed they were in the hall, grabbed her arm and pulled her through the door into the blinding sunlight – straight into one of the Band of Kloor standing in their path!

Tuan slashed out blindly with the sword in his right hand, his knife stabbing upwards at the same time. He heard the sword deflected with a dull metallic clang and his knife arm was wrenched to one side. He became aware that Cliona was screaming at him, and got a look at his attacker before something flowed up his arms striking him hard in the chest . . . It was the bard. And then his weapons fell from his nerveless fingers and he began to shake uncontrollably, his lungs and heart contracting in spasms. A deep pit opened up beneath his feet and he fell forward into it, unconscious. Paedur caught him as he slowly folded. He slipped one arm about the stricken mate and hurried him into the shelter of the ruins. Cliona stooped to pick up the knife and sword and ran after them.

But a shout followed them from the balcony of the house; they had been seen.

The bard led them down seemingly impassable streets; streets clotted with tumbled masonry, rank with rotting vegetation, strewn with the debris of ages. Cliona helped Paedur guide the semi-conscious mate over the more difficult stretches. They ran for what seemed like an eternity to the priestess, until she begged the bard to stop. 'Soon,' was all he said. They continued on, down streets, across alleys and lanes, until she reckoned they must have crossed over half the Old City. She was just about to ask the bard to stop again, when he led them down a lane and into a plaza, in the centre of which was a tumbled street shrine. Paedur stopped and eased Tuan to the ground. 'We can rest here,' he said quietly.

Cliona nodded dumbly and fell down by Tuan's side, exhausted. She looked up at the bard, but he showed no sign of fatigue.

It was now mid-afternoon and the desolate city was silent, even the moaning wind having died during their flight. They had left the warriors of Kloor far behind, puzzling over the fugitives' disappearance down a seemingly blind alley.

The bard knelt by Tuan's side and began to slap his face, at first gently, but then, when there was no reaction, he began striking him more forcefully until his head was rocking from side to side with the force of the blows. Cliona grabbed his arm and begged Paedur to stop.

Suddenly Tuan opened his eyes. 'Stop . . . it is . . . I thought . . .' he mumbled, shaking his head. Paedur produced a flask from within the folds of his cloak and forced the mate to sip from it. He passed the flask to the priestess and, when she shook her head, he ordered her to drink also. She sipped the dark liquid, feeling it burn down her throat; it was foul and bitter, but she felt her fatigue-numbed brain begin to clear almost immediately. She looked across at the mate; he met her eyes and nodded, smiling.

'What happened?' Paedur demanded, returning the flask to his cloak.

'I thought you were . . .' Tuan began.

'Before that!'

'We were . . . we were standing on the balcony looking out over the ruins when I saw movement below. It was the Band of Kloor; we must have been followed . . .' He sat up suddenly. 'Followed? But how; how did the Band know where to find us?'

The bard waved the question aside. 'You forget that Thanos is a powerful magician . . . Continue.'

Tuan pressed his throbbing head against the cool stone. 'We hid beneath the stairs while the warriors searched the ground floor. Then they went upstairs, leaving one on guard. I knifed him, took his sword, then . . . then we . . .' He shook his head. 'Where did you come from? I thought you were one of the Band. I could have sworn you were garbed in the fashion of the warriors. But . . .' He looked at the bard's travel-stained cloak, and shook his head again. 'Then you were there . . . and I had almost killed you.'

The bard laughed softly. 'Don't trouble yourself with that – it wasn't your fault. I had used a *glamour*, a spell, call it what you will, to assume the outward appearance of one of the Band. I had to get close to you. And then when you struck out, I had to defend myself . . .' He raised his hook slightly, 'But I only dazed you.' He stood and listened carefully. 'Come, we must seek shelter, there is a storm coming.' He pulled Tuan up and then helped Cliona to her feet.

'Which way?' Tuan asked, swaying slightly. The priestess looped one arm around his waist and caught hold of his thick belt with the other.

Paedur nodded. 'This way; it leads down to the oldest part of the city . . .'

Tuan looked up at the square blocky buildings that surrounded the plaza, noting their obvious great age. 'Was Maante not the first city in the world?' he asked as they moved off.

The bard nodded. 'One of the first. I would tell you its tale, but I only know fragments, and I never tell a broken or half-finished story.'

'I know it,' Cliona put in; 'before I came here, I did some research on it.'

'Tell us then,' Tuan said eagerly.

'Many thousands of years ago, before the Demon Wars, even before the Isles of Monatome had risen from the sea, this was the original city of Maante, a flourishing thriving sea-port. Where the New City now stands was once part of the Sea Lords' domain. The bay was so wide and deep that even such Culai warships that still survived and which were capable of holding a thousand fighting men could berth and dock safely here. Some say the city was Culai-built, but I do not think so. It lacks the solid grandeur of the Culai-built relics that dot even far-off Monatome.'

'It was built by the hand of man, but designed by the last of the Culai architects, a link between the two worlds and times,' the bard said unexpectedly.

Cliona paused uncertainly, then, with a sign from Tuan, continued. 'Then came the Demon Wars and the Cataclysm when the very surface of the earth was rent and the Southern Continent sank beneath the waves. New lands rose and others fell; islands appearing where there had been none before; whole chains of islands sinking without trace. There were three days of absolute night, when many believed the Time of Reckoning was at hand. And when the sun shone again, it was found that the Bay of Maante had receded, and the sea-bed risen, and that there were now almost three leagues of beach between the wharves and the sea – and thus the Old City became useless almost overnight.' She laughed suddenly. 'Of course, the Cataclysm that ruined the Old City of Maante, created the Isles of Monatome, my home.'

'And how did the New City come to be divided into two parts, the Upper and Lower; who built the Quarter Wall which divides them?' Tuan asked.

Cliona shook her head. 'I don't know; I never thought to check.'

The bard spoke again, his voice seemingly lost in thought. 'The citizens of Maante feared the sea would one day return, and the wall was intended to act as a breakwater. But as the population grew, so too did the need for space, and the land beyond the wall was utilised, thus creating the Upper and Lower sections of the city.'

'There are some who hold that the sea is still retreating,' Cliona said softly.

'That may be so. Our world is still a new world. These past ages are but its childhood. The land and the sea will have to settle, to shift and shape themselves. The land is constantly changing, but slowly . . . slowly, you could not see it unless you lived a hundred lifetimes. Even the sea is working towards this change; it is forever expanding, slowly eating away at the coastline, until . . . who knows? Perhaps some day when even Nusas the Sun grows old, perhaps then there will only be water on this world, a vast seething ocean.' He turned and smiled thinly, at Tuan and the priestess. 'But not in your lifetimes.'

'But in yours?' the mate asked in a whisper.

Paedur smiled, but said nothing.

They continued winding their way through the ruins late into the afternoon until the light was fading. Paedur at last stopped outside a high-walled building, in better repair than most. 'We'll stop the night here.'

And Cliona suddenly realised it was her own Temple of the Mother.

There was a hint of incense from the night before still in the air, overlying the dry odour of must which permeated even the very stones of the walls. Cliona shivered suddenly as they passed into the darkness and Tuan put his arm around her and drew her closer. This time she didn't shrink from his embrace. They paused just inside the door while their eyes became accustomed to the dimness.

Paedur meanwhile had wandered on into the desolate fane, his restless eyes noting the signs of the night's events; the scuffed prints of boots about the altar stone where the people had gathered around the priestess when he had entered. He smiled a little bitterly. Would he always be feared? He shook his head and then grinned ruefully – as long as man feared the unknown, the unnatural, they would fear, and even hate, him and his kind.

Cliona had left the wand he had ignited with the Dannu-fire on the altar stone, and he reached across and picked it up. It still felt warm to his touch and he felt the residue of power trickle along it and into the metal of his hook. He twirled it once about his head, spinning it with his fingers, bringing it to a brilliant blazing life, tremors of blue fire bathing the temple in azure light.

Tuan and the priestess came running, stumbling over the rubble littering the floor. They stood back and watched the bard in silence. He raised the wand high, holding it by one end, and the streamers of fire slowly died until the bard was left holding a brilliant blue rod. Then the light began to pulse, and Tuan imagined he could see rings of blue fire travel slowly up the wand to gather about its tip.

A small circle of light surrounded the bard, radiating from the rod;

slowly it began to expand until it encompassed the trio in a ring of pulsing blue-white light. And then Paedur suddenly reversed the wand, extinguishing it. But, although it was now nothing more than a wooden branch, the light encircling the companions remained, bathing them in waves of shifting azure. 'Now, we are joined in the Fire of the Goddess,' the bard said; 'we are Companions in the old – and full – sense of the word.'

Paedur handed the wand to Cliona. She accepted it gingerly and then almost cried aloud when she held it, for it was hot and it throbbed warmly, pulse-like – heart-like.

Paedur sat at the foot of the altar, resting his back and shoulders against the altar stone, watching them from beneath the shadow of his cowl. Cliona looked at Tuan and then turned back to the bard. And then she suddenly noticed that while the mate was clearly visible in the cold revolving Dannu-fire, the bard remained in shadow. It was as if he absorbed the light, or as if he could not be lit by the fire of the Mother. Did that not make him a Duaiteoiri?

'No,' he said coldly, 'I am not a Duaite, but neither am I Auithe.'

Cliona started and opened her mouth to speak, but Tuan laid his hand on her arm, pulling her down beside him. 'I think it's time we talked,' he said slowly, softly, looking at the bard.

Paedur nodded. 'It is time.' He looked at Cliona, 'You have decided to accompany us to the Blessed Isles.' It was a statement more than a question.

The priestess was silent for a moment, then she looked from the bard to Tuan. 'Yes, I have decided.' She turned back to the bard. 'This was why I was called to Maante . . .?'

'You were brought here for a purpose; to aid me on the Culai Isle. But a choice was left you, for we would not force you against your will.'

'*We?*' Tuan asked, sitting forward.

'*We,*' Paedur repeated. 'You know, Tuan, I am not alone: "*The Gods of the Pantheon on my right hand, the Duaite on my left*",' he said with a thin smile, quoting the old proverb.

'I don't like to think I've been manipulated,' Cliona said sharply.

'You get used to it,' Tuan said, glaring at the bard.

'Be quiet,' snapped the bard; 'you're acting like children. Now attend me. The priests of Trialos seek to open the vessel that holds a fragment of the Chrystallis; the result would be to wipe out everything that has been created by the Soulwind; that includes this plane and every other plane of existence. It even includes the gods. Now, it appears the gods themselves cannot act directly to stop the priests and, similarly, Trialos and the Trialdone cannot aid their followers, for the Culai Isle is a Place Apart, where time and the gods have no sway. Thus while the gods of both Faith and Religion look on helpless, we, their instruments, shall do their will; Thanos on the one hand will attempt to open the vessel, while I, on the other,' he smiled and pressed his hook to his chest, 'will try to ensure that the vessel remains sealed.

'Now Thanos and the priests of Trialos know that I am in Maante, and because of my reputation, he has brought a legion of the Band of Kloor, the Fist of God, with him. Their task is to guard the High Priest – and to slay us.' He looked at Tuan and Cliona, 'What do you know of Thanos?' he asked suddenly.

'He is the High Priest of Trialos,' Cliona said, closing her fist in a Sign, 'he is called the Hand of God.'

'Anything else?' Paedur asked.

'He is reputed to be an evil man,' Cliona said slowly, but Tuan shook his head. 'No, I've heard he is a good, holy man, but influenced by evil men.' He looked from the priestess to the bard. 'Is he?'

Paedur laughed gently, humourlessly. 'See his cunning? Your facts disagree even upon such information as you have.'

'What do you know of him?' Tuan asked.

'I knew Thanos as a boy,' Paedur began, 'and I would say that I knew him better than any man alive. His was not an auspicious birth, for he was born in death. His mother died before he was delivered, and he would have perished also had not his father torn him from his mother's womb. His father was a blacksmith, a hugely muscled man, strong in mind and body, strong in the Faith. Yet he questioned the Faith thereafter. Why had his wife died? Why had the child lived? And in time he spurned the Faith and grew to hate the child. In time also his mind went and he took to wandering about the town, talking and laughing to himself, imagining his dead wife was with him. He was found dead one morning in his forge; he had cut his belly open in much the same way as he had delivered his son from his wife.

'Thanos was a strange boy, and some people said that he carried the shadow of his mother's death over him; that Mannam had set a *bainte* to watch him; that he was already dead and his spirit claimed by the Dark Lord.'

211

The circle of blue light revolving about the trio suddenly quivered, rippling like a stone-disturbed pool. 'Hah, they search,' Paedur said softly, 'and they're closing in. We must hurry. But to continue . . .

'Thanos and I played together as children. Folk would laugh to see us together, for he was as pale as I am dark; he was – *is* – albino. We were as brothers until the time came for me to enter Baddalaur, the bardic college. We wept together to be parted and swore we would be re-united one day. I never saw him again.

'When my mother died I was allowed home for her burial.' His voice grew soft, and his eyes saw another time, a time past.

'Aaah, her death was a great ending in more ways than one. It was the last time every member of my family would be gathered together in one place. Even when my father died there were not so many present. And they have all gone now . . . all gone. I am the last . . .' His voice suddenly changed and his head snapped up. Whatever he had briefly experienced had vanished just as quickly. 'Thanos wasn't there, though, and yet my mother had treated him like another son. And, although I tried to find out what had happened to him, no-one knew – or at least no-one admitted to knowing – except for one, my great-uncle Gahred, who was bard of the Ordivian line that ruled the western lands'.

'I heard of him,' Tuan said suddenly. 'Did he not compose the *Lay of the Reiver*?'

Paedur smiled. 'Aye, he did:

> *The Reivers return,*
> *with blood and death,*
> *and fire and storm,*
> *the Reivers return.*'

Tuan's strong voice broke in;

> *'Their swords are singing,*
> *bright and keen,*
> *fearing neither god,*
> *nor man nor beast,*
> *the Reivers return.*'

He stopped. 'I didn't know Gahred was related to you.'

'I did not know the lay was still remembered,' Paedur said gently.

'All the Taourg know the *Reiver's Return*.'

'That would have pleased Gahred.'

'Does he live still?' Tuan wondered.

Paedur shook his head. 'No, his bones rest in the grounds of Baddalaur.' The bard continued on in a voice grown harsh with some emotion. 'Time, time, there is little enough left. Gahred told me that Thanos had left the village the previous year . . . to study in Maante. Aye, here is Maante. He is returning; returning to the place of his beginning as it were. For it was here that he first came into contact with the priests of Trialos. They were not as active then as they are now, but they took the youth and schooled him. Perhaps they were aware of his potential, for Thanos received training above and beyond that of the ordinary novice.

'Something attracted him to Trialos and the New Religion; the power, the wealth, or a combination of both. Who can tell? He advanced quickly through the ranks of the older, more experienced priests. Some resented this, but they met with accidents. Eventually there was no-one standing in his way, except Sutar, the High Priest.'

'He died horribly,' Cliona said with a shudder.

Paedur bowed his head slightly. 'Aye, he died horribly. Someone – something – attacked him as he lay sleeping. A beast it was said. But what beast could scale the glass-smooth walls of a sheer tower, enter through a slit window, decapitate, disembowel and dismember a man – and do all this silently?'

'A demon?' Tuan asked.

The encircling light flickered once more. Paedur glanced at it, then hurried on. 'Perhaps it was a demon. But who invoked that demon? In any case, it left the way open for Thanos to assume the role of High Priest.'

'Is he not supposed to be a recluse?' Tuan asked.

Paedur nodded. 'That is an image he has worked hard to create. He has always stayed very much in the background, preferring to work through intermediaries, thus fostering his image as a simple man of prayer. Yet he is the real power behind the strength and resurgence of the New Religion today.'

'And he is here in Maante?' Cliona asked.

'Aye, he is here. Thanos, his new acolyte Xanazius – whom I fancy I have come across before – and a full legion of the Band of Kloor. And tomorrow they sail for the Sea of Galae and the Blessed Isle – the Culai Isle.'

213

'When do we go?' Tuan asked.

And for the first time, the mate saw indecision on the bard's face. 'I suppose it must be soon,' he said slowly.

In the silence that followed the Dannu-fire flickered and died. Then high above, where the ceiling should have been, a small cerulean clot of fire began to throb. It expanded, pulsing outwards, in ever-widening concentric circles. Cliona, gazing at the blue whirling cloud, felt as if she were falling up into the centre of the maelstrom. Abruptly the light swooped and expanded and was all about them, enfolding them within its warm embrace. They were blind and deaf, totally unaware of the ruined temple in which they had been scant moments before; totally unaware of one another; they were enrapt, encircled by the whirling, throbbing, gently susurrant, sapphire cloud all around them.

Light, vast streamers of vari-coloured belts of liquid light floated past their blind eyes, felt more than seen. Rainbow-hued fireflies danced intricate patterns across their skins, the touch of the tiny creatures needle sharp and painful.

Then a voice – a female voice – spoke from within the colours; the clouds trembled, the delicate notes of the whispered voice sending ripples of colour through the cloud, azure, violet, turquoise, beryl and aquamarine chasing one another in flowing patterns about the solid cloud of light. And now the rainbow colours were gone, just the pale and dancing shades of blue remaining.

'You have served us well, Paedur-shanaqui-Hookhand. And yet there is the one final task to be completed, but still you linger . . . linger. Your companions are at hand, why do you linger . . . linger . . .?'

Paedur spoke, his usually mellow voice now harsh and raw, sending crashing waves of discordant non-colour through the delicate shades. 'I would know what the future holds before I act.'

And as the patterns gradually settled, the voice whispered gently once more, in reply to the bard's question. 'There is no future . . . future. There is a darkness . . . darkness. Only you have the power to change the future . . .'

'Is that future not fixed?' Paedur demanded.

'It is what may be, not what will be . . . will be.'

Again the crashing wave of white non-colour. 'What help can you render me – us?'

'There is a boat ready . . . ready. A favourable sea and winds

have been arranged . . . arranged. But our power does not extend
on to the Sea of Galae . . . Galae. For there all mortal time ends
and timelessness rules . . . rules.' The voice slowly faded and the
shades of blue began to pale, revealing the three figures. It
continued to lighten until a thin film, almost a mist, surrounded
the trio. Suddenly the mist was shattered as Paedur stood up,
breaking the spell surrounding them. Cliona slumped forward and
would have fallen had not the mate caught her. He looked at the
bard. 'What was that?'

'The Goddess,' he said, but he refused to be drawn further.

'What now?' Tuan asked then.

Paedur shrugged and sighed. 'You heard. To the shore, and
then . . .?'

The door suddenly crashed inwards and the Band of Kloor
poured in, weapons ready. 'Kill them!'

Tuan counted ten of them as his knife came clear of its sheath. It
was the only weapon he had; the sword he had taken from the slain
warrior had been lost as they fled through the ruins. He began to
pray, silently, desperately. Two against ten. He looked about for
something to use as a weapon, something to give him extra reach;
his short knife would be little use against a sword.

The wand the bard had fired earlier lay on the altar. He reached
down to pick it up, but a slim white hand stopped him. He looked into
Cliona's deep eyes, seeing himself reflected in the pools of light.

'No, this is mine,' she said desperately.

The mate had no time to argue as the first of the Religion's
warriors came upon him.

The Band had divided into two groups, five men to a group.
They were attempting to encircle the two men. One man broke
ranks and ran swiftly towards Tuan, his sword held high, poised
for a downward swing that would decapitate its target.

Tuan threw himself forwards and down, coming up directly in
front of the startled youth, the sword whistling past Tuan's head,
moaning almost regretfully as it parted only air. The mate grabbed
the youth by the throat and plunged his dagger into the extended
jugular. Blood spurted over Tuan as the body fell forward,
pushing him down on to his knees. Using the body as a shield,
Tuan prised the sword from the dead man's locked fingers. Two
more were coming at him; he pushed the body in his arms at them,
felt it twitch and jerk as they hacked at it in a vain attempt to reach
him. He stabbed upwards, blindly, with the sword, felt it connect,

215

grate along bone, heard the shrill animal-like scream; he heaved the bloody burden away from him, into the faces of two others, stepped back to Cliona's side, parried a thrust with his knife, slashed with the sword, felt it tremble in contact with metal, then bite into flesh.

In the lull that followed, he found he had slain three.

However, the warriors treated the bard with a little more respect. They didn't know what to expect from this black-clad figure of whom they had heard so much. But Thanos had said that he was human enough to be killed by a blade, and a fortune to the first man who brought in his head and hook. A kingdom to the one who brought the bard back alive. The five warriors surrounded Paedur, ringing him with steel. One probed with his sword, then was abruptly wrenched forward as the bard caught and trapped the blade with his hook, using it to pull the man in. Instinct made him retain his grip, his free hand clawing for a dagger. The bard struck out with the palm of his hand, catching the warrior beneath his nose, just above the lip, striking upwards. The warrior felt his head explode as jagged splinters of bone and cartilage were driven up into his brain. He was dead before he hit the ground.

A shrill scream coming from his right distracted another of Paedur's attackers. He glanced aside for a heartbeat – a fatal heartbeat. The bard's hook flashed out, a gleaming silvery blur, catching the warrior under the chin, cutting upwards, opening his throat like sliced fruit. Another warrior struck out, only to find his target was no longer there but rather behind him; he felt the hook cut deeply into his throat, pull, tear . . . then no more. Three down.

As the rest of the warriors fell back, the bard joined Cliona and Tuan by the altar stone.

The four surviving warriors of the Band of Kloor fell back, rejoining and looking about in amazement and horror. Six men, slain in no more than a score of heartbeats. By two men. And one of them with only one hand.

'I think they will try to rush us from both sides,' the mate whispered. 'They're going to be more careful this time.' Paedur nodded silently.

The four warriors whispered amongst themselves and then divided into two groups, taking up positions on either side of the altar, their swords and knives held ready. This time there would be no mistake.

Tuan and Paedur placed Cliona between them and then they turned to face the remaining warriors.

Tuan found himself facing two youths, their eyes wild, jaws clenched. Their faces were sheened with sweat. Tuan was gambling that they were not seasoned warriors; gambling with his life. He feinted to his left then suddenly fell at the feet of the two young men. One stumbled against his companion, putting them both off balance; Tuan's sword ripped upwards striking one in the groin, his knife slashing at the back of the other's knee. Both fell heavily on top of him, but he was trapped, pinned to the ground by the weight of their armour.

Paedur was not facing youths but seasoned warriors. They approached cautiously, one from either side. Almost imperceptibly a signal passed between the two, and they attacked together. The bard, however, had caught the signal and threw himself forward between the two men, rolling easily to his feet and coming up behind them. One screamed a warning and spun around in time to receive the bard's hook across the mouth, severing his jaw, cutting almost back into the spine. The other stabbed with his sword, and Paedur felt the blade grate off his belt buckle. He grabbed the warrior's extended sword arm and squeezed. He felt the bones pop beneath his grasp. The warrior threw his head back to scream, and Paedur sliced his throat, ear to ear.

Tuan was in trouble. Both of his attackers were still alive and conscious, although one was severely wounded and the other hamstrung, but the mate lay helpless beneath the one he had stabbed through the groin. The mortally wounded warrior grinned at him, a ghastly rictus of his facial muscles, blood dribbling from his mouth where the mate's blade had pierced upwards into the base of his lungs.

'You . . . will die . . . for the greater . . . gl . . . glory of . . . Kloor!' he screamed as he died and then his hamstrung companion raised himself on one arm, his knife held high. There was a sudden keening in the air, then a sickening thud as if rotten fruit were being crushed. The warrior stiffened and fell forward, the back of his head crushed. Cliona dropped the shattered wand and fumbled desperately at the two bodies on top of Tuan's, vainly attempting to pull the armoured bodies off him. She was weeping and laughing at the same time.

'I had to . . He would have killed you . . . to desecrate the wand . . . and such a good wand too. A powerful wand . . . one of the best . . . but I had to.'

Paedur gently lifted her by the arms and led the shaking priestess to the foot of the altar, catching her face, forcing her to look up into his eyes. 'Sleep,' he commanded. Her eyes abruptly glazed and she slumped, unconscious.

Tuan meanwhile had succeeded in freeing himself from beneath the two dead bodies. He stood with the bard and surveyed the carnage. Ten bodies, ten unknown warriors, some no more than youths, their spirits abruptly torn free of their bodies, their sprawled bodies looking almost alien, and some hideously comical.

Paedur looked at the mate's gore-splattered form. Tuan was covered from head to foot in drying blood; it clotted in his hair, encrusted his clothing, even smeared his teeth. He grinned ruefully. 'I must look a sight, eh? Well, you're no beauty either.' Suddenly all the humour left him. He dropped the sword and cleaned his knife on the corner of his shirt before slipping it back into its sheath. 'Come on, let's get out of here.' He bent down and lifted Cliona in his broad arms, his hands leaving bloody prints along the white and blue samite of her dress.

Paedur nodded absently. 'We had better find someplace to clean up. Then . . .'

'Then . . .?' Tuan asked.

Paedur looked over at him and smiled thinly, without humour. 'Then we'd better see about that boat.'

13   The Sea of Galae

And the bard and his companions sailed the Sea of Galae in search of the Blessed Isle

Life of Paedur, the Bard

The Blessed Isle is marked on many charts, but none have ever come to it, for no-one has yet navigated the Sea of Galae.

Lilis' Geographica

Tuan shaded his eyes against Nusas' glare and nodded at the bulging sail. 'Why is our craft the only one that seems to be moving? Everything else is becalmed.'

Paedur, who was kneeling in the prow of the small frail-seeming fishing smack, looked back over his shoulder. 'Faurm, one of the Windlords, aids us now.'

'And we're not the only ones moving,' Cliona said, pointing aft to where a long sleek coastal cruiser moved away from Maante's harbour walls.

The bard stood up and shaded his eyes. 'Thanos,' he muttered. 'Aiaida, the Religion's Lord of the Sea Wind, must be helping him.'

'Can we outrun him?' Tuan asked.

'No,' Paedur smiled thinly, 'but neither can he catch us. The two windlords are fairly evenly matched. If they do battle . . .' he hesitated and then shrugged, 'well, the only winners will be Mannam and Libellius, the Dark Lords of the Faith and Religion.'

'What about magic; could he not attempt to sink us that way?'

'No. Even I would not attempt a sending – or indeed, even a minor working – so close to the Grey Wall.'

'Why not?' Cliona wondered.

'The wall is Culai-fashioned, but to maintain itself it draws upon the magic of this and the many other planes of existence. Every time a spell of any nature is worked, a tiny fraction of it is drawn to the wall. However, it also distorts any spells that might be worked in its vicinity.' He smiled at Cliona. 'How many magicians did you know in Maante?'

She thought about it for a moment, then shook her head. 'None; some minor spell-makers, and most of those were charlatans.'

The crafts were swept out of Maante Harbour and on to the Aangle Sea by their respective windgods, with neither gaining on the other. This part of the coast was completely devoid of islands and the sea stretched flat and unbroken to the horizon where it met the Grey Wall.

Cliona moved down the craft to stand beside Tuan who had the tiller. 'What is it?' she asked, pointing to the horizon.

Tuan smiled. 'Fog.'

The bard, who was standing in the prow, staring straight ahead, glanced back over his shoulder and smiled. 'A little more than fog, surely?'

Tuan nodded. 'A little. How long before we reach it?' he asked then.

'We should have reached the wall by nightfall.' And what then, Paedur wondered, staring towards the distant wall, what happens when we reach the wall? He knew of it from his tales and legends; he had read the factual accounts of travellers and mariners who had sailed – either by accident or design – too close, or even into the fringes of the shifting fog banks. But no-one knew what lay within the heart of the Grey Wall. Even the Culai Isle – which he had visited once before very briefly – did not hold as much fear for him as the Sea of Galae which lay behind the wall.

Their craft reached the Grey Wall just as the sun was sinking, tinting the shifting cloud a dull, bloody pink. It towered above them like a great bastion, its height lost in the clouds, and it dwindled away on both sides seemingly to infinity, curving with the distance. From afar it had the appearance of a solid wall, yet as they neared the Culai-fashioned barrier, the silent watchers could see that the wall floated above the waves at about the height of a tall man and was in constant motion, weaving and twisting, shifting as if blown by winds not of this world. Strange shadows slid past behind the grey veil, but the silhouettes were not of any animal either Tuan or Cliona knew. As night fell, there were a series of animal and bird cries and snarls and screams that floated across the still air, and again neither of them could recognise the sounds. With the onset of night the wall brightened and then gleamed with a strange milky opalescence, as if the Lady Lussa bestrode the heavens, but it was not the time for the Moon Goddess to ride out in her swan-drawn chariot.

And then the wind died, leaving their craft bobbing on the oily swell half a league from the fringes of the Grey Wall. Tuan turned to Paedur, 'What happens now?'

'The gods' power must fade here.' His hook gleamed silver in the light from the wall as he pointed aft, 'The Religion's power also. Sleep, if you can; I don't imagine you will find much sleep once we are on the Sea of Galae.'

Tuan glanced at the priestess. 'I don't think I could sleep with that thing looming over me; the gods only know what might creep out under cover of dark . . .'

Paedur pressed the blade of his hook against his lips, covering a smile. 'I don't think anything will come out. Even so, I think I'll remain awake . . .' He looked down at Cliona. 'You could try to sleep though . . .'

The priestess shook her head. 'No, I don't think so . . .'

Paedur inclined his head slightly. 'As you wish then . . .'

A score of heartbeats later, she and Tuan were both asleep.

Tuan awoke suddenly, his mariner's instincts telling him that they were moving again. He found the bard in the stern, his hook curved around the tiller. 'We're moving,' he said, unnecessarily.

'A current came up just before dawn and began pulling us in; we have been picking up speed.' Paedur nodded to the priestess. 'Wake her up, and then hold her – I'm not sure what will happen when we hit the wall.'

Tuan kissed the priestess, bringing her awake with a whimper. 'Hang on,' he murmured, 'we're moving in to the wall.' Even as he was speaking the craft began to pick up speed, a double wake of churning white spreading out behind them. Tuan crouched over the priestess holding her with one hand, the other wrapped around the mast, and then the tiny boat struck the shifting, misty wall, and shuddered to a standstill. Grey tendrils of freezing fog reached out and enveloped them. The freezing fog thickened, and soon they could barely make out each other.

'What now?' Tuan asked, his breath pluming whitely on the air.

Cliona shivered. 'We're going to freeze to death,' she said, her teeth chattering, every breath she took searing her throat and lungs.

The bard shook his head, 'No, we're just passing through the Place Between the Worlds; the chill will soon abate.'

The banks of fog abruptly lightened, and the chill was replaced by a thick cloying heat. Tuan felt the rime that had formed in his hair and beard melt, and he looked down the craft at the bard to find his heavy cloak steaming. 'We have passed through the wall; this is the Sea of Galae,' Paedur said with a rare genuine smile.

The fog remained, although it was not as thick as before, but it served to muffle all sounds and a deathly silence hung over the sea. Even the normal sounds aboard ship were muted, and when someone spoke their voice was faint as if heard through thick glass or from a distance. They had no idea whether Thanos and the Band of Kloor had made it through to the Sea of Galae, although the bard felt they must have. Even here, on the haunted sea, he would have known if someone as powerful and malign as the Hand of God had died.

Time became meaningless within the wall; there was neither night nor day, and the grey half-light, not unlike the northern winter twilight, persisted. But the bard seemed to be able to keep track of the hours, for he would indicate when a meal should be prepared, or advise Cliona when her devotions to Dannu were due. However, Paedur seemed disinclined to speak and the constant, oppressive sameness of the sea depressed both Cliona and Tuan and so they spent much of the time sleeping.

It was the morning of the fourth day on the sea, by Tuan's reckoning, when he noticed a change in their surroundings: the fog had lightened in colour and thinned considerably. He was about to speak to the bard when Paedur handed him a blindfold; Cliona was already holding one in her small hands, examining the eye-patches which had coins sewn into them to ensure that no trace of light seeped through.

The mate held up the length of cloth. 'I assume this has something to do with the change?' he said.

Paedur nodded. 'As you can see the fog has begun to lighten and soon it will seem as though it is about to dissipate completely – however, I'm afraid it is but part of the sea's defences. Shadow-figures will then appear – drawn from your own minds and hereditary memories – and they will be of people close to you, your mother or father, brothers or lovers, but they are only shadows. You will also feel touches and caresses; and they will also speak, enticing you, talking in terms of love and endearment. Again, you must not heed them; the voices – like the images – are only those of your own memories animated by the magic of the Grey Wall, and the caresses will be nothing more than tendrils of mist drifting across your face and arms.'

'What do we need these for, then?' Cliona asked.

'I think you might find it easier not to listen to the voices, if you cannot see the wraiths.'

'There are only two blindfolds,' she added.

'I won't need one,' the bard said, with a wry smile.

'Just where are we?' Tuan asked. 'I have sailed across the oceans and seas of this world, but where are we now in relation to Maante, or the Aangle Peninsula, for example?'

Paedur glanced up into the lightening sky, judging how much time he had left. 'This sea is not in your world,' he replied. 'We have sailed through the space between the planes – the Ghost Worlds, where we experienced the chill – and now we are sailing the fringes of Sea of Galae, which belong to the Prime Plane but which touches the edges of all the others.'

'I'm not sure I understand,' Cliona said.

Tuan nodded, agreeing with her. 'How can this place be on the charts of our world – and yet not in our world?'

'You know the legend that the Culai still abide on the Blessed Isle, and although this isle is positioned on the charts of mariners, few sailors – if any – have ever succeeded in reaching it. How can I explain it . . .?' He looked around, at a loss for words, but then turned back and continued quickly. 'What you see on the mariners' charts is but a reflection, the like of which you must surely have seen hovering above the dunes of Nasgociba if you ever visited there with Duaize.' Tuan nodded and was about to speak, but the bard had pressed on. 'From a distance they seem tangible, yet as one nears them the mirage fades, like the morning mist on a summer's day. Like the Culai Isle one may never reach them, no matter how close one approaches.'

'And the Grey Wall?' Tuan asked.

'You might liken it to a doorway between the worlds.'

'And is there traffic between the worlds . . . the planes?' the priestess wondered, for though she had been told the tale of the creation of the Prime Plane and the lesser planes of existence, she had always thought them nothing more than parables.

'There is some traffic,' the bard said quickly, 'though it is not as frequent as it once was. But at one time the creatures that roam this world – and even man -- freely migrated through the Grey Walls.'

'Walls?' Tuan wondered. 'Are there more than one?'

'Many years ago, in my grandfather's time, there were many walls and gates scattered across the Seven Nations, but now, alas, they have all disappeared. This is one of the last, and it has survived because it was the most powerful of all the walls, and the only one which leads directly to the Prime Plane; although,' he added, 'I have heard that there are still walls and gates standing in the strange hotlands of the south.'

'What happened to the gates?' Tuan asked.

'Neglect mainly; the gates thrived on use – they fed on a little of each user's essence.'

'Are they alive then?'

'Yes, they have life of a sort, but not as you would recognise it. And now they are slowly dying, fading in the strong light of Nusas, like mist burning away before sunrise. Even this wall is not as it once was.' He looked at them, his eyes flat and expressionless. 'There is an end coming to all things.'

'And perhaps it is coming sooner that we think,' Cliona whispered, but if either the bard or Tuan heard her they said nothing.

'Put your blindfolds on now,' Paedur ordered them. 'And remember, ignore everything you hear or feel. I will not let any harm come to you.'

The priestess bowed her head and pulled back her hair and Tuan slipped the blindfold around her head, settling the two coin-filled patches over her eyes. He felt the tension in her neck and shoulder muscles and he kissed her lightly on the forehead, whispering that she need have no fear – he was with her now. The mate looked over at the bard, and Paedur nodded once, and then Tuan pulled on his own blindfold and sat down with the priestess, with his back to the mast.

Paedur looked down at the two huddled figures by his feet and then he sketched a quick sigil of protection above their heads. If the circumstances had been different perhaps Cliona and Tuan might have had a life together, but then, Paedur realised, without the present circumstances it was unlikely that a priestess of the Old Faith and a Nasgociban pirate would ever have met. He felt his hook begin to warm, and he knew that something was approaching. He tugged his cloak close about his shoulders with his right hand and pulled up the hood; he was not afraid, but nor was he foolish enough to do anything rash. He glanced down at the priestess and the mate again and wondered would he be able to protect them, and then, in that instant – although he was not gifted with true foresight – he knew they would not be returning from the

Culai Isle. A smile touched his thin lips; he had a feeling no-one would be returning from the Culai Isle.

The muffled silence was disturbed by a faint moaning sound, like a summer breeze blowing through leafy copses. It began as a wordless drone but it soon broke up and single words and then fragments of conversation became distinguishable . . . and then the wraiths appeared.

They were fog-wraiths, creatures from coalesced mist and fog and drawn from the memories – both recent and hereditary – of Cliona and Tuan. Strangely, there were no memories generated from the bard's unconscious. Paedur watched the figures with interest. Some were recognisable, the resemblance to either the man or woman being marked, but as the figures continued to file past and the clothing, armour and weapons changed, belonging to earlier ages, the resemblances became less marked, except for the occasional feature which was definitely Cliona's or Tuan's. And the fog-wraiths reached forth with long misty fingers and stroked and caressed the cringing mate and enticed the terrified priestess. When there was no reaction to their caresses or blandishments, the figures moved on and vanished back into the fog.

Paedur suddenly stiffened as his arcane hook burned painfully into the bone of his wrist. He had thought the wraiths were gone, but there was another group gathering now; there were only four figures, and the bard realised that these must be the earliest memories of man – they were the Culai, the First Race.

They were tall and sharp-featured, and they strode up to the small fishing smack with all the arrogance of gods. The Culai had often been worshipped as gods – and it was a title they had taken for themselves – but although they wielded their awesome powers with god-like negligence there was still something about them which marked them of the race of man. Perhaps it was in their eyes, which were hard and cruel – and only man can be cruel; the gods have no time to indulge themselves.

They paused and gathered about the craft, their great height dwarfing it. The bard's hook was blazing with the cold white fire that warned him of Power, but he didn't need his hook to tell him just how powerful these Culai-wraiths were. He could feel the awesome force radiating from them, and even the shivering pair became quiet and blindly turned their cloth-wrapped faces towards the Culai, like a blossom turning its head towards the sun. One stretched out his hand to the priestess, and though she could not see it she still reached instinctively for the long slim fingers.

'Come.' His voice was strong and resonant, unmuffled by the mist, carrying with it the trace of an accent. As his hand approached the priestess it became more solid, taking on a definite shape and form, the veins becoming defined, the tendons rigid, the nails long and slightly curved. Suddenly the bard lunged forward, his hook glittering whitely, slicing through the outstretched arm. The wraith screamed, a high-pitched jarring sound that bit deep into Paedur's skull and set his hook vibrating. The hook blazed with a brilliant incandescence as it passed through the fog, and then long ribbon-like streamers broke away, and the entire shade tattered and was shredded as some ghostly wind pulled it apart.

Another tenuous hand slid across to grasp either the priestess or mate, but again the bard struck through it with his hook, the white fire coursing through his body, and again the Culai was torn apart by the unseen wind.

The two remaining Culai drifted away from the craft and hovered at about the height of the main mast, watching the two humans almost hungrily, Paedur thought. He wondered then what would have happened if they had actually managed to touch either of them. He sketched a sign in the air before them, and their forms wavered and then abruptly drew in on themselves and disappeared. 'It is over,' Paedur said, exhaustion settling over him; the Culai-wraiths had drained him.

As Cliona and Tuan peeled off their blindfolds, they plainly heard screams coming from the direction where they had last seen the boat carrying Thanos and the priests and warriors of Trialos and Kloor.

'What is it?' Tuan murmured.

'The sea's defences have attacked them.'

'Perhaps those same defences will destroy the evil ones,' Cliona whispered. She looked at the bard and found that his face was bone-white, his eyes sunken and dead in his head. 'You are ill!'

Paedur shook his head. 'Not ill, just tired. As for Thanos, well he may have lost some men, but Thanos is powerful and cunning and I have no doubt he will outwit the Cul . . . the defences.' He looked over at the mate. 'Take the tiller. Hold our course as best you can. I will try to rest.'

Tuan and Cliona watched the bard sink into a cross-legged

postition with his back to the mast and settle his cloak about him, and almost immediately his head dropped forward and he was asleep.

'I've never seen him sleep before,' Tuan whispered, more frightened now by the bard's exhaustion than by the danger of the Sea.

'I wonder what were the sea's defences?' Cliona said; 'something powerful and terrible if they were able to exhaust a creature like the bard.'

'What do we do now?'

Cliona ran her fingers through her thick hair, dragging it back from her face. 'We hold the course and wait for Paedur to waken.'

'How am I supposed to keep to a course with neither sun, moon nor stars to guide me? And when will he awake?'

Cliona knelt by the bard's side and felt for a pulse in his wrist and then in his throat; she could find neither. And yet his chest rose and fell slightlty. She lifted his head and peeled back an eyelid, but she could only see a white expanse of eyeball. She looked up at Tuan. 'I'm not sure when he will awaken – I'm not even sure if he's alive!'

Paedur awoke two days later, just as the temperature began to fall and the fog wall was darkening. 'We're nearly through,' he said, coming smoothly to his feet, catching both the priestess and mate by surprise. 'The Sea of Galae, the sea between the worlds, ends here, and now we're about to enter the Prime Plane.'

'You're well again?' Cliona asked.

Paedur glanced over his shoulder. 'Exhaustion merely,' he smiled.

'I don't suppose you want to say what you defended us from, do you?' Tuan asked.

'It's unimportant,' Paedur said, turning away and making his way down the small craft to stand by the prow.

Although the temperature fell dramatically, it was not so cold as when they had entered upon the sea, nor was it as dark. The transition came quickly: one moment they were still within the mist and then it thickened – and vanished. They had passed through the last obstacle, they were upon the Prime Plane. They had come through the Sea of Galae unscathed, but the Blessed Isle lay before them, and neither man nor beast had ever returned from the Culai Isle.

They came out on to a wide, featureless ocean – whose waters were startlingly white, a bleached harsh absence of colour that pierced the eyes, the type which would surely bring a sudden blindness to those who stared too long into its alabaster depths.

'It reminds me of the deadly ice-fields beyond northern Thusal,' Tuan said, his voice falling to a whisper, the white water bringing back terrifying memories of the haunted ice-lands where even the very elements conspire to wipe the land free of all living creatures, animal and vegetable.

'We're moving,' Cliona said, turning to look at the Grey Wall that was now shrinking rapidly behind them, the featureless, almost colourless rolling fog stretching to the horizon, marking the boundary of their new world.

She suddenly swore, and as Paedur and Tuan turned they saw the sleek black craft that broke through the wall and they knew then that Thanos too had successfully navigated the Sea of Galae.

'I never expected otherwise,' Paedur said quietly, turning away.

They sailed across the alabaster ocean for five long days, five days indistinguishable from each other, with no change in the bleached seascape. For five short nights also they sailed, pursued always by the black ship of Thanos. At night the bard would take the tiller and the mate and the priestess would lie sheltered in the lee of their craft's single sail, and they would gaze up at the strange stars that studded the cloth of heaven and the bard would name the stars for them and tell their histories and their attributes.

Here was the Sceptre and Orb, and these were the property of the Emperor, and they had been won from the Princeling, and in the battle he had been cast down and no longer occupied the Throne of Heaven. And there, faint behind the Empress, was the Emperor, for the Empress had come to usurp the Emperor much as he had done to the Princeling, and his light was already beginning to fade. These were of the House of Royal.

And Paedur also pointed out the Houses of Astrios, the Winged Ones; of Baaste, and of Wand, and finally as they rose late in the night, the Twilight House of the Culaithe, the Sign of the Culai.

On the morning of the sixth day, when the mate arose, he found the bard standing by the prow, staring intently ahead.

'What is it?'

The bard pointed with his hook, ahead and a little to port.

'What does it look like?'

Tuan shaded his pale eyes and squinted towards the smudge on the horizon. 'Land,' he said finally.

Paedur nodded, turning away. 'The Blessed Isle.'

As the blistering day wore on, the smudge resolved itself into an island, which rose up out of the ocean with an almost frightening speed. Around noon, it was still distant but so large that Tuan turned to the bard, shaking his head in astonishment. 'That's not an island – it's a continent!'

Paedur smiled slightly and shook his head. 'It's an island, I assure you.'

As the afternoon moved into evening, the island rose up out of the water before them, and they could make out the high and lofty cliffs, carved from what looked like glass and worked with the effigies of men who were not truly men, and beasts that were not wholly beasts. And in the low afternoon sunlight it looked as if the figures were animate, for the shadows writhing and twisting across the glass cliffs gave them a semblance of life.

There was a wall on top of the cliff. But a wall the like of which even the giant builders of Necrosia could not have built. A wall that would have defied the abilities of the builders of the Tomb City of Ellian whose architects knew the secret of softening stone. Brick upon massive brick, it towered above the cliff, almost doubling its height.

'It's incredible,' Tuan murmured.

'Each brick is as tall as a single-floored dwelling,' Paedur remarked almost absently.

It took Cliona three attempts to count the number of blocks. 'But it's eighty blocks high!'

A series of shifting cross currents took their craft then, spinning them in beneath the cliffs, and then they rounded a promontory and found they were facing a broad shingly beach. The currents had died, and the natural pull of the sea swept them up into the shadows in a welter of creamy foam. Tuan was about to leap into the water to secure the craft further up the beach when the bard stopped him. 'On no account must you touch the beach with your bare flesh.' His eyes were hard and cold, and the mate could see tiny white sparks running up and down the bard's hook, gathering in the etched runes, almost making them move. 'Watch!' Paedur said.

The bard lifted a fruit from their supplies. It had been wrapped in its leaves to preserve it and was still firm and unblemished. He tossed it out on to the shingle beach. It had scarcely touched the smoothly polished stones when they began to move, sliding towards the fruit. They piled around the fruit, then they rolled over it, smothering it in a wave of shingle. With a spurt of juice it was crushed to pulp.

Tuan climbed back into the boat, rubbing his bare arms, smoothing down the small hairs which were standing upright. 'What do we do now?' he asked, his voice trembling.

But the bard laughed shortly and leaped into the shallows, splashing up on to the shore. 'The stones only scent living matter,' he said. 'If you're wearing shoes, you're safe.'

The bard led them with an easy familiarity across the now quiescent stones, which however still moved threateningly, a tiny rattling off to their right and now a rasp of stone to their left. They were halfway up the beach when the priestess began to shiver. Her lips turned blue and tiny particles of ice formed on her clothes and in her hair. Yet the mate and the bard were unaffected.

'*T-t-t-uannnn . . .*'

The mate spun around, his knife coming into his hand but he almost dropped it when he saw the state Cliona was in. She looked as if she had been caught in a blizzard. Her hair was frozen in long thick tresses and the frost had turned it white. Her skin was pinched blue and there was a thin coating of ice on her skin. Her clothing was solid. The mate reached out for her, but the bard's hook caught in his sleeve, pulling his hand back. 'The cold is such that it would sear your own flesh – and hers if you touched.'

'But what's wrong with her?'

But the bard didn't answer, he merely used the point of his hook to direct the shivering priestess back on to the beach, almost to the water's edge. The ice melted almost immediately but left her soaking in freezing water. Tuan and the bard both threw their cloaks around her shoulders, but her teeth were still chattering as she told them what had happened.

'It was as if I had plunged into an icy pool, every breath was ice-fire in my lungs, and I felt as if my eyes were about to burst. I was going to die,' she said, shivering now, not with the cold but with reaction.

Tuan looked over at Paedur. 'What caused it – and why did it affect only Cliona?'

The bard shook his head slightly, staring up at the lifelike carvings. 'I'm not sure . . .' He looked at Cliona. 'Show me where you first felt the chill.'

'About there,' she pointed.

Paedur nodded, smiling thinly. 'It's the shadow of the cliffs, I'll wager. Did you not tell us of your halfling blood – you're a child of human man and Nightfolk woman, are you not? And the Nightfolk are the last preservers of the Culai magic. So . . .' He pointed upwards with his hook. 'These cliffs were not raised by the hand of mortal man . . . nor by the Culai, for in their last days on our world, when the infant kingdoms of man strove against the elder power of the Culai, there arose one amongst the First Race who was to change their world as never before. He was Kuallan, and was later called the Friend of Man.

'He saw his own race for what it was, and he had enough of the sight to realise that its days were numbered, and so he gathered together a group of Culai – visionaries, like himself – and he sent these out as missionaries to instruct man in that part of the Culai lore which might prove beneficial to the new race. When Kuallan knew that the Culai had very little time left, he devised a plan so that his race might not be totally annihilated. He travelled through the Grey Walls to the other planes of life and gathered together the greatest magicians and sorcerers on these worlds. Some were human-kind, but others had the likeness of beasts or demons and, although they were usually mortal enemies, Kuallan had bound them all together by extracting one promise from each of them. Until they fulfilled that promise they were his to command. And so he brought them here and they numbered one hundred and three, and should you care to count the effigies carved into the cliffs you will find the same number, for they left their likenesses carved here as the creators of the Isle.

'For that was their task; to build a home for the remaining Culai, an island safe and inviolate, unreachable and . . . inescapable. Thus they created the Blessed Isle. And these cliffs, carved from pure quartz and the massive wall atop the cliff, and the strange and hidden city in the valley behind the wall, all of this is the creation of the Kuallan Oathbound, and it was the greatest single feat of magic in the myriad planes of life.'

'But what has this got to do with the chill Cliona felt?' Tuan demanded.

'Because the Oathbound drew upon the stuff of the Void when they created the Isle. Kuallan had stipulated that they create a barrier to contain the First Race on the Isle; he knew they would attempt to escape once they had recouped their powers. And so the Oathbound wrought the essence of the Void into a wall – a barrier – which creatures of Power, and non-humans, may not pass. Cliona is sensitive to the chill of the Void because of her Nightfolk blood.'

'What can we do?' Tuan asked, looking up and down the beach, but he could see no way around the cliffs.

'You must leave me,' the priestess said, 'I must not hinder you.'

Paedur shook his head slightly. 'No, I won't leave you behind. Night will fall soon, so I suggest we return to the boat and wait and see what the morning brings. Perhaps by then I will have worked out a way to get you past the cliffs.'

They reached the fishing smack just as the sudden night fell, the last rays of sunlight turning the white water to blood and sending shadows rippling up the cliff face, bringing the carvings to life. Sleep didn't come easily that night; they all felt the unseen eyes on them, and occasionally stones rattled on the beach and there were sounds of what might have been a furtive whispering on shore – or it might just have been the sound of the surf on the stones and sand. Once, quite close to midnight, the bard called out in a strange tongue and all sound ceased, and in the silence that followed they plainly heard something hurry up the beach, stones clicking and rattling under its feet.

But far more potent were their imaginations; the night was dark and there were neither stars nor moon, and the white water gave no light. In the darkness their imaginations populated the parasitic beach with all manner of strange beasts and men, creatures woven from what they had glimpsed of the carved cliff face. Only the bard seemed unperturbed, and he stood by the mast for most of the night, wrapped in his black furred cloak, his chin sunk on his chest.

Morning came with the same swiftness as night had fallen and, as the first tints of crimson dawn spilled across the horizon, he awoke his companions who had fallen into an exhausted sleep in the late hours of night.

'We must set out for the city this day,' he said. 'The Band of Kloor and Thanos cannot be far behind and we must reach the city before them at all costs.'

'But how?' Cliona demanded. 'I cannot pass beyond the shadow of the cliffs.'

'There is a way,' Paedur said. turning to look at the priestess. 'It's dangerous, and it will mean revealing my presence here, but I can see no other way . . .'

'What do you want to do?' Cliona asked, something in the bard's carefully neutral expression sending shivers up her spine.

'I want to turn you into a *quai*.'

'No!'

'There's no other way,' the bard said, turning away.

'But a *quai*,' Tuan protested, 'a mindless thing. It's too dangerous.'

'It is dangerous,' Paedur agreed. 'But a *quai* is completely under the control of its creator, and it neither feels pain, heat nor cold. Cliona will be able to walk past the shadow of the cliffs, and once we've reached the other side I'll return her consciousness.'

'And if something should happen to you in the meantime?' Tuan demanded.

'Then she would remain a *quai*.'

'Leave me behind, I can try to delay Thanos and his warriors when they arrive,' Cliona insisted.

But the bard shook his head. 'It's not as easy as that. I'm going to need you when we find the vessel of the Chrystallis . . .'

The priestess stared at him for a long time, then she turned away. 'What choice do I have?' she said bitterly. 'Do it.'

'What choice do any of us have?' Paedur said softly.

'What happens now?' Tuan asked, putting his arm around the priestess, but she shrugged it off.

'We wait.'

As the morning wore on, Tuan grew restive and suggested that he should scout the trail ahead. 'There's no need; I already know the trail, and I need you here to watch for Thanos.'

The second craft appeared about midday, coming in fast on the current. Tuan could see the warriors of the Band of Kloor lining the rail, and behind them the tall white-robed red-eyed figure standing up by the figurehead, one hand shading his eyes, staring across at the fishing vessel. 'They're here,' he said quietly, pulling his knife free.

The bard began to work his magic then, using his hook to reflect the wan sunlight into Cliona's eyes, his trained voice dulling her senses, robbing her of her will, turning her into a *quai*, a mindless creature controlled by himself.

Tuan saw Thanos stiffen and raise his head as if troubled by a distant sound or a strange odour. The bard's magic had disturbed the Ghost Worlds, sending ripples of power coursing through it. Thunder rumbled distantly, and a sudden swell rocked the crafts.

'Thanos will wonder what we're up to,' Paedur explained as he took the priestess by the hand and helped her overboard into the shallows. 'He may think I was attempting to attack him, or setting up a spell here. It will slow him down and, more importantly, it will confuse him.' They were now up on to the beach, and with stones rattling, clicking and sliding threateningly all around them they set off at a run for the path he knew. Cliona ran blindly by his side, untroubled now by the shadow of the cliffs, while the mate took up the rear.

Thanos' craft was actually washed up on to the stones as the rising tide pushed them in. One of the Band, eager to bring back the head of the bard, leaped overboard. But his bare feet had scarcely touched the beach when the shingle began to move. Then it was as if a vast ripple ran across the stones and they flowed towards the stricken warrior, rolling in over his feet crushing them beneath their stone embrace. He floundered helplessly, as his legs gave way and the weight of his armour bore him down, hacking at the stones with his sword and then he fell and disappeared beneath a wave of pebbles. There was a single shriek and then the heaving mass of stone cracked and cracked again and then spurted red liquid. The stones continued to rattle for a few moments later, but the cairn was still.

The bard led Cliona and Tuan along the mazy rock paths that wound about the base of the carven cliffs before they finally led upwards. The cliff sides were smooth and polished, the tracks slippery and treacherous and, although Paedur and Cliona – who was still under his control – had little difficulty, Tuan was soon struggling. When they reached a broad natural ledge, the bard stopped and waited for the mate to join him. He flopped down on to the glass-like stone and took in great sobbing breaths. 'I seem to remember the last time I climbed a cliff with you, it almost killed me,' he gasped.

Paedur nodded briefly. 'But the enemy then was not so dangerous,' he said, and pointed downwards, his hook gleaming scythe-like in the early afternoon light. Tuan crawled out to the edge of the ledge and looked over. On the beach far below the Band of Kloor had disembarked, leaving Thanos standing tall and white in the prow of their craft, his garments fluttering on the light breeze. And then one of the Band pointed upwards, and all heads lifted up to where the bard stood outlined against the stark skyline, his hook burning silver against the dark night of his cloak.

Thanos pointed and Paedur and Tuan saw his mouth working. 'We had better move,' Paedur said, and the mate thought he detected a note of weariness in his voice. 'We've a long journey ahead of us.'

The cliff path soon gave out, and now their way sloped downwards through a long defile with the crystal wall of rock still rising up on either side, which at times also arched across the gully over their heads, so that it seemed as if they fled through a series of tunnels. Finally, as dusk was falling, Tuan called for the bard to stop awhile, for although he was a strong man he was now close to collapse.

'I'm sorry, I sometimes forget about the frailty of the human form. The defile finishes up ahead; we'll rest there.'

The track opened out a hundred paces further on to a broad rocky plateau that was perched high above a forest. The bard called out to the priestess and she stopped obediently. 'Rest awhile,' he said to Tuan. 'I will restore Cliona.'

Tuan dropped down with his back to one of the glass walls and stretched his legs out in front of him, massaging the stiffening muscles. He looked over at the bard, watching him order the priestess to sit down, and then he saw the bard raise his hook, gathering together her essence which he had scattered about the Ghost Worlds and drawing it back to her body, restoring her to full life. Tuan knew it was a frightening and delicate business, for should the bard falter then Cliona would remain a *quai*, and her body might be inhabited by some creature from beyond the Gorge.

And neither of them heard the stealthy approach of one of the Band of Kloor down the long defile. It was just one man, a tall blond-haired warrior, a native of the cold lands of Thusal, both swift and strong and accustomed to the rough trails of his homeland. The cliff face had presented him with no problems nor had the slippery trails – it was similar to walking on ice – and the bard and his companions were in too much of a hurry to disguise their trail, so he had caught up with them easily. The warrior paused in the mouth of the defile, feeling the power of his gods flow into him. He drew his sword and kissed the relic set into the hilt – his would be the honour of slaying the *shanaqui* bard.

He crept along the rough path noiselessly, moving nearer towards the *shanaqui* who was bending over one of his companions. He would kill them both together and carry their heads back to the Lord Thanos.

Yet even as he ran forward and leaped at the bard, his sword raised high, he was struck by a sudden thought – were there not two with the bard . . .?

He heard a hoarse shout off the rocks behind him. Aye, there was another – well, he too would die . . . but first he would take the *shanaqui* . . .

Something hard struck him in the back between the shoulder blades; it burned hot then cold – and he had taken enough knife wounds to know what it was. He could feel his blood flowing hot and warm down his back, but if he could take the *shanaqui* with him . . . And then the bard was turning and his arm raised and his hook rang shrilly as it cleaved the air and . . .

And silence hung heavily over the stone maze of the carven cliffs of the Blessed Isle.

They camped that night in the fastness of the rocks and of the three only the priestess slept for she was wearied and sickened by the *quai* transfer. The night was completely silent, and it even seemed to make the bard nervous, for he kept staring at his hook which glittered and sparkled as if it had been dusted with sand. In the early morning the silence was broken by the sound of sucking which passed their sheltered spot, and the mate was thankful there was no moon to illuminate the desolate rockland – and what roamed abroad.

As the night moved on a mist drifted in from the sea, a thick rolling white fog that blanketed the rocky terrain with waves of shifting smoke. The fog clung to the ground and didn't rise above hip level, and the bard told Tuan to rouse Cliona and move as far back into the rocky niche as they could, for the mist was bound to bring out other night creatures to hunt and stalk.

And as the short night sped towards a bloody dawn, they heard screams behind and below them, echoing and re-echoing off the crystal walls, and they knew that another of the Band had fallen to the guardians of the Isle.

Dawn burned across the alien skies, but the fog did not lift, it merely deepened in colour to a bloody crimson, until even the air seemed to reek of the charnel odour of blood. The mist gathered on the cold stones and ran in twisting streams down the rocks, so that it looked as if they bled.

'It's nothing to fear,' Paedur said, his voice calm and detached. 'This fog is merely another of the island's defences. It is designed to terrify, but it has no other power.' He looked at the terrified priestess, and noted Tuan's strained face, and realised what he was saying was having little effect. He knew what was causing the red fog, he knew it was merely an inanimate defence, and he also realised that he was no longer human enough to fully comprehend the effect it was having on his companions. 'Watch,' he said simply. He stretched out his left arm, his hook a red scythe dripping blood, and then he began to whisper softly. The bloody fog began to lift almost immediately, it swirled away from Paedur's hook in concentric circles, moving away from them. The red liquid on the stones steamed and dried up into a fine rust-coloured dust, and then it scattered on a warm breeze that blew up from the valley below.

They set out for the City of the Culai. About mid-morning the rough winding paths they had been following through the crags changed and became a wide and carefully tended road. It continued to lead downwards, down to the level of the scattered clouds that hid the valley lying below them. Through the clouds they could just make out the tops of the tall trees, lush and almost painfully green after the starkness of the crystal rocks. The track wound down into a gully – and then the wall to their left fell away in a sheer sweep of rock to the lush greenery of the valley, leaving them standing on a track that was barely a sword-length across. The track led sharply downwards, although the lower it went the broader the ledge became. The crystal rock also changed, becoming darker and cloudy, more like quartz, until it finally became a smoothly polished basalt. Further on, they began to notice markings in the rock that were too regular to be the work of nature.

Cliona ran her fingers along the notches, until she finally noticed a pattern. 'They're glyphs,' she said in surprise, looking more closely at them. Some were sharp, irregular notches that bit deeply into the rock, others were twisted spirals and helices and there were blocks and half-finished squares that looked almost painted on the rock. In places pictograms and ideographs marched sedately along, whilst underneath long flowing lines of script swept past. She looked at the bard in wonder, 'What are they?'

'What you see are the one hundred and three languages of the Oathbound,' he said, looking back along the rock, frowning slightly.

'What do they say?' she wondered.

'The message is the same; it is a warning – a warning: *"Lifeless yet shall live, deathless ever be, ye who pass beyond."*'

'But does it refer to any of the Culai who might be attempting to escape, or to someone – like ourselves – trying to get in?'

The bard shrugged. 'I'm not sure.'

The track rounded an outcropping and then opened out on to a broad ledge. Paedur stopped and pointed out over the broad forest below towards a massive walled and moated city.

'Ui Tyrin, the Last City of the Culai.'

From their high vantage point, the city was a solid – almost featureless – mass of ochre sandstone, surrounded by a lush dense forest which encircled a broad golden plain around the walls. The city itself was in the bowl of the valley, running in strict lines of unwavering straightness within the precise geometric pentagon of its walls. Even from the distance they could see that it had been built from massively hewn blocks of stone that only the First Race knew how to work. If it followed the pattern of other Culai buildings, the stones would be laid mortar-less, but such was the perfection of their craft that a knife blade could not be placed within the seams between the blocks. Unadorned in the manner of the Culai, it yet conveyed an aura of stark beauty and harsh simplicity. But it had one curious feature, for in the centre of the city was a single vast building built in the form of a goblet.

'That,' Paedur said, pointing, 'is the Inner City; it contains the Circle of Keys, and the Chrystallis.'

Above its broad almost flat base rose a squat spire, as functional and as sombre as was the rest of the city and atop this spire rested another flat-topped building – which completed the image of a cup. There were no windows as far as they could see, and from the distance the whole building looked as if it had been carved from a single piece of stone.

Tuan and Cliona stared at the city in wonder for awhile, and then the bard urged them on. Night was falling as they descended into the valley and they then realised that there were neither lights nor evening fires from Ui Tyrin, giving it a deserted, haunted appearance.

They camped that night in a cleft in the rockface off the track and, at the bard's insistence, Tuan built a small wall across the opening, for they didn't know what creature might wander down from the heights or up from the valley below. 'But I haven't seen any living thing here,' he protested. 'Where are the sea birds that

238

should have circled above our heads as we came ashore; and what about the lizards and goats that we should have found living in and around the cliffs? We're coming down into a valley which is rich in forest and grassland; where are the *bothe*, the beasts of milk and meat, and what of the *cuine*? Is there anything living on this cursed isle?' he demanded, his voice becoming shrill.

The bard remained silent for a while. He was using his hook to prise flat rocks and stones from the ground to use in the wall. Finally, when Tuan was about to ask him again, he said, 'There is life upon this island, though perhaps it is not recognisable as such. The life that lives here is not the life fashioned by Adur, for the Old Gods hold no sway here upon the Culai Isle. There is a life of sorts here; for the Gorge and Abyss lie adjacent to this plane, and sometimes when the fabric of the world ruptures the damned escape here.'

Cliona sat up and peered out through the gloom. 'Are they here now? Why haven't we seen them?'

'They do not exist in your perception, but so, too, do you not exist in theirs. However, you both have life – and you both exist – and often in the same place at the same time.'

'But how can two creatures exist in the one space?' Tuan asked. 'It is inconceivable.'

'Not so. For you are attuned to your plane of life in the same manner as they are attuned to theirs. You are like threads woven into a tapestry; each thread is separate and individual, yet each combines to make up a far greater pattern. The interweaving, intertwining threads do not break to allow another thread to pass through them; rather they bend and twist. Thus the isle is part of a pattern which uses many threads, for it stands at the hub of many planes, and no two threads will ever break upon one another, rather will they bend and twist . . .'

'And what is the pattern?' Cliona wondered.

'The pattern is creation, and its threads are invisible to all but a few.'

'Can you see these threads?' Tuan asked, but Paedur smiled gently, and shook his head.

'I have been taught,' Cliona said suddenly from the darkness behind them, 'that Life is patterned like a tapestry, that its threads are destiny and its knots are choice. I've been told that there are some – and these may be the god-sought, god-taught – that can see the pattern and conceive its complexity.' Paedur and Tuan heard her voice change, becoming almost accusing. 'Strange that you should speak of the invisible life on the isle in terms of tapestry and threads.'

The mate saw the bard incline his head towards the priestess. 'You have learned correctly and remembered well. But I will tell you this: it is whispered in the darkened corners of man's mythos that the Spinners of the Tapestry were once Culai, but that they, unlike the majority of their kin, attained godhood.'

'I'm not sure I understand. How did they become gods, for example?' Cliona wondered.

Paedur shrugged. 'No-one knows – all that is known is that they were rewarded by the Elder Gods, the First Gods, in return for some favour, and they were allowed to spin the threads of destiny for man, for remember – the Culai were once men. There is a lot on this isle that is unfitting and unsuitable for mortal sight, the merest glimpse of which might send you screaming into the domain of the Nameless God – and so I warn you, do not probe too deeply into the island's secrets.'

'Why?' Tuan asked, looking around.

Paedur smiled, his teeth white in the gloom. 'In case you might discover them.'

When the Culai left this world, they took with them the sum total of their knowledge, and they set it into the ground about their city . . .

Tales of the Bard

Tuan and Cliona were awakened by the bard as the first tinges of dawn were breaking across the distant horizon. They made a hasty meal of dried bread and drank a little from the mate's flask, and then they continued on down the valley towards the city of Ui Tyrin.

The track levelled out on to a rocky decline and then down into a broad and well-tended avenue which led directly into the forest they had seen from the mountains. The track was covered with a strange fine golden sand, in which, curiously, they left no footprints or marks.

'It is similar to the shingle on the beach,' Paedur said suddenly, before Tuan could ask the question, 'the grains of sand flow into our footprints and feed off the parasites and mud and silt deposited by our boots.'

As they neared the forest they began to pass curious plants growing by the side of the track, mingling with other, more familiar plants. They were delicate, beautiful shrubs that looked almost like gossamer tendrils of spun glass, and they shone blood-red in the alien light. Tuan reached out to pluck one of the crystal buds for Cliona, but although they were web-thin and looked fragile they were incredibly strong, and he only succeeded in bruising his toughened fingers. He attacked it with his knife, but the blade screamed and screeched off the branch leaving it unmarked. He glanced over at the priestess with a wry smile. 'I'm sorry . . .' he began, and then the bard's hook flashed out, its razor edge gliding easily through the hardened stem. He deftly caught the bud as it fell and handed it to Tuan with a slight smile. Tuan nodded his thanks and then, as the bard turned away, he quickly examined the stem Paedur had cut through – it was straight and perfectly smooth, with neither ragged edge, crack nor split in the clear crystal.

When the priestess wove the translucent bud into her raven hair, it

241

was as if it had disappeared it was so clear and her hair was so dark, and yet occasionally the blood-red light would catch the crystal, looking as if a crimson teardrop glistened wetly on her head.

But the low delicate crystal shrubs soon gave way to strange distorted trees that writhed in ugly contortions, looking almost as if they were in pain. Their bark was rough pitted wood, covered in bloated pustules that leaked a black syrup, and their leaves were slim and edged with jagged serrations, like thorns. As the bard and his companions continued on down the track, the trees took on even more grotesque shapes – which strangely, Cliona thought, looked almost familiar. The track dipped into a hollow and entered a long grove that stretched arrow-straight into the distance. The trees changed again and now it looked as if the road that ran through the grove was lined with the bodies of men and women frozen in aspects of terror.

Cliona stopped, feeling her heart hammering. The bard was unaffected, and Tuan during his voyages would surely have seen some gruesome sights, but this avenue of tortured bodies . . .

Tuan looked back over his shoulder, and then stopped, seeing her wide frightened eyes. 'What's wrong?'

'Look!' She pointed down the avenue and then gagged, pressing both hands to her mouth.

'What's wrong?'

'The bodies . . .'

Tuan looked around again. 'What bodies?' he asked.

'Those . . .' she almost screamed, and then stopped and looked again: they were not corpses, but rather the blighted remains of trees, older and more worn that those they had just passed, whose shape and appearance was similar to man. And then she suddenly knew why the trees were familiar – they were giant mandrakes. It was impossible – and yet she had handled enough mandrake roots to recognise the shape now – but she had always thought that the mandrake was only found under marshy fens at certain phases of the moon, when the Lady Lussa hid her face from man.

She looked at Paedur and opened her mouth to ask him when he said, 'They are kin to the mandrake of your own plane. The mandrakes are the aborted children of the *Curiahe*, who are kin to the *Crinnfaoich*, the Wood Folk, and also kin to the dark and ancient trees of the Silent Wood, the abode of Mannam, the Dark Lord.'

'Have they life?' Cliona asked, looking nervously at the tall mis-shapen trees.

'I feel as if they're looking at us,' Tuan said nervously.

Paedur laughed softly. 'Aye, they do have a life of a sort, and I would not doubt but that they are following our progress with their own strange senses. But, you needn't worry, we're safe for a time, for these have not yet reached full maturity and are still confined to the ground. They are also sluggish with the morning air, for the sun has not yet fired their sap.'

The mate slid his knife free as he looked around. 'Are you saying that these trees can move?'

The bard shook his head, smiling. 'Not these but others of their kind, that are a little more mature.' He nodded at the knife, 'And that will be of little use against skins of toughened bark.'

'Are they trees or men, then?'

'Both,' Paedur said. 'They are the *Curiahe* – and it is said that the *Crinnfaoich* are the sons of the *Curiahe*, much as man is the offspring of the Culai.' The bard stopped and pointed back along the path and then forwards into the hazy distance. 'The evolution of the Woodfolk is laid out here – from the glass star-shrubs that legend tells once fell upon the world in uncounted crystal raindrops, thence to the grotesque trees that are neither bushes nor trees and thence to the mandrake that have the first glimmerings of sentient life in them . . .'

'And then?' Cliona asked.

But the bard just smiled and whispered, 'Wait and see.'

As they continued on down the carefully tended path through the watching groves the mandrakes gradually became more man-like in appearance, their forms became straighter and taller, features became discernible, and as they moved deeper into the grove the features became finer and more delicate, and slowly the mandrakes regained something of the haunting beauty of the star-bushes.

Finally Paedur stopped. Ahead of them the grove ended and opened out on to a broad flat plain of rustling golden grain. He pointed to a series of broken craters that lined the track; soil still trickled into some of the holes as if the trees had just been uprooted. There was no sign of the trees in the fields before them. The bard pointed to the ugly pits by the roadside. 'The most mature form of the mandrake must stand here.'

'They can move?' Tuan asked, and when the bard nodded, he continued, 'Then they must have risen very recently . . .'

The bard walked on. 'Very recently,' he agreed. 'They must return to the soil by nightfall, else they rot and wither, for they are creatures of the day.' His hook swept out, encompassing the fields of grain. 'We may see them as they wander through the fields, but they are surprisingly shy creatures and avoid contact with others, particularly man.'

Tuan shielded his eyes and looked out over the wavering fields. 'I can see nothing.'

'Count yourself lucky then, for though they are shy they will not tolerate trespassers in their domain. And they make fearsome – and almost invincible – foes.' He glanced over his shoulder at Tuan and Cliona, and then nodded to the fields of rustling, whispering golden grain. The grain shifted and moved, bending its laden heads in sinuous waves as if some snake-like creature rippled through the crops. 'These are the Fields of Knowledge; eat all the ears of grain here and you will become a god, for here is gathered all the knowledge and wisdom of the Culai and mankind.' Something like bitterness crept into his voice. 'But all this wisdom and knowledge is unsorted and uncategorised, and of course the grains of knowledge are unnamed, and so one could spend all eternity searching for a single fact. But, as you can see, the fields are far too big for any single person to assimilate. Of course, some have tried. On all the planes of existence there are growths like this, shadows or reflections of the Fields of Knowledge – they may be trees or bushes, pools or streams – but they all hold some faint glimmerings of the knowledge that these fields contain . . .' His voice trailed away, and his usually expressionless face tightened in pain.

'What causes the ripples in the grain?' the priestess asked. 'There's no breeze.'

'They are the ripples of man's seeking as he merely brushes the surface of knowledge – but it is rare for him to grasp the whole kernel. Look,' the bard pointed with his hook to places around the field that were set apart from the rest, circles of stillness and tranquillity, and yet within these circles a single ear would waver and shudder as if a fieldmouse gnawed at its stem. 'You can see there where man reaches out and grasps that which he cannot understand, taking isolated facets of useless information and dangerous knowledge – an ear here, a sheaf there – but he doesn't know what he's grasping, nor how he will use it.'

'But there must be a plan,' Cliona protested, 'someone must harvest the fields.'

The bard pointed to the dim and misty walls of Ui Tyrin in the distance. 'It is said that a plan to the Fields of Knowledge is contained in the Inner City in the Circle of Keys. Legend also tells of a scythe, a scythe forged from part of the essence of man and the whispers of one of the very first emotions created by man: curiosity. Take that scythe and reap the fields with the plan in mind and you might reap the knowledge of the ages.'

'But what about the dark lore?' Cliona asked.

'Use the plan and one could leave that part untouched. But one must take care, for knowledge – no matter how much it is intended for good – must be controlled, for knowledge is power and power is dangerous.'

'Why has no man reaped and harvested the Fields of Knowledge before this?' Tuan asked. 'Surely there are men of power who know about these fields and the scythe?'

Paedur laughed as he began to walk down the long path that cut through the high grasses. 'Oh, men have tried in ages past and some have even succeeded in reaching the Circle of Keys, and I know of one sorcerer who even succeeded in grasping the scythe, but he, like all the others, failed – betrayed by his curiosity about the Circle of Keys itself, and the need to explore it. All have failed,' and there was a note of sadness in his voice. They walked in silence for a time along the strange path with its scratching, shifting, sandy covering, by the side of the Fields of Knowledge that towered above their heads and wavered in an ethereal wind that was the fumbling curiosity of man.

'I wonder why all those who came before us failed to reap the fields,' Cliona remarked softly to Tuan, 'I wonder were they all evil men?'

The bard turned and looked into her eyes. 'No, they were not all evil. Though there were some that would have used the knowledge they obtained for their own ends, most of them would have used their knowledge for the good of man. Some had found the fields through the shadowy reflections of knowledge on their own planes, and had used the knowledge they had found there to gain entry to the Blessed Isle and the Fields of Knowledge.' He stopped speaking and continued walking, his head bent forward, the fingers of his right hand clenched. 'These fields and their reflections might be likened to a poison; diluted they will cause little harm, yet in a pure state they are fatal. And most of the seekers did not know this. They thought the fields here were similar to the shadow-growths of their own planes and they reasoned that they must eat the grain much as they had eaten the buds or fruits of the trees and drunk the water on their own planes. Some were lucky with the first few mouthfuls, because the knowledge they absorbed was not harmful, but sooner or later it killed them for they could not comprehend or encompass all that they had learned and their minds snapped under the sudden mass of knowledge.'

'Why?'

'Because one must learn in steps, slowly, slowly, building upon a foundation of known facts, but they did not wish to build like that.'

'But if one had the plan?' the priestess asked.

'Aye, if one had the plan of the fields, then it would be possible to learn and reap profitably and with proper care.' The bard turned suddenly and rested his gleaming razor hook against the priestess's soft cheek. 'Do you aspire to this knowledge and wisdom?' he asked softly.

'If I had the proper guidance . . .' Cliona said slowly, feeling the almost flesh-warm curve of the metal.

Paedur looked over at Tuan. 'What about you; do you wish for this knowledge, bearing in mind its power for destruction as well as greatness?'

'I have sailed with the Taourg; I have known many lands, some of which men banish into legend, and many races which men speak of only in myth – and if I've learned anything, I've learned that man is happy only when he has a goal to attain. Take away this goal and you destroy the man. And this goal might be power or knowledge or conquest, but even so it is something to strive for. I think if you granted any man the wisdom and knowledge of the ages, then in one swift move you remove his very reason for existence.' The mate suddenly laughed, and then coughed in embarrassment, 'Listen to me, I must be going soft. Such thoughts are for the market-philosophers and roadside sages and not for honest warriors.'

Paedur placed his hand on the mate's shoulder. 'You have a wisdom beyond your years; treasure it, never mock it.'

About mid-morning they passed an area of the Fields of Knowledge that was stricken with blight. Around it, the ground was seared and withered, and it looked as if a fire had raged here. The bard told his companions that here had once grown the most evil and dangerous knowledge. It had originally grown up out of the nightmares of the One, and had been compounded by the terrors of the First Men. It had lain for countless ages and festered and drawn into itself every abomination from the earliest ages of man and the twilight of the gods when they were wont to walk the worlds.

Then there arose a creature who had learned of the Primeval Lore and had striven to use it; and after many trials which damned his essence to the furthest howling chaos of the Gorge, he had finally reached the Fields of Knowledge and had eaten the dark grains of the Primeval Lore. Somehow, he had survived the terrible and shocking knowledge he had gained, for his studies had prepared him somewhat for it. Then he challenged the gods themselves to admit him into their company, but they had refused, and there had ensued a terrible battle in which even the very restraints of the Gorge were breached and the planes were flooded with the evil creatures that even now beset man. The would-be usurper was defeated and cast into the Gorge, stripped of the form of man, and there it had writhed in unspeakable agony until, one day, man in his stupidity called upon the usurper by name and released him.

'What happened to him?' Cliona asked.

'That creature was Trialos!'

The bard then pointed out the burnt stems of corn within the blasted area, which were writhing and swaying as if a gale blew upon them, but which was man's seeking the knowledge. 'The Dark Lore always attracts man, much as the bait lures the unsuspecting fish, and like the bait for the fish it too often proves fatal.'

Suddenly the bard stopped and raised his face to the alien sky, tilting his head to one side as if he were listening. 'Move!' he hissed, and grabbed Cliona and Tuan and pulled them into the tall grasses. 'Listen,' he said, 'listen.'

'I can't hear anything . . .' Cliona began, and then Tuan's hard fingers bit into her shoulder muscle. 'I can.'

'What is it?'

'It sounds like something crying . . .' Tuan said slowly.

And then the priestess heard it also. The sound was faint, a doleful crying that echoed and re-echoed across the fields. Then they heard a deep, throbbing booming and at first Tuan and Cliona thought it was Baistigh, the Lord of Thunder, riding across the heavens on his clouds of sombre grey – but the sky was clear and cloudless . . .

And then above them flew six huge birds – the first living creatures they had seen on the island.

The birds were huge – larger even than the fabled roc – and Tuan guessed that from beak to tail they would have measured greater than a Taourg pirate ship. Their plumage was a pure white, save for their eyes and beaks and the tips of their tail feathers, and these were black but of a shade so intense that it appeared almost purple. They flew in a perfectly regular diamond formation, and the sound the three companions had heard was their singing. It was a bitter-sweet sound, lovely and pathetic, and Cliona felt tears well up in her eyes. She looked up at Tuan and found that his eyes were glistening. The six birds circled above the Fields of Knowledge and then they swooped down back along the trail, and now a new note entered their songs, one of rage and defiance.

There were shouts and screams from behind as the birds dropped even lower. 'Thanos,' Paedur muttered, and then the birds folded their wings and swooped, their claws extended. One disappeared into the grain for a moment, and when it rose up again there was something hanging limply from its ebon beak. The birds rose cawing and screaming into the air, and then they circled once above the fields before setting off towards Ui Tyrin, leaving the grasses rustling angrily in their wake.

Paedur dragged Tuan and Cliona to their feet and urged them back on to the path. 'Hurry, now, hurry.' He set off towards the city at an easy run. Tuan dropped into place beside him easily enough, although Cliona began to feel the pace very quickly. More to slow him down she asked about the six huge birds.

Paedur glanced back over his shoulder. 'They were the *Aonteketi* . . .'

She frowned, 'The name is familiar, but . . .'

'They were once gods of men, but are now the servants of the Culai.'

'What turned gods into servants?' Tuan wondered.

'Briefly, then,' Paedur murmured, and then his voice changed, taking on its professional tone. 'In the latter days of the First Race, when they had mastered the science that almost made them equal to the gods, there arose amongst them a group of savants and philosophers who believed that, since they had now equalled the gods, then in time it should be possible for the Culai race to become greater than the gods themselves. But there were some amongst them lacking the patience to wait for that future day and they sought to attain godhood without delay. Thus they devised a plot to steal from the gods the essence of their knowledge. Therefore they set out to capture six of the lesser gods, and when they did the Culai tortured and abused them for seven days, until they revealed what little they knew of the essence of godhood.

'But the Culai were not satisfied with what they had learned, and resolved to capture one of the Great Gods to wrest from him the secret of godhood. But the gods had become aware of the plan and sent Mannam, the Dark Lord, and Maurug, the Destroyer, to the Culai, and the Silent Wood was rent with the wailing of the damned and Alile the Judge Impartial was drawn from his cavernous chamber and remained in judgement for many days thereafter. But when the gods had dealt with the Culai, they refused to take back the six who had betrayed them, banishing them to those they had been forced to serve – the last of the Culai. And thus when Kuallan, Friend of Man, had the Blessed Isle built, he brought the six gods with him and commanded them to watch over the enchanted island. They were transformed into the shape of great birds – the *Aonteketi* – by the power of the First Race. Thus they watch . . . and wait; for it is written that when the last of the Culai have gone into the Gorge then the huge birds will regain their rightful form and take their place once more in the Pantheon.

'On occasion they travel through the Grey Wall to our plane and the other planes of existence, and thus have given rise to the legends of the great and mystical birds that are said to haunt the lands of fable.' The bard suddenly stopped and then pointed off to one side, striking out along a thin barely visible path that cut through the tall grasses. 'This way.' He led them to a squat standing stone that sat in the middle of a neat circle deep in the midst of the fields.

'This,' Paedur said, patting the smoothly polished rock, 'is the foundation stone upon which all of man's knowledge is built. It was a gift from the First of the Elder Gods to the First Race, and it was with such basic knowledge that the Culai survived their earliest days on the harsh world.'

They camped about the Foundation Rock that night while the grain whispered and sighed all around them. There were other noises too, less distinct but even more frightening, and at one stage during the night Tuan surged to his feet, his knife in his hand, almost expecting to find himself facing . . . he wasn't sure what he could be facing.

The night wore on, but neither the priestess nor Tuan could sleep, and so Cliona asked the bard again about the *Aonteketi*. 'What were the six minor gods who were taken by the Culai and later renounced by the Pantheon?'

The bard remained silent for such a long time that the priestess thought he had not heard her question and was about to ask him again, when she saw Tuan shake his head.

When the bard spoke, his voice was low and seemed almost weary. 'Aye, I know the six lost gods of the Pantheon, and I could never understand why the Old Gods did not show greater kindness and forgiveness.

'But the gods were these: Scmall, the Spirit of the Clouds, who ruled the misty wastes and cloudfields of heaven. When he disappeared the clouds became the property of all the Pantheon and are now used by many of the gods, such as C'lte and Baistigh.

'Kloca, the Lord of Stone and Rock, was lost also, and thus was lost the great art of fashioning in rock and the dressing of stone. His loss is one of the reasons why no great stone monuments are raised today, for the Culai took from him the secret skill of working stone – that is how they raised their cities and roads which still endure.

'The Culai captured Aistig, the Lord of Subtle Harmonies, and that is why if you listen carefully you will find the elder songs and chants more delicate, haunting and subtle than their modern counterparts. You've both heard it said that there are no great song-smiths alive today, but that's not true – their songs are as good, even better, but Aistig is not there to breathe life into their tunes.' Paedur's head dipped slightly, 'Aye, we lost much when the Pantheon refused to recognise and accept the six.

'Danta, Lord of Verse, was captured, and a great beauty was lost when the Verse-Maker was taken, though I suppose there are few alive today that know that. But ask yourself; why is it that the old tales are always welcomed and the old lays always chanted; why is it that a bard is never refused a welcome? Why? Because the old tales were touched by Danta and, like Aistig, he breathed a subtle life and fire into them, a haunting resonance, a depth of feeling that one doesn't find in the verse-makers of today.' He paused and added quietly, 'And those two, Aistig and Danta, were brothers.

'Now,' he continued, 'you should ask the workers in gold and silver why their craft lacks the delicacy and beauty of the works of their forefathers. Of course they will deny it, and claim that their craft is greater now than ever before, and that it has improved down through the ages. But compare the old and the new and it is very obvious that the modern works lack . . . a something. You probably wouldn't be able to say just what this something is, but you would be able to tell the difference.'

'Aye,' Tuan said suddenly, 'and the antique work fetches higher prices, even for pieces which, by today's standards, would be considered crude. I've seen the Taourg cast aside satchels of gold and silver ware for a piece or two of antique work.'

Paedur nodded. 'That is my point; people can tell that there is a difference – though they may not know what it is – and they find the earlier pieces more pleasing to the eye. The reason for the difference is simple, for the Culai captured Dore, the Lord of the Smiths, and so man lost the art of working metal. Even the workers in base metal lost the secrets of their craft.' He looked up at Tuan, his face a dim oval in the night. 'Why are the few antique swords and armour that still survive so much sought after?'

'Because of their strength and durability – which cannot be found in today's weapons.'

Paedur nodded, the cloth of his cloak rasping softly together. 'When the six were taken, some said it was no great loss and that they would not be missed. HAH! Little did the fools know.'

'That's five gods; who was the sixth . . .?' Cliona asked.

'Aye there was one other, but a goddess rather than a god. She was Fifhe, Lady of the Beasts, the daughter of Lady Adur, and while she was with the Pantheon there was peace between man and beast and also between beast and beast. That peace was shattered when she was taken, and now man hunts not only for food but also for sport. Even the nature of the beasts has changed, and there are some now that hunt and kill but don't eat their prey. The old harmony between man and beast is lost. Once the beasts worked freely alongside man, but now they are constrained by bit and bridle, spear and whip, to carry for their masters. Once man took only what he needed from the beasts for food or clothing, and only then with the permission of the Lady Fifhe, but now he takes when he wants and not what he needs.' The bard's voice changed in timbre and faded into a whisper.

'Scmall, Kloca and Aistig, Danta, Dore and Fifhe,' Cliona murmured; 'henceforth, I will include them in my prayers, for surely they did not deserve their punishment.'

Paedur smiled gently and shook his head. 'They did not.'

The remainder of the short night was spent in silence, and the three companions watched the dawn coming up like blood from a wound.

They continued along the winding track and by mid-morning the walls of Ui Tyrin, the City of the Culai, rose before them, and looming high above the massive city walls was the tall bowl of the goblet-shaped building, the Inner City. From the distance the walls seemed to float on a sea of grain, like a vast stone ship sailing the Seas of Knowledge, thought the priestess as she stood with Tuan gazing up at the city.

'The end is in sight,' Tuan said softly, almost to himself.

Not quite, Paedur thought, staring up at the walls; the journey was only just beginning. His non-human senses felt that disturbance of Thanos and his warriors off to their right. They must have marched through the night, and he could sense the mingled auras of exhaustion and anger, overlaid with the sour stink of fear. 'Let's go – it wouldn't do to be caught by Thanos now . . . would it?'

As they neared the walls the grain shrank back almost to normal size and the track began to broaden and wind erratically. The priestess noticed a new plant growing amongst the golden grains; a short thick-stemmed weed edged with wicked hooked barbs. The weed itself was a strangely baleful colour that was neither black nor the deepest purple but a curious mixture of both. She was reaching out to touch one of the broad flat leaves when the bard stopped her.

'Don't touch it – it's deadly.'

'What is it?' Tuan asked.

'It is alien lore from the furthest planes, and it presents a far greater danger than even the Primeval Lore, for while man knows of its danger he knows nothing about this, nor what its effects on the user will be.' He pointed with his hook. 'And see how it is already shivering in the breeze of man's curiosity.'

Tuan knelt and examined the plant. 'It's an ugly thing, and I wonder why we've only come across it here, so close to the city . . .'

'It came from those who have passed this way before us – undoubtedly a new species of weed is already growing up in your wake, having absorbed what knowledge you have.'

'Have there been many before us?' Cliona asked.

'Many have come to Ui Tyrin – no-one has ever returned. It is said that Ui Tyrin's great beauty holds them enthralled,' he added with a smile.

But the city itself was plain – almost ugly.

Paedur stopped and led them off the path once again, and then he pulled back a tall sheaf of grain and they stepped out on to a broad close-cropped plain that led down to a moat surrounding the city of Ui Tyrin. 'Let's wait awhile,' Paedur said, moving deeper into the grain.

Tuan and Cliona followed Paedur into the heart of the grain and then settled down. From where they were they had a clear view of both the track and the city. Their first impression of Ui Tyrin was of size, of vast overwhelming, impressive size. It sat upon the wide plain like a great beast slumped in noonday slumber. There was an aura of strength and durability about it; it had stood for a hundred generations, and it would last for another hundred, and even in that dim and distant future it would remain unchanged and untouched by time. Its high castellated walls dominated the skyline, and the sharp angles of the pentagonal walls jutted knife-like against the wide and ominously swirling moat. The huge double gates were neither wood nor metal but seemed carved from a single slab of stone, and were set well back into the walls and fronted by a thick portcullis of shining steel. And the gates and portcullis looked particularly new, almost as if they had just been furnished and erected. But there was no drawbridge to lower across the moat, and a small tree grew in the crack in the earth where the door joined the walls. Obviously the gate had not been opened in a long time, and with no drawbridge it looked as if it had never been designed to open.

Suddenly the turgid water of the moat was disturbed and something long and sinuous appeared briefly, then sank again, leaving the smallest of ripples in the milk-white water. Tuan was just about to speak when the water parted once again and the creature reappeared. It was a serpent, but covered with sleek black fur and with a long almost flat head. It heaved itself up out of the water, coil after rippling coil, and spread itself out on the soft margin, soaking up the warmth. Its head waved about, its long black tongue tasting the air before it settled down.

Cliona shuddered. 'It's a nightmare.'

'I have seen creatures similar to it in some of the islands far to the south,' Tuan whispered, 'though they were not so large, nor were they covered with fur.'

'It is a creature from the earliest days of man,' Paedur said quietly. 'Beware: for there are many such beasts,' and he nodded towards the slumbering monstrosity, 'some of them a lot more hideous than that.'

'But what is it?' Cliona asked.

'That is the seast; it is said to be the ancestor of the serpent and the rat and it has the characteristics of both. See the sinuous length of the serpent and the eyes and tongue of one, but see also the fur and chiselled teeth of the rat. In some of the earliest manuscripts, it is written that the Culai, in their stupidity, raised some of the seasti to knowledge, and that they were the Serpent Folk of legend who once ruled the Southern Kingdoms of Teouteuchal.'

'I've heard that,' Tuan said; and Cliona nodded also, 'Aye in Monatome . . .'

Paedur smiled slightly. 'Like the tale of the Creation, the legend of the Serpent Folk is universal to all the planes of life.'

The morning whispered on to the accompaniment of the grain, and the huge bloated sun crept higher in the sky, casting its lurid light across the plain and the walls of the city. The seast slept on, and even Tuan and Cliona dozed in the heat.

Shortly before midday Paedur shook them awake, and they heard something crashing through the grain off to their right, something large that was moving rapidly. There was a shout – a human cry – and then they saw Thanos and the remnants of the once proud Band of Kloor stumble out on to the beach before the moat.

The journey had taken its toll on them. The band of men that had once numbered upwards of twenty-five of the Religion's finest warriors had been decimated, and now no more than ten bedraggled youths remained. They were dirty and unshaven, their weapons and armour rusted and uncleaned, their eyes hollow in their heads staring out in dull apathy. They bore little resemblance to the arrogant fighting men of Kloor.

Even Thanos, Hand of God, High Priest of Trialos, looked exhausted – even more so than his men for he, like the bard – knew just how dangerous the Blessed Isle was, and how deadly an opponent the bard could be.

But now they had reached Ui Tyrin; their goal was in sight; soon, soon the bard, and all his foul gods, would be no more. Trialos would reign supreme. In sight of Ui Tyrin's walls Thanos gathered his men around him and explained to them for the first time what he knew of the City and their mission. In the afternoon silence, his voice drifted across to the three companions.

'I have told you before about the City of the First Race, and the great treasure it holds, and now I must tell you the nature of the treasure.' He paused, searching the closed faces for any trace of interest but finding nothing more than apathy. 'It is no material treasure of precious stones or metals you seek, neither is it cloth nor workings in stone nor clay nor metal, but something far greater. You have been chosen by the Lord Trialos to seek out and find this treasure for his use. Now – and attend me carefully, for there is a reward that far surpasses gold and silver for the finder.' His exhausted warriors began to show some interest and he paused and took a deep breath. 'You are seeking a vessel, a delicate urn of metallic glass of a greenish hue, that is fluted somewhat in the manner of the minarets of Maroc. And there are runes carved about the rim of the vessel and these are like and yet unlike the glyphs of the Culai, for they are the sigil of the Chrystallis. Furthermore, the vessel is stoppered with a gem of the purest water, colourless unless one should look into its depths, and then it will gleam with a hundred changes of colour, and if you should put your ear to the glass, you will also hear a keening, dirge-like and soulful. Now,' continued Thanos, 'should one of you find the vessel, seek me out immediately and, as you value your very life, do not attempt to open the vessel of the Chrystallis. You must remember that you are bound to me and I am ordering you to guard the vessel with your very lives; it is very precious.'

'My lord, what are we to do should we not be able to find you?' one youth asked. Unlike the others, he was clad in the remnants of a priest's robes and carried no weapons and stood apart from the warriors close to Thanos. As he turned, the three companions saw he had a broad curving scar across his cheek.

Paedur stiffened. 'I know him . . .!'

The albino remained silent for a moment, his pink eyes moving slowly from face to face before finally returning to the youth. 'Should you be unable to find me, then you must capture one of the First Race, or better still, one of the companions of the bard, should they still live. Then pray – pray to the Lord God Trialos for strength – and sacrifice your prisoner in the old manner, tearing out the still pulsating heart. You must then bathe the vessel in the smoking blood, and then – only then – you may open the vessel . . .' His voice which had risen to a shriek, now fell back to a whisper, 'Your reward will be great indeed.'

The scarred youth spoke again, 'My lord, what is in the vessel? It is very precious?'

'It has a value beyond value, a price beyond price. I have told you what the vessel holds: it is the container of the Chrystallis, the Soulwind.' Now his voice took on a new note, a note of fanaticism, of madness. His pale eyes widened and became suffused with blood, until they looked as if they were about to burst. 'It holds the Wind that Blew through the Soul of the One and created the four Old Gods. I will release the Soulwind upon the world, and I will wipe out the unbelievers. There is but one god, Trialos, and his servant is Thanos!'

'And the Lord Trialos is well served,' the youth murmured, with a sly smile; 'there is none to equal Thanos.'

Paedur leaned close to Tuan and whispered softly. 'I've met that young man before. I gave him that little memento on his cheek. His name is Xanazius . . .'

The mate grinned broadly. 'Aye, I've heard of him,' he said. 'He is called the Fingers of the Hand and it is said he is more than servant to Thanos . . .'

'Now come, you have rested long enough. We must needs enter the City of the Culai,' Thanos called.

'But my lord, the creature . . .' said one man, pointing to the slumbering seast. 'We must pass it.'

'Coward! Is this what the Band of Kloor has come to – snivelling cowards that flinch at a simple dozing serpent. You,' he snapped, pointing to the man who had spoken, 'do you doubt my leadership, do you question my commands?'

'N-N-no, not I, my lord,' The suddenly terrified man moved back away from the advancing High Priest. The youth Xanazius slipped up behind the warrior and pinned his arms by his sides. Suddenly Thanos reached out and placed his right hand on the face of the terrified man. 'Never doubt me,' he hissed, and the warrior screamed, his body convulsed and stiffened, and he fell back, obviously dead.

Thanos silently gathered his men about him and pointed to the fallen body, slowly looking from face to face. The bard and his companions could feel, even from the distance, the chill of his stare, and the threat and warning were obvious. Without another word Thanos led the Band of Kloor off towards the city, bearing to the right, away from the seast-guarded gate, in search of another entrance.

As soon as they had disappeared, the bard leaped to his feet and ran to the body of the warrior, Cliona and Tuan close behind him. When they reached it, the priestess cried out, sickened, and even Tuan, inured as he was to the atrocities of the Taourg, looked away.

The man's face, where Thanos had touched it, was burned to the bone, the flesh peeling away in blackened strips in the shape of a human hand. 'I've always wondered why he was called the Hand of God,' Paedur murmured, composing the body. They stood still and silent while Cliona recited the prayer of the dead, although she doubted the soul of this creature would find rest here in the wastelands of the spirit, the abode of the godless.

Then the bard led them back into the grain again, striking deep into the heart of the great Fields of Knowledge, and though they pushed through the tall waving grass they never broke nor snapped the blades, and the grass they trod underfoot quickly rose upright behind them, and the bard pointed out that this was a reflection of the durability of knowledge. They were following no marked path – save that the city was always to their right – the bard led them unerringly to a wide dell, a perfect circle within the gently waving grasses. Here the grass was short, startlingly brilliant, and the whole circle exuded an almost physical aura of peace and solitude.

In the centre of the circle was a pillar, a broad cylinder of stone, marvellously worked in the manner of the Culai with the abstract representations of the Elder Gods carved into the sides of the flat square of jade that topped the cylinder. About the base of the pillar were carved the representations of the Culai, one figure for each of the nine races, for when the gods made man they suited him to the nine climates; but the First Race was unique in that, though they were nine separate branches, they remained united as a race.

And incised deeply into the jade was a pentagram.

As the companions neared the pillar, walking carefully across the circle, they could see the jade was inset with five tiny points of light that winked and sparkled in the wan light. Each of the points of light turned out to be a diamond, the size of a man's thumb, set into the five points of the pentacle. The centre of the star had been inset with quartz and ruby respectively, giving it the appearance of a staring eye.

Tuan and Cliona looked on it in wonder; it was solidly built but somehow it seemed almost fragile; but it was very beautiful. Paedur walked over to it, and leaned back against the tall stone.

'This is the Circle of Innocence, and in it is contained all the knowledge of the innocent; see how smooth and even the grass is, unruffled and untroubled by the inquiring mind of man. A child's questions have no malice, no hidden meaning to them; when they enquire, it is with a genuine curiosity.' He patted the stone with his hand. 'This is also called the Cylinder of the Covenant, as it was fashioned to celebrate the union of gods and man in the first days of the First Race, when the Culai were free and innocent – childlike almost.

'The gods walked with man in that time, and there were many who could claim the blood of the gods ran in their veins, and some saw this as the beginning of a new age, an age of godlike men and man-like gods, and so they fashioned the Cylinder to celebrate that New Age.

'But it never happened; the First Age of Man was destined to fall. For the offspring of god and man thought themselves greater than mere men and sought to subjugate them. And this angered the gods, and thus the fields of Ab-Apsalom were made a battle-ground for the first time. The halflings lost and were cast out beyond the very edges of the universe, though they were to return generations later during the Demon wars.'

'And the Cylinder?' Tuan asked.

'Aye, the Cylinder. Well, it remained as a symbol of the great age of peace.' The bard shook his head sadly. 'We shall not see its like again. When Kuallan and the Oathbound fashioned the Isle, the Elder Gods took the Cylinder and placed it in the Circle of Innocence in the Fields of Knowledge, and they set these fields about Ui Tyrin as a lesson to the Culai. For though the First Race may walk along the paths that lead through the fields, they may never leave the paths and they may never taste the grain – perhaps because they, in their arrogance once thought themselves the masters of all knowledge – and now, although surrounded by wealth, they have nothing. That is why the Circle is placed within the fields; the Culai know of its existence but they can never reach it; they can never regain that lost innocence. The Cylinder is a symbol of what might have been . . .'

Paedur turned and pointed to the five glittering diamonds with his hook. 'But it has another use.'

As Tuan and Cliona watched, Paedur touched each of the shining points, starting with the topmost and moving anti-clockwise, striking them with the point of his hook.

258

Abruptly the eye of the quartz and ruby flickered and glowed, and the air above it began to shimmer as if the stone gave off heat. Then, at the edge of the circle of grass a faint tracery of lines appeared, as if etched by fire, but the grass didn't burn. And these lines formed into the shape of a pentacle with the Cylinder at their centre, and, at the points, fist-sized pools of light burned with a cold radiance. As Paedur ordered his companions to place their hands on the stone, these cold liquid lights began to shift and spin about themselves until they were nothing more than lines of white fire. And the lines began to expand round the circle of grass, and pulse along the rim of this circle until it seemed as if the circle was slowly starting to revolve. It seemed to spin faster and faster, and the Field of Knowledge dimmed and faded, and they were in utter darkness . . .

Cliona and Tuan screamed aloud, but there was no sound. There was nothing.

15 The Three Cords

No human ever penetrated Ui Tyrin and lived – except the bard, but the bard Paedur was not truly human . . .

Tales of the Bard

There was only the Cylinder. Tuan and Cliona clung to the sole remaining tangible form in the wheeling void, their minds shocked, their fingers frozen on the icy stone.

And then there was sound as the bard spoke. 'Remain calm; there is nothing to fear, but you must hold fast to the stone . . . the stone . . .' His voice echoed as if they were in a vast chamber or tunnel, but it was calming, soothing the terror that was threatening to overwhelm them both. Sensing this, Paedur continued. 'The City of the Culai has nine gateways. Some are situated in the walls in the normal manner but the others flicker through the Ghost Worlds and lead beyond the city walls. However, the gate through the Circle of Innocence is the one most rarely used, for many of those from the world of man who reach the Culai Isle had bartered the last vestiges of whatever innocence and humanity they possessed for the route through the Grey Wall to the City . . .'

As he was speaking the shifting darkness lightened and paled towards greyness, and then the white light at the points about the rim of the star flared brightly once again, and then they began to slow down, gradually fading. The cold fires separated into five distinct parts – and stopped, and abruptly the three companions found they were standing in a great hall that stretched to dusky infinity in all directions.

Paedur sighed and stepped away from the Cylinder, absently rubbing his hook against his cloak. Tuan and Cliona followed him, clinging tightly to each other, their heads still spinning. As they stepped across the traces of the outline of the pentacle on the stone floor, the hall abruptly contracted and dwindled in size until it was no more than a large square room. 'A matter of perspective,' was all the bard would say, refusing to elaborate further.

The room was much like those found in the ruined temples of

the Culai on the mainland. It was stark, and bare of adornment, and there was a thick layer of dust upon the floor, unmarked and undisturbed as if it had lain through the ages. The air was dry and acrid and a complete silence enfolded the place.

There was no doorway in the room and the single murky window set high in the sheer wall was barred with a lattice grillework.

Paedur looked around in amusement. 'There have been some improvements since I was last here,' he murmured to Tuan, his voice sounding flat and dull in the silence, robbed of its usual resonance.

'There is no door,' Cliona whispered.

'Aye, they have blocked the door – probably to prevent me returning,' Paedur said, pointing to a spot on the wall where a rectangle of smaller newer stones was faintly outlined against the older darker stones of the rest of the walls.

'You never told me you had been here before,' Tuan accused him.

'Did I not?' the bard murmured absently. 'It was a brief – very brief – visit in . . .'

'We're trapped,' the priestess said, a thin note of hysteria in her voice. Tuan went and held her, but his own expression was troubled as he turned back to the bard. 'She is right . . .' he whispered.

Paedur slowly walked around the room, brushing the grey walls with the tips of his fingers, pausing when he reached the lighter shading of stone which had replaced the door. And then Tuan suddenly noticed something. Where he and the priestess had walked, the dust on the floor was scuffed and imprinted with the marks of their footwear – his thick-nailed, rib-soled mariner boots, and Cliona's smaller, sharp-toed sandals. But where the bard had walked there was no mark, no impression.

'Can we get out?' he said, looking up and catching the bard staring at him with a strange almost feral smile on his lips.

'Aye, there is little trouble in doing that and yet . . .' the bard turned back to the bricked-up doorway and paused indecisively.

'Yet?' Tuan persisted.

'Yet to do so I must use a little Power and that will undoubtedly alert the Culai and Thanos. I wish to avoid a confrontation with both groups for the moment. The former outnumber us, and the latter, if he were to feel a ripple of Power, might overreact and do something rash if he thought, or even suspected, we were within the City.'

'But can you get us out of here without calling on your Power?' Tuan asked.

Paedur shrugged, shaking his head slightly. 'No, there seems little else we can do.' He suddenly tapped the brickwork with his hook, the sound ringing sharp and musical. 'Tuan, look at this . . . what do you think . . .' The mate stepped away from the priestess, and squatted down to look at the wall. 'Look . . . here,' the bard said, and then his voice suddenly echoed cold and chill within Tuan's head, terrifying him. *'You must forgive me for this intrusion, but what I must say to you is for your ears alone . . .'* The voice was sharp and insistent, but there was also a slightly breathless quality to it. *'At all costs Cliona must be kept safe,'* the bard continued. *'She must not fall into the hands either of the Culai or Thanos. Do you understand me?'* he demanded, staring hard at the mate. *'At all costs.'*

Tuan nodded silently.

'I'll have to call upon some Power, then,' the bard said aloud, glancing over at Cliona.

The mate nodded, 'I can see no other way for us to get out.'

'Move back,' Paedur commanded. Then he laid his hook flat against the joining of the new and old brick and he began to whisper in a strange lilting tongue. The runes on the curve of his hook darkened and then they began to sparkle. They turned black, rust-coloured, and then red, until they finally glowed with an intense white heat that even Tuan and Cliona could feel across the room, although the bard seemed unaffected. Then slowly, like a knife cutting through butter, the edge of the hook sank into the stone, biting deeper and deeper until it was almost up to the bard's wrist. Paedur began to move his arm up along the seam in the door; mortar and chippings spat and ran in molten globules down the stonework and the air reeked with sulphurous bitter fumes. Stretching to his full height, Paedur traced the outline of the door, from threshold to lintel and back again to the threshold.

There was a grinding sound and then suddenly a large section of the brickwork fell inwards, narrowly missing the bard, the sound echoing and re-echoing through the building in a long rolling thunderclap. The bard slumped back exhausted and waved Tuan and the priestess through the opening before him. 'We must hurry,' he panted, his thin face sheened with sweat.

They looked out into a long arrow-straight corridor, stretching into the dim distance. Tuan went first, his knife in his hand, moving quickly through the hole, straightening and pressing his back to the wall. But the corridor was deserted. He lifted Cliona across the tumbled bricks and then reached out to help the exhausted bard through the jagged rent in the wall, but Paedur shook his head, and almost visibly seemed to draw upon some inner store of strength. 'Come on,' he panted.

The bard led them at a run down the echoing corridor, ignoring the iron-studded doors that were set into the wall at every score of paces. And then rolling down the corridor came the slow solemn booming of some great bell tolling out a warning, reverberating against the walls, raining grey gritty dust down on them. But the bard ignored the bell, only urging them on. He knew they were racing against time now; his use of Power had – as he had expected – alerted the island's almost sentient defences and the Culai would soon rouse themselves to investigate.

The high, slit windows admitted little light, and Cliona and Tuan stumbled on the cracked and uneven flagstones; the lack of light didn't seem to affect the bard. The walls were stark and without ornament but, in contrast to what the bard called the 'gate-room' whose walls had been dry, the walls in the corridor dripped with sluggish moisture, and deep channels set into the floor carried the water away to overflowing grills. The whole corridor had a desolate air of disuse about it.

And then the bell ceased its mournful tolling.

The bard stopped and raised his hand for silence. 'What is it?' Tuan whispered, but the bard shook his head impatiently. The mate could hear nothing except the monotonous drip-drip-drip of moisture. He was turning to the priestess when she stiffened, and stifled a cry. 'Listen,' she whispered, and then Tuan heard it. He half turned, feeling the familiar burning in the back of his throat, and the deepening pounding of his heart. Faint in the distance a stealthy padding came whispering along the corridor.

'Let's go,' Paedur said quietly, but now Tuan heard a new note of urgency in his voice.

They ran then – and a nightmare began for Tuan and Cliona. The corridor loomed endlessly ahead, the high windows and tall doors on either side never changing and no end in sight in either direction. They ran, but it was as if they stood still while the corridor just flowed endlessly past.

The padding behind them grew ever louder, and then its tempo changed, becoming swifter, as if whatever nightmare was pursuing then now also ran. They could even hear the click of claws on the stones, and the faintest suggestion of deep chuffing breathing.

Tuan suddenly grabbed the bard by the arm, hauling him to a stop. He was red-faced and bathed in sweat, and there was an agonising stitch in his side. He bent over double and placed both hands on his knees. 'We must rest,' he gasped.

'We cannot – there is no time, the beast will soon be upon us.' 'Fight it!'

But the bard smiled almost sadly and shook his head. 'I cannot.'

'You . . . you go on then. I . . . I will stay and try . . .' he left the sentence unfinished, and merely tilted his knife slightly, but his meaning was clear.

The bard hesitated a moment and then nodded, seemingly almost unsurprised by the mate's decision. He placed his hand on Tuan's shoulder, and the mate immediately felt a new strength flow into him. But it was a false, dangerous strength – he recognised it from his Taourg days. It would be short-lived and ultimately debilitating. Cliona looked from one to the other in confusion. 'Tuan . . .?' she asked.

But the mate only smiled and pressed a finger to her lips, and then he kissed her gently. 'I love you,' he whispered.

Then she understood. She turned to the bard and her dark eyes filled, shining silver in the wan light. 'Paedur, you cannot leave him here. You cannot. Use your Power . . . please,' she begged.

'Priestess, I would not *ask* Tuan to stay here; it is his decision. And I wish I could use my Power, but at this moment I am totally drained . . . I cannot.'

'Then I will,' Cliona said defiantly, 'I will call on the Mother . . .'

'Priestess, you will need your strength soon enough; do not use your Power now. I do not ask this lightly.'

Tuan pulled the priestess tightly against his chest, and she clung to him weeping bitterly. He gently brushed her long thick hair. 'Do as the bard says,' he whispered; 'it's for the best, trust him – I do.' Then Paedur took the priestess by the arm and half carried, half dragged her away from Tuan.

Tuan watched them in silence and, as they were gradually swallowed up in the dust, he called out, 'I'll re-join you soon.'

But they all knew he lied.

The corridor suddenly turned and the bard paused and looked back. Tuan had half turned and was watching them, but in the dusky light it was difficult to make out details, and only the blade of the Chopt knife was clearly visible. The bard lifted his hook and Tuan raised his hand in a final salute, and then he turned and prepared to face whatever followed. But the bard, turning away, silently pledged himself to find the mate again, whether he be in the Gorge or the Silent Wood.

The corridor now widened and branched. The bard did not hesitate but led the sobbing priestess down the left-hand corridor, which seemed to be leading downwards. It was colder and damper here, and the slit windows were so high as to be almost invisible. The bard reached out and caught Cliona's small hand in his, leading her over the broken flagstones. She was surprised to find his flesh warm and dry, and even more surprised to find sword callouses on the palm of his hand and about the base of his fingers.

As they neared the bottom of the corridor, a long shrill scream – chokingly silenced – echoed off the stone walls. The sound brought Cliona to a halt, and she half turned, as if waiting for another scream. 'That . . .?'

'It was Tuan,' Paedur whispered, turning her face slightly, staring into her eyes. 'There's nothing we can do for him in this life,' he added, his grip tightening as she attempted to pull away. 'All we can do now is to ensure that he did not die in vain.'

Cliona struggled against the bard's grip for a few moments then she suddenly nodded, her face hardening and her eyes beginning to glitter dangerously. Tuan's death had given her a new strength and the determination to avenge him!

They continued on, moving slowly in the dim light, when the bard suddenly felt a faint plucking at the fringes of his consciousness, a touch that was at once alien and yet strangely familiar. Again and again it attempted to breach his guard, but each time he repulsed it. But the battle of wills was taking its toll and, exhausted as he was after his massive use of Power earlier, he could not continue on for much longer. He staggered and Cliona caught his arm – and felt the tingling residue of the assault flow up her arm. Recognising the mind-touch, she allowed a portion of her own strength to flow into the bard.

Paedur felt the warm rush of new strength and power and he savagely lashed out, using the remnants of his own strength, and felt the intruder's touch fall away, but in that instant he recognised

265

it. He had felt that touch once before . . . it was the mind-touch of his boyhood companion: Thanos. The Hand of God was in the City.

The corridor now sloped steeply and dipped below ground level into total darkness. The priestess stopped in confusion, tightening the hold which she still had on Paedur's arm. The bard's enhanced senses flared, and what was now a tunnel became visible for him in shades of pale blue-green. He continued on, leading Cliona along the winding tunnel, warning her when the roof dipped, when the flagstones were broken, or when there was a step cut into the rock. The tunnel seemed endless, and she quickly lost all sense of time in the echoing lightless chamber of stone.

Finally Paedur stopped and his voice echoed whisperingly around the tunnel. 'Ahead of us lies an obstacle. We have avoided the rest – pits, clawed traps and the like . . .'

'You didn't tell me,' Cliona accused him, her voice falling to a murmur.

'I thought it best not to say anything. However, the next obstacle stretches right across our path; it is a growth of sharp-spined razor-leaved bushes. Now, I must ask you to draw upon your fire.'

'In this place . . .?'

'If you so will it – you can,' Paedur said.

And the priestess composed herself and, calling on the goddess, attempted to fire the unseen growth ahead of her. The effort left her shaking with emotion, but nothing happened!

Then the bard whispered to her, 'Now you have seen that your magic will not work here, because the Old Gods have no sway on this isle. But you have been trained in the Lore of the Nightfolk, and their magic is akin to that of the Culai; draw upon the knowledge your mother taught you.'

'That was a long time ago, Paedur, I'm not sure . . .'

'Some things are not easily forgotten. Try it.'

The priestess composed herself and concentrated once again, recalling dim childhood memories of kneeling beside her strange mother while the pale woman spoke in her whispering voice, and taught her the legends and magical lore of her own race. She invoked the image of fire, held it, and then she poured forth all her anger and hate and pain, fuelling it. A green levin bolt spat across the tunnel sending her reeling backwards. The bramble bushes erupted in licking yellow-green flames that quickly and silently consumed them.

Paedur took her hand and led her through the blackened

branches and snapping cinders into a narrow side tunnel that was so low she had to bend double, and the deeper they went the narrower it became. And the priestess was suddenly gripped by a sudden fear, a fear that the low ceiling might collapse or the walls close in on her. She felt her chest tighten and her heart begin to pound, and she was conscious of a pulse throbbing in her temples, pounding and pounding until it felt as if her head were about to explode. The sudden heat was becoming unbearable, suffocating . . .

She stopped, her only thought to leave . . . to leave now, return to the mouth of the tunnel . . . for now the walls really were closing in . . . constricting . . . the ceiling was surely lower now . . .

Then the bard was beside her, quiet, reassuring, his voice ringing through her confusion and turmoil. 'Fight it, priestess. This is but another of the tunnel's defences. Fight it, fight the fear. Fight it . . .'

And then his voice was swept away in a wave of suffocating constriction, and then she could actually feel the walls moving, closing in on her and the pressure of the roof on the top of her head . . .

'Fight it; if not for your sake, then for the memory of Tuan. Do not let his death have been in vain; he fought to save you. He died for you. You can fight. Fight!'

Cliona felt the cold anger of Tuan's death return and grip her, and the soul-destroying fear receded. In those brief moments she cleared her mind and recited the simple incantations she had been taught as a child to ward against the ffis flowers of her native Monatome that induce fear and then feed on the emotion. Gradually the simple repetition drove out the last vestiges of the claustrophobic fear and barricaded her mind against further assault. 'I'm fine now,' she said simply.

In the darkness Paedur smiled slightly in admiration at her self-control, and he wondered what the priestess might have become had her destiny not been woven with his.

They rounded a curve in the tunnel and found an irregular circle outlined greyly ahead of them. It was the mouth of the tunnel. They stopped when they reached it, and looked out into the cavern beyond.

The cavern was of awesome dimensions, and the distant walls were lost in the dimness. The walls were slimed with a phosphorescent fungus that glowed with a pale milk-white light, creating figures and leering shadow faces within itself. Stumps of stalagmites were dotted along the floor close to the walls, but the centre of the cavern was smooth and flat, with the natural floor polished to an almost mirror-like brightness. High in the roof of the cavern was a tiny circular spot of a blood-red colour – which, the bard said softly, was an opening to the sky above.

Paedur waited, using his senses, both natural and enhanced, to ensure that the cavern was empty before he hurried the priestess across the floor, their footsteps ringing hollowly on the stones. Cliona slipped on the smoothly polished stones and begged him to slow down, but he pointed with his hook to the tiny red spot on the roof and then to the floor directly beneath it. 'The sun shines through that opening directly into this cavern close to this time every day; aye, every day – this plane has no seasons, and every day when the sun is directly overhead the Culai gather here in this, the Cavern of Power, and who knows what rites they perform, what beings they invoke?'

'You fear them?' she asked, her voice beginning to shake with exhaustion.

The bard smiled gently. 'Only a fool would not fear the First Race. Yet, I am somewhat protected, for I have been gifted by a god, but you . . .' He shook his head slowly, 'You have no protection save your magic, and that would be of little use here in the inner sanctum of the Culai.' His hard dark eyes caught and held hers. 'There is something else you should know, priestess; I would rather see you slain – and by my own hand, if need be – than let you fall into their hands alive.'

'Tuan knew that, didn't he?' she asked.

'Aye, he knew. He knew you were too important to our mission to be captured, and that was one of the reasons why he stayed behind. And he too would not have allowed you to be captured and used by the First Race. For they would not slay you, oh no, they would bend you to their will; then you would be mindless, a *quai*. Remember the warning carved into the sides of the mountain?'

'"*Lifeless ye shall live, deathless ever be, all ye who pass beyond*",' she whispered.

When they reached the far side of the cavern, they found that there were three tunnels leading out from the Cavern of Power. Paedur stopped and raised his hook, his head tilted to one side, listening.

'What . . .?' Cliona began, but the bard's fingers crushed her hand, silencing her.

And then, suddenly, the cavern was ablaze with blood-light,

glittering, shining, reflecting from the luminous mosses and fungi, winking with a thousand points of light. Paedur flung his cloak over the priestess, but too late – the sudden light had all but blinded her.

The tiny circle in the high roof blazed with a blistering light, for the sun was now directly overhead, and a bar of almost solid light shafted down into the cavern. Directly beneath the light was a pool of slate-coloured, viscous liquid, which reflected the alien sunlight about the cavern. Around the pool were set ten stones of varying colours, which had been polished so smooth so that they too caught and reflected the light in different colours off the walls, the ceiling and the polished floor.

A slow throbbing began, sounding as if a great heart were beating in some distant cavern – and then a slow susurration whispered across the emptiness, sounding almost like a breeze disturbing dead and dry autumnal leaves; but the throbbing gradually intensified and the whispering resolved into a sharp liquid twittering.

Then silence.

And the sudden silence was all the more terrifying. There was shadowy movement against the lichened walls, and tall figures began to file into the cavern from scores of darkened openings in the walls. Paedur pressed Cliona back against the wall, forcing her down as the Culai approached.

More and more of the Culai arrived; they all wore the metallic sheath-robes favoured by the First Race in their latter days, and which reflected the light like so many burning beacons. They were unnaturally tall and thin, beautiful after a fashion, but their fine, delicately pointed features were blotched and marred by the changing colours.

Most of them passed within an arm's length of the bard and priestess, the reflected light from their robes almost blinding them, but then a small group came towards them, their heads bent deep in conversation . . .

Paedur closed his mind to the sight-destroying light from their robes and began to weave a web of emptiness about himself and the priestess, attempting to slip them fractionally from the present plane into the grey Ghost Worlds that exist between the planes of existence. Normally, it was a simple enough manoeuvre, one he could achieve by merely willing it. But now nothing happened. He pulled Cliona closer to him and rested the point of his hook against her smooth throat, while desperately attempting to complete the spinning. But the Culai were too close . . . too close . . . he would never . . . Abruptly he felt the chill given off by the edge of the planes and he was in the Ghost Worlds, with the priestess still in his arms. He was still able to see into the Cavern of Power, and he jerked back automatically as the four Culai seemed to pass over and through them. Cliona was still wrapped within his cloak, her eyes streaming from the blinding burst of light earlier.

The Culai had gathered about the large pool in the centre of the floor in long straight lines, like spokes radiating from a circle. Paedur did a quick calculation and found that each line was made up of one hundred Culai, male and female alternating, and that there were one hundred lines. These ten thousand were the last of the First Race, a race that had once numbered tens of millions. But they had not bred for many generations, and these were the same Culai who had been settled on the Blessed Isle when it was first created. In all that time age had not touched them.

They bowed their heads and began to chant, and in their voices were the haunting resonances of Elder Days. The sounds chilled the bard, dredging up memories he had long thought forgotten; his uncle had used those cadences and his grandfather before him, for they were amongst the purest of the bardic forms. The voices soared, thin and high, seeming to venture into those regions inaudible to human ears.

While the bard was entranced, Cliona struggled free of his cloak and blinked her watering eyes . . . And felt vertigo and sickness grip her.

For about her was a swirling grey nothingness, an abstract void reminiscent of the Grey Walls, but before her she could see into the cavern and the lines of chanting Culai, almost as if she were looking through a window. She reached out and touched the bard's forearm and, when nothing happened, she shook him. He turned his head slowly, and stared at her with no trace of recognition, his face hard and closed, almost inhuman. 'Paedur . . .?' she breathed. Something moved behind his eyes, and then he shook himself like a man awakening.

He smiled slightly, and then turned back to the window looking in at the Cavern of Power. '*Now is our opportunity, while the Culai are deep in their devotions.*' His voice rang in her head, ice-cold and terrifying. He told her to hold on to him and she felt his body tense as he attempted to move them out of the Ghost Worlds.

270

But now the chanting of the First Race had taken on a new note, a higher, more insistent keening . . . a calling. It was another reason for leaving the safety of the half-world; he had no idea what might soon be coming through it.

And then he felt the tug, the tiny giving of the fabric of the planes, as both he and Cliona slid back into the cavern, but not before they were both abruptly chilled by a sudden gust of icy wind that had rippled through the Ghost Worlds.

And as they scrambled for the shelter of one of the tunnels ahead of them, there was a high exultant cry from the assembled Culai. Paedur glanced back over his shoulder and saw a thin wavering line appear above the pool, a snake, a cord of absolute blackness.

And as the line twisted and wove back and forth, it seemed to gain substance from the vari-coloured lights in the cavern, for the colours paled and dimmed . . . and then suddenly it flickered once and was gone . . .

It reappeared, and this time it was not alone. Now there were two wavering cords of darkness, pulsating, twisting, weaving together . . . and then they too disappeared. And reappeared. But now there were three.

As they spun and interwove, the bard felt his eyes drawn hypnotically towards the three cords, and the swirling after-image on his retina suggested something . . . something he could not name, except that he was sure he had seen it before. The image was familiar – frighteningly familiar – and the very sight of it chilled him to the bone.

With a start he realised Cliona was pulling insistently at his arm. He looked around and found he had stopped in the mouth of one of the tunnels – in full view of the First Race, but he doubted if anyone had seen him. The Culai acted as if they had been drugged or entranced as they stared mindlessly up at the weaving cords.

He turned and ran up the tunnel behind the priestess, the image left by the serpents still burning in his brain, tantalisingly familiar. He had seen it long ago, of that he was sure. Three twisting black lines . . . there was a symbol, a sign as old as the gods themselves, a sign of three twisting lines . . . a sign . . . The Sign of the Three Cords!

And suddenly he remembered!

And the memory terrified him.

Perhaps he fell – he didn't know; the next thing he knew he was sitting with his back against the cold stone wall of the tunnel, with the priestess bending over him. He started up, but Cliona pressed both hands against his shoulders and pushed him down, and he felt so weak, he allowed her.

'What happened?' he mumbled.

The priestess shook her head slightly. 'I'm not sure. One moment you were behind me, and when I looked again you were on your knees, not exactly unconscious but not fully awake.' She paused. 'Do you want to tell me what happened?' she asked.

'I'm not sure myself.'

'Do you want to tell me what are the three cords?' she asked quietly, and then watched his face tighten in pain and beads of sweat begin to trickle from his hairline.

'How do you know about the Cords?' he asked.

'You spoke about them while you were unconscious,' she said. 'What are they?'

'I think they are the reason we were sent here,' he murmured, almost to himself.

'I thought we were here to prevent Thanos gaining control of the Chrystallis,' Cliona said.

'So did I.'

'What are these cords?' Cliona demanded. 'You've seen them before, haven't you?'

Paedur nodded.

'Tell me,' Cliona almost screamed, shaking him by the shoulders. 'Tell me!'

Paedur ran his fingers through his hair, pushing it back from his eyes, and when he spoke his voice was so low that Cliona had to stoop forward to hear him. 'I was a boy at the time,' he began, 'no more than eight years, I think, younger possibly but certainly not older. I found a stone in the ancient ruins in the hills above my home, a stone etched with three curving lines. I can remember my fingers finding the lines and tracing them over and over again and, innocently, I carried it home in my left hand. My father saw it and asked what it was, and when I showed it to him he wouldn't touch it, but he sent my brother for Gahred, my great-uncle, who was staying with us at the time. When I showed it to him, Gahred silently took me to the mountain stream that gushed from the ice hills further north and ran through the gully close to my home. There, he ordered me to strip and bathe in the icy stream; I refused and then he struck me, and I think it was only then that I realised the old man was terribly frightened.

'While I was bathing, Gahred cut a branch from a Lady Tree and, in that terrifyingly powerful voice of his, he called forth the Dannu-fire. I'll never forget it; it was the first time I had ever seen the blue-white cold fire of the goddess. Then Gahred ordered me to stand by the water's edge and stretch out my left hand, the hand in which I had carried the stone home. I did as I was told, although I remember it took an effort to hold my left arm steady, because my hand now stung as if it had been burned and it twitched and trembled of its own accord. My great-uncle then cried aloud in the Old Tongue that had been suppressed a generation before and the white fire on the branch had frozen in jagged ice-like streamers. I had never seen such magic before and, while I was mesmerised with that, Gahred brought the branch down on my arm, severing my hand at the wrist.' The bard lifted his left arm, and looked unseeing at the silver hook, remembering the hand he once had. He took a deep sobbing breath and continued. 'I can remember looking at the stump of my arm and feeling no pain, merely a soft warm glowing that rose up from my feet until it reached my head . . . and then I remember no more. But, before I lost consciousness, I do remember noticing that the wound had not bled.

'And all on account of a stone with three wavering lines cut into it.

'The days thereafter were the stuff of nightmare, and there were further ritual purifications. Afterwards I learned that the door of the house had been torn down and burned because I had touched it, and all the clothes I had worn also.

'I can also recall a twisted little man – a dwarf – who was seemingly of great age, whom even Gahred called "*Heer*" which is "father" in the old speech. He fitted an oversized silver hook into the bone of my wrist, and although I know he had cut and sawn into the bone, I don't remember feeling anything, although I do know Gahred laid his gnarled hand on my head and whispered strange words that buzzed and vibrated like a thousand insects inside my skull before the old man started his work.

'And when the hook had been fitted, the old man – and now I suspect that the dwarf might have been Toriocht the Smith, brother to Chriocht the Carpenter, the halfling servants of the gods – carved runes into the length of the delicate curved blade. He thought I was asleep but I heard him explaining to Gahred that the hook would grow with me, so that when I reached manhood, the hook would be the full and proper size for a man. My uncle asked about honing, but the old man said that there was a thin band of metal running along the edge of the hook. This, he said, was forged from the head of one of the spears of the Stormlord, it was knife sharp and would never dull . . .' Paedur lifted his hook, and looked up into the priestess's eyes. 'And all for the sake of a stone. A stone with three waving lines cut into it. The three lines of Disruption, Annihilation and Chaos. The first is slow, the second total and the third ultimate. The most ancient legends say that they co-existed with the One, but they also hint that they existed before all things, before the One and the Void and the Chrystallis.'

'Are they more dangerous than the Soulwind?' Cliona wondered.

Paedur glanced back down the tunnel, and then he shook his head. 'Thanos and his warriors are a threat, but they are minor – a mere irritation – when compared to the forces the Culai are invoking.'

'But what can we do?' the priestess asked, desperation edging her voice.

The bard stood up, the fingers of his right hand tracing the runes etched into his hook. 'I'm not sure,' he said wearily, 'I'm not sure the Three Cords can be destroyed.'

'But which do we attempt first – the Chrystallis or the Cords?' Cliona asked.

Paedur turned to look at the woman, her words sparking something deep within him, nudging some fragment of his bardic lore. He allowed his mind to go blank for a moment, knowing that whatever he was looking for would come to the fore if he left it alone.

'Paedur . . .?' Cliona asked harshly, finding his silence disturbing.

'*The Magician's Law*,' Paedur breathed, and in that instant he conceived a plan, a desperate measure to attempt to save the planes of life from complete destruction. It would mean death – death on a scale never even imagined but tiny when compared to the potential destruction of either the Three Cords or the Chrystallis alone. It never occurred to him to wonder by what right he made that decision – he never even thought of it – but deep within him he knew that this was his destiny. The Magician's Law – the force of equals.

The priestess shrank back from him, seeing him change almost

274

before her eyes, seeing his features harden and close, his eyes become hooded. He had sloughed off that part of him that was still human and what remained was . . . godlike – and terrifying.

When he spoke she found that even his voice had grown harsher. 'Come. We must hurry; we are racing time, the knowledge of the Culai, the readiness of the Cords, and Thanos. We don't know how soon the First Race might release the Cords upon the planes of life – if indeed, the Culai still maintain any control over the Three, which I doubt.'

'Where are we going?'

'To get what we came for – the vessel of the Chrystallis.'

The tunnel wound upwards in a slow spiral, and once they had left the flickering light that burned around the entrance, they were in total darkness. Paedur held Cliona's hand and dragged her roughly along. She struggled to keep up, frightened of running into something in the dark, frightened of falling, or cracking her skull against the ceiling. Frightened also of the bard. He had changed; the man that she and Tuan had followed on this doomed mission was gone, and had been replaced by . . . by what? She wondered then, had they ever been following a man – or merely a creature that looked and walked like a man? Had the bard actually changed back there in the tunnel – or had he just shed his human skin and become his true self?

What was it Tuan had once said to her: *I feel my destiny lies with him; I am drawn to him*. She smiled bitterly; his destiny had lain with the bard, and his destiny had been death. And what of her own destiny – was she, too, doomed? The bard needed her, he had needed her to come through the tunnel; he needed her in some way to preserve the seal on the vessel of the Chrystallis. Did that not give her some bargaining power? Power to bargain with him for her own life . . . and the life of Tuan. She felt sudden hope swell within her. The bard had admitted before his dealings with the Dark Lord, Mannam; might he not be able to bring the mate back from the Silent Wood?

And then there was a sudden light ahead of her, an orange circle against the black throat of the tunnel. The bard was outlined against it, a tall, inhuman, shapeless figure. He slowed and released her hand as they neared the opening, finally stopping in the mouth of the tunnel. He stood, half in shadow, his hook resting against her right shoulder, and then he turned and looked down at her, his shadowed eyes burning with a strange fire. He did not seem to speak, but his voice was ice in her head.

'*Your thoughts do you no honour, priestess, and you belittle the*

275

memory of Tuan. I did not ensorcell you, nor draw you here by
force of my will, nor are you following a Duaiteoiri. You followed
a man and your choice was a free one – for the followers of the
Old Faith are not like the minions of Trialos, who seek to force
their will on others. But . . . but we are all puppets; even the very
gods themselves are used by forces far greater than they. I have
always been a puppet of the gods, and Tuan knew this. But you
should also know that I have always retained my free will. I was
not forced to come here, no more than you were. I chose to come,
and my decision was based on a sense of duty and what I felt was
right, and now that I am here I will do what I feel is right.

'I do not know why Tuan came; he had his reasons, but he, too,
made what he considered to be the right decision.

'And you. Why did you come? Because of your dream? And do
you always heed your dreams? Or did you come because you felt it
to be right?' He turned away and went to the mouth of the tunnel
out into the lurid sunlight; behind him Cliona wept silently.

'But I will tell you this,' Paedur said, without turning around,
his voice ringing ice-cold and painful in her head, 'I have sworn to
find Tuan, whether he be in this life or the next. And I took that
oath by the Pantheon when I last saw him, as he prepared to face
that which followed us.'

Suddenly he turned around and spoke to her. 'I am going on
now; to reach the vessel before Thanos has now become even
more important. You may stay here in the tunnel and I will return
presently – if I can. Or you may accompany me. The decision is
yours and yours alone.'

And in a voice that was barely above a whisper, Cliona said, 'I
will come with you.'

She joined the bard outside the tunnel and looked around in
amazement. They were on the roof of a building, a broad square of
rough sandstone, unrelieved by ornament or decoration, and without chimney or balustrade. Behind her the roof rose to perhaps
twice her height, forming a high wall, the mouth of the tunnel the
only opening. The tunnel must have led upwards through the core
of the building.

Paedur saw her astonishment and said, 'It's common in Culai
buildings.' He pointed across the flat roofs of the city spread out
before them, and in each case the roof was on two levels, each
displaying the black circle of a tunnel mouth. 'They lead down to
the Cavern of Power; it is at the very centre of the Culai way of

life, and thus at the same time each day, no matter where they are or what they're doing, they must retire below and worship.'

'But that means we must have passed a door in the tunnel on the way up,' Cliona exclaimed.

'We passed several, but they would not open to us.'

'And where is the centre opening through which the light comes?'

Paedur turned and pointed with his hook. Cliona followed it and there, behind her, towering above the rest of the city, was the goblet-shaped building of the Inner City. Its size was enormous; its base alone, which from the distance had seemed almost flat, was huge and almost topped the building on which they stood, and the spire which rose from the base was colossal, taller than the lighthouses that dotted the coast of her homeland and at least three times as thick. And the spire melded into the base of the building that squatted atop it without trace of a join or crack. As Cliona looked at it, she realised that something was missing. She puzzled over it for a moment – and then she realised that there were no windows or doors in the building.

Paedur nodded towards it. 'The vessel of the Chrystallis lies within the Circle of Keys in the Inner City,' he said.

'There is no door,' the priestess protested.

'There is always a door,' Paedur said. He walked to the edge of the roof and looked down into the silent empty streets far below.

Cliona called over to him, desperation edging her voice. 'How are we going to get off the roof, never mind getting into the Inner City?'

But the bard remained silent.

'Are we going to jump?' she asked bitterly, coming up to stand beside him and staring into the streets below.

'Aye, perhaps,' he said, squinting up into the orange sun. 'We have a little time, the light still burns below, and there are features of the Inner City I would point out. Come, sit here.' He drew her back from the edge of the roof and made her sit on the warm stone.

'What does its shape remind you of?' he asked suddenly.

'A goblet,' she said immediately, and the bard looked so surprised that she continued, 'See there, a base, a stem, a bowl.'

Paedur nodded absently. 'I see it now, though I must admit I have never thought of it that way before. Do the philosophers not say that life is like a rare wine, to be sipped slowly and enjoyed to the full. If we take your comparison, then that bowl is full of some rare vintage, for it holds the keys not only to our survival but also to the continuance of Order and Life on all the planes of life.

'But look again. Is the shape not reminiscent of the *naekt*, the glyph for fulfilment, discovery and completion in the Old Tongue?' He continued on as she nodded. 'Within the Inner City lies what we seek, the vessel of the Chrystallis. It is kept within the Circle of Gates or Keys. That is our destination. Once we reach it, our task is almost complete . . .' his voice died to a whisper, and then he stood up and reached for her hand. 'Come.'

'But how do we get off the roof . . .?'

The bard walked over to the edge of the roof and pointed down with his hook. 'This way.'

Cliona went over and stood beside him and looked down into the street, but she could see neither ladder, steps nor rope. 'How . . .?'

'Trust me,' Paedur murmured, and then, before she could ask him what he meant, he gripped her arms, pinning them tightly to her side, and jumped!

She screamed – but there was no sound. Her eyes watered in the wind that streamed upwards past them; she squeezed them shut, cutting out the sliding blurring sandstone side of the building they were falling past. But she could not shut out the sensation of falling . . . falling . . . falling into a limitless space and then there was . . .

16   The Vessel of the Chrystallis

Faith lends Substance.

Ancient proverb common to the Seven Nations

This day the gods themselves walked amongst us once more . . .

Song of the Teouteuchalai

Consciousness returned to Cliona as she lay in the shade of the tall square building, the bard bending over her, his ice-cold voice calling urgently deep in her head. '*Awaken . . . Awaken . . .*'

Her eyelids trembled and opened, and then closed again as everything shifted and spun. And then something bitterly cold was pressed against her cheek, bringing her fully awake. Paedur lifted his hook from her face, and smiled in apology. 'Come, we must hurry. The sun has shifted and the light will have died out down below. The Culai will soon be coming up from the cavern.' He pulled the priestess to her feet and propelled her across a wide street in the direction of the massive base of the Inner City. 'Hurry!'

His touch suddenly repelled her and she roughly shook off his hand and, head still spinning, staggered towards the featureless block of stone and into the shadow of the huge spire and bowl. Once out of the sickening glare of the red sun her head cleared and she began to think more clearly. 'There's no door . . .' she said thickly.

Paedur gripped her by the wrist and gestured with his hook to a portion of the wall. And though his lips didn't move, his voice cut through the remnants of the fog in her head. '*There! Visualise a door there. A door such as you have seen in the Order House of the Mother on the mainland. There the lintel, and now the posts . . .*' Gradually he built up in her mind the image of a door, a door similar to the Houses of the Mother; her imagination and memory supplied the rest, filling in the details, until she could almost see a door there.

And suddenly a door was there! A door such as she had visualised. A door from her memory, and past. She reached out to touch it; the brukwood felt warm and oily and the iron studs rasped against her fingers as she pressed on it.

Paedur pressed his hand flat against the door, and it swung silently inwards. He pushed Cliona through the opening just as they heard the sounds of high, musical voices approaching. She caught a glimpse of the Culai as they rounded the corner of a building further down the street, their heads bent in conversation; and then she was inside the building, and the door . . . had vanished.

The bard pressed her back against the smooth wall, his hand raised for silence as he listened. He took a few noiseless steps forward. 'Stay here, don't move,' he hissed.

Cliona nodded, glad of the opportunity to gather her wits and look around. They were in a huge chamber that was so vast the far walls were invisible in the dim light. It had been constructed in the manner of the First Race, with the massive blocks of stone welded together without trace of mortar or clay. The stones were ice-smooth and portions of them had been polished to a mirror-like sheen. The floor was of black marble, and was worked through with tiny threads of gold and silver in a pattern of some sort, but the design was so vast that she could make little sense of it. The impossibly high ceiling was also of the same black marble and the constellations and planets were picked out with tiny sparks of light, like the stars in the heavens on a sharp winter's night. Something caught her eye and she looked again – there was something vaguely wrong with the constellations . . . and then she realised that what she was seeing was a representation of the night-sky many generations ago when the Culai walked amongst man. There were no windows in the huge room, but a vague sepia light emanated from some of the wall stones, giving the place an almost twilight atmosphere.

Paedur materialised out of the dimness and took her hand. He led her across the floor, and then stopped before a section of the glass-like unadorned wall of the chamber. 'I want you to visualise a stairway here.' He tapped the wall ringingly with his hook. 'A stairway built in the manner of the Culai, the ruins of which you will have seen surviving in the Nations and the islands off the coast.'

Cliona nodded. 'I've seen them.'

'Imagine it here!' Paedur commanded.

The priestess closed her eyes, concentrating on the image of a

Culai stairway. They were nearly always the same; single blocks of stone laid haphazardly one upon the other. The steps were usually of differing heights and thicknesses, and of varying sizes, jutting crazily at all angles. This chaotic arrangement was at complete variance with the stark symmetry of all other Culai architecture. Some scholars maintained that the Culai had no use for stairways but had built spiralling ramps that ran around the outside of their buildings. However, they explained all absence of such ramps from the many Culai ruins by pointing out that external ramps would have been the first things to succumb to the ravages of time and the elements. There was little evidence to support this theory except that the crude mismatched stairways were only found in the later buildings, when the time of the First Race was drawing to a close.

Keeping his voice low and using all his bard's powers, Paedur built up a vivid word picture of a typical Culai stairway and Cliona added to it, drawing upon her childhood memories, for Monatome, her homeland, was one of the great centres of Culai ruins.

And gradually the flickering image of a stairway began to imprint itself upon the blank wall, winking in and out of a shadowy existence. Cliona tensed, forcing her mind to accept the image she was seeing; like all magics, she knew she must believe in it. Faith, she must have faith in it, faith lends substance. But she knew she had neither the strength of mind nor spirit to bring the stairway to reality.

And then the bard stepped up beside her and rested his hook upon her shoulder. There was a tingling transference of power and suddenly she felt new strength flow into her. The image immediately hardened and solidified, the blank wall faded . . . and the stairway was there.

The stones felt solid and real under her feet as the bard urged her up them. She slipped and fell upon the angled irregular steps, barking both shins, and she knew then the steps were no illusion. They were real. The bard pulled her to her feet and continued on without speaking.

The stairs wound endlessly upwards, weaving back and forth erratically, with neither rail nor guard and with a fall that grew steeper with every step they took. Cliona clung to the bard's cloak, keeping her eyes fastened to the stairs, blanking her mind to the terror that gibbered at the edges of her consciousness and threatened to overwhelm her at any moment. At one point she had tried counting the number of steps, but had given up somewhere around twenty-two hundred. She reached the point of exhaustion and begged the bard to stop, but he ignored her, and only seemed to increase the pace. Her leg muscles cramped, but she forced herself to go on, realising that the bard would probably leave her behind if she stopped now. She stumbled on, exhausted, almost sleep-walking on leaden feet.

Paedur abruptly stopped and Cliona staggered into him, and then slid down to her knees on the rough stone steps, gasping for breath, the pounding of blood roaring in her ears. She dimly realised the bard was speaking, but she couldn't make out the words. She looked down at the steps, her whole body shivering, her leg muscles twitching of their own accord, and when she looked up again the bard was gone. Something like terror gripped her, leaving her breathless, and she staggered to her feet . . . and then she heard the clatter of metal on metal – ahead!

Fear lent her strength and she ran up a few steps, and suddenly found that the stairway had ended and led out on to a short broad corridor. Midway down the corridor the bard was bending over the body of a ragged man, his hook dripping thick blood on to the polished stones. He looked up when the priestess appeared, and then silently lifted the dead man's arm in the curve of his hook. There was an iron band encircling it.

'The Iron Band of Kloor,' Cliona panted.

'Thanos has beaten us.'

'But how?'

Paedur shook his head in frustration. 'I don't know how. Just as there are several ways into Ui Tyrin, I suppose there must be more than one way into the Inner City also.' He turned and walked to the end of the short corridor, stopping before a high glass door set flush into the wall. He examined it closely, running his fingers over the opaque crystal, tracing out the curious design that was etched deep into the glass. Cliona walked slowly down the corridor, avoiding the grotesque and still bleeding body, and joined him, steadying herself against the wall.

'Do you recognise the design?' Paedur asked, tracing the hour-glass shape in the glass with his hook.

Cliona looked at it and then slowly shook her head.

'Look again,' Paedur snapped.

She ran her finger over the shape and then she suddenly saw within the design the outline of the Inner City.

'The *naekt*,' she said wearily, 'the symbol for fulfilling, finding and answering.'

Paedur smiled thinly. 'Just so. And that is what we must do now. Find the answer to the puzzle.' He deliberately struck the door with his hook, but the crystal remained unmarked.

'What puzzle?' the priestess asked, the bard's words slowly sinking into her fatigue-numbed brain.

'This design holds the key to this door; something about this tracery will open the way for us. And it cannot be too difficult either,' he added, pointing back down the corridor to the still body of the warrior. 'It was not beyond Thanos.'

'I still can't work out how he got here before us; I thought we left him beyond the city gates.'

'I would have thought all the gates on the far side of the city wall would be well guarded . . . but Thanos is cunning, and it is a dangerous – and usually deadly – mistake to underestimate him. One fact remains . . .' He tapped the glass door. 'He is already within; we have to get inside soon.'

Paedur turned back to the symbol etched into the glass. This was the key to the door; all he had to do was to charge it. Given time he would inevitably find the answer – but there was no more time left. Thanos and his men had already passed through the door – perhaps they already had the vessel and were even now preparing to open it. He pounded on the door with his fist in frustration; he had come so far – he would not be cheated by the Hand of God, not now, not so late in the game. He would not allow it! At any instant all creation might be swept away in a swirling chaos of the time before Life, the era of the One and the Void and the Chrystallis – and the Cords.

And what of the Three Cords? They posed an even greater threat than the Soulwind. Should the Chrystallis sweep all the planes back to the Void, it would mean an ending to everything, but it would not be a final, ultimate ending. The process of creation could begin again; there might be a future. However, if the Cords should scour the planes free of life, rending through the soft fabric of time and the wafers of fragile space, then Disruption, Annihilation and Chaos would render the Void lifeless for all eternity. Even the One might not survive the passage of the Three Cords. They had to be stopped, but what could a mortal – even a mortal gifted by the gods – do against Disruption, Annihilation and Chaos?

Cliona slumped at the bard's feet, too exhausted to even think, images of the last few days – was it only days? – chasing each other in ever decreasing circles around in her head. Numbly, almost emotionlessly, she felt the salt tears fall to her roughened hands and splash on to the dry stone floor. Idly her fingers moved in the wetness, tracing the symbol of the *naekt* on the stone.

The bard knelt beside her, hunched and silent, his eyes darting about the corridor, seeking; seeking anything that might suggest the key of the door. If the Culai used this door with any degree of regularity, then it must be something simple – magic of any sort, no matter how minor, was draining. Therefore it was something built into the door, a crude static spell which could be charged by a simple process. And all he had to do was to find it.

His eyes fell on the priestess, and he saw her trace the shape of the *naekt* repeatedly. He watched her finger move . . . left to right, then down to the left-hand corner again, then across to the right, then back up to the left-hand corner, making two stylised triangles, one atop the other.

And realisation blossomed in the bard, and suddenly he had the answer – he had the key to the door. 'Reverse the process,' he murmured, 'reverse it . . .!'

Pulling the priestess to her feet and supporting her with one hand he began to trace the shape of the *naekt* on the door in reverse with the tip of his hook.

Almost imperceptibly the crystal door began to split, a tiny crack at first beginning at the top in the centre and widening out in a long wedge until it touched the floor. The long triangular split seemed almost to be painted on the gleaming crystal, black velvet on white silk. 'Are you ready?' Paedur asked Cliona, but, without waiting for an answer, he pulled her through the opening . . . into a suffocating cloying blackness that was tangible, an absolute featureless sightless nothing that the mind refused to accept.

Cliona opened her mouth and screamed, but there was no sound, and then she choked on the gate's foul inky ichor that enfolded her. Her limbs began to tingle – at first almost pleasantly, but then they quickly turned numb. The blood pounding in her ears and temples threatened to explode with the violence of the throbbing. Her eyes opened and closed, straining to see something . . . anything!

And this is what it must be like to die, she thought; perhaps this is death, and I am on my way to be judged. 'Is this death?' she screamed silently.

Something brushed her mind, a feather touch, a caress, and then she could almost feel the bard within her head, and not chill like the last time but solid, comforting . . . and real, something she could cling to.

'*This is like the space between the planes,*' Paedur whispered, his voice echoing hollowly within her head. '*You have passed through it twice before and, though it was not as powerful or as pure a force then as it is now, you need not fear it.*' Even as he was speaking the blackness had begun to lighten, and the utter darkness was replaced by a dull grey semi-light, something akin to a winter twilight, which was shot through with darting points of white light . . .

. . . They emerged into a large circular courtyard that at first glance seemed open to the sky, but the priestess immediately realised it couldn't be the sky of this world, for the sky was a delicate pastel blue, the clouds were smoky white, and the sun, low on the horizon, was an orange gold. The familiarity of it all brought sudden tears to her eyes. The ceiling – for that was what it was – had been created by a master-craftsman and artist from tiny flakes of differing marbles, white and blue, red and gold. It was very beautiful and yet it looked almost out of place – it did not belong here amongst the starkness of the Culai Isle.

The large circular room itself was featureless, except for a simple stone pedestal set into the centre of the floor. But set into the walls were doorposts and lintels, and these opened out on to different views; a snowscape, a seascape, summer fields rippling beneath a gentle breeze, a barren plain. Cliona first thought that they were pictures, tapestries perhaps, but the bard took her to the empty pedestal in the centre of the room and from there she could see each of the nine openings. 'Look closer,' Paedur said quickly.

She looked – and found that there was movement in the pictures: the seas crashed against high cliffs; the wind whirled tumbleweed across the dusty plains. 'They're like windows to other worlds . . .' she whispered.

The bard laughed. 'Priestess, do you not recognise them? They are openings to other lands . . . they are the keys to our plane, for we are now at the hub of the Inner City, the Circle of Keys. Behold the Keys!' His hook swept around the room, encompassing the nine doorways.

'I have never seen anything like it,' she whispered, looking in wonder from opening to opening.

Paedur went over to one of the gates, through which Cliona could see a swirling snowscene, with desolate ice-fields beneath a leaden sky and a wan sun burning low on the horizon. 'Ah, but the gates were once quite common,' Paedur continued. 'They provided a magically swift method of transport between any two points on our world. They were similar to the Grey Walls in that respect, except that the walls shift the traveller through the planes, whereas the gates confine the journeyer to one plane. Did you know, priestess, that there are still working gates on our plane?' He laughed gently. 'Can you tell me where?'

'It can only be the Great Henge,' Cliona gasped.

Paedur nodded. 'That is the last circle of gates on our plane,' he said slowly, walking from gate to gate, looking out at the Seven Nations. 'But now they may not be used. They were the focus for much evil upon the Southern Kingdoms down through the generations of man, and evil draws evil to itself . . .'

'But if the gates are simply used for moving people from place to place,' Cliona asked, 'what's the harm in that?'

'The gates proved to be unreliable, and before they came to be no longer used they sometimes lost people, and occasionally admitted shadow creatures from the Gorge which had grown tangible with man's belief.'

'Are these doorways usable?' she asked.

Paedur nodded silently.

'And what about Thanos?' the priestess asked.

'He has escaped us – with the vessel!' Paedur nodded to the empty pedestal in the centre of the room. 'He's gone through the gates – but which one, which one?' He stood beside the pedestal and slowly turned, looking at each gate in turn. A thought struck him, and he suddenly darted to an opening across from the priestess.

'What is it?'

But the bard silenced her with a wave of his hand and stared intently through the opening. Beyond the gate a crude stone and mud-bricked village shimmered beneath a blistering sun. The tiny dwellings were bleached colourless and the rough windows and doors looked dark and ominous in the harsh light. Even the sky seemed bleached, with a delicate metallic blue only showing close to the horizon; the world seemed lifeless.

'Where is it?' the priestess wondered.

Silently the bard pointed to a mound beyond the village. Cliona squinted into the harsh light, already feeling the heat on her face and hands. The mound was a crudely shaped pyramid with a levelled top and had countless steps inset in its side.

'Teouteuchal,' Paedur said slowly, almost triumphantly, nodding to himself. 'Aye, it would strike Thanos as fitting to open the vessel of the Chrystallis atop the pyramid.'

'Why?'

'The pyramids of Teouteuchal are amongst the earliest symbols of man's devotion to the Gods of the Pantheon. The Teouteuchalai have always worshipped Nusas, the Lord of the Sun, and Thanos would take great delight in defiling the god's altar.'

'But how can you be sure he is there?' She looked around at the other gates. 'He could be anywhere,' she said, a note of despair touching her voice.

'He is there, I know it,' Paedur said confidently, stepping up to the gateway. 'Come.'

He reached for her hand but she flinched away, and he saw the fear in her eyes. 'What are you frightened of?' he asked quietly, and then he added, 'The passage between places on the same plane is not as traumatic nor as severe as travelling between the planes. Trust me,' he said.

Cliona nodded doubtfully, and then Paedur stepped through the opening, taking her with him into the Southern Kingdom of Teouteuchal. She clung tightly to his hand, squeezing her eyes shut, but all she experienced was a sudden chill, nothing more, and then the heat struck her, a heavy, dry, desiccating blast of leaden heat. The bard spoke softly by her side. 'We are through.'

It still took another moment or two for the priestess to muster her courage, and then she carefully opened her eyes, peering through slitted lids. The first thing she spotted was a cluster of small dwellings ahead and to her left. They looked almost like part of the ground, with the dried earth and baked walls burnt to the same shade of ochre. One house, slightly larger than the rest, had been thatched with wisps of straw that were so old they looked brittle enough to crumble.

The bard touched her gently on the arm, startling her. 'We must make haste – Thanos is here, I can sense him.' He set off through the huts, moving like a shadow personified, but Cliona noticed with a tingling chill that the bard himself cast no shadow.

She ran after him, glancing back once . . . and stopped in

sudden wonder. The gateway through which they had come was gone, but in its place stood two upright pillars, topped by a crossbeam, beautifully wrought in an unusual emerald-green stone. Countless tiny intricate pictograms were worked into the stone, and the square blocky carvings winked and sparkled as chippings of metal or crystal caught the light. Beside the two uprights stood two tall fluted urns of baked clay, both painted in soft flowing colours. Tall reeds drooped in the urns, their golden petals or leaves lying scattered on the brown earth at the base of the pillars. Cliona found it interesting to see that although the reeds were now wilting with the heat they were still reasonably fresh and therefore could only have been placed there earlier that day. The priestess felt the bard by her side. 'It's a holy place for the Teouteuchalai. They worship it as the doorway of the gods.'

'But I can see right through it,' Cliona protested. 'I cannot see the Circle of Keys; how then do they know it's a gateway?'

'Through tales passed down from generation to generation. The legends also prophesy that the gods themselves will one day come through that gate . . .' He stopped suddenly. 'Of course . . .' he breathed.

Cliona shook her head. 'I don't understand . . .' but the bard had already turned and was running towards the pyramid that rose beyond the town.

'Paedur, wait,' Cliona called desperately after him. 'What's wrong?' But the bard had gone, his shadow-figure seeming barely to touch the unyielding baked earth. The priestess struggled after him, the fear of being left alone lending her speed. As she ran from the pillars, she suddenly realised that Thanos and the remnants of his Band had come through the gate – and the Teouteuchalai people would have thought them the promised gods. They probably thought he was the Lord Nusas himself. And they had gone with Thanos . . . gone to the mound where the Hand of God would undoubtedly open the vessel of the Chrystallis with a blood sacrifice. The Teouteuchalai would refuse him nothing, not even one of their own number to be torn asunder atop the stepped pyramid.

She ran through the deserted village, heading down the single street towards the pyramid, which she could now see was swarming with tiny ant shapes. She wondered if she dared call upon the Mother's Power – and if she did, would she be answered? On the Culai Isle the Old Gods had no power, but she was not on the isle now. But it would alert Thanos to their presence . . .

Still undecided, she followed the rough pitted track that led out of the village, stumbling over the ruts and potholes. The track wound through tall thorny scrub and then dipped down a sharp slope. At the bottom of the slope she sprawled across a ragged body lying in a pool of still-flowing blood. Dragging herself to her feet she noted the look of horror etched into the features of the dead man. His throat had been torn out. He still clutched a stiletto blade, and as Cliona bent to pull it from his fingers the thick metal band about his wrist caught the light – Thanos had lost another warrior.

She followed the track up out of the hollow and found that it opened out into a wide plaza lined with short pillars. Across the plaza the first steps of the pyramid began. The pyramid itself was not large, nor was it pretty – this was no king's burial mound, with gilded stones and delicate paintings. It was a squat, broad-stepped mound, six or possibly seven floors high. The workmanship was crude and looked unfinished, although the pyramid itself looked ancient. But it was nothing more than an elevated sacrificial slab.

She ran across the plaza, and then found that it dipped down on the far side, so that the pyramid actually began in a hollow, making it taller than she had thought at first. On the slope she came across two more bodies; they too bore evidence of the bard's sudden and violent passage. But, curiously, there was no sign of the Teouteuchalai. She hesitated, and then heard the soft, chanted murmuring. Following the sound she found that one side of the plaza dipped down to a broad lake, whose waters seemed impossibly blue and bright against the drabness of the rest of the landscape. The Teouteuchalai had gathered on the lakeside, and seemed to be engaged in a ritual purification. When the rite was complete, they would undoubtedly gather about the base of the pyramid to salute their god, but by that time, Cliona realised, she and the bard would have to be well away from it.

When she reached the first steps of the pyramid, she looked up and could just about make out the black shape of the bard ahead of her. She took a deep breath and began the long climb.

Atop the pyramid, a sacrifice was in progress. Two short brown bodies lay in pools of blood about the base of a stained flat slab, gaping wounds in their chests leaking blood across the flat roof. A third youth lay spreadeagled across the dripping slab, his eyes wide open in terror. His arms and legs were held by two of the Band of Kloor, while Xanazius, Thanos' acolyte, stood beside him, his arms caked in gore up to the elbows. At his feet two shapeless lumps of meat still quivered. Thanos stood behind the altar, a delicately carved, tall-necked jar clutched in his arms. In the sunlight, his pale skin and bleached hair were almost translucent, causing his eyes and lips to look startlingly red. And about them the priests of the Teouteuchalai worshipped in watchful silence.

Thanos raised the jar high. 'Behold the vessel of the Chrystallis. It has lain too long on the Culai Isle, and now it hungers. Feed it!' He nodded to Xanazius, who raised his butcher's knife high . . .

And then the bard burst on to the top of the pyramid. In the eyes of the Teouteuchalai priests he appeared as a Duaiteoiri, a demon, with blazing eyes and a curved talon dripping blood on to the scoured flagstones. They saw him raise the bloody talon and describe a design that burned with a cold white fire on the still air before the God-Priest who had come through the Gate of the Gods. The white-haired, red-eyed priest snarled in a guttural tongue and held the delicate-looking gem-stoppered vessel close to his chest. Immediately two of the priest's seven acolytes advanced on the Duaiteoiri, knives glittering in their hands.

Cliona heard the shouts and clash of metal as she struggled up the countless worn wooden steps of the pyramid. Calling upon the Mother for strength she redoubled her efforts to reach the top and aid the bard. There was a short shrill scream that was choked off in a liquid gurgle above her head, and she looked up – just as a body flopped over the edge of the pyramid and began to slide down the steps, arms and legs flailing in a grotesque parody of life, trailing a stream of glistening red-black droplets. The priestess cowered to one side as the body crashed past her and lodged a few steps below her. A terrible fascination drew her eyes to the upraised face. A scream caught deep in her throat; the face had been torn from forehead to mouth, down the left side, obviously slashed by a blade . . . or a hook. Fear, and the sudden need to be away from those ghastly staring eyes, made her turn and run up the planks of wood that had once been brought from the far Northlands to serve as steps to the god's throne.

She eventually reached the top, but stopped before the steps ended and raised her head to peer over the edge of the broad platform. She noted the miserable huddle of natives, now terrified witless by the sudden violence which had erupted on their holy place. And then she spotted the bard, who was surrounded by the five remaining warriors of the Band of Kloor. Paedur was standing over the body of another, and his hook and left arm were thick with blood. Behind them Cliona could see the white-robed albino, Thanos, his bloodless hands clutching what could only be the vessel of the Chrystallis. His eyes were wild with a burning madness as he hissed curses at the bard and urged his followers to attack.

The warriors hung back, however, for they knew the power of the bard: they had lost too many of their number to his razor hook and extraordinarily fast reflexes. They shifted continually, jabbing with their swords and knives, probing for an opening. And then one suddenly lunged, his curved knife plunging towards the bard's unprotected back. As if on signal the remaining four made their move, knives and short-swords darting towards the bard.

Cliona screamed. And the Dannu-fire blazed blue-white across the roof of the pyramid, lapping fluidly about the three nearest warriors. They fell, writhing in agony as the cold flames ate through them with startling swiftness, burning through flesh to expose the white bones beneath before they extinguished themselves. The bard caught a blade on his hook while another shattered on his cloak as if it had struck stone instead of cloth. His hook flickered and blurred and sliced through flesh as easily as a knife through cheese, opening a throat, severing another man's jugular – and the last of the Band of Kloor fell.

The bard bowed slightly to the priestess as she joined him, stepping over the charred remains. Together they faced Thanos. Behind them the moaning priests scrambled down the steps, and the sacrificial youth slipped off the altar stone and ran down the steps followed, a moment later, by Xanazius. Thanos watched him go without comment. A brittle silence settled over the pyramid and, although the noonday sun beat down directly overhead, the priestess was chill.

Paedur took a step forward, his hand outstretched. 'Give me the vessel.' His voice was level, completely emotionless.

Thanos laughed.

The bard took another step forward, but Thanos raised his hand. 'Come no further, *shanaqui*, else I will cast this vessl to the ground below.'

'That would not serve your masters,' the bard said, measuring the distance that separated him from the wild-eyed priest. 'Break it now and you have no control over it.'

'You will never claim the vessel,' Thanos spat. 'I would rather destroy the planes than surrender the vessel to you.'

'But it is of little use to you now. You have lost . . . again. As your faith has lost for a hundred generations. The Religion is but a wayward child compared to the parent Pantheon. How could you even hope to threaten the Faith armed only with the best elements from a score of lesser faiths and beliefs and aided by a Usurper from the Gorge?'

Thanos began to laugh wildly. 'But you're wrong, bard, you're wrong! The Religion has been growing, and we have more converts now than ever before. We are growing. And as we grow, so the Faith weakens and dies. Like a child growing to maturity as the parent comes to senility.'

Paedur began to speak again, but Cliona abruptly felt his ice-cold touch brush her mind. She couldn't make out what he was saying, all she received was the impression that she was to make a move now, to act while Paedur held the Hand of God distracted. 'Your converts are tricked, your priests entice them into the Religion with false promises.'

'It is for their own good,' Thanos said passionately. 'Once they have joined the ranks of the faithful, they will see the error of their past and recognise the Religion for what it is: the one true belief. Our gods are real, they are living . . .'

Cliona took a deep breath and began to move back away from the bard, keeping him between herself and the priest. She stopped when her heels moved off the edge of the flat roof. Her foot found the topmost step and she stepped down on to it. She moved down another ten or so, desperately wondering what the bard expected her to do. He obviously expected her to distract Thanos, while he grabbed the vessel of the Chrystallis. But how? She could attack him using the Dannu-fire – but what would happen to the metallic green jar? she couldn't allow it to be damaged. But if she managed to get around behind him . . .?

She looked up the dozen or so steps that led to the flat roof. The steps ran almost the width of the pyramid, long flat slabs of polished black wood, slightly curving in the centre with the passage of countless feet. She moved to the edge of the step on which she stood. It ended just short of the corner, and she had no idea whether the steps continued around on the far side. Wiping a trickle of sweat from her eyes, she carefully slid one hand around the angle where the two sides of the pyramid met, fingers groping for a handhold on the far side. Using the edge of the step as a base, she extended her right leg around the side. But she couldn't feel any steps. Finally, her foot found and rested on an irregular outcropping and, resting her whole weight on it, she pulled herself around the corner. There were no steps; this side of the pyramid was unfinished. Pressed flat against the baking earthen bricks, she began to edge her way along the rough-hewn stones, chippings of mud and stone crumbling beneath her torn fingers.

Above her head Thanos' voice rose to a hysterical shout, 'There is no god but Trialos, and I, Thanos his Hand, I am his representative upon this plane. Trialos is the one true god . . .'

Cliona glanced down. Below her, she could see tiny insect figures running to and fro, yet always returning to gather at the foot of the pyramid. Light glinted off metal, and she could hear a muted angry buzzing, and the priestess realised the Teouteuchalai were arming themselves. They would storm the steps at any moment to avenge their god's priest. Desperation lent her strength, and she dug her tattered sandals into the crumbling side of the pyramid and pushed herself up. And her fingers brushed a rough fibrous root. She wrapped her fingers around it and pulled; it gave a little, displacing a long line of mud but also showing her just how far it ran across the side of the pyramid. She pulled on it again – harder this time – and it didn't move. Breathing a silent prayer to the Mother, she used the root as a guide-rope and moved swiftly across the slope, dislodging chunks of dried clay and mud from between the stones. She stopped when she heard Thanos speaking directly above her head.

But now the root had disappeared back into the mound, and there were only the sun-baked stones above her head. The stones here were of differing sizes, crude and ragged; obviously the better stones had been used for the front of the pyramid. She reached up and pulled one of the stones – it came away in her hands in a shower of dried clay. She tried again, and a huge chunk of the dried earthen covering came away, revealing the hard packed earth beneath. She could go no further.

Above her, the voices rose to a crescendo, the bard threatening to call down the power of the Old Gods and Thanos threatening to throw the vessel off the pyramid.

Cliona suddenly remembered the stiletto she had picked off the corpse on the track. She had stuck the long thin-bladed knife into the laces of her sandals, and then forgotten about it. Pressing herself flat against the slope, with her left hand closed firmly around a chunk of coal, the priestess carefully felt for the blade with her right hand; her fingers slid down the dry clay, then gently

293

crept inwards until they were poised above the top of her right sandal where the hilt of the knife protruded. She was reaching for it when the coal crumbled to powder in her white-knuckled grip. In one swift movement she snatched the knife from her sandal and, as she began to fall backwards, plunged the knife into the side of the pyramid, deep into the hard packed earth. The knife shook and the thin blade bent, but it held, leaving her hanging by one hand as her precarious footholds crumbled beneath her feet. Her left hand scrambled for a fingerhold, prising loose chunks of stone and mud, and she kicked into the brittle clay with her pointed shoes. She lay there, trembling violently, the blood pounding in her temples, feeling the slickness of her palms seep into the dry mud.

She also became aware of the silence above her head, and then the voices seemed to be reaching a conclusion; the hysterical shouting of the priest had a terrible ring of finality about it. She desperately began working the blade from side to side, loosening it, and when she eventually eased it free she clenched it between her teeth. The fingers of her left had reached for and found a handhold, and she pulled herself up – and over the edge of the roof. She was behind Thanos.

Cliona rested a moment, then she rose to her feet – just as the priest turned!

The albino froze in shocked surprise, and backed away from her, then suddenly realising that the bard was behind him, he turned, raising the vessel in both hands. Cliona lunged, the thin warped blade of the stiletto held at arm's length. The priest opened his mouth to scream as the blade entered his chest but blood suddenly welled from his lips – and with one last convulsive effort he threw the vessel of the Chrystallis from him . . .

Cliona lay where she fell, unconscious of the priest's blood trickling down her arms, unconscious of the body that had fallen across her legs, conscious only that they had failed. She had seen Thanos throw the delicate vessel of blue-green metallic glass over her head; desperately, futilely, she had reached for it, but she had already been falling and her fingers only brushed the base as it arched over her head.

It had all been for nothing.

She wondered dimly about the bard as she waited for the vessel to shatter on the ground below; she waited for the howling winds of destruction to sweep across the planes of existence, returning them to the Void from whence they came . . .

She heard the winds then, an almost human sound of exultation, a triumphant howling. So the vessel had struck the ground and shattered, and now the Chrystallis was howling through the Void, descending upon the plane . . .

She waited another score of pounding heartbeats and then wondered, where was it?

Cliona opened one eye. Beneath her face the grains of grit loomed large as boulders. Shakily the priestess pushed aside the body lying across her and sat up – and then an arm enfolded her waist and helped her to her feet. It was the bard. He laughed in genuine amusement at the look of astonishment on her face and then, with a dramatic flourish, he produced the vessel of the Chrystallis from beneath his cloak. The priestess reached out with trembling fingers and touched it. And then she wept.

Before they began the long climb down the wooden steps, Paedur sketched the Sign of the Dead over the body of Thanos, and bent his head in a brief silent prayer. 'I'm sorry he's dead, in a way,' he said suddenly, pausing on the top step and looking back at the pale corpse.

'I thought he was your enemy,' Cliona said, surprised. 'He would have destroyed everything in his mad lust to see the Pantheon overthrown.'

Paedur nodded absently as he manoeuvred around the body of the man he had killed earlier, which was still lodged on the steps. 'I know; but he was a worthy foe, cunning and resourceful. He reminded me of Mannam in many respects.' He was silent for a moment. 'But he did truly believe in his Religion. And I wonder were we so different in our devotion to our beliefs?' He shook his head. 'Aye, well, he was mad of course, and towards the end his petty god finally deserted him.'

'And the vessel . . .?' Cliona prompted.

'Aye, the vessel, the vessel . . .' He lifted the jar and ran his hook over the curious opaque glass, tapping it gently. It sang with a high musical note, the sound quivering on the still air. 'The vessel of the Chrystallis. Before I saw you clamber over the edge – and I think it surprised me as much as Thanos – I had begun to call upon the Windlords, Faurm and Faurug, and their father, Feitigh. The pyramid is old in the service of the Pantheon and the very power that Thanos sought to defile finally worked to his own destruction. The Windlords came and gathered about the pyramid . . .' Paedur suddenly laughed and shook his head. 'And when Thanos threw the vessel as he fell, it was caught by the Windlords and clung seemingly in mid-air, and all I had to do was to pluck it free.'

'I heard the wind and I thought the vessel had fallen and shattered and that the Soulwind was coming,' the priestess murmured, 'and I cursed you then as I cursed myself for not catching it.'

'I tried . . . I tried,' he said gently, 'for I must admit I feared the Windlords might not be able to hold it.'

At the base of the pyramid, the Teouteuchalai were gathered in silence, their bronze and stone weapons burning in the afternoon light. They watched as Paedur and Cliona stepped off the last step and prepared to start back along the rough track to the village. Some of the natives moved in threateningly. The bard eyed them coldly, his gaze seeming to burn through the still air, and they shuffled back in confusion. Gradually, the ranks of the Teouteuchalai began to part like receding tide waters, until they lined the track in a parody of a guard of honour. Swiftly Paedur and Cliona made their way through the people, the eerie silence unbroken on either side. When they passed, the natives closed in behind and as the bard supported the priestess along the winding track and through the pitiful village the entire population followed the terrifying despoilers of their altar.

When they reached the twin pillars of stone, the bard turned and faced the people and his hook gleamed in the dull light as it sketched a glyph that burned silver in the still air. 'Accept this as my payment,' he said clearly.

And suddenly the clear afternoon sky began to darken rapidly with swift-moving billowing grey clouds. Soon the sun had disappeared behind a leaden shield, and the faces of the Teouteuchalai turned upwards in wonder and sudden hope. And as Paedur and the priestess stepped through the gate the first large and heavy drops of rain began to fall . . .

17 The Magician's Law

Life comes only through Death, and destruction is, in itself, merely the starting point for a new beginning . . .

Culai proverb

The Magician's Law, the force of equals, allows a balance to be maintained . . .

Grimoire Magnum

. . . And they stepped back in the circular gate-room in the Inner City.

The brief passage left Cliona dizzy and slightly sickened, and Paedur took her arm and led her to the centre of the room to the jade and gold pedestal that had once held the vessel of the Chrystallis. He returned the metallic jar to its place and then put his hands to her shoulders and made her sit down with her back to the smooth cold stone. 'Rest a moment,' he murmured. The bard then returned to the Gate of Teouteuchal and stood gazing out at the puzzled faces of the natives. Rain sluiced down, turning the baked earth into a mire, but the Teouteuchalai knelt before the gate, their heads bent, arms outstretched in prayer.

'Why?' Cliona asked suddenly.

Paedur turned to look at her, his face impassive.

'Why did it rain?'

The bard moved his hook across the opening and the gate behind him immediately darkened and the Teouteuchalai vanished. 'Payment, I suppose, payment for our trespass or for undedicated bloodletting on their altar, for invoking gods other than Nusas . . .' He shrugged. 'And it has not rained there for many seasons.' He began moving around the gates, drawing his hook across them, darkening them all in turn.

'What will we do now?' the priestess wondered, watching the bard.

The bard joined her at the pedestal, squatting down to stare into her eyes. 'Now we must return to the Cavern of Power.'

'But why?' she whispered. 'We have what we came for.'

'I know,' he sighed. 'But now we must face a far greater threat than Thanos ever posed.' He saw her look of incomprehension. 'We must face the Three Cords; the Cords of Disruption, Annihilation and Ultimate Chaos before the Culai loose them upon the planes.'

'But how do you know they will free the Cords?'

'I don't think they will have any choice in the matter – they will have to release the Cords soon before they become too powerful for even the Culai to control.'

'I'm frightened,' Cliona whispered, suddenly shivering, 'more frightened now than at any other time.'

'I know,' Paedur said softly. His emotions has been blunted when he had been given eternal life, but he was still able to experience the most powerful emotion of all – fear. He stood up and lifted the vessel of the Chrystallis from its pedestal. He held it up to the light and watched as the gemstone stopper came alive with sparkling, shifting lights. Cliona, however, was looking at the way the green light of the metallic glass reflected back on to the bard's face, giving him an aged, dead look. And suddenly she was filled with a terrible foreboding, an abrupt chill fear, not only for herself but for the bard also.

'Why must you do this? We have prevented the vessel from falling into the hands of Trialos' followers. We have saved the planes of life. Thanos is dead, and the Religion has been dealt a mortal blow. Can you not rest now?'

The bard knelt by her side again and, placing the vessel on the floor, took both her hands in his single hand. 'Priestess, I can never rest,' he said softly. 'It is a price I pay . . .'

'What price . . .?'

'For a "gift" I received and a vow I took some time ago,' he murmured, his voice lost in the mists of memory.

'But how can you fight the Three Cords?' she demanded.

Paedur shook his head. 'I'm not sure I can,' he said softly, 'but I can try; I'm going to use the Magician's Law.'

'What happens if it doesn't work?'

The bard smiled. 'Then we'll never know.'

The chilling benighted passage through the glass door was shorter than the priestess remembered it, the darkness not so complete nor as heavy and cloying. The stairs were as they had left them – the creation still held, although its edges were becoming ill-defined and hazy. They passed the body of the warrior the bard had killed in the corridor, but it stank now as if it had lain there for many days.

Paedur paused, looking at it. Cliona glanced briefly at it, and then turned back to him. 'What's wrong?'

'Time,' he said very quietly. 'We've lost a few days. Come; we must make haste!' And then he turned and ran silently along the length of the corridor, and started down the steps. Cliona struggled along behind, hesitating only for the space of a single pounding heartbeat, before dashing down the stairs, her fear of losing him greater than her fear of falling. She ran with her left hand brushing the wall, her eyes fixed firmly on her feet or the few steps ahead of her. She knew that if she looked either up or down she was lost.

However, the lower she went, the more fragmented and unreal the steps became. After a while she realised that her feet were sinking slightly into the stone, and actual holes were beginning to appear in the steps. She finally caught up with the bard, only to find that he had stopped because the last stairs disappeared into a shifting, swirling fog.

'The illusion is fading. Come now, concentrate, create once again a Culai stairway.' He stepped behind her and rested his right hand and hook on her shoulders and poured strength into her.

Cliona drew upon her own strength and the power of the bard, and set about creating the illusion of the stairs from the agitated fog. Gradually the angles and planes of the chaotic stairs, the differing sizes, the irregular shapes and mixed stonework began to appear. And solidify – and abruptly the stairway was complete.

The priestess was soon staggering with exhaustion, her movements automatic, her brain numbed. Eventually Paedur took her arm, fearing that she might actually reel off the edge of the stairway, and led her down the final few steps back into the great marbled hallway of the Inner City. Cliona slumped at the bard's feet as they stepped off the last step, and as she drifted into unconsciousness she was aware that the stairway was just dissolving back into mist. Her last conscious impression was of the bard lifting her up . . .

As Cliona awoke there were a few terrifying moments of disorientation, and then she became aware that she was in one of the small side tunnels that led into the vast Cavern of Power beneath the City of the Culai. The bard sat by her side wrapped in his enveloping furred cloak, the dimly glowing vessel between his feet, his hook touching the stopper, firing the gemstone, bringing it to life so that it glowed with a soft blue radiance. When he saw she was awake, he removed his hook from the glowing gem, and the light faded, leaving them in darkness.

Beyond the tunnel the Cavern of Power was empty and in silence, the phosphorescent fungi giving it a ghostly sub-aqueous appearance. This, she thought wildly, must be what the Netherworld, beyond the Silent Wood, must look like.

They did not speak; there was nothing to say. They each had their own thoughts; Cliona's were confused and sluggish, the events of the past few days – was it days? – crowding in, one atop the other. In contrast, the bard had but one thought, one fixed immutable idea – to destroy the Cords, if he could.

Cliona dozed again and was awakened by the bard's hand pressed over her mouth. His ice-cold voice echoed in her skull. '*Culai!*' She sat up; beyond the dark circle of the tunnel the Cavern blazed with liquid fire-colours, bringing tears to her eyes. Shadows moved before her streaming eyes, and when she brushed the tears away, she found that figures were passing across the mouth of the tunnel.

The Culai were arriving.

Their metallic, mirror-bright skin-sheaths reflected back the burning light so that it looked as if the delicate elfin features of the First Race floated in a shifting sea of liquid colour. The Cavern of Power was filling swiftly and silently, the only sound the gentle susurration of the Culai's cloth slippers on the stone. They gathered about the light-burning pool of reflective liquid, looking up at the long beam of light stretching upwards to the tiny glowing eye in the roof through which the sun shone. They took their places, the lines radiating out from the pool, their shadows hard and sharp and black against the colours.

The chanting began then, a high, thin keening, their voices soaring aloft, the sound pure and fragile. Cliona strained, attempting to catch the words, some of which sounded almost familiar. It seemed to be a single sentence or phrase, repeated over and over again. The chant picked up in speed, becoming faster and faster until there was just one long continuous sound, wail-like in its intensity. The priestess didn't know the words, but she recognised the meaning – it was a call.

And then it stopped – almost as if the First Race had heard an answer.

The chant was taken up again. But now each line of Culai intoned the chant in turn, the other lines taking up the chant sequentially until a piercing crescendo was reached and the insistent calling was such that even the priestess felt the primeval pull of it, the sudden compulsion to move forward into the centre of the cavern. Cliona suddenly felt the bard stiffen, and simultaneously the air above the shimmering pool darkened and began to flicker. The Culai chant took on a new note, a note of triumph. And abruptly above the pool a long thin snake-like band appeared, writhing in convoluted circles.

The first of the Cords, Disruption.

The Culai had fallen silent with the appearance of the first of the Cords, gazing at the weaving strip of nothingness as if entranced. And then the Cord was gone, and for the space of a single heartbeat the grey swirling mists of the Ghost Worlds seeped into the cavern, only to be dispersed like wind-blown smoke.

And then two Cords winked into the Cavern of Power, and the second was Annihilation. Together they interwove and spun in silence, drawing substance from the colours and light and the faith of the Culai. Then they too were gone, and the air above the pool was suddenly flooded with rich, warm, vibrant colours to replace those leached out by the two Cords.

A third Cord winked into existence – Chaos.

And now the Cords began to swirl and twist with ever increasing speed, weaving pattern after pattern in the paling air, until they had assumed the shape of three interconnected black rings orbiting one another. The colours faded from the air above the pool, leaving a misty greyness in their wake, and then the circles began to thicken and grow in size. Immediately, the light in the vast cavern dimmed and a chill and bitter wind swept down the tunnels and howled about the gathered Culai.

Now the colours were almost totally gone; the rainbow-hued stones that had encircled the pool were now only slabs of black and grey, and the beam that shot down into the pool was nothing more than a milky grey sliver of light. The Cords were beginning to move out above the Culai, spinning in flat circles, leaching the last vestiges of colour that lingered about the assembled group, until only a gritty black and white and grey remained. The three spinning bands now came together with an audible crack that echoed and re-echoed about the cavern, reverberating off the walls, shivering through the stones. Loose rock and stalactites rained down on the Culai, felling some to the floor, but the others paid no attention. They were enthralled by the Cords.

The Cords had now melded to become one, and above the First Race wheeled a flat disc of total darkness, darker than the furthest reaches of the Gorge, colder than the Land of Muirad. The high glittering roof of the cavern was lost behind it and the distant walls began to waver and shred in a wispy darkness, for the fabric of the plane was beginning to break down under the onslaught of the Cords. The vast circle of darkness began to descend upon the heads of the Culai. The Cords would feed.

A cold blue radiance flared from beneath the bard's hand, and the priestess realised Paedur had fired the gemstone in the mouth of the vessel of the Chrystallis. The sudden colour attracted the Cords, and sable tendrils began to snake towards the blue circle of light that outlined the mouth of the tunnel.

The bard handed the delicate vessel to Cliona. 'Open it!' His voice was harsh and strained, belying his slow careful movements and emotionless features.

For a moment, his words didn't register – and then the full enormity of what the bard had asked her to do sank in. She looked at him, slowly shaking her head, her eyes round with horror. She opened her mouth to protest, but Paedur raised his hand, pressing his fingers to her lips. Glancing desperately at the approaching darkness, he shouted above the roar of disintegrating stone and the twisted rending of the fabric of space.

'Only you can open the vessel. The gem is merely another aspect of the Dannu-fire; only a priestess of the Mother can open it. But you must hurry, the cords are growing stronger . . .'

Cliona shook her head, struggling to make sense of what he was saying. How could she open the vessel when all they had done so far, all they had suffered, and Tuan's death, had been to prevent that from happening? The bard's chill voice suddenly spoke in her mind. '*You must open the vessel . . . it is the only chance we have of wiping the Cords clean from this plane. Do it!*'

The Magician's Law, she suddenly realised, the force of equals, the Cords and the Chrystallis!

Her fingers fumbled at the gem, attempting to prise it free. She looked out into the greyness of the cavern – the snakelike streamers from the Cords were very close now, leaving in their wake a total absence of light. Frantically, she pulled at the gemstone, lacerating her fingers on the sharp points, but the gem wouldn't move.

The streamers of night coiled about the mouth of the tunnel. '*Priestess . . .!*' Paedur cried.

Praying desperately for strength, Cliona raised the vessel in both hands – and smashed it down into the mouth of the tunnel . . .

The gem splintered into minute flecks of blue light that winked and glittered like a myriad fireflies, then they too were lost as the encroaching darkness swept in. The bard turned, his face floating, disembodied, towards her, his mouth working, his eyes alien and completely terrifying. She was aware of a terrible soulless howling, a bass moaning that plucked at the consciousness with black insistence, and then – there was nothing . . .

The Chrystallis erupted from the tunnel in a burst of vivid blue light with an exultant – almost beast-like – roar that reverberated through the disintegrating cavern. The shock shattered slabs of stone, sent them tumbling from the ceiling where they were absorbed into the chaos of utter night that was the Cords. The Soulwind began to encircle the cavern in a whirling vortex that sucked everything in its path into a seething maelstrom of destruction.

Jagged rents ran along the wall, lumps of stone flying into the vortex of azure-touched wind, revealing not another wall of rock but the twisting grey mist of the Ghost Worlds. The fabric of the planes had been breached. Tendrils of the Cords venturing out to the edge of the cavern were shredded and torn in the gusting silent Chrystallis.

But in the centre of the cavern, the eye of the storm, nothing stirred.

And then the encircling Chrystallis began to close in, tightening like a closing fist. Some few of the Culai still left standing were whipped into its embrace. The flat disc of the Cords was rent along two irregular streamers and dispersed in the Soulwind. The circle of the Chrystallis grew smaller and smaller, strangling everything within its grasp.

The Cords – torn to shreds – separated with a crack that staggered the Chrystallis, and for a moment the Soulwind remained motionless, pulsing insistently. The Cords shot out tentacles of blackness deep into the semi-visible sheet of the wind.

The Chrystallis recovered, and began to move again – and the probing streamers were gone, lost in the whirling depths of the Soulwind.

With the spell of the Three Cords broken, the last of the Culai came to their senses. Terrified and dazed, some moved back to the pool in the centre of the cavern, huddling together, while others ran screaming into the wind – only to be torn to pieces in its grasp. A few attempted to defend themselves, calling down their magic, but even the most powerful sorcery was useless against the raw elemental power of the Cords and the Chrystallis. Worse, it only served as a focus for the shrinking Cords, calling them in . . . and then the last of the Culai race were absorbed into the blackness of the Cords.

The grey slabs of stone about the pool were ripped apart by the Cords, chunks of jagged rock exploding outwards, only to be pulverised into dust by the encircling wind.

The Cords were now confined to a small space above the pool. They compacted into a tight ball of pitch-like darkness and began to spin. Tendrils of night snaked from the ball, darting into the Chrystallis, and were instantly destroyed.

And now the nameless liquid in the pool boiled upwards and was absorbed into the Soulwind, giving it shape and form, so that it came to look as if a circle of liquid glass encircled a black sphere. The centre of the cavern was now a tightly compacted mass of pulverised rock and shattered stone, the torn and mutilated bodies of the Culai, and at the heart of it, the tiny ball that was the Three Cords of Disruption, Annihilation and Chaos. Tighter and tighter the Chrystallis closed, the black ball flickering wildly. Abruptly, a part of it had gone. And then another part. Now, only a tiny mote of darkness remained like a black star – then it too flickered and was gone.

And the Chrystallis crashed in upon itself with a roar that rippled through the myriad planes of life in a cataclysm much as there had been in Elder Days. Seas boiled and rose; lowlands were lost beneath the waves; islands sank without trace and others rose where none had been before. Mountains fell and rose again in new configurations and open-mouthed cones spewed forth, burning filth, while the northern and southern ice-caps shifted, crashing into the warming seas and immediately beginning to melt.

And many went to Mannam that day to be judged by Alile the Judge Impartial.

But the Chrystallis and the Three Cords were no more.

But they left behind in the cavern a seething cauldron of indescribable chaos. The Chrystallis and the Cords had ripped vast swatches of matter from the plane, and now jagged rents in the delicate fabric between the worlds caused the thin grey mist of the Ghost Worlds to leak into the plane – but the material impacted upon entry, slowly sealing the holes. However, had the Chrystallis or Cords been allowed to continue, they would have rapidly broken down the entire fabric of the plane, returning it to the Void or Chaos.

The remnants of the cavern rippled with the exploding matter, rebuilding the fabric of the shattered plane. Nothing could have lived through the passage of the Cords or the Chrystallis, both of which were the very antithesis of life. The imploding matter rained chunks of incandescent material about the cavern, destroying even the creatures of the halfworld which had come to investigate the disruption in the fabric of the planes.

Nothing human could have survived – but through it all wandered a tall figure, clad in a stained and worn cloak and hooded like a monk. His face was lined and pained, worn, but his eyes were expressionless. They were now flat and reflective, like mirrors. And once a curved silver hook rose to etch the Sign of the Pantheon on the turbulence, and a row of flickering figures, godlike and serene, appeared briefly to place their mark upon the newly fashioned place: '*This is the Ending; go now in peace for you have served us well . . .*'

The hooded bard turned away, shaking his head slowly, and when he looked back there was nothing human left in him. 'No,' he hissed, 'you are wrong. This is not the Ending – it is merely the Beginning!'

'A wonderful, magical novel'
MARION ZIMMER BRADLEY

THE FINNBRANCH
PAUL HAZEL

From the wintry land of the mountains came Finn, the warrior
whose legacy was both a blessing and a curse.

His mother was a witch and a wanderer upon land. His father –
from what they knew – had risen up like a god from his
kingdom beneath the sea.

And so Finn began his odyssey in search of his birthright:
drawn deep into the secret world of sorcery, braving waters
that would drown a man in dreams, roving among people
who would answer riddles with fresh riddles . . .

'Dark and intriguing, at once wonderful and strange . . . one
of the best fantasies in some time' Publishers Weekly

0 7221 4545 4   FANTASY   £4.95

Continuing the enthralling chronicle of
Ann of Cambray

Gifts
-of the-
Queen
Mary Lide

Lady Ann of Cambray has wed Lord Raoul, Earl of
Sedgemont, Count Sieux in France, and now awaits
the birth of his heir. But the alliance – a tempestuous
one – has aroused the hostility of the King, Henry II,
who has long coveted Ann as his bedmate.

Their English estates now seized by the monarch, Ann
and Raoul must flee to Normandy and her husband's
ancestral home. But even here they cannot escape
Henry's cruel vengeance: they find the castle sacked,
and their hopes in tatters around them . . .

Also by Mary Lide in Sphere Books:
ANN OF CAMBRAY

0 7221 5564 6   GENERAL FICTION   £3.50

A selection of bestsellers from Sphere

FICTION

CYCLOPS	Clive Cussler	£3.50 □
THE SEVENTH SECRET	Irving Wallace	£2.95 □
CARIBBEE	Thomas Hoover	£3.50 □
THE GLORY GAME	Janet Dailey	£3.50 □
NIGHT WARRIORS	Graham Masterton	£2.95 □

FILM & TV TIE-IN

INTIMATE CONTACT	Jacqueline Osborne	£2.50 □
BEST OF BRITISH	Maurice Sellar	£8.95 □
SEX WITH PAULA YATES	Paula Yates	£2.95 □
RAW DEAL	Walter Wager	£2.50 □
INSIDE STORY	Jack Ramsay	£2.50 □

NON-FICTION

A TASTE OF LIFE	Julie Stafford	£3.50 □
HOLLYWOOD A' GO-GO	Andrew Yule	£3.50 □
THE OXFORD CHILDREN'S THESAURUS		£3.95 □
THE MAUL AND THE PEAR TREE	T.A. Critchley & P.D. James	£3.50 □
WHITEHALL: TRAGEDY AND FARCE	Clive Ponting	£4.95 □

Cash sales form:

All Sphere books are available at your local bookshop or newsagent, or can be ordered direct from the publisher. Just tick the titles you want and fill in the form below.

Name_____

Address_____

_____

Write to Sphere Books, Cash Sales Department, P.O. Box 11, Falmouth, Cornwall TR10 9EN

Please enclose a cheque or postal order to the value price plus:
UK: 60p for the first book, 25p for the second book and 15p for each additional book ordered to a maximum charge of £1.90.

OVERSEAS & EIRE: £1.25 for the first book, 75p for the second book and 28p for each subsequent title ordered.

BFPO: 60p for the first book, 25p for the second book plus 15p per copy for the next 7 books, thereafter 9p per book.

Sphere Books reserve the right to show new retail prices on covers which may differ from those previously advertised in the text elsewhere, and to increase postal rates in accordance with the P.O.